THE WATER'S EDGE

TIMBER PHILIPS
JARED KINGPACAL LAIN

COPYRIGHT

DEDICATION

Timber Philips would like to thank Jared KingPacal Lain for picking up the broken pieces of this book and re-forging them into something amazing with her. She would also like to thank Ben McCarter for giving her the much-needed infusion of laughter and light, joy and smiles that were required to finish this endeavor. Thank you for helping my heart sing again, Ben.

Jared KingPacal Lain would like to thank Timber Philips for the great opportunity presented in the repair and completion of this, his first publication. He would also like to thank his wife, Heather, for putting up with his particular fascinations and literary dilettante habits. Thank you for being there and giving me your love and support, Heather.

PROLOGUE

LAST DAY OF AUGUST 1731

*E*amon Bligh...

The *Queen's Mercy* listed beneath my bare feet. The hold was empty except for the complaint of broken wood and the sighs of the sea as it seeped in through the hull. The cargo, what little there was, had already been pulled above. Forty hogsheads of sugar, bales of cotton and sundry goods as such a ship would carry to provision its crew, and their scant possessions; seemingly a meager cargo for a crew to fight to the death to protect.

The *Queen's Mercy* sat low in the water too.

Captain Blaine had thought taking the *Mercy* would be easy—fire a few shots, they would strike their sails, and trade their cargo and rum rather than face cutlass and cannon. It had turned into a no quarters red slaughter. They fought like madmen and animals. My own shirt was wet with blood, though most of it was not my own.

It had been so damnably senseless. Slaughtered for some sugar and raw cotton. What crew would be so devoted to their captain or charter? Blaine's own men had almost faltered themselves, but the shouts of the captain and his first mate cursing God and King kept them in the fray and manning the guns.

Now that the battle was done, and the *Mercy* was taking on water, the survivors had plenty of time to curse God.

Nay, there was a reason they had fought so, and why even empty and holed, the *Mercy* set low in the water like she had a greater load. She had a secret, and by the blood spilt and dead stacked like wood, I intended to find it.

The hull of the ship groaned. Whatever burdened it was still aboard. The crew had been excellently armed with pistols, cutlass, and had fine cannons – twelve pounders, and a full dozen of them. Most merchantmen that ran armed carried eight pounders and deck guns. *Mercy*, you were well-armed.

I eventually found myself in the bottom of the ship, atop the bilges. The water was slowly filling the holds, but certainly not enough to cause worry. She'd float for another day or so before taking her dive down to Davy Jones and his submarine navy. The wood was new, unaged and unworn, the edges still raw from the lumbermill. I pried one of the boards up with my dagger, revealing darkness and water. The stench of the bilge was strong and stung my eyes. I had no desire to plunge my hands into that fetid place.

Curiosity be damned, I had to!

The water was oily and brackish, and made me feel more stained by it even as some of the blood was washed away from me. I grasped, fingers sweeping through the bilge, and then felt something smooth and hard. Metal. I traced the edge and found more of them, before I found a corner to wrap my fingers around. I pulled the strange heavy bar out of the bilge, and in the twilight of the hold, dripping with bilge water, there was no mistaking what I held in my hand.

"God be praised," I whispered aloud. I furiously wiped the muck from the bar, and it gleamed. It shone like the sun. I turned the bar over, smooth on all sides, polished to a mirror finish, no rough cast gold, but the king's own. His damned face was stamped into the bar, underscored by the emblem and words of His Majesty's South Seas Trading Company. I kissed the bar before laying it at my side.

I started removing the other bars from the bilge. They kept coming. When I could reach no more, I tore more of the boards away and found more gold.

~

THE SUN BATHED ME AS I PULLED MYSELF FROM THE HOLD, MY FIND wrapped and tucked into my belt, a weight that could not be ignored. Mister Baxter regarded me with his one good eye. His face was speckled black with powder as he was a fine master of the cannon.

"It be good of you to join us, Mister Bligh," he growled. "Did you have a fair rest in the hold?"

"I had a search of the holds, for the rest of the *Mercy's* cargo," I said.

"We have the full of it," Baxter said.

"We have the full of it, now, Mister Baxter," I said. "There was just a small bit more, concealed, as it were."

"What did you find, Mister Bligh?"

The surviving crew had gathered around Baxter and I, curiosity warring with exhaustion in their expressions. My lips cracked from a scowl to a smile, then a great full grin. I withdrew the rag wrapped ingot and tossed it to the deck. It landed solidly, like a cannonball and the sun set it ablaze. Mister Baxter's good eye went as wide as a boiled egg.

"Bloody hell."

"Here is the *Queen's Mercy*, she has the king's gold in her belly," I said. "Hundreds of those each stamped with the king's face and crest, packed stem to stern down in the bilges. She was no simple merchantman, my fine fellows, she was the king's treasure ship."

Mister Horn, one of the mates, picked up the bar and hefted it in his hands. "This is His Majesty's gold." He ran a rough and calloused thumb across the face of the king's likeness.

"Nay, Mister Horn," I replied. "This was His Majesty's gold."

He gave a grin. "Aye," he said. "Aye it was."

~

OF THE TWO SCORE AND FIVE WE HAD ONCE BEEN, JUST SEVENTEEN OF us remained. Captain Blaine had done his dying, and when he was dead, we heaved him over the side. He was joined by his first mate, the quartermaster, the pilot, and the rest of the dead. They had been fine men. We few were left to our own machinations. We stood in a ragged circle, still living, but a few still bleeding. They would mend, in time.

We all looked at our gathered prize, rescued from the hulk of the *Queen's Mercy*, stacked neatly and square on the deck of our own ship. Caution dictated that we not create too large a pile in one place for risk of breaking through the deck or upsetting the balance of the ship. The gold was brilliant, the tropical sun making it come alive.

Nothing in the world gleams like gold, nor so fiercely.

Eighteen score and fourteen bars in full count – a score and two bars for each man of the crew. A single bar was more than an honest man could hope to earn in his lifetime, and a lucky pirate might make that, but his life was likely to be a might shorter than the laboring man's. Each of us, every man, was entitled to twenty and two of them.

"I don't believe it," young Mister Hawkins, our cabin boy and newest mate, muttered. His pale blue eyes wide. "I-I just don't believe it!"

"My cod be getting tight just lookin' at it," Mister Forsythe said with a dark grin, running a hand over his matted beard.

They all had words to say, and they were said—whores, whores in great number, feasting the likes of which had not been seen since Henry VIII or Nero, fine clothes like proper gentlemen, spirits and new boots. Mister Baxter even exclaimed he would get a new eye rather than wear the patch. We were a crew without a captain, and until that vacancy was addressed and occupied, the disposition of the ship and its bounty would remain an open question.

"Lads," Mister Dougal said. "We have matters of great import to make words of." His thick Scottish brogue cut through the chatter, and the men fell silent. He was no captain, but when the cook spoke, the men listened.

"What's that, then?" Mister Hawkins scratched at the back of his neck, blond hair blowing in the breeze. He was still young enough that his cheeks stayed smooth without a razor's attentions; pale fuzz taking the place of a proper beard.

"Now that Captain Blaine is done dead, that leaves us sorely lacking a captain," Dougal replied, scratching at his round gut. He was a heavy man, well into his years, and his red beard and sideburns were salted with white. His head was almost smooth, but no less a fierce fighter and a cunning pirate. I reckoned him for the next captain.

"We keep to the code, any man may throw his hat in and speak his piece, then we cast our lots" Mister Baxter said. "Any feel like wearing the captain's hat?"

"I nominate Mister Eamon Bligh!" Hawkins said before anyone else could speak.

"Mind your tongue," Forsythe said. "I nominate myself." I wasn't surprised.

Forsythe was a cruel and ambitious man. He wanted the captain's hat but was never so unwise to say it aloud. He was a brutish man, who took pleasure in his abuses, and was the sort of pirate that caused the crown to give pirates to Jack Ketch rather than lock them up in a gaol. He glared at me, his eyes hard and dark. He was not educated and knew that I was. That made him suspicious of me, even to the point of hatred.

Hawkins stood undeterred, his youth giving him more courage than common sense. "Why not? Bligh's a fine choice. He's a good fighter, he knows navigation, he can read, write, and do sums."

"He's in the right," Mister Horn said. "And it was Mister Bligh who found the king's gold. I'll second the nomination of Mister Bligh."

One by one each of the crew accepted my nomination, and I was nearly struck dumbfounded. I hadn't said a word to being captain, and at the count, there were fifteen votes for myself, a single lot for Forsythe, and I myself had cast no lot.

"What say you, Mister Bligh?" Mister Dougal regarded me with a jovial smile. "You willing to take the hat?"

"If the crew wills it, I'll do it," I said, eyeing them each in turn. Forsythe brooded; he had gained no second, and none of the other men saw fit to toss their hat into the circle. Mister Baxter had Blaine's hat, mostly unharmed, and he presented it to me.

'Blaine took his sash with him to Davy Jones, so we'll not have one of those for you to wear, Captain," Mister Baxter said.

"I will manage. Last I saw of it, the thing was holed and bloody," I said.

"Indeed, it was," Dougal said. "So now that we have a captain again, we can look to our next matter of import." He nodded once in my direction. "Well, Captain, what's our heading?"

I felt a tremor of excitement, not for the two shares of the gold that I would receive for the captaincy, but for something far more valuable, at least in my eyes. It was my decision as to where we would set sail. The others would have some say in it, but I was the captain and the helmsman, the choice was mine. "It's time we set our course, gentlemen," I said.

"Port Royale," Forsythe shouted. "I say we pull into Port Royale and have the time of our lives!" Some of the other men perked up at this idea. Mister Dougal and Mister Baxter stood, watching me. They were taking my measure. Forsythe had lost the captain's hat and he had already started to undercut me. It was a shame that of all the men dumped overboard; he was not among them.

"Here," I said, picking up one of the ingots, and tossing it at his feet. "Pick it up, that's every whore in Port Royale. Take another, it's part of your share. There is enough rum to pickle you and put you in an unmarked pirate's grave." He looked at me coldly. "And while you're drinking and whoring, every thief, scallywag, and bastard fit to be called a pirate is looking at you, figuring out where to stick the knife between your ribs, and nick your score of gold you haven't even thought about yet."

"Men talk, and the king's men listen. When a group of bloody pirates wash up at Port Royale, carrying gold like the Pope, they'll know." I looked at Dougal. "Some of you used to serve in the King's Navy, you know they listen for these things." Dougal nodded his head slightly. Some of the others did too.

"Maybe you'll be drunk, lost in your cups, when the king's men come and clap you in irons, when they come for all of us, irons and nooses enough for all of our necks. No sir, Mister Forsythe, we will not be making for Port Royale, unless you'd like to take your share and a dinghy and make your own way."

"This is a matter for a vote," Forsythe sputtered.

"The captain has the right of it, Mister Forsythe. That gold is a lifetime of whores and rum, and in Port Royale, that's a week or two," Mister Horn said solemnly. "I'd venture Tortuga would be little better."

"Lads, what we have here is the wealth of King Midas," I told them. "We cannot affix ourselves with petty dreams when the God Almighty has seen such a treasure into our worthy hands.

"With wisdom, we go to where the reach of the king is weak," I said calmly. "We go to a place where the men won't care about the king's face, or the marks of the South Seas Trading Company stamped into each bar of our hard-won lucre."

"The colonies!" Mister Hawkins proclaimed. Forsythe made a scowl and spit on the deck at the suggestion.

"The colonies, Mister Hawkins, what do you know of the colonies?" Forsyth said sharply. "I'll tell you of the colonies, they are teeming with savages, the red man. They cut the scalps from the men they kill and wear them as decorations."

"Those words almost sound fearful," I said. "Especially from a man we know cuts ears to wear as a necklace.

"There are savages in the colonies, aye, that's true. But they have bow and arrow, and tomahawk. We have pistols, cannon, and cutlass. The Spaniards cut them down like wheat. The French have made them their allies. The colonials bed them almost as fast as they shoot them. I am afraid of no savage; I will meet him with the same vigor that we gave those men on that treasure ship," I said. My words seemed to find ground as the men looked more convinced of mine than of Forsythe's words.

"In the Carolinas, they are blessed with a great bounty of land. More land than they can farm, more land than they can even draw a map of. We make port there, we take our fortunes ashore, and we become landed gentry there. In the colonies, we can carve out our own fiefs and become wealthy with the bounty of the unexplored continent."

"We can find smithies who would smelt and strike our gold," Baxter said. "Be rid of the king's glower."

"There are stories that the colonies are so rich in gold that it is almost normal that a common man strike great wealth and become rich," Hawkins said excitedly.

"A fairy tale, boy," Forsythe said.

"If it be a fairy tale, where did all this gold come from Mister Forsythe?" Hawkins said, putting a pitch of defiance in it for Forsythe calling him a boy.

"I can vouch for that," Mister Hawkins said. "I've heard stories of men doing it – striking it rich in the colonies, I mean." I blessed him for speaking up and hoped it would be enough.

"In the colonies," I looked at Forsythe, "a man need not be of noble blood or title to command respect. He need only wealth and confidence. Even the lords who visit must tip their heads to the men who hold the iron and the gold."

Forsythe was silent but I could tell I'd caught his interest along with several others. Forsythe was a cruel man, mean and low, but he was not truly an idiot. He dreamed of wealth, of power, of other men bowing and scraping to him. He longed for it. If he fell in line, he would have his chance, and I hoped that he would realize this.

"It is a fine idea," Mister Baxter said.

"Do you bloody take me for a farmer?" Forsythe's face was scornful, but his tone was less harsh.

"You would be a plantation master, Mister Forsythe, not tilling a row yourself. A far cry better than a dance with Jack Ketch," Mister Horn said.

"I'll second sailing for the Carolinas," Dougal said. "It's a better plan than visiting any of the free ports or taking our luck in Spanish or French holdings."

"We sail for the Carolinas and fortune," I said. "We stow the gold the same way we found it, in the bilges. Then we bring the bow around, to the north."

"Aye," Dougal said. He turned and raised his voice. "You heard the captain... get a move on! We're about to be rich men!"

The crew hustled to obey, cheering and laughing as they worked. Even sour Forsythe took to his tasks without complaint. Or at least much complaint. I didn't join them in their celebration; I knew better. The captain kept his own company, and the crew to theirs. A foolhardy captain never gave his men room to breathe. As I watched the massive pile of treasure gleaming in the sun at my feet, more wealth than any man who wasn't a king could dream to possess, I knew...

Our troubles had only begun.

CHAPTER ONE

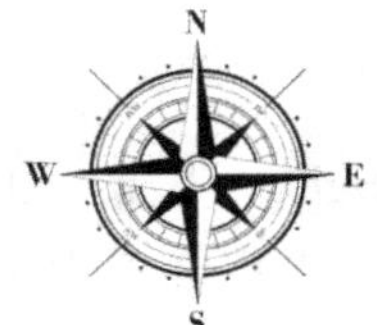

*A*very Barker...

I sat in my expensive silk blouse and pencil skirt and wanted to scream. I wanted to go stark raving mad, run up the hallway back to the elevator and take myself as far away from here as I possibly could. I *hated* these restrictive uncomfortable clothes. I *hated* having to prove my case over and over and *over* again just to have doors slammed in my face – just as many times.

All it takes is one, baby. The voice inside my head sounded suspiciously like my daddy's and I was okay with that. I wished he could be here. He'd always been better at talking with potential investors than I. This was *his* arena, not mine. Mine was below the waves. I knew he believed in me, and I knew I was right about this.

My *dad* knew I was right about this. We were willing to bet the entire fucking farm on this endeavor, take loans out on our houses, put a loan out on *the boat*, risk it all... the only problem? It wasn't enough. It was *never* enough. We needed backers. We needed at least one financial backer with the money to push us the rest of the way.

Which is why I was here, singing for my supper, the way people in my profession always had to. I hated doing it, but reality was what it was.

"Avery Barker?" I looked up and smiled my best professional smile while my heart leaped into my throat. Sweat stood out along my spine and beneath my arms, hidden by the stifling prim gray suit jacket that matched my skirt to perfection. I tucked a stray strand of blonde hair behind my ear from where it had escaped my French twist and stood.

"Yes, I'm here."

The woman smiled brightly, her makeup perfect, not a single hair out of place. She was my age, lithe and fit, but whereas my fitness came from hard work, with regular swimming and diving excursions, hers was likely a byproduct of a strict gym regimen. I rose and held out my hand and she looked at it and laughed awkwardly.

"I'm not one of the people you have to convince," she whispered and smiled. The smile was both kind and a little apologetic. My heart immediately sank, and I steeled myself for another tough battle ahead, trying to convince a bunch of boardroom-dwelling yuppies to take a chance on me and mine. That apologetic smile told me everything I needed to know. That this, like every other venture I'd tried to date, was going to be all uphill. I could taste the edge of defeat already. A bitter taste for sure, but me being me, I wasn't about to give it up until the door had been firmly closed in my face.

I followed the secretary down the expensive marble hall, past doorways made from rich mahogany, our high heels clicking sharply and echoing back at me from the vaulted ceilings. I swallowed hard. *Last stop.*

She opened the door to a board room to rival the swank of the hallway and waiting area and I stepped through, briefcase in one hand, portfolio in the other. I was greeted by four stern-looking men and one iron lady gathered around one end of a long boardroom table. The table was of a rich, equally impressive wood as the rest of the building, and gleamed with a soft luster. Antique stained-glass lamps hung above it at regular intervals, casting a soft golden gleam along its surface.

The table easily sat twelve, yet only five were here, leather blotters beneath their tablets, laptops, and in a case or two, old-fashioned paper and pen planners. I was led to the end of the table opposite the five and set my portfolio and briefcase down. I made eye contact – down all that gleaming wood – with the portly, balding man in his sixties who sat at the head of the table.

"Ms. Barker," he said and inclined his head.

"Mr. Bancroft, I presume."

He smiled, and it wasn't unkind. "Yes. These are the members of my board, Mr. Lennox," he said, indicating the youngest man at the table, easily in his early thirties with dark, perfectly clipped brown hair and blue eyes who was sitting to Mr. Bancroft's right and closest to me. "Mr. Abrams," he said, indicating his direct right-hand man, a thin, gaunt man with sunken eyes and gray hair in a fringe around his balding pate. He wore silver wire-rimmed glasses that I almost wanted to call a throwback to nineteen-twenty's fashion.

Mr. Bancroft put down his right hand with its gold pinky ring and lifted his left with its simple wedding band. "Ms. Moira Caldwell..." who was a pinched woman, in an outdated power suit, likely in her fifties with her red, graying hair pulled into a severe bun at the back of her head. "... and last but not least, Mr. Murray, one of the Bancroft Investment Groups top-tier accountants."

I smiled politely and inclined my head in Mr. Murray's direction as I had to each individual in turn, saying, "It's a pleasure to meet all of you."

A soft chuckle escaped Mr. Lennox and I turned my smile up a little brighter. Mr. Bancroft leaned back in his expensive leather seat and said, "What do you have for us, my dear?"

"Right, well, in the interest of saving your valuable time, I'll get right to it," I said, opening up my portfolio to make use of the easels and stands set up behind me to display my proposition to Mr. Bancroft and his board.

"What if I told you that not only was there a fortune of gold bullion, but that it was both unmarked, and with the added benefit of being located on American soil?"

I knew it was sure to grab their attention, and I wasn't disappointed. Mr. Abrams leaned forward in his seat, while Mr. Bancroft's eyebrows went up. It was Ms. Caldwell who seemed the most skeptical, crossing her arms beneath her small breasts and leaning back in her seat, mouth drawn, in a disapproving downturn. Mr. Lennox merely looked amused, propping his elbow on the edge of the table, pressing his ring finger into his lips, laying his index along his cheek. It was the same thing I would have done to keep from laughing.

It was the perfect motivation for me. I loved disproving smug bastards; making them eat their tittering laughter and amused looks. While we weren't quite there with Mr. Lennox, it was close enough to light my fire.

"I'd say that is quite the claim, Ms. Barker," Mr. Bancroft replied.

"I'd have to agree with you, were I in your position, but I assure you, it's not only true, I've found the proof of it." I whipped out my first display piece and propped it up on one of the easels – a lithograph print, blown up and a bit grainy from the original of a large East India merchantman named the *Queen's Mercy.*

"On August 22nd, 1731, the *Queen's Mercy* set out from Port Royale bound for Great Britain with a listed cargo of sugar, molasses, and cotton. She never made it, and she wasn't carrying just trade goods, either." I paused for dramatic effect and waited for one of them to break and ask.

Mr. Abrams was the one to do it. "Did it sink?"

"No, she didn't, actually. She was beset by pirates." I put up the next image out of my portfolio, preferring the old-fashioned method to the digital PowerPoint presentations that had taken over as technology had inexorably continued its march forward.

The next lithographic image I presented was of another, much smaller ship. A Brig known as the *Honor's Price.* "The pirates captured the *Queen's Mercy,* plundered her, and found the treasure she harbored."

"And just how do you know that?" Ms. Caldwell demanded.

I smiled. "I'll cut to the chase." I put up the next image I held on the easel. A sea-level view of an island off the North Carolina coast. A mocking laugh came from Mr. Lennox and I paused just long enough to gather the reins of my famous temper.

"The Isle of St. Elsewhere is part of a chain of islands that make up part of the North Carolina coast. It's one of the largest of the outlying islands and goes by another name, *Fade Isle.*"

"The island where people disappear and fade from memory?" Mr. Lennox asked and rolled his eyes. "You can't be serious. For *years* they've claimed some kind of buried treasure to be there, and for years, every expedition that's gone there has come up empty. Why would yours be any different?"

"Because I have it direct from the pirate's mouth, so to speak." He wanted to be a condescending ass? Okay fine, the gloves were off. I opened up my briefcase and pulled out six copies of my spiral-bound ace in the hole. I passed them out myself and flipped through several of my foam boards to get to the goods.

I put the one I wanted up on the easel and said, "One of the pirates on the *Honor's Price* kept a journal. Eamon Bligh was purportedly hanged for piracy in Charleston in October of 1731, but his encoded journal wound up in the hands of a wealthy tobacco plantation owner in Virginia. You see, Bligh's sister was sold into indentured servitude on the plantation and before he died, the captain of the *HMS Norrington,* which was the ship responsible for Captain Bligh's capture, had the journal sent to his sister as her brother's last effects. You see, they were completely unawares that *she* had died in childbirth the previous year."

I watched as the men and woman at the table flipped open the spiral-bound books to digital images of the journal's pages. While the journal had been encoded, the flowing script nonsensical to anyone without the key to crack it, in the digital images they held, Photoshop had been used to overlay the translations just below the spidery script for effect.

"How do you know what this says?" Mr. Bancroft asked.

"Once I figured out it was written in code and cipher, I sent it to Wilhelm Fischer, one of the world's most renowned cryptographers. If you turn to the back of your booklet, you will see the various certifications of authenticity from not only Wilhelm but the Smithsonian Institute detailing both the authenticity and provenance of the journal." I looked Mr. Lennox in the eye and said, "I'm not making this up. This is as real as it gets."

"I see," Mr. Bancroft said and frowning asked, "What precisely are you looking for from the Bancroft Group, Ms. Barker?"

"I have the personnel, I have most of the equipment, I even have the permission of the United States government to go looking on Fade Isle, which is an uninhabited wildlife preserve. I just need the funds to get down there and *find* it."

"How much are you asking for?" Bancroft asked and I leaned forward, palms flat to the shiny wood of his fancy boardroom table.

Without blinking, without fear, I named my figure. Mr. Murray immediately balked, choked, and picked up his water glass to take a sip. Mr. Bancroft gave him a sidelong glance and leaned back in his seat, coolly appraising me.

"You must be joking!" Ms. Caldwell demanded.

"I assure you, she's not," Mr. Lennox said, eyeing me critically, a debonair smile gracing his lips. He looked like I'd finally done something interesting enough for him to take notice. I knew what I was asking was pretty ballsy. I also knew it was going to be tough with two utter failures in a row at expeditions under my family's belt. No one really wanted to look at the success rate that came before the failures, especially when the failures had been so spectacularly monumental in nature.

Those failures also hadn't been mine and my father's, but rather lay solely at my cousin Gwen's feet; not that you'd know it. Her misdeeds and mishandling of things had been right up under the Barker family name. The only daughter to my father's brother, my father's kindness had led us to near ruin where she was concerned, and we were hardcore feeling the effects of it now.

This expedition was more than just finding treasure. It was

about a last-ditch effort at mine and my father's survival, as well as redeeming the family name. Gwen had ruined more than just our finances, she'd taken down reputability, and some things, like the things she'd pulled, were near impossible to come back from.

"I'm sure you have questions," I said, and settled in for the long haul. I could tell I had Mr. Bancroft, Mr. Abrams, and surprisingly, Mr. Lennox on the line, and I needed to bide my time and reel them in slowly. If I could get Mr. Murray on board, all the better, but Ms. Caldwell seemed almost an insurmountable odd. I'd take three out of five in my favor, but more would be better, and honestly, Lennox was hardest on the fence.

I would need every bit of smooth-talking ability, every trick, every bit of charisma my father possessed that could have possibly been passed down to me... I had to make this pipe dream a reality and make these people believe as hard as I did that Eamon Bligh, a man I'd never met, who'd died two hundred and thirty-seven years before I was even born, was telling the truth.

CHAPTER TWO

Eamon Bligh...

I sat alone in the captain's cabin, gazing into the lantern. Not Blaine's cabin, mine. I had much to consider, and the privacy afforded to me by my new accommodations was a blessing. The rest of the men considered the appearance of the gold to be a gift from God Almighty but gave no thought to the future. A navigator always had to know what lay ahead, and I knew better, but far be it from me to make them question their newfound fortunes. Just as they had made me captain, they could as easily un-make me.

It wasn't my competency in question. Mister Hawkins had the right of it during his speech before the vote. I was the only man among them with the wit to steer the ship and end up where he intended. The only one who knew a star beyond the star of the sea, or read a map, write, or even dance with numbers. The great and terrible problem lay with the remnants of Blaine's crew, the survivors who were now my new crew.

Fate would see that brave men, bold and true, those with sharp wit and sharp steel were the first into the fray. In the case of His Majesty's bullion ship, these fine lads were also the first to die, and most recently, were gifted to Davy Jones. Those who remained among my crew, aside from wise veterans like Horn and Baxter, who knew oft that discretion was the better part of valor, and young Mister Hawkins, the rest were the sort better known for hanging back. Better to retreat if the fight turned against us, or to rush in once the tide had turned in our favor. They were the dimmest and more brutal among what had once been a fine crew.

Under our circumstances, without careful planning and a fair measure of luck, the treasure stood to be more bane than boon.

There came a knock at my door. "Come," I called out.

The door opened, letting darkness and salt air in, as well as Mister Dougal. He grinned. "Thought I'd find you still awake."

"You have a need?"

"I'd describe it as a wish, Captain." He held up a leather flask. "I wish to share drink and have words."

I gave a nod and kept my face neutral. Dougal was one of the wary veterans and a right fellow, but he was also a pirate and a canny one, and I was now his captain. We had been friends before. Before I was captain. Things can change, and quickly.

"We made an ample amount of words before the vote," I said. "If you had concerns, then was the time to voice them."

"There are matters which don't concern the crew, or the gold." He crossed the room, picking up two tin cups and setting them on my desk. "Rather they concern myself, personally." He opened his flask and poured a dark amber liquid into the cups; I caught the peaty scent of highland spirits. "But for now, a taste of the homelands."

"For you, perhaps."

Dougal grinned and tipped his cup at me. "I'll not hold that against you, sir, have a taste."

I did – a small sip. Liquor dulled wits and I needed mine sharp, but aside from insulting his family or his heritage, the quickest way to incense a Scotsman was to refuse to drink with him.

"Quite fine," I said, but the harsh smoke and peat taste was far from my likings. In truth I preferred a brandy, but Dougal needn't to know that. Pirates such as ourselves were seldom afforded the luxury of our tastes in spirits.

"Been saving it for a special occasion, I have" he said, easing into the chair across from me.

"Taking the king's weight in gold, that would certainly be the most special of occasions," I said.

He laughed. "The truth sir, that be the truth"

The ship heaved beneath our feet in time to the heavy creak of rigging and timber. The captain's inkpot slid toward the edge of his desk. *My inkpot, my desk,* I caught myself just as I caught the inkpot before it could topple to the floor. "Now, what troubles you, Mister Dougal?"

"You've convinced the crew to set a course for the colonies," he said. "I'd like to know why."

I took another small taste of his highland spirits. "I told them why," I replied. "Such an action isn't the folly making that Port Royale would be."

"You gave them a right reason, sir, one they'd believe." One bushy gray eyebrow climbed toward his hairline. "You have your own plans. I would like to know them."

I contemplated the contents of the cup. In truth, I wanted to keep my words to myself, but knew that I had to trust at least a few of the crew if I had any hope of success. Which of my men to trust remained the burdensome question?

"You need me, Eamon. Captain Bligh." He took another sip of his scotch. "You've no fear of the King's Navy and I know that to rights. You wore the king's colors; you know their tactics and their will. We can and will sail rings around them." He grinned slowly. "No, your worry is elsewhere. With this much treasure aboard, you worry about fighting among the crew. After all, if one man dies, the share of all the living increases many times, and we both know the quality of men who remain aboard *Honor's Price.*"

I sighed. "The gold, divided among each of us, is more than we could spend in a brace of generations."

"Be true, as it may," Dougal said, "but we both know that won't bide some of them. You know what gold does to a man's soul. He doesn't see whores, or wealth, or his cups. He can only see gold that isn't in his grasp." He set his empty cup aside. "This is why you will need me. So, indulge me... for what true purpose are we heading for the colonies? It isn't for wise investment in tobacco or sugar plantations."

I sighed. "Mister Dougal, I meant what I said to the crew."

"Indeed, sir, you did." He regarded the empty tin cups between us. "This is a treacherous current we ride, no slack tide. I would know your true destination. That is unless you think you are above the need for help and good council." He studied me with gull's eyes, hard and sharp. "You wear the captain's hat well, sir, but these are base and low men, and they know you are not their kind. No whore's son has the schooling you do, and the men know it. They already distrust you for it. If they get it in their heads that you've hidden something from them, that will set their suspicions true and you might see ole Captain Blaine on the way down."

I leaned back. I had already considered the situation, but if I gave pause, and acted as if I had not, Morgan Dougal would be more likely a confidant and less a future mutineer. He was to rights, but that is how a man survived on a pirate ship – wary and knowing the importance of scuttlebutt and the insecurities of his fellows. "I have family, yet, in Charleston. A sister, and fate has seen her cruelly sold into servitude. I aim to purchase her contract and liberate her from her employers."

Dougal stared at me in disbelief. "We've looted the king's treasury, and no small price," he said, "and your first concern is your sister scrubbing some colonial's laundry and pots?"

My fingers tightened on my empty cup. "The men who hold her contract have no intention of allowing her to pay off her debt, and news from those plantations is that the most die without ever tasting their freedom again." My voice came out low and harsh, and little wonder.

I could not imagine my sweet, bookish Emma cheated and bound to servitude and not feel rage. I knew well her lot; abused by the lady of the house, manhandled and fondled by the lord of the estate when he felt the urge for something less a harridan than his wife. There could be even greater trespass, but of that, I could only speculate, darkly. I thought of the Blighs, the diminished and tattered remnants of my family. Emma had certainly fared poorly. I thought of those who were dead and buried or lost. The shades of their memory rose within me, but no amount of gold could raise the dead. They were beyond my ability, but Emma. Emma was not.

Morgan refilled his tin cup, gave it a moment of quiet, before sipping from it. "Eamon, sir," he said. "You confound me."

"To what end?" I asked.

"The gold... without that sister of yours, you'd have no use for it."

"At the moment, it is nothing more than the Devil's ballast," I said.

Dougal laughed. "You would care to explain that, sir?"

I put aside my ghosts and my anger. Morgan Dougal might not have had much of an education, but long experience stood him in good stead. Of those remaining, I had a chance of making him see sense.

"Mister Dougal, gold becomes wealth only when it can buy a man what he needs and wants," I said. "What can we do with it? We can't eat it. We can't drink it. The only thing we could do with it is load it into our cannons and shoot it at His Majesty's fleet. As we sail now, the only purpose it can serve is the one it already is, as an exceptionally pretty form of ballast that the crew could tear itself apart over."

Dougal nodded, slowly, the wheels turning behind his eyes.

"If we can't find a safe place to spend our newfound wealth, all we will gain is a meeting with Jack Ketch. I'll be happy to be a rich man once the ballast no longer threatens my life."

"You're a wise man, sir," Dougal said. "But what of the crew? I doubt many of them have sweet sisters held in bondage"

"There is no scarcity of spirits or whores," I said. "From Newfoundland to the tropic of Capricorn, let them fritter their gold on such vain pursuits. If we make a safe port, we are all wealthy and free men, and that suits me. I will liberate my sister. They can have their fill of whoring and vice."

"A sister means so much to you?" he asked.

"I have a score of gold ingots," I said. "But there is only one Emma."

Dougal was silent, his frown a ponderous one, but I knew I had him. Kith and kin were a situation any Highlander would understand. I reached across the table and squeezed his shoulder.

"I chose not to speak of Emma, not when we had words of destination with the crew. What care would they have for me and mine? Precious little. At best, such pleas would find deaf ears. At worst, they might think me untrustworthy, and as you said, fit to swim to the colonies. Another thought, there is a chance one or more of them may be unwise with their gold even if we make a safe port. The less they know of my plans, the less they can give up if put to the king's questions."

He laughed, and flipped his cup upside down, now not even a film of moisture left inside. "Fair point."

"Are you satisfied?"

"Aye," he said. "And more, I'll help you."

"It is well appreciated."

"What do you need from me?"

"That our fine crew of men remain as such, a fine crew. Distrust and gold fever can undo us before we even lay eyes on dry land" I said. "*Honor's Price* is reduced to but seventeen men, certainly enough to handle the ship, but nothing more. We can lose no more men, and if there is..." I hesitated. "A mutiny, regardless of the outcome, there will not be enough hands to man the ship. Without me, there is no navigator, and no helmsman. I need trust that they remember this."

"Your surest threat is Mister Forsythe," Morgan said. "He's a black-hearted bastard, and he'd as soon sell his kin into servitude if it put a few coins in his hand."

My brow lowered; my mouth twisted. "I've no argument there," he said. "John Forsythe is a bastard, even for a pirate."

"I saw when he found that poor woman hidden in the hold." Morgan shook his head in disbelief. "A whore, for God's sake, a whore and a pitiful one at that. His pockets were fat, and her need was obvious. What he did, it was cruel and his making a jest of it later sits poorly on my soul."

"There will be no tears shed for Mister Forsythe," I said. Morgan Dougal was trustworthy. It had long been my greatest measure of a man's character, whether he treated the fairer sex with dignity and what he thought of men who didn't. It was my experience, men who were amused by harming women, who could jest of such things, were the worst sort. The sort of man who would take a woman by force; the sort who thought little of fists and his own pleasures, that was the sort of man who knew no honor. His shipmates were victims, not brethren. The code only protected him, never stayed his hand. When he fell into the king's hands, he sang and helped Jack Ketch. There was a long silence. Morgan was likely contemplating the same. The ship pitched sharply to port, and I was forced to snatch both inkpot and cup, lest they be dashed to the floor.

Morgan Dougal spoke, "The longer I let your words sit in my head, the more true they become. In this hour, the gold is no treasure, though it may be yet, it is a tribulation," he said. "Turning it from sin to gold will take our measure."

"That will be so," I said.

"It stretches my imagination, sir, we changing our lots, trading days as sea dogs to become landed men, proper gentlemen."

I regarded my cup, wiped at my mouth and gave Morgan Dougal the only answer which was even remotely honest.

"We will try."

"Aye, lad, that we will." He gave a determined grimace. "And I'll make you an accord, if it is pleasing to you. When we succeed, I'll buy us a bottle of the king's finest, and we'll drink it together and curse his name."

"Aye, Mister Dougal, aye."

Morgan touched two fingers to his forehead in the ghost of a salute and made for the door, returning his flask of scotch whiskey to his pocket. I yawned once he was gone, the fatigue of the Devil's day had conspired with the potent drink, and I was weary to the bone. I discarded my weapons – the cutlass, the brace of pistols, the dagger, and my shirt and salt-cursed boots. When this day had begun, I could have hardly fathomed that by its end, I would find repose in the captain's bunk.

My bunk.

CHAPTER THREE

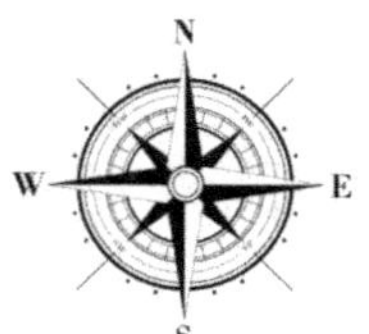

JUNE 2016

*A*very Barker...

A ghostly touch tickled down my back and I moaned softly. I think that was what woke me more than the touch itself. That impossibly low, sexy, and sultry moan that vibrated my throat startled me awake the rest of the way. I mean, I'd never quite made a sound like that in my entire life.

I blinked my eyes open and focused on a very masculine, very nude, thigh, inches from my face. I sucked in a shuddering breath and held it, my eyes flicking up past the jutting cock, which was uncut, interestingly enough. My eyes continued to climb up the flat, muscular stomach, across the swell of muscular chest, skating along the reddish-tinted beard to a set of the most incredibly vivid green eyes I have ever seen.

Dreaming. You're not awake, you're dreaming.

He smiled this incredibly sexy and endearing crooked smile, and I felt a mischievous answering one of my own. His rough fingertips slid over my heated flesh, trailing in light, nonsensical patterns over my bare skin and another of those moans, along with some gasping little breaths, slipped out of me.

God that felt good.

I didn't remember closing my eyes again, but I must have, because they opened when his weight shifted, and the mattress beneath me dipped. He'd gone up on one knee and his lips landed on the back of my neck as he swept my hair aside for better access. I went limp, melting into the bed at the sensation it wrought, even as my pussy throbbed with an aching need.

You're dreaming, and you should let this happen.

I was absolutely going to let this dream-man do whatever he damn well pleased. His lips touched again, slightly lower than the first kiss and he interchanged those butterfly kisses with hot, wet, flicks of his tongue and *God,* it was nice. He moved slowly, and I got the sense he was worshiping my body as well as exploring it, and that was… beautiful. A kind of gentlemanly you didn't encounter in most modern lovers.

He found a particularly sensitive spot, kissing my lower back, where it dipped before the swell of my ass and I sucked in a sharp breath. I heard him smile. That's right, I *heard* him smile and he lowered himself so he straddled my thighs, pressing my lower half into the sheets.

He explored me lightly with his fingers and I writhed a bit against that probative touch. His teasing had set me on fire, and I needed something to satisfy that burning desire for sex like nobody's business. He eased forward, and I arched, to allow him to do what I so desperately wanted. He eased himself inside of me and I sighed out. *God, that felt good!* He lay atop my body which felt even better, despite the thick, summer heat pooling in my tent.

I moaned and he stroked deep, his palms finding the backs of my hands, his thick, rough fingers finding the spaces between mine. I swallowed hard, and he brought my right hand between my stomach and the sheets, delving down the front of my body, pressing my fingertips into my clit.

He made it pretty fucking clear what he wanted, and I was in no position to deny him, nor did I want to. Instead, I slicked my fingers through my growing wetness and teased my clit, while he thrust evenly, stroking in and out of me with, dare I say, practiced ease; flipping just about every one of my switches as if we'd been old bed partners.

You're dreaming, of course he knows what you like.

I pushed the thought away, concentrating on his gasping breaths, letting the sounds of his desire, his passion, push me just that little bit further along. I cried out gently, came, and woke up for real to Jacob Lennox's voice saying, "Oh now that *is* a sight…"

I glared and felt heat that had nothing to do with desire or sex rise in my face. I wanted to kill him, but I was also so *humiliated.* My famous temper roared to life to compensate.

"Just what the hell are you doing here?" I demanded, dragging the sheet up over my back to cover myself from his decidedly lecherous gaze.

"Well," he started, dropping into my desk chair and rolling up to the edge of my bed, "as your top investor, the Bancroft Group decided your little operation could use some oversight."

"So, they sent *you?*"

He gave me a thin-lipped smile and let his deep brown eyes roam over my body from head to foot, leaving an oily, disgusting feeling coating me wherever they touched and that no amount of showering was going to get rid of.

"I volunteered, as both the youngest and fittest of the board of directors."

Of course, he did.

"Mind giving me a little privacy so I can get up?" I asked, arching one brow pointedly.

He smiled, and it wasn't friendly, at least not to me. He opened his mouth to say something when Mac's booming voice from outside the thick, sun-bleached canvas of my tent cut him off.

"Ave! You awake?"

"Yeah, Mac! A little help?" I called back.

Mac was my father's best friend and was basically an uncle to me. In fact, I'd been calling him 'Uncle Mac' just about all of my life. A strapping man in his late fifties, I couldn't and wouldn't find a better dive master to run things for me on the surface while I was down below.

Mac pulled aside the tent flap and took in the scene before him. He immediately went apoplectic with rage, his face turning an ugly shade of red which damn near went into purple.

"Mr. Lennox is with the Bancroft Group," I said quickly to get Mac back under some semblance of control. "I'm guessing he arrived with the supply ship this morning, and he seems to be a little lost. Mind showing him to where he can bunk?"

"Not a problem, baby girl. Want I should teach him a lesson about walking into places uninvited?"

"That won't be necessary," Mr. Lennox said coolly, eyeing Mac's lumbering frame.

"Mr. Lennox is a smart man, Mac. I think he gets the picture."

"Uh-huh," Mac said, eyeing Jacob Lennox closely. He stuck out a meaty paw in his direction and said, "The Bancroft Group did yah say?"

"Yes, sir," Lennox agreed and made the mistake of taking Mac's hand. Mac did his classic death grip of a handshake and I choked on a laugh at Lennox's expression. Mac didn't let up right away but kept Lennox's hand in his for a touch longer than necessary.

"Well, at least you dressed right for the occasion," Mac said, looking Lennox up and down. He wore a pair of light-colored khaki cargo shorts and a white button-down shirt loose over them; the sleeves turned up over his forearms which were tanned a golden brown like the rest of him. It remained to be seen if he came by the tan honestly or not. It could have been an expensive spray job.

When Mac looked down at Lennox's footwear, I couldn't help but let my gaze follow suit to the expensive pair of brown boat shoes. Sensible footwear, until he needed to get up to the caverns.

"I'll get dressed and join you boys down in the mess," I said and Mac gave a nod, pointedly looking any direction but mine. I could tell my state of undress, covered by only the sheet, was making him uncomfortable. Hell, I wasn't exactly happy about it either, but the rest of the team knew better than to just barge into my tent.

Mac held open the tent flap and ushered Jacob Lennox through. Lennox got the hint and went and as soon as the canvas dropped behind Mac's broad back, so did my shoulders, with relief, just before the embarrassment set back in.

Way to go, Avery. Of course, they would send the pervy investment banker and of course the universe would let him walk in on you while you were masturbating. Since when has it been that the universe ever thrown you a bone?

Okay, I was being a little unfair there. The universe had thrown me plenty of blessings and bones since my father's accident. He was alive, for one, and for two, I was here with the funding I needed to find Eamon Bligh's treasure.

I stared at my feet against the canvas floor of my tent as I sat on the edge of the bed my father and I had built one summer when we realized we were going to be doing more land-based operations than by sea for a while. After all, what was the point in living aboard a vessel when you could reach a site by a short swim off a dock? Maintenance and upkeep of a research vessel was much more expensive than glorified camping. Just because you had the funds, didn't mean you should waste them. You never knew when something was going to go tits up, and it was always good to have the funds available from doing a little penny pinching than it was to scramble to squeeze more pennies out of an already limited supply.

Such had been the lessons my father had taught me, and that man knew the business of treasure hunting and maritime salvage both inside and out. It was a lesson I was glad to know, because just as the universe decided to throw me a bone, it was just as likely to take it away. It just seemed to love to lead me around by a carrot on a stick.

Take this expedition, for instance. We'd barely gotten started and already we'd been delayed by a week and more by mechanical failures with the ROV. That would be remotely operated vehicle, or a mini-sub operated by a trained technician up here on land.

It was safer, where I was concerned, to send it in over me, especially when it came to this operation. I was no stranger to cave diving, but when you factored in both the dangers of cave diving and add in the depths we were having to go to? Every time I went down, I was playing a reverse lottery with my life and the chances were growing slimmer I was going to continue getting lucky and keep it. That was one jackpot I didn't want to hit. Hence, the use of the ROV over my skinny ass going down there, as frustrating to me as that was.

I pulled the sheet aside and forced myself to my feet, digging out some clean clothes from the footlocker by my desk. I pulled on a pair of cutoffs and a tank over my head, forgoing a swimsuit. I wasn't getting in the water today, so there wasn't a point. I stopped and dropped into my desk chair, waking up the laptop by rolling the mouse back and forth over the pad sitting on the scarred metal surface. The screen lit up and I pecked out my password. One of the images of Eamon Bligh's journal appearing on the screen. PDF's were a beautiful thing, allowing for the preservation of the actual journal which sat in a fireproof safe on the corner of the desk.

Sometimes, I liked to hold it and look at its real pages. It'd taken some time, but Wilhelm had been patient and had taught me the code and cipher particular to Bligh's journal, to the point that it was almost like watching a subtitled movie. Watch long enough, and the subtitles just seemed to melt away, and it was almost as if the characters on the screen spoke the language you read.

Now, once I got going with the cipher, I could almost hear a low, soft, masculine voice reading the words in my head. Of course, it was purely my imagination what Eamon Bligh sounded like. I didn't even know what he *looked* like. There were no portraits from the time and photography had a long while yet before its invention. The best description I had was of the clothing Eamon Bligh wore on the date of his execution, and that he was a tall, white man, with a trim beard.

I sighed and put my laptop back to sleep. I had a small generator here in my tent which I only ran for about an hour or two at night, depending on the needs of the equipment I had to charge, which was only the laptop, and satellite phone in here.

We were in a semi-permanent basecamp. Once upon a time, before the island became a wildlife preserve for the Piping Plover, a summer camp operated here. Throughout history, ever since the island's discovery, legends of disappearances had been a thing. As the stories went, when someone disappeared, it was always at night. Everyone figured that it was a ghost story meant to terrorize children, but it was the disappearance of a seven-year-old boy in nineteen-eighty-five that finally closed the park to campers and overnight visitors.

When people actually bothered to go digging, it was to find that the island held many stories of actual disappearances – not a campfire ghost story after all.

For a long time, the camp simply languished; falling into disrepair. Then, it was discovered that the Piping Plover had taken up residence on the island and with the bird's endangered species status and an infusion of federal funding, the island became a nature preserve.

Now it was open to the public a few weeks out of the summer for daytime visitors only. The old restrooms and showers from the days when it was a summer camp had been repaired and brought up to code for the island's birdwatchers and beachgoers. The ranger station, which used to be the camp councilor's cabin, even had a little gift shop. Suddenly, Fade Island was one of North Carolina's premier tourist attractions. Some for the birds, some for the surfing, some for the exploration of the paranormal, and some for the legends of pirates and buried treasure.

I suppose we were guilty of the last just as much as anyone else, the only difference being, we were the professionals.

We'd set up a mess in one of the covered picnic areas, and the other we used as a sort of barracks, stringing canvas on all sides and pinning it to the earth on the edge of the concrete slabs. Rows of cots were set up for the guys in that one. My tent had been set up just up the path from the buildings, near what was called the Mirror

Pond. It was so named for its smooth, glassy surface and near mirror-perfect reflection it gave of the sky.

"Avery!" Mac called from outside and down the path. "Come get your breakfast before its gone, baby girl!"

I smiled to myself, and rose, shrugging my feet into a nearby set of flip-flops. My hiking boots were down near the four shower stalls, which we'd added doors to with permission. It was only cold water, but in this heat and humidity, none of us minded that terribly much.

"Coming!" I called back down and thrust my tent flap aside.

It was promising to be a long day fraught with annoying questions given Jacob Lennox's presence. I always hated it when the investors hung around an expedition. I especially hated it when that investor was a banker or accountant. This was going to be worse given that this particular investment banker was attractive, and thought he was God's gift to women. It would be unprofessional of me to disavow him of that notion, no matter how pervy he got. He held the purse strings, and he who holds the purse strings, like it or not, holds the power.

Fucking asshole, I thought bitterly. Which was just fine, as long as I kept it in my head and didn't let it out of my mouth.

Hopefully, Mac and the rest of the boys would keep him in line for me, because if it had to resort to *me?* Those purse strings would be cut real damn quick and this would all be for naught. I couldn't and wouldn't accept failure as an option, not when we were so close, I could almost taste it.

I took the last turn in the path to the outbuilding housing the restrooms and did what needed doing. It was already hot, but the cinderblock, no-nonsense building that held three bathroom stalls, two sinks, and a blower, always seemed to remain cool. I half thought about setting up a folding chair and TV tray in here to work at when the heat became totally unbearable.

I did my business, washed up in the sink, and headed for the mess, leaving the cool respite of the bathroom reluctantly. The nice thing about it was there was a reprieve coming by way of the caverns where we were finishing up getting set up. Everything was ready to go except the ROV, and Pete would have it working now that he had his spare parts.

I pulled aside the canvas and stepped into the little antechamber we'd made. Satisfied there were no flies or other winged pests trying to make it in, I stepped through the mosquito netting and into the mess.

It took a second for my eyes to adjust to the dimness, but I was pleased to find pancakes, bacon, and eggs were the breakfast choices today. I picked up a plate and went along loading it up. I scanned the room and the four picnic tables for Mac and found him closer to the unused fireplace at one end of the shelter. Unfortunately, Jacob Lennox was with him.

I refused to let Mr. Lennox run me off, and went that direction anyway, taking a seat beside him, and across from Mac, asking him, "You see Pete?" before shoveling in a mouthful of scrambled eggs.

Mac grunted and nodded, swallowing his own mouthful of food before answering, "Yeah, he's gone up to the caverns already."

"Kind of figured now that he can get his baby up and running," I said dryly.

"I thought Pete was just your mechanic," Lennox said looking at me, but at least not openly leering this time.

"Pete *is* our mechanic, but if it's something he repairs, it's his baby."

"So, who drives the thing? I thought that took some kind of special technician."

"I do, and I'm called a pilot," Keith said and dropped his plate with a splat on the other side of Lennox, waving at him to scoot over. Lennox obliged gladly, scooting right into me and putting his leg right up against mine. Mac and I both glared daggers at Keith who never knew when to quit joking. He gave us a secretive shit-eating grin right back and I raised an eyebrow at Mac. Mac smiled back at me conspiratorially and gave a single nod in my direction. Keith lost his easy grin and ducked down, shoveling food in his mouth.

"Mr. Lennox, meet Keith Aldridge, our ROV pilot."

"Please, call me Jake." Mr. Lennox held out his hand and Keith wiped his greasy bacon fingers off on his shorts before shaking.

"You're the investment banker, huh?"

Lennox laughed and nodded. "That I am."

"Word to the wise, try not to get in the way. It makes Avery angry, and you wouldn't like it when she's angry."

"Keith, shut it!" I barked.

"Oh no," Lennox said, laughing. "Looks like she's about to Hulk out."

I took a deep breath in through my nose and let it out slowly, trying to contain my irritation. When I got angry, I tended to lose my mastery of the English language and started dropping f-bombs like they were a comma. Around the regular crew, big fucking deal, but around uptight investment bankers handing me the boatload of cash allowing me to make this work? Probably not a good idea.

"Avery!" I looked back over my shoulder at Kurt Wallace, my diving partner. He waved me over to his table, and I took the life ring he was tossing me.

"Duty calls," I sang out and stood. "Don't mean to be rude, but when Kurt calls, I answer." I put on my thousand-watt smile and picked up my plate, stepping out from the bench seat and tried like hell to not make it look like I was scurrying away.

"Who's that?" I heard Lennox ask, the note of jealousy in his tone totally not lost on me.

"That's Ave's diving partner," Mac grunted, but he gave Keith a sharp look. Keith zipped it and ducked his head back down over his food.

I laughed to myself and took the seat next to Kurt who had the kind of physique that could put an Olympic swimmer to shame. He wasn't just a hot body and a pretty face, either. In his mid-thirties, Kurt was a retired Navy Seal. We'd known each other since we were kids, although Kurt was older than me. When he'd decided to join the military, we'd already been diving for years together. When he went to boot camp, I'd felt the loss keenly. The best thing about

Kurt, at least for me, wasn't that he was such a badass, it was that he was my best friend and safe to be around. I'd played his girlfriend for just about every military function he'd needed to have one at, because another thing about him? He was as gay as the day was long. In fact, the first thing he asked me when I dropped onto the bench beside him was, "Who's the hot guy?"

"That would be Mr. Jacob Lennox," I said dispassionately and Kurt lost his shiny hopeful expression immediately.

"The pervy one that's been bothering you?"

I sighed. "That would be the one and Jesus *fuck*, word gets around fast."

He shrugged and glanced back over his shoulder at Lennox saying, "Damn, I thought for sure he was batting for *my* team." He sighed. "Guess he's just metro, not gay."

"Sorry to burst your bubble," I said with a shrug but I wasn't really sorry at all. Kurt could do so much better than the likes of Lennox.

"Seriously, way to be a killjoy," he said with a smile and bumped his shoulder into mine. I had to laugh.

"Is that the only reason you called me over here or did you have any business you wanted to talk?"

"Nope, just wanted to know about tall, dark, and handsome."

I grinned. "Trust me, if you could get him off my scent, I would be forever grateful."

He harrumphed and chewed the bite of food he put in his mouth and I took the opportunity to shovel mine full again. We chewed in mutual silence before he said, "I want to get in the water."

"I do too, but you know Mac isn't gonna let it happen until we have a target, and as detailed a map of the cave system as we can get with sonar and the ROV."

"I know," he said and visibly pouted.

"I'm right there with you, partner," I said, grinning.

"Let's finish up and see how deep these caves go, shall we?"

I snorted. "With how high we have to hike, and with how filled with seawater those caves are, it's going to be tri-mix all the way.

Those caverns are *deep*, and the water has to be coming up from the bottom."

"I know." He grinned wide. "Challenge accepted. I really can't wait to get some idea of what we're up against."

"Me either, but safety before anything."

"I know, I know…"

"And you're supposed to be the *reasonable* one of the both of us."

Kurt grinned happily. "Always."

I rolled my eyes.

IT WAS NEARLY DUSK BY THE TIME WE CAME DOWN FROM THE CAVES, and I was tired, hot, grimy, and just wanted a *shower*. We'd made a ton of progress in fixing the ROV which had been damaged when we'd offloaded it from the *Sapphire Horizon*, mine and my dad's research vessel, which was now in hock up to our eyeballs.

Pete had sworn up and down that it wasn't an accident, that someone had damaged her on purpose. Per usual, we'd butted heads over his drinking and argued until Mac and Kurt had to get between us. Luckily, Lennox hadn't been around to see it. He wouldn't understand it anyhow. These people, this team, we were like *family* in a lot of ways. Half of them I'd grown up around, then a good quarter I had grown up *with*, and finally, the rest of them had been with me and my father for years *before* Gwen had nearly destroyed us with her shady shit.

Anyway, it had been a mentally and emotionally exhausting day. We'd been here a week already and hadn't even gotten in the water once. It was a waste of time, and a waste of money. None of these guys worked for free. Their paychecks needed to be cut for their time whether we were or were not getting anything accomplished. Likewise, they all needed to be fed, the parts for the ROV needed to be bought and *those* weren't cheap; neither was the fuel to get the *Sapphire Horizon* back and forth from the mainland to resupply our food and pick up those parts.

Yep. Frustration had been the rule of the day today, and I wasn't pleased. I just wanted a shower, and to spend some time with the reason we were all here to begin with... Eamon Bligh's journal.

I went into my tent and fired up the generator to make sure everything was charged up. I figured by the time I was showered, everything should be topped off on their battery power. I took my time cleaning up, the cool water soothing after the sweat, grime, and grind of the day. We had a small gator all-terrain vehicle, but it still took muscle and elbow grease lifting equipment on and off the thing.

As I stood under the stiff jet of cool water, letting it pound between my shoulder blades, I let my mind drift and where should it go? But of course, the erotic dream from that morning. I had no idea *where* that had come from, but I couldn't deny, I'd liked it. I'd liked it very much and couldn't help but harbor the secret hope that I'd meet my dream lover again.

Usually, I dreamed and then I forgot all about them after ten or fifteen minutes awake. Very rarely did a dream hang with me all day like this one. In fact, if I closed my eyes, I could see those startling green eyes of his. Like pale emeralds set in his strong, handsome, sunburned face. I sighed out, shivering, but not from the icy cold sinking into my bones from the shower spray. No, this shiver had nothing to do with the cold at all.

I shook my head. *Who are you?*

He didn't look or act even remotely like any former lover of mine, or any from-afar crushes I'd ever had either, celebrity or otherwise. It was like my imagination had simply made him up out of whole cloth. It was beyond strange, especially when I recalled all the details; a small scar on his right shoulder blade, another over his left eye, a crude tattoo of a spray of feathers on his bicep... Christ, the dream was so vivid it was difficult to remember it hadn't actually happened.

I made sure my hair was rinsed well of shampoo and conditioner and turned the single tap, shutting off the spray. I took my oversized beach towel down from the hook outside the shower's door and wrapped myself up in it before stepping out of the stall and shrugging my feet into my waiting flip-flops.

When I got back to my tent, I pulled on a pair of black boy short panties and a spaghetti strapped white cami so I wasn't nude, then took the time and care to braid my wet hair over my shoulder. I sighed. Not wanting to risk dripping water on the journal, I instead booted up the laptop, keying in my password and calling up the transcription of Bligh's journal.

In among describing the events of any given day, Bligh had recorded many personal and philosophical observations, covering his views on just about every subject imaginable. A few of them had made me blink in surprise; for a sailor and a pirate, Bligh had been way ahead of his time about a lot of stuff. Some of it was pretty personal, the way journals always were.

The thought of my sweet sister locked in demeaning slavery never fails to provoke the spectre of guilt, I read. *Had I only been at home, instead of away fighting the king's wars I might have been able to prevent the travesty of justice which destroyed my family. With the treasure I now possess, I will do my best to apologize to Emma for her needless suffering.*

Wind and wave push me closer, and I count the days. Would that it were possible for me to tell her I am coming, that a new life of comfort awaits us both. For I am coming, Emma. I will find you.

The words made me frown. I was just enough of a romantic to feel a twinge, because I knew the truth; by the time Eamon Bligh had penned these words, his sister had already been dead almost a year from a botched childbirth. I kept reading, drawn in as I always was by Bligh's story. Parts of it read like a thriller novel.

A venture such as ours is ever uncertain, but one private fact remains in my heart, locked away from all others. Justice was denied to my mother and my sister. I cannot change the past, and there is no purchasing justice for my dead mother, nor will there ever be.

A chill went up my spine as I kept reading. I could almost feel the anger radiating off the words. *Whether I will live to spend the gold I have pilfered is unknown, but one truth remains... I will not let the king and his cronies have it back. Even if I must send it to the bottom of the ocean, His Majesty is now the poorer for its loss, and will remain so. Gold cannot pay for blood, but carving such a fortune from the Empire's flank is better than letting my mother's murderers remain unscathed. For it was the crown which murdered her.*

If justice is denied, to her and to me, I shall settle instead for base vengeance.

I leaned back with a sigh. Reading the personal details of Bligh's story brought me no closer to finding the gold, but I couldn't help it – his life made for damn good reading. Not for the first time, I wondered what he looked like. He'd never sat for a portrait during his life, and the only contemporary description of him I'd been able to track down was a few lines penned by Bligh's former captain during his time in the Royal Navy. I'd memorized it – *Tall and clean-shaven, of good natural parts and personal bravery, yet possessed of a contrary intransigence which surfaces at odd times and defies all logic.* It wasn't much to go on.

I glanced at the last words once again – *If justice is denied, to her and to me, I shall settle instead for base vengeance.*

"Pity you didn't make it," I murmured.

Exciting as it was to read, Bligh's story was pretty damn sad. He'd lost his family, and had been caught, taken into port at Charleston and jailed. There had been a prisoner uprising, but as far as records showed, he'd been hanged without accomplishing any of his goals except for making sure the English crown hadn't gotten their treasure back. If we were successful in finding the gold, I planned on opening up a museum exhibit somewhere so that people other than me could know the story. It *deserved* to be known.

I reread the words I'd read probably a thousand times before until my eyes began to droop. Satisfied that everything was sufficiently charged, I shut down the generator and went to the Coleman lantern hanging from the tent's ridgepole, illuminating its interior like a captive star.

I twisted the knob to douse the light until it stopped hissing and wearily took myself to bed. The last thought I had before I slept was of a warm, masculine body, pressing me into the thin mattress.

CHAPTER FOUR

SEPTEMBER 1731

*E*amon Bligh...

There is a strange place that exists between wakefulness and true sleep, and I am aware of this gray predawn time. I am also aware that I am not alone in my bunk. There is a weight, warm and soft, pressed against my own. A woman, nude, her own eyes open, staring into my own.

By the Lord?

I did not fly from the bunk, my hand did not seek dagger or cutlass, and that was how I knew this was not waking, but that I was still on the cusp of dreaming. Her eyes were as blue as the sea and just as bright, her lush lips turned up into an imp's smile. She had the semblance of the angels painted by the Italian masters, but fairer. I thought to speak, to ask her name, to demand how she made her way into my bunk, but when my lips parted, she placed hers against mine. Such thoughts fled, and I was drawn into this kiss from my strange goddess.

This is a dream, nothing more.

I let my hands wander along the curve of her shoulder and down her back. Her hand grazed my face, her fingernails traced lines down the side of my neck. She was supple, her body smooth and perfect, clean and flawless. She moaned softly into my mouth and wrapped one of her legs around me. I was keenly aware of her nudity, and she was completely shameless. Perhaps she was more a siren and less an angel.

Did she know my thoughts? Because her mouth wandered away from mine. Her breath was warm on my neck, and on my chest. She traced an old scar from a sword wound with her lips, and I lost my breath when she found my nipple. Her hair was soft, golden as the first blush of sunlight as it rose over the horizon, and she smelled curious. Perfumey, but clean, not the overly sweet or cloying way a whore did. She moved lower with her kisses, undoing buttons and laces.

I groaned aloud.

Her angel's face hid the Devil's temptations. She took me into her mouth, and I could not breath. Her fingers ran down my chest, my stomach, and I was still breathless. If this was the dream I was going to have, I wasn't going to fight it. It was a damn good dream.

She eventually released me from her mouth, and I groaned. She straddled me, pinning me beneath her, her face glowing with angelic lust. The shape of her smile was wordless desire. The look in her eyes reinforced that. She rolled her hips and I felt her, hot and wet, against me. I shuddered, and thoughts of reservation, sin without shame, left me. I could take no more of her teasing and I grabbed her hips. I had to have her, I needed her. Her eyes shone! I thrust.

God!

I bolted up with an inarticulate shout, my heart pounding in my chest. I was rigid and indisposed, that much remained unchanged, but my bunk was empty, I had no siren atop me. I rubbed my face with my hands, my fingertips sought out my own eyes as if they could press the sleep from my skull. I pulled down the hem of my shirt and redid my disheveled laces. Thankfully, without the siren, the fallen angel, my ardor had cooled. I contemplated sleep but thought the better of it. The gentle rolling of the ship, the creak and groan of the hull was familiar, almost enticing me back to sleep.

I was still alone in the captain's bunk. I half expected her to appear, as if she were real and not some creature from the land of dreams.

"Bloody *hell*," I muttered, staring at the rough timber above me. I dug through the effects of the former captain and found in his locker, a bottle of some sort of rum, though if it had a label it had since been rubbed away smooth. I took a small pull from the bottle to ease the nerves. It seemed my nerves were ill at ease most of these days. My sleep was frequently disturbed. We were near a week's travel north from where we left the better part of the crew and the wreck of the *Queen's Mercy*, but still some distance from the coastline we sought. These were still the king's waters, and he claimed the colonies, but it was where he sent those men he disliked, those he would have far away from him, their backs bent to breaking the new land and filling his ships with the bounty of the New World. There were many among them who were no friend to the crown. The sea lanes were not empty, and we passed several ships – Dutchmen, free traders, mostly. We alternated between flying those same free trader colors, or the king's colors when it was wise.

Her hair, it was so fine, so soft, and her skin almost glowed without flaw or imperfection. Could someone exist so, outside of those Renaissance paintings of the angels? Even those, glorious as they were, were somehow even flawed in my mind's eye.

It would be difficult to shake her from my mind. Most of my other restless slumbers were easily brushed away, cobwebs that fragment upon too close and inspection. The more I thought on her, the more real she felt, and not the opposite. Her memory should decompose, snap away like pipe smoke on watch, or billow and vanish like hot breath on a cold morning. The impossibility that she represented haunted me. Her teeth, straight and white, not one turned a bit, not a dark spot. She had been taut as canvas in full wind, but yielding and supple. She had strength in her body and was no frail thing. Her skin, her damned skin – not a scar, not a ghost of pox, no bruise or blemish – it was impossible.

Then there were details I could recall as easily as if I were describing a member of my own crew, or a family member. There was a beauty mark above her lip, in and of itself no rare thing, but hers was no painted-on whore's decoration. Around her waist her skin was pale, the sun shadow of some garment she must wear, like the island girls favor, but smaller. She had been completely free of lice, and her lady's tuft was trimmed as neatly as a dandy's beard. I have never seen as such.

She was so real. *God's wounds!* I could still feel the memory of her kiss; warm, and strangely, tasting of… mint.

"Who are you, my siren," I whispered.

I tried to shake this base lust from my head. I had my own reasons and refused to let such ignoble passions consume my mind. Every man has his phobias, his unmaking fear. Some shrink back from bared steel, others from great height, some the bottomless ocean and the creatures that dwell in it, the touch of the dead, crawling things and biting creatures. I was no different, though none of those things stirred my gut. I knew comfort on the sea, and feared neither man, nor beast, nor battle, and I was well accustomed to Death and when he came for me. My only question would be if I met the harvester with bared steel and resolve, or if I would welcome him as a friend.

No, my phobia was something else, something far more common, and frequently overlooked. *A man's wits are what sets him apart from children and beasts,* my father had told me. That was the end of my fear, the loss of my wits, the rot of the mind. That was how much I had believed his words. But that was the end result, not the object itself. I saw my fear almost every time we put ashore in some free port or pirate-friendly harbor. I saw in in the brothels and taverns where the men would slake their lusts in whatever would have them.

'The French malady," I said aloud, to no one in particular.

I knew the ravages of the disease, the toll it took on sailor and prostitute alike. The skin would be marked with lesions, rashes, and eventually their minds turned to jelly and they couldn't care for themselves. Their constitution would fade, and their breathing would fail. Their hearts would give out, and it was a horrid wasting death.

I swallowed another mouthful of Blaine's rum. The burn helped clear my thoughts.

I would one day meet my end. It was an inescapable fate, but I hoped that it would be on my own terms, and that I would meet the Reaper and dance with him, my wits and cutlass against inevitability and the harvestman's scythe. I wouldn't wind my way to the grave down a madman's path from a few minutes purchased or stolen passion. This fear had resulted in keeping far more coin in my purse, and limiting the intimate charms I had exchanged to a select and rather small number of the fairer sex.

And none had been as flawless and talented as she had been.

I shuddered as my flesh remembered her phantasmal touch.

Mind your tasks, Mister Bligh, I said to myself. *You're no fresh cabin boy, nor poet to be seduced by dreams and imagined pleasures.*

"Captain, sir!" Hawkins knocked and called at my door. I rose to my feet and donned my captain's hat before heading up to the deck. The ocean breeze was warm and heavy. I knew that such meant fog could be likely on the morrow. There was a different scent in the air as well, something that I didn't care for – not a stink or foul smell, but a hint of cool air, storm scent. That wasn't important, not yet.

"What do you see?" I questioned Hawkins. He stood on the forecastle, arm raised and pointing excitedly.

"Seabirds, sir, seabirds!" He whooped.

I drew out the spyglass and lifted it to my eye, it was indeed seabirds. A number of them coasting above the waves, they wheeled and took turns diving at the surface of the sea. "Good eye, Mister Hawkins," I said. "You know what that means?"

"Land, sir. It means we're close to land," Hawkins said.

"Indeed, it does," I said. I turned and let the spyglass chase the horizon, and the seabird smile faded from my lips. It died. That cold scent, behind gray clouds churned and grew. It was a storm. No squall line, but a great storm.

"Full canvas!" I called. The men on the deck jumped to their stations, half puzzled, half alarmed. "Storm to aft and closing fast. Give me every inch of canvas you can, and we'll try to steal its own winds to outrun it!"

"Can we outrun it?" Hawkins asked nervously. This was likely the first time he had seen one of the great storms from the deck of a ship.

"God willing," I said.

The fact that my golden-haired, glowing-skinned siren had finally left my thoughts was of no concern, *Honor's Price* had to fly.

CHAPTER FIVE

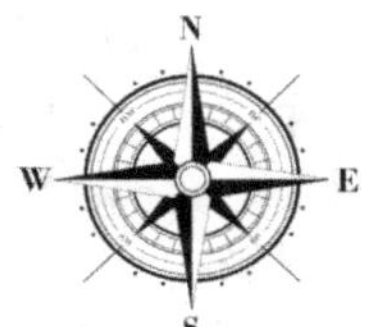

JUNE 2016

*A*very Barker...

"Ave get up!"

I groaned and sighed out, frustrated. It'd been such a pleasant dream with the mystery man of the morning before. I'd liked it, too, because this time *I'd* been in the driver's seat and had gotten to ride *him* on what looked to be some old ship in the captain's quarters.

"Avery, damn it, *get up!*"

"Whaaaat?" I whined and Kurt ripped the canvas aside, stepping into my tent.

"Doesn't look like we're going down any time soon at this rate, dammit. If we want to send the ROV down, we'd better get on it. The Doppler says a storm front is moving in."

I shoved up off of my bed and twisted, demanding, "How bad?"

"Batten down the hatches, it's going to be a blower."

"Whhhhhy?" I whined and pouted.

"Universe isn't quite done with the cock and ball torture I guess," he said, rooting through my footlocker and throwing clothes at me.

I sighed and shucked out of my cami and panties, not caring about doing any of it in front of Kurt.

"Gross," he teased, and flung my bikini bottoms at me off his finger like a rubber band. I caught them, snatching them out of the air with one hand, just in time for the top to follow. I grabbed it out of the air with the other hand and stuck my tongue out at him.

"You don't know what you're missing," I told him.

He snorted and looked at me dubiously. "Trust me, Avery, baby; I know *exactly* what I'm missing, and I'm *glad* for it!"

I laughed and tied my top behind my neck, adjusting the girls into the cups, before pulling on the navy-blue board shorts he held out to me over the bikini bottoms.

"Presentable enough?" I asked and he looked down into my foot-locker and back up at me, critically. He finally pulled the white tee shirt he had on off over his head and held it out.

"Pervy-Perverton is still out there. I wouldn't put it past him to help himself to a handful. Better throw this on until a time you have to get in the water." I rolled my eyes but took the shirt. I wasn't at all surprised that Kurt would literally give me the shirt off his back. It was how we were.

"Kay, come on. I want to take a look at the Doppler myself, make sure this is going to be as bad as the stormpocalypse you're claiming it's going to be."

"It isn't a hurricane, but it's still pretty significant. Wind, rain, thunder and lightning are expected."

I made a face and laced up my Keds. "We get thunderstorms through here all the time."

"Yeah, rain, thunder, and lightning, sure, but not so much wind. Not like what's predicted."

"Ugh, why couldn't you have just let me sleep?" I finished tying off my shoes.

"Having some good dreams?" he asked, amusement lighting up his face.

I narrowed my eyes, suspiciously and sat up. "Maybe," I said. "Why are you asking?"

He grinned even wider and I felt the hot rush of blushing humiliation from the morning before return to my face.

"Never mind, forget I asked," I muttered and he *howled*, laughing so hard he had tears leaking out of the corners of his eyes.

"Keith is never going to let you live it down," he said and I froze.

"Just what the fuck did Lennox *tell* you guys?" I demanded, knowing Mac might have told Kurt, but he *never* would have said *anything* to Keith – not in a million years.

"Come on, I'll fill you in while we walk. Time's a wasting and I've got some of the guys bringing us breakfast burritos up at the caverns."

"I really don't want to hear this, do I?"

Kurt's toothy grin didn't diminish in the slightest and I felt nauseous. I wasn't going to want to hear this *at all*.

HIS PLAN TO GET ME UP TO THE CAVERNS AND TO BYPASS THE MESS hall was an utter failure. By the time we reached the mess, my temper had not only been ignited, it was a full-on California wildfire chewing through acres of self-control, that like the mansions out there, I could only ever *dream* of possessing.

"Lennox!" I barked and he looked up from the table where he sat with Pete, Keith, and a couple of the other guys. Keith blanched and immediately went back to his food, suddenly finding his scrambled eggs totally fascinating.

"Avery…" Kurt murmured, his tone one full of warning. *Be cautious,* it said, *we still need his money,* it said, and he wasn't wrong. I was pissed, but I'd like to think I could keep it together enough to not blow our one and only shot at this before we had a chance to do it.

"Ms. Barker, what can I do for you?" Lennox asked coolly and I gritted my teeth.

You can get the fuck off my island and leave me to my goddamn work, I thought, but what came out was, "A word if you please?"

Kurt gave me a look like, *you want me to stick around for this?* I gave him a nod, because *absolutely* I wanted witnesses.

Lennox strode toward the front of the picnic shelter turned mess hall and followed me and Kurt out, I kept walking to get outside of earshot, up the trail toward my tent just a bit short of the edge of Mirror Pond. I stopped at the trailhead and turned on my heel to face the boys.

Lennox laughed slightly and said, "What is this about?" I gritted my teeth and gave him my best scathing look, counting silently to three before I opened my mouth.

"You may be one of my investors but let's get one thing straight, you are here because *I* allow it. Furthermore, *while* you are here you will abide by the following rules – one, you will respect my privacy and you will announce your presence before you *ever* enter my space again. Do I make myself clear?"

He looked down on me, amusement sparkling in his eyes, and said, "Go on."

"Two, you will conduct yourself like a *professional* with my team. This isn't a holiday and I am their *boss*."

He chuckled lightly and Kurt scowled. "Something funny?"

Lennox reared back unconsciously from Kurt's formidable scowl as well as his menacing stance before he looked back down at me. "Don't you think you're overreacting just a little, Ms. Barker?"

"Because I don't find anything about sexual harassment amusing?" I countered. "Because I expect my operation to run clean and drama free and you're fucking that up right now?"

"Avery…" The warning was back in Kurt's voice and I tried like hell to get my temper back in check. If I didn't, I was going to start using the word 'fuck' like a comma and I was *so* going to lose points if I did that. I was a woman, and this was a boy's club. I needed to hold it together or I was going to be shrugged off as a hysterical female and that wasn't going to happen. Still, I wasn't going to allow this piece of shit yuppie scum to piss on the respect I'd hard earned from my team, either.

"Ms. Barker –" Lennox started and I cut him off.

"Unless you're going to follow that 'Ms. Barker' up with an apology for violating my privacy and behaving like a lowlife frat boy perv, then going one step further and trying to undermine the rapport and respect I've earned with my crew, I don't want to hear it." I paused for dramatic effect and let what I thought of him sink in. "But you wanna know who *is* going to hear all about this in my next status report if you don't shape up?" I raised my eyebrows as his look turned almost murderous. His jaw clenched and he smoothed his lips together as he tried to decide if I were bluffing about running to Mr. Bancroft.

"I may joke about a lot of things, Mr. Lennox, but I don't bluff about being a jackbooted feminazi. You picked the wrong woman to sexually harass. I've played this game a lot longer and a lot harder than you could ever dream. Welcome to the big leagues. Either show some respect or you can take your ass out of here on the next supply boat."

His mouth dropped open and Kurt stood there, shoulders shaking with the laughter he was trying to suppress. Lennox looked at Kurt and said, "You let her talk to your investors like that?"

"I let her talk to men who have zero respect for women like that. You underestimate everyone here by thinking we're all on your side by virtue of sharing the same anatomy. About the only ones you'll find any solidarity with are Keith and Pete; and Keith *likes* Avery, while Pete at least knows who signs his paychecks."

"I do believe the Bancroft Group is the one signing *all* of your paychecks." Mr. Lennox's look was dark, and I gave him an exceptionally nasty smile.

"Right you are, *the Bancroft Group* does sign our paychecks and last I checked, your last name was Lennox." I was beginning to sweat, and it had nothing to do with the heat and humidity. I was beginning to gamble here, and hard. I needed to quit while I was ahead and so I did.

"You'd better think about some things, Lennox," I said, starting back down the trail, walking backward to keep him in sight. "As I said before, my crew actually *likes me*, and Mac? The one who found you in my tent? Yeah, he's been my father's best friend since before I was born. I somehow doubt he'd have a problem embellishing the truth in my favor."

"I know I wouldn't," Kurt said, having my back all the way. Then he smiled and flipped the script on Mr. Lennox. "Besides, if you want a lover while you're here…" he looked Lennox up and down with a slow sweep of his chocolate brown eyes, before cocking one eyebrow, lips spreading in a slow, sexy smile that typically made girl's panties spontaneously combust. "I'll show you a really good time," he finished and it was everything I had in me not to explode with laughter at the look on Lennox's face.

All presence of anger was wiped away and I filled right up with joy. Just one of the reasons why I loved Kurt as much as I did. Not only did he have my back, he always knew the right thing to say or do just when it was needed the most.

I stopped just outside the mess and took a deep breath before letting it out slowly before I stalked inside. "Finish up and do it quick. I want to try and get this show on the road before this storm hits," I said before quickly dishing myself up some oatmeal, grabbing a couple of bananas, and heading out and up the trail leading to the caverns. Breakfast burritos were Kurt's thing, I didn't like them that much.

I ate on the go, my body trembling finely from the aftereffects of my anger and adrenaline. Just because I was as feminist as they came, didn't mean I wasn't fully aware a man outstripped me physically any given day of the week. If Lennox had swung on me, he could have hurt me and bad before Kurt could react. Plus, what would happen if Lennox cornered me when Kurt wasn't around?

You'd fucking hurt him back, but what would it cost you? I asked myself.

It was a fifty-fifty chance putting a man on notice like that. On one side, he could take what I'd said to heart and back the fuck off like he was supposed to. On the flip side, I may have just presented an irresistible challenge. We'd see which way the coin landed eventually. Right now, I had other things on my mind.

I reached the caverns and sighed, slowing my march into an easy stroll so I could take them in. It was at the highest point of the island, the brown rock hollowed out and the entrance big enough to roll a couple of big rigs through. When you went in, it was a marvel of nature's beauty – vines and ferns growing on the ledges of rock until the sunlight couldn't be reached.

We had folding tables with equipment set up just inside the cave, as close to the water as we could get while still maintaining contact with the satellite uplink. From the tables it was a wide swath of fine silt beach to the gently lapping water. We'd set up a catwalk that ran down the center of the beach and out over the water. In the center of the dark pool was a platform, square, with a center square cut out of it. Hovering over the cutout by its hoists and winches was the *Wet Dream*.

I drew up even with the tables sporting monitors, radios, and all manner of technowidgetry involved with our craft and glanced at Mac who was peering through his glasses at the Doppler's screen. Patterns of fierce red and orange started at a point offshore and meandered their way in double and triple time over the pin set on the island's map denoting our location.

I asked him, "Is it as bad as Kurt is saying, or is he just being a drama queen?" Mac looked up at me, expression both solemn and grim. I swore and sighed out harshly. "What's it looking like, Mac? Are we packing it in and weathering the storm or do we have time to take the *Wet Dream* down for an exploratory run?"

"Trust me, baby girl, as much as I want to get *Dreamy* in the water, with the way this storm is shaping up, I think our time would best be spent battening down the proverbial hatches. We aren't gonna get shit else accomplished if *Dreamy* gets damaged worse than she was before. We also don't have the money to replace equipment. I'd rather be safe than sorry, sweetheart. Move you into the sturdy shelter with us guys tonight and tie down anything that might wanna take flight."

"*Son of a bitch,*" I muttered. I blew out my cheeks, hands on my hips, fingertips tapping against one of my belt loops before making my judgment call. Mac didn't even need to hear me say it, he just wordlessly passed me the radio sitting next to the Doppler's monitor.

"Attention all personnel, Avery here. Lock it down people, we're in for a rough bit of weather. There won't be any dive today."

Someone cued their radio mic in the mess, likely Keith, to all the moaning and groaning going on and I had to smile, I felt the same keen disappointment as they did. I cued my radio mic and said, "Pete, Keith, as soon as you wrap it up down there, I need you up *here.* I want to bring in *Dreamy* and get her snug as a bug in a rug."

Pete's grizzled, gnarly, voice came over the radio, "For once you have some goddamned sense. Be right up."

Mac and I exchanged a look and laughed a little. "Glad we finally agree on something, Petey. Avery, out."

I sighed and looked into the cavern where the *Wet Dream* hung forlorn and a little sad, her bright yellow fiberglass hull sparkling from the care Pete put into her. I looked off to the side, and behind me at the mouth of the cave where she'd come from – a fiberglass housing unit we used for ground transport, attached to a small trailer. We'd hauled her up the trail carefully with the Gator, but that still hadn't stopped her from shifting inside the hard shell, damaging one of her servos. No matter what damn fool alternative theory came out of Pete's mouth, I was damn sure that was what'd happened.

"Think she's gonna weather okay up here in just that?" I asked Mac.

"I think she'll be fine. Chock her wheels but good and maybe drag her back here into the cave a little bit more, she should be fine. I'd stroke Petey's ego and ask him, though. You know how he gets."

I rolled my eyes. "Pete's becoming a regular high-maintenance bitch."

Mac laughed, blue eyes sparkling under his bushy graying eyebrows. "I don't disagree, baby girl."

"How much of this can we start breaking down?" I asked.

"I'd wait for Keith on *Dreamy*'s controls, but everything dive related, any of the scuba gear, that's our world, girly."

"Let's do it," I said and we got started on what was bound to be one seriously long day of going in the wrong fucking direction. *Damnit!*

~

"WELL I WAS *GONNA* TAKE A SHOWER!" I DECLARED, RAISING MY VOICE to be heard above the rain.

"Might as well just hand you a bar of soap and let you go at it," Keith yelled good-naturedly, and he didn't mean anything by it; he was right. We had everything crated, boxed, and stowed under the picnic shelter we were using as a mess hall, the canvas staked and lashed down as good as it was going to get. All of the digital equipment we couldn't afford to have tossed around by wind, or to have it get wet, we'd managed to stow in the ranger's station doubling as the island's gift shop. It was locked up as tight inside the sturdiest four constructed walls as we could get.

I wish I could say the same for *us*. The best we were going to get was the roof of one of the picnic shelters over our heads and the concrete slab of it beneath our feet. We'd reinforced all four sides as best we could with tightly lashed canvas, as we had with the mess shelter, but I still found myself worried. I wished hard that the camper's cabin hadn't burned down over ten years ago. It was where the concrete foundation of what was now the second picnic shelter had come from.

"Well, we aren't going to get over there standing around like this," Mac stated and I shrugged.

"At least I'm dressed for it," I said.

"Me, too," Kurt added, but didn't sound at all happy about it. I was with him; I would have much rather gotten wet by way of diving than dashing through the onslaught of rain between us and the next shelter over.

We took two steps and were soaked, the white tee I'd thrown on over my bikini top plastering itself to my skin which made me groan inwardly. By the time I got into the open maw of tent flap that was the barracks, all I could think about was who was going to be the first to say –

"Competing in a wet tee-shirt contest, Avery?"

I gave the man who'd spoken a withering look. "Shut up, Carl!"

I looked back over my shoulder at Kurt, who'd lashed the canvas doorway to our shelter shut, and listened to the rain beat on the roof and pour from the eaves. We'd moved my collapsible bed from my tent, had taken the entire tent down and brought it in here too. It rested in a heap of canvas on my desk next to where my bed had been put back up. I was set apart from the guys, the desk and pile of my large tent between my bed and the canvas wall, providing more of a wind break.

Under my desk, sitting on an overturned milk crate to keep it up off the concrete, sat the little fireproof safe with Eamon's journal. On top of the safe, sat my industry standard, super rugged laptop. The kind of thing you saw in the movies that required you open a catch to unfold it and had a built-in handle to carry it like an attaché case.

We had lights, the Coleman lanterns hissing loudly. We had the generators piled in the middle of the room, out of the rain. I didn't want to admit I worried still about their safety, even as the wind began to pick up, the canvas snapping, the lashing holding it to the pillars and beams creaking and groaning.

If the generators still weren't safe from the storm in here, what did that say about us?

Best to leave that question unasked and to weather this with a sort of bravery I for sure didn't actually possess, which was another lesson I'd learned early in the game about being a woman in a leadership position… *Fake it 'til you make it.*

"Avery, get your skinny ass over here and warm up," Mac said gruffly, and I nodded, making my way between the long lines of bunks to the fireplace at the end. He had a fire going, and it looked like we were actually going to need it with how blustery it was. The storm had dropped the temperature, and even though it was still warm, add wet and cutting wind, it felt much cooler.

I pulled Kurt's soggy tee over my head distastefully and took the towel Mac held out to me, running it over my hair, wringing water from the ends while a bunch of the guys looked on from their bunks – light, aluminum-framed things with a heavy, nylon material lashed with paracord to act as a mattress, and sleeping bags rolled out on their tops and good for a single man.

They actually weren't too bad; pretty comfortable, if I did say so myself, and I would have used one but I had some serious sentimental value attached to my bulkier camp bed. It was almost like if I couldn't have my dad here with me, I wanted to surround myself with as many things that were his or that he had a hand in making for or with me. Hence, why I'd had his old, battered desk brought up from our research vessel.

Things just weren't the same after his accident. He just couldn't get around as easily as he used to and it killed me, to see him robbed of so much of his joy.

"Here." One of my guys passed me a steaming tin cup full of stew and a heel of hard crusted bread. I smiled and gave a nod.

"What next, oh Captain, our Captain?" Carl asked. I looked at him, a younger guy in his early twenties, his dark hair pulled into a man bun, his close clipped beard fitting his face. He looked good, muscular and lean, and sometimes I thought it was a shame that I was the boss and couldn't go there. Then again, as hot as some of my guys were, none of them held a candle to my dream guy. I pushed those thoughts away and answered Carl's question as it'd been legit.

"Now," I said, chewing a bite of stew and swallowing, "now we weather the storm. Tomorrow, we put the camp to rights and then, we dive. Doesn't much matter what time we send *Dreamy* down, day or night, makes no difference at that depth. We clean up, then we stop fucking around and go find what we came for."

"Passionate speech," Lennox said, rolling his eyes. I had to give it to him. He hadn't sat on his ass today. He'd surprised me by pitching in and taking things down, hauled equipment as much as my regular crew had, and had really pulled his weight. I was guessing it was a bid to get inside my good graces enough for me not to go and tattle to daddy, and I was actually okay with that.

Lightning flashed and thunder boomed outside. Lennox flinched, and I didn't, but only because of a lesson Mac and my father had taught me long ago. We'd gone to a gun range when I was something like twelve or thirteen, with both of them having every intention of teaching me to shoot. It'd been loud, the cracks and booms of guns going off making me flinch.

My father had looked at me and asked, *Are you flinching?* I'd been raised to be honest and had told him the truth, that yes, I was flinching from the loud noises. He'd looked at me critically – in the way that had always made me take notice – that whatever he was about to tell me was going to be of grave importance and a lesson in more ways than one. He'd driven the magazine home in the gun we were going to use and had told me point blank, *Stop flinching,* before he jerked back on the slide and began to fire at the target Mac had set up.

His words, *stop flinching,* had been like magic. I hadn't flinched from more than just gunfire ever since. The thunder rolling over-head? That was nothing.

I tried to do for Lennox what my father had done for me. I made eye contact and asked him, "Are you flinching?"

He looked at me and paused before nodding his head. I nodded once back and with grim determination, said the magic words… "Stop flinching."

I got up and went back down the line of cots to my waiting bed. Shucking out of my wet board shorts after kicking off my Keds, I declared, "Lights out in twenty minutes. We get a stray gust of wind; I don't want anyone burning up in their beds because a lantern fell on them or exploded."

"Sounds good, Avery," someone called, and I heard Keith quietly say to Lennox, "There's more than one reason she's the boss."

I smiled, my back turned to the room, and hoped that would

sink in. I was tired, and I wanted so badly to crack Eamon Bligh's journal, but it just wasn't a good idea. Neither was turning on the laptop. So, instead, I tucked under my blankets in my damp suit and huddled down, closing my eyes.

A strong gust caused the canvas to snap and my eyes flew open. I pushed myself up into a sitting position and looked down the two rows of cots, only to find them empty, the fire beyond them in the hearth completely out; not even embers remaining.

I twisted slowly, taking in the shivering canvas walls, the interior of the shelter lit an eerie blue, as if by moonlight, between the brighter, white hot flashes of lightning. I swallowed hard, the fear of the storm and for the sixteen men, here but not here with me, gripping me.

As I panned to my right, toward the entrance to the shelter, I realized that I was hearing another sound, the soft spatter of dripping water against the cement floor. Heart in my throat I expected some jungle Swamp Thing like monster, but what or rather *who* I found kneeling there startled me further.

It was my dream lover, his green eyes wide in fear and disbelief, likely a mirror of my own. His face was twisted in a grimace and a mask of blood. Panic seized my heart and I threw the blankets back where they were pooled at my waist and went to him, taking up his hand which hung limp, cold, and dripping at his side. I looked at him, cupping his cheek, the stubble rough against my palm, and he collapsed against me, unable to hold himself up in a sitting position any longer.

I pulled back, not liking how cold he was, and drew him up so I could look at his face, to figure out what was wrong. He dropped his head in a bow and more blood gushed, dripping down to his face and I realized he had a serious gash in the back of his head, near the crown.

Thunder crashed and he tensed. I shivered and cuddled him into me, laying my lips against his shoulder as his arms went around me, holding onto me. We kneeled like that for a series of heartbeats while my panicked mind got it together for me, listing everything I would need. The tempest raged, and I struggled with the weight of him draped over me, to get him up, to help him stand. He got the picture and struggled with me and I got him to my cot, seating him on the edge.

I looked down at him. His eyes both dazed and bright with curiosity, his expression filled with confusion. I felt a sort of stillness, a feeling like this was where I was meant to be, right here, right now, helping him, and it made me turn with grim determination to root through the pile of crap nearby for the emergency med kit.

The stranger in my dream, in my heart, and in my head, watched me, clearly hurt and dazed but appearing as if a sense of safety fell over him. Good, that was good. I found the industrial-sized med kit and went back to him, kneeling on the floor in front of him and opening it up.

He reached out and laid a rough hand along my face and I looked up, startled, into those green eyes of his, a silent beseeching coming from them and I smiled, laying a kiss in the center of his palm that tasted of salt and copper.

He would be fine. I would fix this, and I promised him with a look while I frantically searched for the damn penlight.

CHAPTER SIX

*E*amon Bligh...

Honor's Price was fast, but we were short crewmen. The storm was faster and was soon upon us. The men clung to the rigging, going to their tasks, but these were not the sharpest of seamen, and as one man attempted to furl the mainsail, a man opposite of him was trying to let out more canvas. It was all I could do to hold the wheel, bracing myself against the helm. The wind howled, and the waves rose, lifting us. At times I could feel the rudder cut nothing more than air, thence back into the brine.

The gambit to outrun the storm had failed, and we were closer in to shore than I expected. Were this the open sea we could heave to, or bring the bow about and show this whore of a storm our teeth, bare with determination. Too close to land, I didn't know the depths, the rocks, and a wide sweep could take ground the hull, or splinter it.

Damn my eyes!

"Reef that mainsail!" I shouted above the gale, throwing a

commanding gesture above. "Furl the topsails! I said furl the topsails!" Mr. Hawkins was ghastly pale, but he took the command and scurried up the main mast and shouted my orders up. The men heard him, and looked to me. I shouted again and pointed at the sails.

Salt stung my eyes, and the world was chaos. The waves broke over the deck, the wind roared through line and canvas. We would be at the mercy of the storm, but as it was, we were so oversailed that the *Honor* was trying to heave and roll, the rudder fighting the rigging and the hull caught between. We could lose a mast, rip canvas. We were in God's hands.

The *Honor* dropped out from under us, cresting a wave and falling into its trough. The wind seemed to howl, like a hungry beast baying for our blood and bones. There was a sharp cracking sound from the main mast, hard as a pistol shot. My head jerked up, and above in the rigging, the men were still fighting the sails. The mainsail was still catching wind, and if they didn't furl that canvas, we could lose the mast.

"Curse you!" I shouted. "Curse you and those sails! Furl that mainsail!"

I saw a man twist on the mast, losing his feet and balance to the wind. Cold dread clenched in my chest as I saw the man, Mister Jenkins, tumble and fall. He grasped for a second at a rope on his plummet but his fingers failed him, and the deck greeted him with a sickening thud, or perhaps I only imagined hearing that sound.

There was no way a man could have survived that fall, and Mister Jenkins did not stir from his repose. There was no time, and no hands to go to him. If we lived through this devil's tantrum of a storm, well then there would be time for words and grief. Now, a single man wrestled the largest sail on the *Honor*, and too much of it was taut in the wind.

What would take us? Would the mast snap, and tangle all the rigging, leaving us completely without action? The ship might catch too much wind and we could watch the bow dive into a wave, then the sea would rush in to embrace us. The rudder bit into the water again and the chains and wood between it and myself groaned. It was a Herculean struggle, holding the wheel true, keeping the wind and waves from taking us in the side.

That sail had to come down even if it meant cutting it free. Better to lose a sail than the entire ship, her crew, and the king's lucre.

"Mister Morgan!" I shouted above the sea's voice.

"Aye, Captain!" Morgan shouted back, his hands holding to the helm.

"You will do me the pleasure of taking the wheel," I said.

"What is your fancy sir?" Dougal shouted back.

"The mainsail will be our damnation; she must be set free!" I replied.

"I must protest, Captain!" Dougal looked alarmed.

"Bide your tongue and tell me later," I said, and clapped him on the shoulder, passing the wheel and the helm to him. "Keep her with the wind, keep her steady!"

I flew across the deck, ignoring Dougal's protests and curses. I came near to ruin twice as I made my way headlong to the main mast – once to a wave, and then to poor footing. Perhaps it was God's mercy, as the wave took the body of Jenkins and washed his blood away. I reached the mast and clenched my dagger between my teeth before taking to the climb. The sky above churned, and lightning split the clouds. Above me, I could see a lone man. He had largely given up fighting the sail and instead clung tightly to the rigging and spars.

I happened to make the mistake of looking down once. I knew the distance wasn't great, but the deck seemed like it was a great and terrible distance away, and the sea itself seemed like something out of a preacher's sermon, the boiling wrath of a merciless god. My ascent seemed like nothing more than a rigorous attempt at suicide.

I was near to the main spar and *Honor* took another gambol over a great wave, and I felt a tremor run through the mast. It wouldn't take much more of this abuse.

"Captain!" the man clinging to the rigging shouted and gave me a hand up to the spar. He had himself steadied with a length of rope tied around his arm. Dangerous, but perhaps less so than the fall that Jenkins had taken. "You shouldn't be up here, sir!"

"Cut the bloody sail free!" I shouted. "Cut the lines!"

He looked at me, and vigorously nodded his head. "Aye, Sir!"

"Hurry, Mister Hammond!" I shouted. I headed to port, wrapping my right hand in the line as he had, my dagger firmly gripped in aching fingers. I started slashing at the lines. Each parted rope loosened the sheet, and the strain on the mast was reduced. The sail was freed to move and the reward for this was to be battered by the heavy wet canvas. Between the storm and bully boy sail I nearly dropped the dagger and my footing.

Fall, damn you, fall, I thought, but the sail remained unperturbed by my ire.

I could not reach the last bit of rope, not without surrendering my line in the rigging. I had hoped that by this point the weight would have snapped the last few bits of rope, and saved us the effort, but the hemp hung strong. I cursed. To cut the last of it, I would have to surrender my senses and self-preservation to walk the spar to near its end.

I could make out the profile of land to port, a great rocky coast. The mast groaned again, and each gust could be the last it would bear. Then I thought of Emma. *I cannot fail to save my sweet sister, I have to live. If I am to live, the sail has to be freed. I am all that is left and it falls to my hands.*

I gripped the dagger in my teeth again and began to crawl the length of the spar. I prayed to God that I not lose my grip. I prayed that the spar remained true, that the mast would hold, that Mister Dougal kept our course and the rudder chain was strong. I prayed that I would see Emma's jade green eyes again, and this, finally, gave me the clarity I needed.

My arms burned with the effort, muscles quivering and my fingers felt icy and numb. All the while the wind and rain beat at me. I tensed every time the spar flexed, the mainsail flapped furiously and the wood groaned in protest.

Just hold. Just a bit longer.

Finally, I reached the last of the line. I attempted to loosen the knot, but the weight of the sail had it drawn tighter than a bow string. I was about to switch the dagger from teeth to hand when the ship gave a great lurch, and the spar sprang beneath me. I came a finger's width away from losing my grip, not down to the deck, but upward, outward.

God be merciful.

I had almost been lost to the storm itself, in that instant. I shuddered, my fingers gripped the spar and line with white-knuckle intensity and fear coiled in my gut. From where I was clamped like a barnacle, I could see the depth of my dilemma. To reach the last line, I would have to use my knife, and there would be no balancing atop the spar. No, that was tricky enough in calm weather and while I knew my knots and sails, it had been some time since I had the rigging barefoot.

With grim determination, I found a loose line still firmly attached to the mast and tied it around my arm. I tested my weight against it, and it held. I would have to dangle from the spar, creep to near the tip, and then while hanging by one arm, cut the snarled line free with my dagger.

I set myself to my seemingly futile task. I sawed at the cursed knot, and I shivered from the relentless wet and sheer effort of my task. My safety line had started cutting into my flesh, but I was so close.

Come on, come on! Blast you!

And then it did. The rope parted, and the weight of the mainsail was gone. Ropes sang through the rigging, and the great expanse of canvas blew away with the storm, releasing its weight from the mast and the spar. I floated for a fraction of a second, the spar flexing upward, and I was following it. Then, with a crack and a flash like lightning, my head met the bottom of the spar. Strange colors swirled behind my eyes, and everything seemed to have become muted. I dangled for a moment, vision darkening around the edges.

I was spent, but the deed was done. I knew I was injured, but the lack of pain was distantly concerning. I had to get down from the mast, and quickly. I grabbed a line that seemed to run to the deck. I pulled and loosened the loop around my right arm and hoped that this was not my second fool's errand of the day. I hopped from the spar and thought to use the rope to slow my descent. It would hurt, but far less than Mr. Jenkin's arrival.

I wrapped my leg in the rope, and even soaked through, it bit. I hurtled toward the deck, and the rope turned into a ribbon of shark's skin in my hand. It was far worse than I had imagined, and I knew that there would be blood, and the ocean's kiss was worse for it.

The deck seemed to lunge for me with supernatural speed, and I thought that I would scream, but my mouth couldn't decide which particular tone of alarm it would sound, so it made none. My heart was in my throat, and had decided that it too was not going to act until after the landing.

I'm sorry, Emma.

That seemed like a suitable last thought, my final words, before I was dashed against the deck planking. I tried, I had tried and found greater success than I thought myself worthy of. These must have been thoughts of acceptance and surrender because as they flashed through my mind, dazed as it was, my grip failed completely and the rope was gone from my hands.

I reached the deck.

The storm exploded into a flare of burning and bloody red. Thunder exploded all around me, and then?

Nothing.

CHAPTER SEVEN

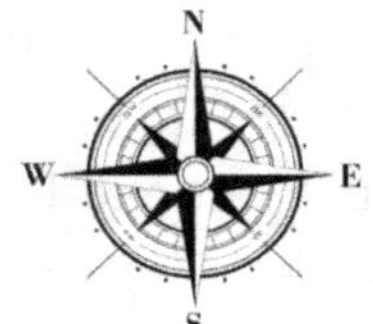

JUNE 2016

*A*very Barker…

It was a bad cut, but his pupils were equal and reactive to the light I shone in them, even though he hadn't been keen on that. Now, I kneeled behind him, his body leaned back against mine, sucking occasionally on the end of the penlight I held in my mouth so that I could see what I was doing.

Both my hands were occupied with stitching his scalp laceration closed, and it was a doozy. It looked like it would take nine of my careful stitches to close it. A nasty sliver of wood that I'd pulled from the injury lay on a bloody piece of gauze by one of his hips and I couldn't even begin to guess what he'd been into, *or why I would dream this.*

I pushed all my questions to that end out of my mind and just tried to enjoy the simple act of caring for someone again. This wasn't my first rodeo when it came to giving stitches. My dad had taught me when I was, ironically, nine years old. *Nine was when I started, nine stitches he was getting... wonder if there's anything to that. Probably just something my subconscious dragged up.*

I knotted and clipped the thread and felt his shoulders ease down from where he'd tensely held them. He really hadn't liked the lidocaine shot I'd given him to numb the area, but then again, when it was me, I didn't let them give me the shot. Once had been enough. It was worse than getting the damn stitches to my mind.

I got up and he jerked slightly, jumping at any sudden movements. I came back around and kneeled on the floor in front of him then turned his hands over. He had his wrists resting on his knees, the palms hanging over empty air and I had a suspicion. I hissed at the bloody and torn rope burns to them and shook my head. Sucking on the end of my penlight I turned and rooted through the first aid kit for the giant ass tube of antibiotic ointment plus pain relief, scoring the big bottle of Tylenol with codeine along the way in the search.

I popped the top on that and held two out to him on my palm. He looked at me and then them with suspicion and I frowned.

Could he seriously not know what they're for?

I pantomimed putting them in my mouth and swallowing and he just kept on with that look, like I was out to poison him or some shit, but finally he bowed his head and took them up off my palm with his mouth, chewing them with the most disgusted look on his face. I laughed and shook my head and held out a bottle of water. He washed it down, but again, didn't try to use his hands. *The poor man.*

I cleaned them as I had his scalp wound and he gritted his teeth. I put a hand on his shoulder rubbing it and grimacing, taking absolutely no delight in hurting him further but knowing it had to be done.

Once I'd managed to disinfect everything thoroughly, I slathered on generous helpings of the antibiotic ointment with the pain relievers in them. He watched me as I carefully wound gauze around his hands to keep the wounds clean and an ACE bandage over that to keep everything in place.

I think the Tylenol with codeine was working for him, *thank you,*

Canada, because his eyes were a bit glassy and he just looked so tired now – tired and relieved. I put everything away in the medical kit and shut off the penlight, putting it back in its place before I closed the kit up. He reached out and traced my face with gentle fingertips that weren't wrapped like the tan version of the mummy's hand and I stopped, looking up at him.

The moment hung between us, thick and almost alive and I kneeled up and leaned in, kissing him lightly and carefully. He trembled slightly under the touch of my fingertips and I drew back and smiled and it felt a bit wan. He'd been through something terrible but for some reason, here in the dreams, neither of us dared to speak. As if speaking would shatter whatever magic there was and everything would disappear never to be again.

I didn't want that. I don't think he wanted that either.

I helped him to lie down on my cot and went around to the other side where there was still room and laid down next to him. He turned on his side to face me and rested one wrist on the rise of my hip.

I smiled at him again and he closed his eyes, but he was smiling too. I watched him as long as I could until sleep overtook me too and when I opened my eyes again, it was to the sun pressing in on the outside of the canvas walls we'd rigged on the picnic shelter and to the sound of the guys waking up.

"Jesus Christ, that was a hell of a storm!" Mac boomed out; his voice strained with the luxurious stretch he was giving.

"Shit, yeah, it was," Pete agreed.

"Weirdest thing ever, I slept like a brick," Carl said, pulling on his hiking boots, sitting on the edge of his cot.

"How'd you sleep, Avery?" I rolled my eyes and pushed the blanket off of my head and sighed.

"Not as good as the rest of you apparently," I said, answering Mr. Lennox, the investment banker. I got up, stretching myself before promptly tripping over the goddamned med kit next to my cot.

"What the fuck you have that out for?" Kurt asked scowling. "You alright?"

"Yeah, fine," I lied. "Thunder gave me a headache, went for the Tylenol."

"Shit, you good to dive today or what?" he asked.

"Better safe than sorry," I said, cursing myself on the inside for painting myself into this corner. "If we can manage to get the ROV in the water, you'll have to make it happy. Nobody is actually diving today."

"Fair enough," he said, looking me over. "You sure you're okay?"

"Yeah, just a headache." I hated blowing him off like that, but there wasn't any way I was going to tell him the truth. That I had dreamed all that I had dreamed and that somehow the med kit had moved over here in real life.

I opened it up and looked, but nothing had been used. While things had certainly been moved around… all of the packaging was intact and none of the things I had dreamed about using were actually missing.

Thank God for small favors. I didn't need to be needlessly replacing medical supplies because I was sleepwalking.

Still, I was rattled down to my very core. This was weird, and beyond weird at that. Still, I couldn't stress about it right now. I had too much other shit to worry about than whether I was going crazy.

"Where do you want to start today, boss lady?" Carl asked.

I looked over at him and said, "You and the rest of basecamp can get basecamp put back together. Kurt, Mac, Pete, and I are going to go up and check things out at the cave system and make sure our babies are safe. Let's hope there isn't any damage to anything important, boys."

Forty-five minutes later, we were standing at one of our canvas walls while Mac and Kurt unlashed them from the standing timbers of the picnic shelter. The canvas dropped and we all looked out and froze.

"This island is frickin' weird," Carl said and his proclamation was met by a bunch of semi-astonished grunts of agreement.

"Don't look a gift horse in the mouth," I said and was the first to venture out.

While there were fallen leaves and small branches, the outside of the shelter didn't match at all what we'd heard going on last night. The guys came out after me and I said, "Load the chainsaw onto the Gator, anyway. We don't know what it's going to look like up the mountain. Maybe there's more damage."

There wasn't. A quiet kind of descended on all of us the further up the incline we rode on the Gator. Aside from a shit ton of mud and a few smaller branches, there wasn't anything we had to stop for or cut out of our way. With how bad the storm had been, there should have been way more damage than this.

"How do they look?" I called out.

Pete had leaped off the Gator while we were still in motion so that he could stride into the mouth of the cave and check things out. God forbid anything happen to any of his precious equipment. He was always far more concerned about it than the humans most of the time.

"Not a scratch on it," he called back.

"Good deal." I gave a nod and cued my radio to share the good news with basecamp.

We unpacked laptops and folding tables and went into the shelter of the rock and the standing pool inside. Our scaffolding, everything, was perfect. Nothing shifted, nothing collapsed.

"Rock on!" Kurt declared and I reached up over my shoulder with a fist. He bumped it and sailed right on past me saying, "Pete, let's get your precious out and ready to rock. We might actually get the ROV down there today."

"Maybe," I called back, giving in to Kurt's good mood.

"If there's any visibility," Mac reminded us.

"Fuckin' killjoy," Kurt teased.

"What can I say? I'm a realist," Mac shot back.

I bowed my head and chuckled as they bantered, making sure the connection to the monitor cable was snug as I moved around hooking things up while Pete worked with Kurt, and Mac got the generator uncovered and ready to go.

It took us the better part of four hours to get everything set up and ready to go. We'd radioed down to basecamp and Carl had told us lunch would be brought up so we could keep going. Kurt was just about out of his mind wanting to send our smaller ROV down to check things out.

I sighed and said, "Suit up. The water's bound to be cold."

"Yay!"

I rolled my eyes. Pete made a disgusted noise while Mac just laughed.

We worked our asses off and got everything set up in record time, the thrum and undercurrent of excitement of any impending dive or action contagious, rippling through the camp like wildfire.

"Hold on Kurt! Gotta get the monitor up at basecamp," Mac cried.

"Tell 'em to hurry the fuck up!" Kurt called back irritated.

"Well, you're the one that jumped the gun and got in the water early," I called back and Kurt splashed uselessly in my direction. I straightened up so that I was sure he could see me over the monitors and flipped him the bird with both barrels.

He laughed and kicked lazy circles around the space inside the floating catwalk we'd erected around where we'd sent *Wet Dream* down. We couldn't do anything until Keith got his ass up here. I radioed down to basecamp and asked, "Anybody got eyes on Keith? We're ready for him up here."

"Yeah, I'm right here!" he called from the mouth of the cave.

"Good! I'm freezing my balls off in here, man. Let's go!"

"Way I heard it, nobody told you to get in there," Keith called back and I laughed.

He sat down on the folding chair and began his systems checks, flipping switches and hitting buttons, moving joysticks left and right, up and down, calling back and forth to Kurt.

"Okay, kids, all systems are a go," Keith declared, and called out to Pete operating the winch, "Slack on the line!"

Pete yelled back, "Slack on the line!"

Kurt echoed with a "Yup!" and *Wet Dream* began to lower. I hated this part. *Dreamy* was a heavy piece of machinery and with Kurt in the water like that to handle her into position and loosen her tether, so many things could go wrong but we were all highly trained professionals and so I didn't micromanage. Instead, I gritted my teeth and gave every outward appearance of assurance that I one hundred percent believed in my team.

That was just it, though... I *did* one hundred percent believe in my team. It was fate, or karma, or the powers that be – mother nature, the curse of whatever treasure – all of that shit that could and would throw monkey wrenches into everything at any given time. You could plan for and train for everything except the unexpected.

"How are we looking?" I asked Keith and he smiled but never took his eyes off the monitor or his hands off the controls.

"Splashdown achieved, oh Captain, my Captain."

"We unhooked?"

"Couple more seconds."

"Sonar's up," Mac declared.

"Good deal, good deal," Keith muttered, then yelled out, "Hey Kurt! Come on up outta there would you?"

"Yeah!" Kurt yelled and I saw him haul himself up onto the edge of the platform.

"And we're diving in three... two... one..." *Dreamy*'s thrusters kicked up a white foam of bubbles and then she was gone, the surface smoothing over. I looked down from the real view to the monitor view and grimaced.

"A lot of particulate," Mac said nonplussed and unsurprised.

"Guess we can only get so lucky for one day," Keith said. "But we aren't down very far either."

He was reading everything, the sonar, what we could manage to see on the monitor, which wasn't very damn much for all the silt and sediment stirred.

I sighed, a real headache brewing. It was not an ideal first dive, and the further down we went, the worse the visibility got.

"What do you think, boss?" Keith asked me.

"How's the current?" I asked.

"Fighting it some."

"*Dreamy* in any trouble?"

"None at all."

"She better not be," Pete grumbled and I had to smile. Salty old bastard who I rarely agreed with he might be, but he always had the equipment in fine working order and the budget's best interest at heart by keeping it as safe as possible.

"Right, I think tomorrow would be a much better day for this, give things time to settle. Go ahead and shut it down," I said.

"Yes, ma'am."

"What, just like that?" I turned to look back over my shoulder at Jake Lennox.

"Just like that," Mac said.

"Did you get *anything* useful out of this or was it just a waste of money?"

"Got plenty of useful sonar," Keith declared.

"Tomorrow will be better, don't you worry," I told him and sighed inwardly. I didn't want to play nice with the asshole, not if he was going to constantly second-guess me, which it looked like that was the road we were headed down.

The headache was for real by the time I got down the mountainside. I was grateful to my crew that they had my tent back up and I had my privacy again. I just wanted to go to sleep and see if I dreamed anymore strange dreams.

CHAPTER EIGHT

*E*amon Bligh...

The world slowly brought me back, and I was aware of a dreadful pounding sound. It took some time to realize that it was my heart. I was yet still alive, and I was not alone. It took several attempts to force my eyes open. When I finally succeeded, it seemed like the ship was sailing perilously close to the sun, and we should have been in danger of bursting into heatless flame. I groaned and closed my eyes. I was cold, laid out on some flat surface. I didn't think it a coffin – pirates are typically afforded either a toss over the side, or to dance a jig at the end of a rope. It wasn't a coffin, but it still felt cold as a grave.

"Water," I managed to croak.

"Ah, there you are, Captain," I heard a voice. I cannot make out who it is, not at first. Thankfully they do not wait for me to name them before giving me a small tin cup of water. I drink a little, and cough. Each cough is like a cannon shot near my head.

"You've taken a blow to the head, Captain," my caregiver said. I thought it might be Dougal, the accent seemed right. "We've been worried that you might be joining Mr. Jenkins for a swim later."

"The ship?" I asked.

"In a more fair shape than you, sir," Dougal said.

"The storm?"

"It's gone," he said. "We've run aground and furled all the sails. Storm blew like something straight from hell, and then you know how the sea is. It kept on howling and roaring and as quick as it was on our stern, she was gone chasing the horizon." I blinked a few times, my eyelids remembering their proper function, and the furious sun was nothing more than an oil lamp lighting my quarters. I could make out Dougal and his great red Scotsman's beard. There were others in the cabin as well – Hawkins and Hammond, grim Mr. Baxter, and unfortunately, the sour-faced Forsythe. Of course, the storm would not have seen fit to take him.

I closed my eyes and marshalled my strength. I thought of the fallen angel again, and how strange and different she had been – strange clothing, and the curious medical implements she had, the attentions she had paid to my wounds.

"Are you still among the living, Mister Bligh?" I heard Forsythe ask.

"That I am. You'll not be rid of me so easy," I said. I forced myself to sit. I was sore, and the ship decided to spin a few times. My vision blurred, but I managed to rub my face until they focused again. There were no bandages on my hands but looking at the upturned palms they were red and angry. I knew that in my plummet to the deck, they had been sawed to the quick by the rope, and there had been blood. I touched my scalp gingerly, where her hands had done strange work. There was a great knot and some remnants of dried blood, but it seemed far better than I should have hoped.

Are you real?

There was no other possible explanation.

"Easy, sir," Hawkins said. "That was a nasty fall."

"Aye, sir, best to err to caution," Dougal said.

"There will be time for caution later," I said, and turned enough to put my boots on the floor. "Casualties?"

"Mister Jenkins took a fall, but he was probably dead when the sea took him overboard. Mister Stebbins was not so lucky and was very much alive when he decided to take a swim," Forsythe said. "And until you opened your eyes, most of the crew was counting you among the deceased.

"We've also run aground most seriously," Forsythe said after a pause. "Onto rocks that you navigated us directly toward."

"A storm does as a storm does, Mister Forsythe," Baxter said. "There isn't a sea without storms."

"The Americas have been quite kind," Dougal said. "Giving a fast place to rest."

I took to my feet and Hawkins moved quick to steady me. I put a hand on his shoulder, and while I leaned on him, to the others it seemed like I was holding him at just slight of an arm's span. The crew streamed out onto the deck of the *Honor* and I walked to the railing on the port side. The ship was struck upon a great mass of jagged rock. The timbers showed great distress, and some were broken. A full crew could free her from this predicament, but for an abbreviated crew of myself and fourteen men, impossible.

I could feel John Forsythe's eyes burning into my back.

"A fine port you've chosen," he said. "We cannot free ourselves because this sea dog steered us wrong. The Americas were wrong, running for the coast was wrong, and I cannot wait to see what folly he aims us toward next. So, Captain," he said icily, "what are your orders."

I ground my teeth for a moment, then unclenched my jaw. I rolled my arm, testing my shoulder. "Mister Dougal," I called tersely.

"Aye!" he said.

"I require a brace of pistols with powder and shot, and a brace of cutlasses." He looked at me curiously. Perhaps he imagined that I was going to board the rock and fight them? The rest of the crew regarded me, and I saw it begin to dawn in John Forsythe's dark eyes. "Our articles are very clear, every man's quarrels are to be settled ashore, with pistol and blade."

Murmurs went through the small group that remained of our crew.

"We all made our marks in Blaine's book, my book now," I said. I gave Forsythe a challenging savage glare. "Is your mark there, John?"

"What?" he asked, startled. "Aye, my mark is there. The same as many man's here."

"We are ashore now, are we not?" I asked pointedly. Several of the men chorused "Aye" but he was not one of them. "And you've made no bones about opposing me. You wanted the captaincy then, and you want it now, don't you?" I asked, not allowing for him to answer. "You have a quarrel with me," I said, dropping all pretense of civility. "I'll have the end of it, one way or another."

"We are wrecked," Forsythe said. "This is hardly –"

"We are ashore!" I shouted. "So, either pick pistol or cutlass, or do you lack the conviction. If you lack the will to face me now, you do not have the fortitude to wear this hat."

There was silence on the deck. I felt my body, quivering and weak, and prayed that Forsythe would not see through my bluff. If he picked pistol, I had a small chance. If he picked cutlass, he was better with a blade than I and would win easily. I was prepared to face him, to have the end of it. The men saw it too. Their faces were worried, nerves frayed, even shocked. Dougal remained stoic. He had spent years in the king's service and that discipline remained.

Forsythe looked down, his eyes on his boots. The ship groaned as a wave shifted its weight, a reminder of our situation. There was going to be no duel, and I decided to follow the articles, and let him off as lightly as possible. So long as he minded his ambition, we would move forward as if there had been no challenge, the conflict forgiven.

"Secure the rigging, make sure those sails are properly furled. We'll be lowering the masts. Won't do for a passing king's ship to find us and decide to make target practice of us." The crew snapped to and went to carry out my orders. John did as well, but his step was a bit on the slow side. He wasn't eager to jump to my commands, and his eyes were dark as night. He had lost again, and there were few things more dangerous than a humiliated man. I would have to keep a sharp eye on him.

IT WAS SOMETIME LATER BEFORE I WAS ABLE TO RETURN TO MY CABIN. Dougal had made me rest, and take food and drink. He had wanted me to retire sooner, and absolutely refused to allow me to help with the rigging or the lowering of the mast. We reached a compromise – I would remain on deck, but would do so as the captain, making sure all was done to rights, but not doing any of it myself. By the time I did retire, I felt as if I had labored as hard as the crew.

The tasks were done, the masts were down, the canvas was squared away, and we were as concealed as possible. The day had not agreed with my injury or exhaustion, but the ship was well enough, and the crew placated. A few were singing as I pulled the door shut.

I dug through the captain's desk and found the maps and charts. I discarded all but the ones of the Americas, and the American coast. I had to determine where precisely we were, and how much of a problem it would be. Blaine had been an avid collector of maps, so I had several to choose from. If things were favorable, we would be able to take the treasure to a nearby shore in the longboats. Two had survived, and we could winch them down the starboard side of the ship. The weight of the lucre would be an issue. They were long-boats and not treasure galleons and could only carry a small amount of gold in each trip.

I unrolled the map I sought and weighed it down with pistol and dagger. This kept the near duel with Forsythe in my mind. That is where it needed to remain.

Figuring our precise location was difficult, nearly impossible. The storm and the winds had been sudden and erratic and there would be no dead reckoning our position. The flora and fauna we could spy from the ship was exotic, so there was no guessing by that. For all we knew, we could be miles from a township, just a spit of land away from a hostile port or marooned on some godforsaken island known only to birds and sea turtles.

I took a reprieve from the map and took *Honor*'s sextant above deck to find our position using the stars. Thankfully the skies were dark and clear, and I found the star of the seas, Polaris, and quickly calculated from that where we were. With coordinates in my mind, I returned to the maps.

I sat and plotted the path we had struck through the storm. I had to focus, the men expected it, and if I couldn't find our bearing, it would do Emma no good. I traced my finger along the lines of the map and found our location. There was a palpable sense of relief. Under my finger was a collection of coastal islands, ringed in double lines, the Ghost Islands. They were known, but they were not properly mapped. With a name like that, they were most likely the demesne of local superstition and uninhabited – an excellent place to be.

The cabin door creaked open. I snatched the pistol from the map table and aimed for the door. I had a bead drawn on Mister Dougal, who promptly held up his hands, they were empty. "Easy, Captain, I come in peace."

"In the future, Mister Dougal, I would advise knocking." Hesitantly, I lowered the pistol, taking my thumb off of the hammer.

"Aye, that would be the truth," Dougal said, keeping his eyes on the pistol until I returned it to the table.

"I assume you have need of something?" I asked.

"Advice, sir, and the giving of it, not the asking for it," Dougal said.

"Out with it, then," I said.

"This is your first time wearing the hat, and for the most part, you've done well, sir." Dougal said. "Those words being said, you've only made a single serious error, nearly a grievous one."

"And of the many mistakes that have befallen us," I asked, "which one specifically do you speak of?" I fetched the worn bottle of the captain's rum and the same tin cups we had shared his good Scottish spirits with. I poured two drams of brown liquor and gave him one. "I would have your honest council, Morgan."

"It was the mainsail, Eamon. Climbing the rigging with a knife in your teeth. That was a poor choice of action, and it would mind you well to not repeat that folly," Dougal said, accepting the cup of rum. He took a sip and raised an eyebrow.

"It's no highland peat," I said. "And the sail had to come down."

"Aye, it's no highland, but it's got its own charm. The sail indeed had to come down, but you are the captain and your duty is to command."

"We are light on the side of crewmen, and there are plenty who could hold the wheel," I said.

"That might be so, but there is only one man among us who can navigate and set our position by the stars. You're the only one who knows where we are, and thus, the only who can set us to the right course," Dougal said sternly. I was sore, tired, and the rum was creeping up on me like a footpad.

"Young Mister Hawkins had the right of it. You are our captain, and if you hadn't woken from your storm nap, we would be in far worse straits for it," he said. "What do you think we would do if Forsythe had the hat, or even Baxter? No, sir, you are the only man among us who has been educated to use his mind and wits. The rest of us are common buccaneers and scallywags. How many do you think can read or know their numbers? Hell, there aren't many men here who can write their own name. The captain's ledger is full of pirate's marks, not blasted names."

"If we lose you, Eamon, we lose everything. You know that," Dougal said. I wanted to argue, that I was just any man, just another member of the crew, but he was right. "In the future, when the Lord God sees fit to send us a tribulation, you give the order. The others take the risk in your stead."

"We could afford to lose a bastard or two from the crew. You know who I mean."

Dougal regarded me firmly. "We lose you, we're damned and dead men."

"Morgan," I said, tipping him some more rum, "you should be the one wearing the hat and barking the orders. You've been at sea longer than I've probably been alive."

"Aye, there may be some truth to that, but two problems. Firstly, the men, they chose you. I cast my lot for you if you recall." I nodded; I did remember that endorsement. "Secondly, I have no want for that damned hat. I've seen what it does, and what it takes to wear it. I'm no captain. I'm a cook, and a fat man, and a bastard."

"I'll drink to some of that," I said.

"You'll drink to all of it, Eamon. You have to learn a few tricks. Know your worth, and when the time comes, don't be afraid to be the bastard. We're pirates, the lot of us. If you aren't at least something of a bastard, you'll not wear that hat long."

"I'll take that under advisement," I said, and finished my rum.

"You know our reckoning?" he asked. I nodded that I did and tapped my finger on the map. "Good, good to know. Now that is squared, you ought to take to your bunk. Rest will take the hurt out of the beating you've taken in the last day."

I had no conviction to argue. Dougal was in the right. I sorely needed to rest. He thanked me for the rum and left of his own accord. My bunk beckoned, and as I undressed and tucked myself into it, I wondered if I would sleep as I had before, would I dream of her?

I had no problem finding unconsciousness.

I DREW IN A BREATH, AND THERE WAS THAT SMELL, SHARP AND CLEAN. I knew she was there, pressed against me. I didn't open my eyes, not yet. She caressed the side of my face with her hand, a feeling warmed through me. I opened my eyes, and she was there, golden hair, flawless skin, her bare breasts pressed against me. I touched her, caressing her face as she had mine, cupping the cheek, brushing her ear with my fingers. I slowly ran my hand down the side of her neck to the roundness of her shoulder.

My dream siren, my fallen angel.

Her smile grew, and her eyes sparkled. As my hand lingered on her shoulder, her own hands were deft, moving under my shirt, tracing outlines against my stomach. I could see her desire without feeling for it, I knew that would come momentarily, but this tender moment, I wanted to hold onto it as long as I could.

I pulled her close and kissed her. Her fingers grasped at me and she kissed me back. I ran my hands across her, feeling how real she was – the rise of her hips, her ribs, my thumb stroking the side of a breathtakingly soft breast. Her kiss was hot, and she tasted of mint and desire. I felt myself rising, I could not resist desire eternally.

The years of self-discipline, the polite and not so polite rebuking of prostitutes, the women I had denied for my own reason, they faded. It was a dream anyway, at least, that is what I told myself. I thought of our last dream meeting, the strange kindness she showed me, the way her hands took the pain away from my injuries. I felt a different sort of ardor grow inside me.

There was no mistake, I intended to have her. I was going to have her, but it was going to be my way. The last time she had appeared to me clad in nothing but a smile, she took me in her mouth, and the thought stiffened me, and I thought of her neat tuft. I pulled her head back, my fingers buried in her beautiful golden hair. I kissed her neck, and she moaned under my atten-tion. I tightened my grip and she made another sound deep inside.

She liked that.

I traced my lips across her collarbone, and down to her upturned breast. The skin was flawless as the rest of her, the nipple a soft pink, and already stiff with anticipation. I kissed around it, teased it as she had teased me. Perhaps she was real, somewhere else, and she lay in her own bunk imagining my lips on her breast, moaning the same in her slumber. I would do her one better than that. I finally took the nipple in my lips and drew it into my mouth. God, she was soft and clean. I shuddered with excitement for what I planned ahead.

I released her breast and traced a southerly course. Her stomach was flat as a board, and there was the faint substance of muscle beneath the smooth, tanned skin. I released my grip on her hair and let my hand trail a lazy track south as well. I lingered in the quiet place above her nether and below her navel. I was long accustomed to patience, so felt no rush, though there was a growing urgency. I felt the soft brush of her tuft against my lips and she squirmed, impatient. Her hips rose, pushing it up toward me.

Her fragrance, here it was. She always smelled clean, of sea salt, and the sun, and the inescapable feminine fragrance. I kissed lower, not quite seeking that treasure, but around it. I took a breast in hand, fingers seeking the fair nipple to give a teasing to. She moaned and arched her back, and I could see the definition in her stomach.

I tasted her.

She shuddered.

As she had once taken me in her mouth, I relished the same attention on her. Where once I would have quailed from such atten-tion, I could think of what sounds I could cause escape from her mouth. I was well rewarded, and her excitement only encouraged me to explore her even more completely.

Perhaps I am her dream lover as well...

I might have been content to do this for the entirety of my night-time fugue, but my ardor had other notions. I stood, but only long enough to remove what nighttime clothing I wore. She regarded me with liquid eyes and I could see the shine between her legs. She was perhaps more ready for this than I was.

It was barely an afterthought, wiping my face, before I placed myself above her. My need was hard, and already it anticipated the heat of her secret embrace. I remembered her teasing ministrations, how she slid up and down my length, and how I woke at the moment of penetration. I prayed to God that that would not happen again, but it could only be delayed so long. I rubbed the end of my cock against her lips. She arched her back, flexing her hips toward me. I withdrew a small distance, just enough so that she did not take me inside her.

Not yet.

I teased her thusly a few times before she made a petulant sound. I relented and gave her the length of it. I sank into her. She made a noise I can scarcely describe, and her fingers clenched hard against my arms. I was not to be swayed, and only ceased when our hips were flush together, my cock buried completely inside her. She shook for a moment, but I felt her move against me. I did not wake, and she was more real than any woman I could recall from my memories.

I pressed against her and savored the sensation, her warmth, and I lavished kisses on her neck, her shoulder. I groaned myself. She was so tight around me, and she was hungry for me. We made love, rolling against each other. A shudder passed through her, and she seemed to surge with heat. I felt my own need coming close, but she wanted something else, something different. I let her push me back.

I felt cool air on my cock as it sprang from her. She looked into my eyes with her angelic sea blue eyes and then turned away from me. She kneeled on my bunk, presenting her bottom to me. My breath caught in my throat seeing her sex presented to me in such a manner. She was shiny and wet, and my passion rose again. I needed no guidance or instruction in what she was wanting.

I will enjoy this.

I took her by the hips and entered her roughly. She gave herself to me. I had her, and it seemed as if my perception narrowed to the pleasure I felt, her pussy wrapped around my cock, the sound of our skin as it came together, and the sounds we both made. I was not immediately aware of the sounds I made, but I couldn't hold to silence. She felt too divine to plunder in silence.

Her music was primal. She had her need as much as I had mine, and perhaps more. My angel perhaps was not as fallen as I imagined. Perhaps, she was a godly and chaste woman. Maybe I was the devil she fancied to take her as no man she knew would. I couldn't hold such thoughts long, her cries of mounting pleasure, her coming release drew my attention away from dream time philosophy.

In a trice, I had her on all fours. I grabbed her hips and thrust into her harder than I'd ever taken a woman. She didn't fight it, didn't submit at all... instead she *helped* me, worked with me, pushing her hips against mine as she made animal cries a primal side of me recognized as shameless begging, a need at least as strong as my own. As her cries became more shameful, I felt my own lust reaching its crescendo. I felt as if my own cock had grown harder, as if her need made me strive for more. I thrust harder.

La petit mort, the little death. The French, for all their flaws and faults, had a word for almost everything. I felt *la petit mort* and I died the little death. There was no ship on the rocks, no troublesome lucre, no close to mutinous crew, there was no angel, there was not even Eamon. I did not exist except for a silent pulse that left my body.

My soul escapes.

I held her for a moment, my senses slowly creeping back into my body. I sagged as if my soul had reentered my body and found it ill-fitting. I was covered with sweat and was close to being winded. She was also glistening with sweat, and reluctantly, I let myself slide out of her. A pearl ran down her leg.

She rose from her kneeling position, and before I could make a sound or form a word, she had her mouth on mine. She was passionate, her kiss strong and hungry, but not like it had been before. I was in awe of this and kissed her with my own desire. She was so bold, and I could not help but be entranced.

I wished that this had been real, and that it didn't have to end

She pushed me back toward the bunk, and curiously, I went to where she wanted me. We kept our embrace, and I let my hands wander across her body, touching her, exploring her. She was perfect and without flaw. The play of muscle and sinew beneath her supple skin, that was a thing of wonder and beauty. I enjoyed such post intimacy distractions, when they presented themselves, and I endeavored to enjoy this as much as I was allowed.

My angel did not object and had a mind similar to mine. As I explored her soft body, her hands charted my own cordy and rough features. She did not draw back from the old scars, the puckers where the Reaper had come close to calling but had withdrawn. She seemed as interested in me as I was with her. Never had I been with a woman so open and unrestrained with her passions.

I remembered the way she had tended my injured hands, the way she mended my wounds and how when I woke, they were far less severe than I had expected them to be. As I was waxing rhapsodic about stitches and scars, she wrapped her slender fingers around my plump sack. She gave it a caress and a gentle squeeze, eliciting a moan from me. Her hand moved up so, as to grip my shaft. Her expression was molten, her lips sought mine again.

She wants more? God, who are you?

I might have withdrawn, but her attention was intoxicating, and her touch was clever and deft. She stroked me, drawing me to the ready again. Once she was satisfied with my hardness, she slid her leg over me, and straddled me again. There was no teasing this time; she mounted me quickly.

She rode me in expert fashion, and for a time longer than our first tryst. I thought of how perfect she was – her breasts and her angelic face. I thought of her fierce need, and how tender her touch had been when I was sorely injured not so long ago. I felt something, a deep and inexorable affection for her.

I wanted to know her name, and to hear her laugh.

Le petit mort, I cannot count the number of deaths she experienced, but I found my second grave, buried deep inside her.

I floated on the edge of consciousness, and felt oblivion seeking for me.

I was spent and had nothing left to resist it, and wrapped my arms around her.

CHAPTER NINE

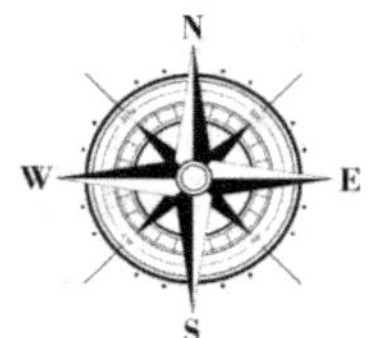

*A*very Barker…

"Wait, wait; wait! Go back, go back! Carefully! No, no, no! Too far!" I'd seen something. Something decidedly man-made and *old* by the glimpse of it on the ROV's camera. I was back-seat driving and I knew it but I couldn't care less. This was potentially big. Excitement bubbled just below my surface and I could barely contain it. I gripped the back of Keith's chair and leaned over his shoulder, searching the monitor. He paused his own visual search and looked up at me.

"Can I have a little room to breathe, please?"

"Get it back on the screen," I ordered but a smile curved my lips as I said it and I'd tried to lighten my tone.

"Jesus Fucking Christ, quit back-seat driving me," Keith muttered.

"Stop, stop, stop, stop; *stop!*" I whacked his shoulder excitedly with my fingertips, *thwap, thwap, thwap, thwap!*

"Okay, okay, okay! For cryin' out loud! Do *you* want to drive?"

"Yes, move over."

"Too damn bad! *I'm* the pilot."

There was light masculine chuckling and laughter around us at our comedy routine as Keith centered the camera on the object.

"Is that…" Kurt tilted his head and I grinned.

"Silver," Mac declared. "Too good a condition to be anything else. It's *old*, too."

"I thought we were looking for *gold*," Lennox said frowning, and I smiled savagely.

"We are, but you know what that is?"

"Looks like a barnacle crusted piece of trash to me," he said nonplussed.

"Use your imagination," Kurt said, peering over mine and Keith's shoulder.

"Get it in the basket, Keith," I said, ignoring them all. Ho boy, I *wanted* this. I wanted it *bad*. This was good, this was *really good*. This was a flask and from what I could make of it from around the encrustations, it was sixteenth century, *easy*.

The rest of my team knew what we were looking at and we all held our collective breath as Keith extended the mechanical arm on *Dreamy*. It had pincers on it, two of them with a flat finger and thumb, basically. Corrugated heavy rubber pads were worked over the aluminum hand to protect and provide grip to whatever object was being picked up, but still, using something so rudimentary to pick something up from the bottom took skill.

Keith had that skill, but it still wasn't easy.

"Damnit," he cursed low as the object slipped out of the pincer's grasp.

Groans on the order of *you were so close, you almost had it* slipped out of every one of my guys and I bit the inside of my cheek from doing the same.

"Come on, Keith, you can do this, you've got this," I said instead.

"I've always been good at those claw arcade games and this. Is. *Easier*, and I got it!"

He retracted the arm, checked the other monitor for the camera view on *Dreamy*'s bottom and released it into the basket mounted to the underside of the ROV's carriage. I immediately got on the radio.

"Carl, this is Avery. We've retrieved an artifact, get a tank up here."

The radio crackled to life over the guys cheering and Carl's voice came over the airwaves, "On it, boss; what'd you get?"

"Oh, it's good. Hurry your ass up and bring my fireproof safe while you're at it."

"Boss?"

"A tank and the safe, Carl. Bring them both, bring them now!"

"Okay, okay! Geez, you got it!"

I tossed the radio on the desk and straightened up, lacing my fingers and placing my hands on top of my head, letting out an explosive breath. It was the only way I knew how to let off some steam. I was anxious as hell for that find to reach the surface and for Eamon Bligh's journal to get up here along with the tank because holy good *goddamn*, I knew I was right. I knew I was right and once I could *prove* I was right, all of these guys would be cracking beers and celebrating tonight.

We needed a win. We needed this win so damn bad. Morale was getting low and Lennox was chomping at the bit and holy Christ we needed this win. I could barely contain my excitement when it came to letting these guys in on what I knew we'd just found. Actually, maybe I could speed this up a bit.

I went for my laptop set up next to Keith and started tapping keys furiously, vaguely aware of Lennox demanding, "What the hell's gotten into *her*?"

Kurt answered him and I could hear the grin in his voice as he shifted from foot to foot behind me. "She's got something. Something important to show us, but she does this. Gets hyper focused and won't spill the beans until she's absolutely sure."

Mac gave one of his low rumbling chuckles. "Oh, I know that look, she's already sure."

My excitement became contagious as the guys picked up what I was putting down despite my attempts to hide it. We were a team and a family, Lennox the only unknown quantity among us, so he was behind on the curve.

"I hate it when she does this shit to us," Pete grumbled.

"I don't want to get you guys excited for nothing is all," I said, blowing out another breath. "Mac or Keith, can one of you go back in the footage and pull up the best shot we have of the artifact?"

"I surely can," Mac said and tapped on some keys on the other side of Keith. Keith took his attention off the monitor with *Dreamy* for half a second and glanced at my laptop monitor, letting out a low whistle.

"Hey! Eyes on the prize!" I chastised and he focused on what he was doing. It was going to be a half an hour or more before *Dreamy* reached the surface and I did *not* want her getting damaged because I let Keith get distracted. Still, that one glimpse had been enough. The set of his mouth had become focused, thinning down into a grim line of determination. He pushed some of his curly mop of brown hair off his forehead and used the one hand not wrapped around *Dreamy*'s joystick to push his glasses higher up on the bridge of his nose.

I checked on Mac's progress and said, "That's good, Mac; right there." Mac pushed a button and the screen flashed in a capture, the inkjet printer spitting out a glossy eight by ten. I picked it up, handed it to Lennox and stepped away from my laptop monitor so he could see.

It couldn't have been a better shot than by Hollywood design. The perspective of the encrusted flask nearly identical to the hand drawn image of it next to a dented old tin cup in Eamon Bligh's journal. It was unmistakably the same flask. Something that Morgan Dougal had likely pilfered from someone that had pilfered it before *him* going back for however long. The flask in the drawing and its real-life counterpart on the screen were both of Dutch origin, probably crafted anywhere from thirty to sixty years before Dougal owned it; and though the real-life version was black, for it to have held up down there for close to three hundred years, it had to be silver under all of the tarnish and encrustations. It wouldn't have held up otherwise.

"That's…" Lennox was speechless, as was the rest of the crew as they stared from the picture he held or bounced between Mac's monitor and mine.

"That's solid irrefutable fucking *proof*!" Kurt crowed. The boys in the cavern erupted in cheers and I grinned, soaking it all in. Relief washed over me. So much so that my emotions almost got the better of me and I choked up, eyes hot and just starting to well. I shut it down quick, my emotions and their slightly premature celebrations. The artifact wasn't in a tank of seawater and hadn't even come close to beginning the desalination process. We couldn't get too comfortable, not yet, but this was, indeed, a *really* good sign.

"Hey, hey, hey, hey, *hey*!" I put my fingers in my mouth and let out a piercing whistle, which echoed back from the cavern walls. The boys piped down. "We aren't done yet, not by a long shot. You can have your beers when *Dreamy's* put up, the artifact is in the tank, and we're back down in basecamp. Look alive, boys. You know the drill!"

Carl had pulled up sometime during the whooping and hollering and stood just past everyone with a fish tank between his hands. He blinked, bewildered through his trendy horn-rimmed glasses and asked, "What the fuck did I miss?"

"Come over here and I'll show yah," Keith said. I went over and took the tank and jerked my head at Kurt. Grinning, he walked with me down the catwalk to where *Dreamy* was supposed to come up.

"For all the time we spent cursing the hell out of that storm, looks like it was a pretty big blessing," he said, and I nodded.

"Remind me the next time a pain in the ass storm blows through to not bitch about it as hard." I think in our eagerness to get any kind of significant work done, we'd all forgotten how storms tended to stir things up. It may be the reason we'd made the find we had today.

$\sim$

THE PARTYING HAD BEEN GOING ON PRETTY HARD, BUT I'D SET MYSELF apart from it. I never actually ended up needing the journal out of my portable safe. Lennox seemed happy enough with the scanned images of its pages on my laptop's screen. He had the fever now, and I was glad for it. It would buy us a little bit of leeway for a while. The search was still just beginning. All the flask had done was prove we were right where we were supposed to be.

When it came to the preservation of artifacts, that was where Max stepped in. Right now, the flask sat on the corner of my desk in a tank of the water we'd pulled it out of. You couldn't just yank something out of the water and let it dry. Corrosion could and would set in and had the potential to destroy significant findings. No, it would be a month-long process of desalination to get them to a point they could be displayed. Max was on the *Sapphire Horizon,* berthed at the mainland, but would be back with some supplies tomorrow. He knew what was up and that Kurt and I knew precisely how he would want things done and so that's how we'd done them.

I tapped the keys on my laptop in my lap and waited, breath held, for my dad to answer on the other end.

"Hey, princess!" His face lit up blue, the house dark behind him, but I could see he was in his office by the placement of the pictures on the wall behind him.

I rolled my eyes for his benefit. "You ever going to stop calling me that?"

"Nope. Now, to what do I owe this pleasure?" he asked.

"You said to call you if I found something." I gave a blasé little shrug as his image wavered on the screen and his eyebrows went up under his signature trucker's hat as he leaned back in his chair.

"You found something this early?"

"We had a storm the other night, a really bad one. It's been setback, after setback, after setback since we got here so trust me," I gave a gusty sigh, "for us, it doesn't feel like we found anything 'early'. It's been one of those hunts where we feel like it's been a long time coming."

"Well, baby girl, for you it *has*. You been the one to find all this from start to finish. This has been all you leading the charge."

I nodded and felt myself temporarily lose focus as I thought about all the things I'd had to pull or do to get here. Even my dad had been skeptical when it'd come to the journal which I had found, literally, completely by chance.

"Well, you gonna keep an old man waitin'? What'd you find?"

I smiled and said, "Sending you some photos."

I watched him put on his glasses for reading and he peered down his nose through them at the screen, tilting his head back and giving me a great view up his nose in the process. I stifled a laugh.

"Okay, what am I looking at here?"

"The drawing of the flask," I told him.

"Okay, alright," he drawled, giving it a close examination.

"Now, here's what we found." I shot him some stills from *Dreamy*'s dive and he frowned, studying them. I watched his eyebrows go up again.

"I'll be a son of a bitch," he said in wonder. He let out a bewildered *huh* and I gave a slow smile knowing what was coming next. Next, he started to laugh, and it was almost a hysterical thing that made my eyes wet to hear it. "Woo hoo!" he cheered, and the laughter rolled out of him as he clapped his hands.

"Oh, baby girl, that's *fantastic!* Jesus, Avery. I am so damn *proud* of you."

"Thank, Dad." I sniffed and held it together but just barely.

"You gettin' in the water tomorrow?" he asked.

"No, sending *Dreamy* down again. We have a pretty good idea what tunnel that the flask may have washed out of but the complex down there is *immense* and safety first."

"You're doing great, baby, and that's exactly what I wanted to hear." I nodded and my resolve to be strong and independent wavered.

"I miss you," I said and emotion gripped me. "I wish you were here."

"I wish I was, too, Aves, but I'm just too old," he grumbled. "It's time to pass the torch and you're carrying it like the pro you are. I mean it, kid. I couldn't be more proud of you."

"Thanks, Dad, and you're not too old. If you hadn't gotten hurt—"

"Now, Aves," he cut me off, tone full of reproach. "There's no use cryin' over spilled milk. You've got this and you don't need me to even tell you that. You've got Mac around and the rest of the team, I hear, is treating you just like they would me. You don't need me there."

"Okay, fine, I *want* you here."

"Tough titty, darlin'."

I snorted a laugh.

"Go on and get some sleep. Its late here, which means it's late there."

I rolled my eyes. "We're in the same time zone."

He gave me a wink. "Get some sleep."

I felt my lips curve into a smile, a mask to hide the fresh swell of emotion in my chest threatening to overwhelm me.

"Night, Dad."

"G'night, baby."

He mercifully ended the video chat so I didn't have to.

I heaved a big sigh and set my laptop on my desk chair after closing it up. I got ready for bed and doused the lantern, the tent plunging into the soft dark. I tried to sleep, but sleep wasn't having any of it. So, I lay on my bunk and stared at the tank and safe on my desk. I felt another wave of emotion. A homesick nostalgia.

It was to the point that it was time to walk it off. I got up and took myself up the small trail behind my tent, further back from the mess tent and the guys' bunk. I didn't want or need any of them up in my business.

The moon was out, the sky clear and full of stars, reflecting in the smooth obsidian pool that was the Mirror Pond at night. It was almost dizzying when you stood at the water's edge. Having both the sky above and below, you almost felt like you were falling while standing still; without having moved at all.

I closed my eyes and took in a deep breath, covering my mouth with my hands to stifle the relieved sobs that started. I couldn't hold it in anymore. I was happy, I was ecstatic, but I was also so incredibly *relieved*. Having concrete *proof* of something, having something that *old* just sitting on the corner of my desk, it was so incredibly monumental but I would be damned if I would cry in front of my team. They didn't need to know how hard we were riding the razor's edge with this one.

I tried to rope it in, taking breath after deep soggy breath when a twig snapped nearby. I whirled and expected I would snap at Kurt or Mac, but it wasn't either of them. It wasn't anyone from this time or place. My dream lover stood wide-eyed in rough spun pants and a loose shirt.

I was dreaming again, and I was safe to do whatever I needed to do here.

I went to him abruptly and put my arms around his waist, resting my forehead against his chest and the tension eased from my shoulders and back. I gave in for a moment and let myself cry, his hands tentatively finding my shoulders, easing around to my back, before he held me and let me cry it out.

I thought hard at him, too overcome to even try to speak; *God I wish you were real.* I couldn't believe how lonely I was despite being surrounded by a whole team of people.

CHAPTER TEN

*E*amon Bligh...

I woke reluctantly, and to my great disappointment, I was alone. It was disheartening, but not unexpected. I sighed and rose from my bunk, and I felt renewed, as if my dance with the storm and then the masts were less than a memory. I felt my head, where the knot had been and it was almost gone. That had been a great knock on the head I had taken, and likewise, my hands were near to completely healed. Such injuries were not so lightly brushed away, and I could not help but think of her, her angelic face as she did her work with dabs and sour bites. I shuddered a moment, remembering the bitter taste of those wretched things.

I took a few minutes and cleaned my black boots. There was no putting a shine to them, they were far beyond worn, but they did take to a cleaner black finish. I gave a few minutes more to mending the captain's great coat. The hat earned a bit of attention as well. I sighed and sat the hat on my head – Captain Bligh was ready.

The crew had roused itself by the time I made it to the forecastle.

The men stopped and took notice. "Ready the longboats, it's time to take a trip to the island," I said.

"Do you know what land that is?" Mister Baxter asked.

"That would be one of the Ghost Islands, not far from the coastline of our desired destination. The Carolinas lie on the other side of this cluster of islands," I said. I withdrew the spyglass and sought out the coast of my destination. We had approached from the worst angle and found the worst of the rocks with the hull. It was an easy enough path around our position and a relatively short span to a forested beach with a bare lip of sand around it.

The men readied the longboats, and I bid men to come with me – Hammond the rope monkey and Bennet, a gunnery man. "Mister Dougal." I made a point of checking my pistol before tucking it into my new sash; it had previously been the shirt I wore when we took the *Queen's Mercy* and the blood had stained it a suitable color.

"Aye!" Dougal said, stepping forward.

"Take care of my ship while I am away. I expect everything to be in proper order when we return." I turned and sought out one John Forsythe. "Mister Forsythe, have you dry powder and sharp blade?"

"Aye… Captain," he said somewhat reluctantly.

"I'll have both at my side while we survey this island," I said. "I expect to find it uninhabited, but should there be savages, it will take good steel and shot to clear our way." Forsythe regarded me coldly but nodded.

We loaded into the boats and Dougal oversaw our lowering into the ocean. It was a rough landing, the sea heaved and threatened to throw us into the hull of the *Honor*. We pulled hard at the oars to move the longboat away from the swirling waters. "Pull you swabs, pull for what you're worth," I shouted, and by the strength of our backs, we moved away from the ship.

There was something of a test to this, with just four men. If one didn't pull, all would know and we would move in a wide circle. I wanted to know if Forsythe would himself, put his will into serving as a member of this crew. He worked his oar as hard as the rest of us.

The shore was sandy and silty, not the coarse coral sands of the Caribbean. This was the sand of swamps and continents, and it was welcome under our boots. Mud squelched under our feet as we pulled the boat further up the shore.

"There is a hill," Forsythe said, pointing with his cutlass. "We should be better able to see the rest of this heap of mud."

"Indeed, Mister Forsythe, indeed," I said. The rest of us loosened our blades and started the tedious business of cutting through the mangrove and saw grass that held sway over this island.

"Does this island bear a name, sir?" Hammond asked. He was a deft man with the cutlass, and he proved it by taking the head off of some island snake before it could strike at him.

"I would call it Eamon's Folly," Forsythe said with a jest.

"A fair name," I said. His tone was far most humor than spite. "But alas, my fine gentlemen, it is already named most ominously on the king's rudders." I paused and examined the most curious of flowering plants that called this island home. Strange things, full of bright and beguiling colors, and the air was alive with the humming sound of many insects and birds. This place was dangerously alive and we would have to keep our wits about us.

"The king's cartographers have seen fit to name this Ghost Island, and to his grace, he doesn't even know how many islands there are here. It's just a muddy thumbprint on his royal map. Here be some fucking islands!" I said. We all had a laugh. Even if we might have been close to each other's throats as pirates were, there was no love lost between us and the wigged tyrant who sat on the throne.

We hacked our way further inland, finding clearings full of the purple flowers that grew up the sides of trees, and that had blossoms as frilly as a French whore's underpants. Purples, and pinks, and all shades of sunset rioted across the island. It was as if we had wandered into some sort of fever dream.

Mr. Bennet found berries and assured us they were safe to eat. More importantly, we found fresh clear water that would be needed to replenish our stores back on the *Honor*. Fresh water, some fresh fruit, some of it quite strange, would go a good way to raising morale. Finding something on foot would be fortuitous as well, but I doubted that we would be so lucky as to find a boar or deer on this island.

We wound a path up to a high point on the island, and I put the spyglass to work. For all our hours of labor at the cutlass, we were still within sight of the ship, and I could distantly make out figures on the deck. Mr. Dougal's red side whiskers made him plain to see.

"How far?" Bennet asked.

"Within range of my eye, but outside of your twelve pounders, Mister Bennet," I replied. He gave a squinting grin.

"I don't know Cap'n," he said. "I bet if I had a twelve pounder here on this hummock, I could put a round in Dougal's pocket fair to sure!"

We shared another laugh, and then passed around a flask of rum. Solid land underfoot was a good feeling, and morale was important. We rested, the breeze blowing fresh and cool, and rest crept upon us, unsuspectedly.

I dreamed of my angel, but it was much different. This tenebrous thing was only a dream, a spectre of my imagination. Her kisses were phantasmal. Her touch was a memory relived in sleep.

I was relieved when such dreams rolled away and I came to waking again.

"It seems that we have been waylaid gentlemen," I said, rubbing my face.

"Aye," Hammond said. The lad had seen fit to climb into the crook of a tree for his rest. So long at sea, I'm sure sleeping on the ground was as unnatural to him as sleeping on a branch would be to any of us. "Nothing came round, 'cept for a few birds and such."

"Shame," Forsythe said. He whittled at a piece of wood with his dagger. "I think I would fancy taking one of those throwing axes I heard tale of from some continental savage."

"Some black-headed woman might take a shine to your beard Mister Forsythe," Hammond said. "She might carry you off, make you her native husband."

There was more laughing.

"We'll not make it back to the ship before dark," I said, looking at the position of the sun, and marking the distance we had come. "I would rather make a camp here than try cranking up the side of the *Honor* in the dark."

The others agreed, and we set to making something of a more proper camp. We would need a fire and something of a shelter for the night. There was no shortage of vine for lashing, deadfall wood for burning, and plenty of green to make a cover above our head. There was a quiet dinner around the fire, hard tack and salt beef we had brought from the ship, berries and strange yellow-fleshed tree fruit, all washed down with spring water and the last of the rum. The tree fruit was a peculiar, custard-like texture, but had a musky sweet taste to it. Hammond had found a great number of them, and we planned to take many back with us to the ship.

The moon was high the next time I woke, thankfully from a regular slumber. I felt the urge to relieve myself and so stumbled away from the camp to do so.

A glimmer caught my eye – bright as silver.

I finished my business and slowly, quietly pushed through a hedge of wild flora. There was no easy path to it. There was apparently no large game on this island and there were no deer trails, nothing larger than a rabbit track. The greenery gave way and I found myself on the edge of the most spectacular of sights.

It was a pond really, nothing more. But the edge was nigh on perfectly circular, and the surface as still as glass. I couldn't guess to its depths but it reflected the light of the moon as if it were made of quicksilver. I stared into the water. This felt like a holy place of sorts, or one of those places where the mushrooms grew in fairy circles. I saw my own reflection, and beneath the water's surface something moved. I saw her reflection in the water, her face turned up, illuminated by the moon.

My angel stood on the other side of this mercurial pool.

CHAPTER ELEVEN

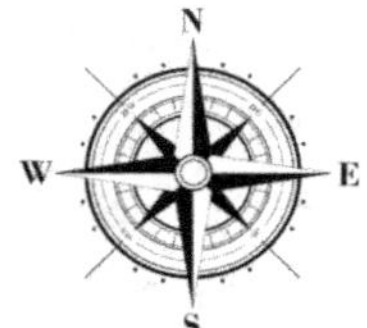

*A*very Barker...

"I'm calling it," I said and the guys all groaned.

"You've got to be fucking kidding me," Lennox grumbled and after several days of it, it was the last straw.

"Avery..." Kurt warned, knowing the look on my face but I shook my head violently.

"Nope, he's earned it," I declared and Lennox looked affronted.

"Excuse me?" he demanded.

"Yes!" I snapped. "Excuse you!" I pushed up off of the chair I was straddling in front of the panel of monitors and stood, my hands finding my hips so I didn't smack the high-and-mighty look off his face.

"Bancroft Group may be the ones bankrolling this operation but *I* am the one who runs it and *I* am the one who says what goes when. *I* am sick and tired of you second-guessing *every decision* I make because *money*. I make the rules, Lennox! If you don't like it, take your ass down to the dock and I'll have transport come get you."

"Now hold on just a minute!" he said ramping up, and I was over it.

"No!" I barked. "You have no *idea* what goes on except for whatever underwater exploration documentaries you binged on the damn Science Channel before coming out here! It is *dangerous* diving at those depths and don't even get me started on cave diving! I won't risk mine, or Kurt's life to satisfy *anyone's* gold fever!"

I was heated and I stepped into Lennox's chest and gave it a sharp jab with two fingers.

"You can just wait, like the rest of us, until the visibility is where it needs to be and we are *safe* to go down!"

"How *dare you* talk to me like this!" he cried, and I flung out an arm.

"Look around you, Lennox! Look at their faces! We've all done this before. We're all disappointed! But disappointed is better than A," I held up one finger, "being dead and B," I held up a thumb, "being so crippled from decompression sickness as a result of a stroke that you can't dive anymore!"

A few of the guys recoiled. Mac's face fell and Kurt turned to Lennox as I sniffed sharply, eyes welling, I was so angry.

"Shut it the fuck down for today!" I snarled, voice cracking, and turned stomping for the mouth of the cave.

"Avery..." Kurt tried, tone gentle, and I flung up an arm waving him off.

Mac told him, "Let her go." I heard him address Lennox with disgust. "You really need to learn to keep your mouth shut every time you think you ought to second-guess the little woman."

I knew the guys would have my back, but damn it, they shouldn't have to.

I wanted my dad. I wanted him to be here, but he couldn't. The stroke he'd had as a result of his accident had left him too weak on his left side to effectively get around without risk of his leg giving out. He had to walk with a cane on a good day, a walker on a bad one now, and it killed me.

It. Killed. Me.

That such a big, strong man, so independent, so fierce as he had been my *entire life*, couldn't get around his own house without a Life Alert button anymore because he might fall and wouldn't be able to get back up on his own without help.

Damn it.

I let my feet carry me all the way back to basecamp but didn't stop in to talk to any of the personnel there. Instead, I went straight for my quarters, such as they were. I dropped onto the edge of my bunk and flopped over, crying myself quietly into a nap.

I didn't dream, which was just another added layer of disappointment to a day that had been absolutely full of them. When I woke, it was getting on toward dark, and though I was hungry, I had no desire whatsoever to join the boys in the mess. I'd honestly rather go hungry.

Now that I'd cooled off, I felt embarrassed. The last thing you wanted to do as a woman in a professional setting was get angry and lose your cool; because then you just became the stereotypical hysterical little lady and you lost ground. Of course, you were damned if you did and damned if you didn't on so many levels it wasn't even funny.

My entire existence was turning into a rock and a hard place and like ninety percent of it was squarely because of Lennox's presence.

It was frustrating.

I got up, stared down at my rumpled bunk and sighed.

I was starting to miss my fictional dream lover. It'd been a while. Only once since the night of the storm, like the day after or two days after? I don't know. Time was beginning to blur together as we rambled into proverbial brick walls of varying heights and thicknesses when it came to our work here.

The last time, we had been on a ship. Which, come to think of it, was every time I dreamed of him – I was affectionately starting to think of the lantern lit old brigantine captain's quarters as 'his place' while any time he visited me was in my bunk at my place, except that one time by the Mirror Pond.

I wasn't sure if that time had actually been him, though... or if it had just been my wishful thinking and imagination.

I sighed and listened to the cricket and frog song outside my tent.

That had actually been the last time I'd seen him. That time, by the Mirror Pond, when he'd held me tight while I'd wept, feeling miserable about my daddy and his inability to be here for this.

I hugged myself and shook my head, leaving my tent to take a short walk up to the Mirror Pond.

I stood, at the water's edge, staring over its glassine surface, calm and serene, the moon hanging low in the sky and perfectly reflected in the pond's surface. I stood, listening to the nocturnal island life and tried to let my feelings of misery and inadequacy go. The impostor syndrome was real tonight and I struggled with the decisions I'd made thus far.

No dive was completely perfect. There was always one condition or another that was out of whack – but the stakes in this particular scenario were absolutely sky high.

Not only were we going to be forced to dive at depth – we were cave diving. As if one weren't dangerous enough, add the other and the chances of something going wrong? *Jesus.* I just couldn't take that risk. Not with my life and definitely not with Kurt's... but it wasn't just us, either.

It was every man on this crew. If we went bust on the first manned dive this whole operation went bust and the ripple effects of that was *huge.* So many of us were all in on this one and I was feeling the weight of it keenly.

"I wish you were here," I whispered into the dark, and I sighed. My father or my dream lover, I would take either at this point.

A flicker of movement below the Mirror Pond's surface caught the corner of my eye and I took a step closer to the water's edge just as a twig snapped behind me and a voice called out softly, "Avery?"

Distracted from the glassy surface, I turned and stepped away, just as Jacob Lennox stepped out of the jungle-like tree line.

"I come in peace," he said, holding up one hand, a paper plate with a sandwich balanced on the other.

"Is that a peace offering?" I asked, ravenous.

"It is, actually. Mac said you were probably hungry but that you wouldn't come and eat."

"Mac knows me the best, except for maybe Kurt," I said, wondering why Mac would tell Lennox of all people.

"Yeah, well, I insisted on coming up here to talk to you and he said if I was feeling suicidal that was on me, but the least I could do was bring you a sandwich."

A smile broke through my misery and I hung my head, nodding ruefully.

"Sounds like Mac."

"So," Lennox asked, stepping out from the tree line further and holding out the plate. "Do I get to live?"

"Depends, is it bologna and mayonnaise?" I asked.

He broke into a smile and said, "Yeah, actually, it is."

"Woo boy." I stepped forward and took the plate from him and went over to a fallen log, a way back from the waterline to perch on it. "Mac pulled out all the stops."

"Seriously?" Lennox asked, skeptically. He joined me on the log and took a seat a healthy distance away.

"My dad used to make them for me when I was a kid. It was a staple in my house."

"Ah, yeah... he and Kurt let me know about that," he said. I was mid-way through chewing a big bite of sandwich and I looked at him sideways. "I'm sorry," he said. "About what happened to your dad."

"Yeah," I said after swallowing. "Me too."

"A lot of it makes sense now," he said and looked a little rueful himself and I sniffed.

"A lot of what makes sense, exactly?"

"Your reluctance to get in the water."

"Ha!" I brayed a laugh and he winced.

"No, not what I meant," he said. "That came out wrong. I mean, your dedication to safety."

I searched his face for a minute and tried to decide if he was yanking my chain, or what. Finally, I had to concede, he seemed genuine.

"He's still alive," I said and set my half-eaten, half a sandwich down on the thick paper plate. "My dad didn't die."

"Oh, yeah, I know. I knew that," he said.

"Sometimes, I think he wishes he had… you know, died."

"Why would you say that?" he asked surprised.

"You didn't know him before the accident," I said. "This?" I gestured behind me in the vague direction of the camp. "This was his everything."

"Not *everything*," Lennox said, looking me over.

"I mean, I know there's me. I also know I'm probably the only reason he's toughing it out and sticking around." I sighed. "Taking him away from all of this, though?" I shook my head. "If there is a God, he's one cruel son of a bitch. I'll tell you what."

"Seems to me God wouldn't have much to do with something like that. You sure that isn't more the Devil's jam?"

I raised my eyebrows and side-eyed him a little. "You getting philosophical on me?"

He grinned and bowed his head, nodding. "It's an interest of mine."

"I believe in science," I said. "I'm not about a bunch of mystical bullshit." I took the final bite of the first half of my sandwich and he leaned back on the log.

"So, you don't believe the stories about this place?" he asked. "About people disappearing and all that jazz?"

"Oh, I believe people have disappeared," I said. "But I'm sure there's a perfectly logical explanation for it."

"Well, whatever the explanation, the myths and legends served your pirates well."

"Ahh, interesting," I said mildly.

"What is?" he asked.

"You believe me," I said.

He laughed a little, shook his head ruefully, and with a grin said, "I'll admit, I didn't at first… but then you pulled that flask up out of the bottom of that cave and I'm sorry… that *can't* be a coincidence. The shape of that thing and what's in the journal? That's just too much."

I nodded and sighed.

"It's down there, Mr. Lennox. It's down there, and I'm going to be the one to find it and bring it up."

"I believe you, Miss Barker. I do. And I want to be here when you do it."

"So, you'll stop with the second-guessing?" I asked and he sighed.

"I will try to do better," he promised. "It's my job to know where the money is going and when to cut the Bancroft Group's losses," he said.

I nodded.

"I know, and I can respect that," I said. "So, if I can't get that, precisely, can you at least knock it off with the lecherous bullshit?"

He laughed outright and said, "I apologize. I get around a beautiful woman and I lose myself."

"What a rich, white-bread, red-blooded American male thing to say." I rolled my eyes and his laughter picked up.

"I'm just every other spoiled trust fund, silver spooner to you, aren't I?" he asked.

"Ah, if we're being honest?" I said and looked sideways at him.

"I don't feel the need to stop now, do you?" he asked.

"Ah no," I said. "And to answer your question? Yup." I popped the 'p' on yup and he howled with laughter.

"You are certainly full of surprises Ms. Barker," he said, wiping a tear from the corner of his eye. "All of that aside, is it because you already have someone?"

I hesitated, thinking about my dream lover and finally hedged my bets… "Yeah," I said and it didn't quite feel like the lie it was supposed to be. "But he's far out of reach of me."

"I'm sorry," he said and he nodded. "I'm sorrier still that I've been inappropriate. I misjudged you."

"Yeah, the blonde does that to people," I said. "Think I should dye my hair?"

He laughed again and said, "You're decidedly different Avery Barker." He stood with a sigh, dusting off the seat of his khaki shorts. "Never change."

"I don't plan to," I said and pushed my luck. "You, on the other hand, have some work to do."

He considered me for a moment staring down at me, searching my face. "You may be right," he said nodding, and I nodded too.

"One thing you'll never get from me, Mr. Lennox, is a load of bullshit. You can count on that," I said.

"I can see that, Ms. Barker. I can see that."

"Good, I'm glad we understand each other."

He smiled then and said, "I would say to drop the hard act, but I'm realizing – it's not an act at all is it?"

"No, it is not, Mr. Lennox."

"I think we have an understanding then."

"Glad that we do," I said softly and looked up. I toasted him with the other half of my sandwich and said, "To better habits, Mr. Lennox."

He inclined his head and said, "To better habits."

I turned my attention back to the still surface of the pond and sighed.

I needed to work on myself, too. There was always room for improvement no matter what you did, no matter how you did things. Always. While I didn't think there was any such thing as *'too careful,'* I had, perhaps, maybe, been a wee bit overzealous.

I finished my sandwich and returned to my tent, turning on my battery-operated lantern on the edge of my desk to get the Coleman gas-powered one hanging from my ridge pole going.

I sat down at my desk with a restless sigh and went over the data again – over the forecasts and weather patterns both past and present before taking a look at the barometric numbers and reported wind speeds. After, I clicked through images of Eamon Bligh's journal on my laptop.

It was humid today, and I didn't want to take it from the safe.

I didn't spend long reading his beautiful flowing script. If there was any hope of diving the next day, I needed to be well rested and alert. I cursed myself for napping for so long earlier in the day as I stripped out of my clothing and got into my bed. It was going to be impossible to sleep, now.

I opened my eyes at the light touch at the hollow of my throat. My dream lover, sitting on the side of my bed, the tip of his middle finger touching me oh, so gently, his eyes fixed to the spot, lips slightly parted in what could only be described as wonder. He dragged that fingertip gently down my chest, between the valley of my breasts, the sheet catching on the extended digit and pulling away, revealing me to his eyes, his gaze growing in both curiosity and lustful intensity.

Watching him, looking at me like that, I couldn't help but get wet. His eyes flicked to mine and he startled slightly when he caught me watching him. I felt the corners of my lips lift in a slight smile.

God, I'd missed him. How I wanted him. How good it felt to be in his arms. I'd been low-key worried that whatever it was that had conjured him in my mind had just as easily and readily dismissed him. I wasn't ready for that. I didn't want him to go. If anything, I wished desperately for him to *stay with me*. I wished desperately for him to be *real*.

His fingertip continued it's slow, lazy, teasing descent down my body when he realized I wasn't upset or angry at his explorations. How could I be, when he brought such joy and general good vibes?

I closed my eyes, lips parting, smile fading as I arched up gently under that slightly ticklish touch that swept my covers away and revealed my body to him like some sort of gentle magic trick.

I loved the way he looked at me, his quick, green eyes rendered near colorless with the moonlight so expressive as he roved my body with his gaze.

He dipped his fingers gently at the apex of my thighs and I

parted them for him, letting him touch my sex, desperate for that deeper touch that I knew would drive me wild.

My fists knotted in the sheet below me, at my hips as he watched my face, expression neutral, passive, as he plunged that single thick finger up inside of me, to the third knuckle. I gasped and arched, grinding my pussy against his hand as he thrust it against me. I moaned and gasped brokenly as he felt around inside of me and came up against that *spot*.

He leaned down to get a better angle and added a second finger to the first, watching my face, eyes intent on my expressions as he teased me to life, stoking the fires of my passion and sending sparks of pleasure through my body that threatened to ignite me and turn me into a living brand.

I moved my hands from down by my hips to up over my head, tucking them beneath the heavy cross bar that served as a head-board to my bunk and pressing up so that I could press my lower body down onto his hand further. He raised his chin slightly and looked down his nose at me, imperiously, his face a study in concentration as he worked me with his hand, studying me as though to discover all my secrets and precisely what made me tick.

I ceded control, *gladly*, in perfect trust, and let him play. Let him explore at his leisure because truthfully it *all* felt good.

I moaned as things ramped up, the wetness from how turned on I was getting, coating the insides of my thighs as he worked me deftly, firmly, but also oh so carefully. A slow build, getting me so damn maddeningly close to orgasm before backing off just enough, edging me carefully until I was torn between dragging his mouth to mine and kissing him or smacking the holy shit out of him for denying me.

His expression remained neutral the whole time he was playing me like some kind of fine instrument and I lived for it.

From the heat in his gaze, the concentration on his face, the strength and the way he dominated my space and yet the absolute care with which he did it is what completely undid me.

I was close, so close, so very close and I didn't know what I needed to get there, to finally plunge over that silver fall of shining pleasure. What I needed for the starlight he brought to earth to fill my veins… but he did.

He leaned down slowly, his eyes locked to mine, his mouth descending toward my chest where he took one of my nipples into his mouth.

Oh, *God.* He knew just what to do, the perfect balance between sharp teeth and suction on the sensitive nib that sent me jerking beneath him, his fingers inside me playing over that spot, his thumb outside of me, swiping through my wetness against my clit. All of it building into the sweetest crescendo until the sensations spilled through me, a rich symphony of sensation that was beyond anything I had ever felt before in my life.

The star fire went off behind my eyelids and I lay limp on my bunk, vision clearing to the man of my dreams kneeling nude and perfect between my thighs, stroking his long, thick cock with his fist, waiting for me to come to my senses enough to plunge inside me and take me for a ride all over again.

Every time with him just kept getting better and better.

CHAPTER TWELVE

*E*amon Bligh...

I paused a moment to admire the fruits of my handiwork. My angel lay on her back, her legs parted for me. I could see her breath was rapid, and though she had tasted *le petit mort* she was far from being finished. I stroked myself a few times, letting my eyes linger on the glistening wetness between her legs. She was beautiful.

I rose and mounted her. She offered no resistance as I entered her.

She gave me her throat and I devoured it with kisses. She arched her hips into mine, her sex hungry for my own. I was in no terrible hurry, so I gave her my full length in a measured deliberate pace. She would moan and nip at my ear as I came near to escaping her and shuddered when I returned and buried myself completely inside.

How long this lasted, I couldn't venture a guess. Time seemed to fall away and the only measure was our rhythm. I brought her close to the edge, and I could feel her tighten around me, vise-like on my cock. When I felt this, I would slow slightly, letting my stroke become longer.

Ah, the sounds she made when I pulled completely out of her. She pulled at me, raking her fingers down my back, across my arms. Then, I would take her again. She felt all the hotter for it. Her eyes burned like coals when they met mine, the tension I was brewing in her loins would not be too long denied.

I couldn't tell her that I felt the same. My cock felt like an iron rod pulled from the forge, pulsing and aching for release, and I knew that I was perilously close to the edge. She began to clench around me again, and her breath was ragged in my ear.

I'll punish us no further; I didn't give her a respite for the urge to wane. I took her quickly, my thrusts fast paced and all the way in. She gave a cry and I felt her spasm around me. Her orgasm sang in my ears, and she was trembling, shaking, as my own passion reached its peak.

I kissed her deeply, and felt it. My sack tightened, and I felt everything collapse to a single point, and then the powerful throbbing sensation. I couldn't breathe, I couldn't move. The only thing I could do was exist, until the little death passed.

We laid together for what seemed like a wonderfully long time, sharing small kisses and intimate caresses. I was loath to move, even with my passion quenched, and my body slick with sweat. My angel gave a deeply satisfied groan when I finally withdrew from her.

And then there was a harsh knock on the cabin door, rousing me from my slumber.

Damn.

"Aye, enter," I said, sitting up and rubbing my face.

"Captain, I have news sir," Mister Baxter said. I rose and pulled my coat on and bade him to speak. He gave a cough. "Mister Bennet and company have finished their labors and are ready for your inspection, sir."

I nodded in agreement and finished dressing myself. We had been stuck at Ghost Island for several days now, and the transition from ship to shore had been going well. Most of the crew and provisions were on the island, and we had struck a fair camp well away from the silty beach. It wouldn't do to be seen by any passing ship, especially if they might have known what colors we flew.

The few men remaining on the ship had been picked for their loyalty, those I knew I could trust to leave with our two most valuable possessions, the *Honor's* cannons, and the king's gold. There was no freeing her from the rocks, *Honor* was lost to us, as true as if she had sunk, and considering the time of year and our location, it could be as simple as one of the great Atlantic storms coming and dashing her further on the rocks, and she would be gone.

The food and water were ashore, most of the weapons were as well. The gold would take time to move, and the consideration to move the cannons had been made, but none of the crew was sure that we could do so. The twelve pounders would be difficult to move from the gun deck, to a longboat, and then winched down the side. No, that course would be folly. We would lose cannons, we could lose a longboat, and even men if the cannon shifted and caught a man underneath it.

It was painful, but the main guns would have to remain behind. We were far from unarmed, though. The swivel guns were ashore, as were the pistols, cutlass, and sundry other tools of piracy. Should things go unexpected, each of *Honor's* cannons were already loaded and packed, so that a scant few men could give one good volley, if need be.

It had been busy work, and packing cannon and shot put the men in good spirits. The gunners had good sport, joking of giving some English merchantman the devil's balls right in the powder room. We were leaving the cannons behind, and there was little chance they would ever be fired again, though it did morale good to pack them anyway.

I had sat in private council with Baxter and Dougal regarding the fate of the *Honor*. We could not unstick her, and if she came loose on her own, we lacked the men and lumber to effect repairs on her stricken hull. Once unburdened of our supplies, arms, and treasure, she was a danger to us. Some English captain might see her and think to take her and hunt us down. The same could apply to a passing Frenchman, or Spaniard. We discussed the wisdom of leaving her on the rocks, or if it would be wise to set a fuse in the powder room or to simply set her alight.

We came to no answer.

It was a hard thing to consider. *Honor* had served us well, and there was a peculiar shame that came from being the captain who gave the order to scuttle his own ship. Such were hard times. My mind was settled as I put my thoughts and misgivings to my journal, working in my own entertaining cipher. The leather-bound book had been my companion for some time and had become all the more valuable since gaining the hat.

Eamon, the pirate, had precious little to worry himself with words. There was plenty to consider, the black fate of the Blighs. I wondered what felonious offence my father had discovered about the king. We Blighs had been no pretense of nobility, but we had been granted lands, and there was some wealth to our names. I had joined the King's Navy as a lad and had been away when the deed had been done.

Treason.

It was a load of bollocks. My father had been an ardent supporter of the king and made no bones about his distaste for the independence and religiously deviant colonists. Master Bligh had been a forward and vocal supporter of the king, and the Anglican church, so much that treason felt like a lie draped in an ermine cape, wearing a jeweled crown. My father was hanged for whatever he learned. My mother had died of some malady that took her in the king's dungeon. My eldest brother hung next to my father, and Emma…

It stung to think of her. She had been sold to some colonial loyalist in Charlestown, like chattel. It was indentured, the man had told me, and that in time, she could buy her own freedom, or someone with enough pounds sterling could do the same. Then, the same man presented me with the warrant for my own arrest and execution as a traitor to the crown.

The crew didn't know these things. I was confident that their illiteracy would keep my secrets as well as any lockbox.

My first act as a pirate had been to shoot that specific man with my pistol.

A month later, I had hopped enough ships to make my way to Port Royale, and that was where I had met one Captain Blaine and a few men of his crew. They were taking names in his book, fresh men to join his crew. I made my mark and left behind the king and his navy.

Now, it was my book, and my ship, and the remnant of my crew.

These were such as the days of the less than stellar Captain Eamon Bligh.

I sighed and joined Baxter and the others on the deck. It was going to be soon upon us, making a decision what to do with the *Honor*, but none of us were ready for that. Until our hand was forced, we were likely to leave her where she rested. There was still the matter of the disposition of the lucre, and that needed to be off the ship sooner than that. We only had to find a place on Ghost Island to stow it away.

We loaded the charts and rudders into the longboat and rowed them to the island.

There was precious little left aboard now, and most of the crew worked and slept on the island. A few persisted in calling it Eamon's Folly, but such was waning. Not even Forsythe took that up much now. Instead, they had made good putting up a pirate's fort not far from the hill we reached on that first trek. The Mirror Pond was fresh water, and likewise, not far from our camp.

The nights when I didn't sleep on the ship, I came to the water. I strove to see my angel when I was awake. She had startled away the one time I saw her, and I hadn't seen her with waking eyes since.

After inspecting the goings on in the camp, and commending the men for their foray to the mainland and returning with a brace of wild pigs, I took to wander. My thoughts led me in no particular direction. I didn't look for anything in particular, not my angel and not a place to hide the gold. If you looked too hard, you'd never find what you were looking for. Such things came from the corner of the eye, where you could see but did not look.

I found my way to the Mirror Pond. Its quiet and stillness was soothing, and even during the day it kept its secretive feeling. I made my way around the edge, and the footing was treacherous. The ground was silty and my boots sank in places, the mud sucking at them. Creatures retreated from my heavy step, and I fancied movement from the corners of my eyes, larger things, of the wind just moving in the green.

I found where my angel had stood, the far side of the pond was the better side, wide and flat with a berm of worn stone rather than ooze. There could be a path here, if a man wanted one. I limbered by cutlass and sought the way she had gone. I shook my head, there was nothing but branch and bramble here, vines covered with flowers and hungry thorns. I gave the green wall a few blows, and I was left dumbfounded.

The worst of the thicket gave to and fell and by God there was a path. It snaked down, away from the Mirror Pond and it was firm and set with rock. It was no road, no animal path, it was rock. I slew a few more of the grasping vines and pushed my way down this new direction. Another hill rose, flanked by trees and the green blanket that covered the island.

The second hill was taller than the first we found, but easily lost in the forest growing over it. I gave a great laugh as I found the thing that pirates tell stories of, a cave, in the side of the hill. I ventured inside, as far as the light of day would carry. It was rough, and there was the scent of years of creatures living inside – bats and birds and crawling things. Some skittered away lest I crush them underfoot.

It extended deep into the ground, further than I would have expected. As the light from the entrance faded, I found a branching, turning path, and beyond it, blackness. I grabbed a few stones and tossed them into the dark. A few bounced and struck things, but several bounced once and were gone. There was a drop off, and a damned steep one at that. This would more than suffice for our purposes.

My return to the camp was nearly a flight. I gathered a handful of men and we returned to the cave, well-armed with ropes, torches dipped in pitch, and other such tools as we might need. We followed the mouth of the cave to the back where it twisted into a throat. Beyond there was another chamber, low topped, but seemingly larger than the first. The walls seemed an almost luminescent stone, almost wax like.

We were beset with a multitude of dark stone maws. The first we took wound back on itself and sank down into the earth. The air became fetid and stale, and we found a shallow pit, the bottom lined with the bones of long dead and decayed creatures. I gestured and we retreated from that cursed twist. Another vein in the stone led us to a chasm that seemed rent in the earth and was at first large enough for a man to venture into, but quickly closed on itself, causing some consternation to Mr. Bennet who volunteered to plumb its depths.

The last circuitous route led us to a large almost theater like chamber, its sides bowled out like the inside of a cooking vessel. At the center of the chamber, there was a black hole in the earth, dropping at a slight angle but quickly straightening itself so that we could only see darkness.

"That would be the devil's gullet, if I ever saw it," Bennet said.

"I'd call it the Devil's Arse," Forsythe quipped. "And that's a fine place to cram the king's gold."

"Mister Hammond," I called. He popped up next to me, eyes bright.

"Aye, sir, aye." he said. I gestured to the hole.

"You're the surest footed of us all. We'll tie a rope around you and you go on down and see what we have down there. Our gold has to be hidden so far up the Devil's bum that even God himself couldn't find it," I said. He gave a nod, and the men set to tying the line fast and checking so that our man didn't plummet to a horrible death. He descended, looped the rope around his waist and leg so that he picked how fast he went down.

It was what I had tried so many weeks ago and had failed so horribly to accomplish. He went down a great distance. We counted knots in the rope as we lowered Mister Hammond, each knot a fathom, so that we would know the depth of this endeavor. After fifteen fathoms, we had to pause and secure more rope to his line. The count continued, twenty fathoms, twenty-five...

How deep was this blasted hole?

After counting a score and six knots, Hammond's perilous descent ended.

"I found the bottom, sirs," his voice came faintly from the hole.

"Mind yourself," I shouted to him, and we dropped him a lit torch. It flipped several times before coming to a rest far below our vantage point.

"Oh, it's a sight, it's a sight!" he called up to us.

"What do you see, boy!" Forsythe shouted down to him.

"I can't say, sir. I don't have words for this, I am no poet. If you are of a mind to come down, mind the shaft, it doesn't fall straight away like a stone well, it kindly... it kindly twists about," he said distantly.

Hammond's words lit a fire in our bellies, and one by one we made our way down the shaft to see what he could not describe.

When I reached the bottom, standing shoulder to shoulder with Forsythe and Bennet while Mister Hammond made his way back up, I completely understood the failure of his words. There was a large chamber, the floor rough and heaving like a ship caught in a storm but frozen in stone, and the roof above us glittered with crystals. Our torches filled the chamber with dancing light and the translucent stone above us shone brighter and more glorious than any of the chandeliers of stained glass of nobles or clergy.

"A moment, lads, a moment," I said. "We have found a secret cathedral here, and the Lord has seen fit to decorate it for us."

The ascent from the cathedral was difficult and slow, and we carried word back to the camp. Over the next few days, most everyone had a chance to shimmy down the Devil's Arse and into the cathedral, to see the splendor that was down there. We all agreed, this was the place to obfuscate the gold.

I heeded Dougal's advice, and for the largest part left the unloading of the gold to the men. We packed the bars two and three at a time around the Mirror Pond, down the stone path and up the greater one through the trees to the cave. Finally, we toted them carefully down into the depths of the darkness under the earth. I made notes in my journal, impressions of the stones, a feigned hand at making a map, and more such observations. It was far better reading than the previous dry angry words of treason. Though, I had to admit, my map-making skills were far less than my skill at reading them.

From first bar to last bar carried down the shaft, three days passed. Even after the gold was removed, there was still work to be done. We emptied *Honor* of everything she carried – every scrap of rope, every stitch of canvas, every keg of powder. When we were done, she was hollow save for her cannons, which were too heavy to move, and the ballast in the bilges. Baxter was heartbroken to leave his guns, but his anguish was lessened by the removal of the ramrods, shot, and other accessories of cannon craft.

Evening came, and we gathered on the shore of Ghost Island, each man facing *Honor* where she was stricken on the rocks. From that soft and gray vantage point we could all see the damage in her side, and how we would never have the ability to rescue her. We took turns, each of us had something to say about the ship. For some, it was our first hand at piracy. For others, she was just the last one.

It was not my first ship, but it was my first captaincy, I confessed to them.

Forsythe spoke of Black Bart and Calico Jack, crewing on their ships.

Mister Baxter and Mister Dougal spoke of *Honor's Price* when she flew the king's colors and not the black. How Baxter had never left the ship, and how Dougal had served on it, left for larger ships, and found his way back to her.

"It's time," Baxter said, his eyes betraying him as he spoke. He had prepared one of the swivel guns on the beach, with incendiary shot. *Honor's Price* had been prepared, and there was lamp oil, pitch, and some gunpowder scattered across her deck. "You should do her honor, sir," he said solemnly.

I had the urge to protest. I had already done enough harm to the ship, and he had served on her longer than any of us, but I caught Dougal's eye, and remembered his council. To be captain was to be the captain. I took the fuse from Baxter and thanked him, thanked all of them, and touched it to the smoke hole of the swivel gun. It barked in response and pelted the ship with burning debris. The fire spread quickly, the oil going quick, the powder going in a flash, and the pitch catching and burning furiously.

I held the captain's hat over my breast, and those among the crew who affected hats held them in their hands, or over their breast as I was. The fire spread quickly and consumed the ship faster than I would have imagined.

We were a quiet and somber lot as we returned to the camp. Our fate was now completely decided, and it lay in embarking in the longboats north, following the coast. We would secure provisions and supplies as we needed and banked on returning to Ghost Island in the near future, to secure our wealth and make among us the wealthy gentry of the Carolinas our peers.

I was weary, but sleep eluded me. I drank and gazed into the remnants of the campfire. With no need to repair *Honor*, we had taken to feeding wood from the ship to the blaze. I had consented to this, save for the ship's wheel. That I would not let them burn to roast plucked birds or the peculiar fruit of the island.

I tired of this navel gazing and sought the most peaceful place on the island, the pond. With the moon high, maybe it would take my mind away from the events of the day, the scuttling of the ship, and the low morale of the crew, or the hollowness that was growing in us.

The dry foods would run out soon, and the spirits would be gone well before the rations. I sighed and once again considered what trouble the gold had been to us, and in what ways fate might have played us a different hand, had I not found it. With no lucre, there was no reason to avoid Port Royale, or Tortuga, or any of the Leeward islands. We could have signed a new crew, and taken back to the sea to plunder and weary the Spaniards and the Dutch.

I looked into the pond and was taken aback. The reflection in the glass-like water was not my own. I looked into the eyes of my siren, my angel. Slowly, curiosity drew me down like some terrible giant's hand, I reached for her...

CHAPTER THIRTEEN

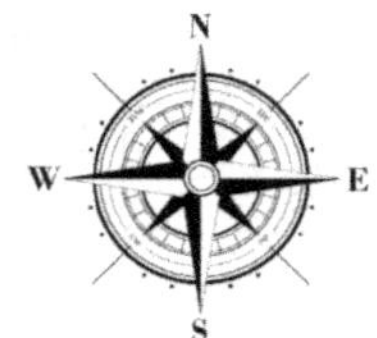

*A*very Barker...

"You sure you're ready for this?" Kurt asked and I looked up sharply from my final equipment check on the edge of the platform. My face felt pinched and squished by the suit around my head and the semi-claustrophobic feeling of the mask over my face was only going to make it worse once it sealed, but it was an easy sacrifice to make so I could get down there to explore the shaft and what we'd marked out as 'tunnel one' in our scans and ROV reconnaissance.

"Absolutely," I said without preamble. I was sure.

"You're not doing this because of Lennox, are you?" he asked and I frowned at him.

"Are *you* sure you want to do this?" I demanded. "Because if you have *any* doubts—"

"I'm sure, Ave," he said hastily and he fixed my gaze with his. I stared into his deep brown eyes and searched out his feelings.

"What's up with you?" I demanded.

"Nothing!" he said quickly. "How did me being worried about *you* turn to questioning my state of mind?" he demanded with a laugh.

"No idea," I said, shaking my head. "But I'd really like to get down there and check things out at the tunnel mouths myself, even if that's all we manage to do today."

"Better not be all we manage to do today," Kurt grumbled and I couldn't help but grin.

"The sea, she is a cruel mistress," I reminded him.

"Don't you *dare* jinx us," he admonished and I laughed.

"Enough of that shit, you two," Mac called and brought over our masks with built-in regulators. It would allow us to speak with both each other and those who remained on the surface. He hooked me up himself, like he always did, and double-checked Kurt once he was through.

"Communications check," came through the earpiece. "Testing, testing, check, check, check."

"Got you loud and clear, Pete. Can you hear me?"

Keith's voice came over the airwaves, "Hear you just fine, Avery."

"Let's do this," Kurt's voice came through and I smiled, the thrum of excitement was palpable.

"How dangerous is this? Really?" I heard Lennox ask from nearby and behind me.

"More dangerous than I'd like," Mac grumbled. "You watch your air."

"You know we will," Kurt answered. "Ain't nobody dying today."

He caught my eye though our respective masks and with a nod, we both plunged over the side of the platform, the weight of our gear dragging us down.

It wasn't long before it was dark as pitch, and neither of us could see. We'd run a guideline down to the bottom with the *Wet Dream*, but only to the bottom. It was up to me and Kurt to set the guide rope through the tunnels.

"Turn on your light, let's see what visibility is like," Mac called through the headset.

"Hang on," Kurt said as I thumbed the switch on the spotlight tethered to my wrist.

At first it was blinding, the emerald-green water flaring bright, the particulate a crazy swirl in front of my mask until I could see beyond it. Kurt was right in front of me and his light flared up too, revealing his thumbs up.

I let go of the guideline just long enough to give him a thumbs up back and asked Mac, "What do you guys see?"

"Got beautiful images coming through up here. Visibility is good. You are clear to continue your decent."

"Copy that, Mac."

We dove, using the guideline to get to the bottom, the visibility improving as we went. The cave structure was *insane*. I wasn't super used to cave diving, but Kurt had more experience with his time spent in the systems throughout Mexico and the Yucatan peninsula.

"Want me to take lead?" he asked.

"Yeah, you know this type of thing better than I do."

"Yeah, but even I've never seen anything quite like this."

"You guys getting this?" I asked.

"We're getting it."

"This place is *massive*." There was no mistaking the awe in Kurt's voice and I was with him on that.

"Tunnel one is to the left," I said and Kurt gave the 'okay' sign with his hand. We hooked a fresh guideline to the bottom, and Kurt picked up a reel of fresh line that'd been placed by *Dreamy*.

He led, I followed, the line unspooling.

"What do you think?" I asked when we reached the narrow passage – too narrow for *Dreamy*, but not at all too narrow for us.

"Definitely not a problem for us, but yeah – *Dreamy's* fat ass didn't stand a chance."

"I lead, you follow?" I asked. If something went wrong, I would rather it be me and not Kurt who got hurt.

"Dream on, Princess," Mac came through the radio.

"What Mac said." Kurt left me behind with a sharp kick of his fins.

"Watch your time, watch your air, you two." Mac wasn't playing but he also didn't need to worry about either of us on that score. I particularly enjoyed breathing.

I followed Kurt through the opening which was plenty big for a person but had stopped *Dreamy*.

We dove tunnel one but it was a relatively fruitless endeavor, there was nothing there. It took us a while with the decompression stops that we had to make, but it wasn't a total waste of time or a complete loss.

"That's one down," Mac said, leaning down to grasp my gloved hand and haul me up out of the water and onto the platform.

"Yeah," I said as soon as I pulled the mask off my face. I drew in big lungsful of fresh air scented with the green growing things outside the cave's mouth.

"What do you think?" Lennox asked. "Going back down tomorrow?"

"They could, but it's best to give it a little longer than that between deep dives," Mac told him as he helped me shrug out of my tanks, taking them off my shoulders.

Pete was over helping Kurt.

"I guess I don't understand. I thought you'd be eager to make more progress," Lennox said and I took pity on him, feeling charitable after our talk a couple nights before.

"Don't get us wrong, we are," I said, breathing hard still.

"We're just not terribly eager to court decompression sickness," Kurt supplied.

"What is that?" Lennox asked. "You keep talking about it but I don't follow."

"I'm starving," I told him. "Tell you about it over some food down at the mess."

"Well," he said, as I peeled out of my wetsuit and to the swimsuit I had on underneath, trying hard not to look as Mac handed me a beach towel. "As soon as you're ready, allow me to escort you."

"How gallant of you," I said, shivering a bit from the colder water, eager to step out into the sunlight shining outside the cave's mouth. "I'll take you up on that. Just let me dry off and we'll go. I'll run you through decompression sickness on the way down."

I climbed into a pair of short jean shorts and threw a loose, boat-neck tee over my head, squeezing out my ponytail as best I could. Mac wordlessly took my towel from me and gave me a look as if to ask if I was really cool walking down with Lennox alone. I gave a nod. Kurt and Pete huddled behind Keith at the monitors.

"You staying up here?" I called over and Kurt waved me off, pointing at something on the screen and telling Keith the firsthand experience from his perspective – what it was and what he thought it meant.

"Pete?" I called, and he waved me off, too.

"Gotta check the equipment, run the tanks down to the *Sapphire Horizon* and get 'em refilled. My job's just starting, you know that."

"Okay, I'll see y'all down there," I called, and to Lennox I said, "Let's go."

"So, decompression sickness?" Lennox asked, and I nodded.

"Just how much *do* you know about deep diving?" I asked.

"I'll confess – nothing at all."

"Cool, I just didn't want to go over that which you already know."

I shrugged my feet into my flip-flops at the mouth of the cave and oh God, did it feel good to get out under the sun! The rays warmed me down to my soul. It'd been a pretty damned oppressive and claustrophobic dive down there. Some of the passages we'd gone through narrower than I would like.

"When you dive beyond a certain depth, gasses build up in your bloodstream," I explained. "Come up too quick and the bubbles aren't given time enough to dissipate, and you could be in for it."

"How so?" he asked.

"Joint pain, and in some cases, like my dad's, something as bad as a stroke. They call it the bends. It's not good, can cause permanent damage and if you do get it? It can be one of the most painful things you ever go through."

"Have you ever had it?" he asked.

"Mild form, once, and I never want to do that again."

"How do you stop it?"

"Regular pauses while you ascend to acclimate your body to the changes in pressure and allow the gasses built up in your blood and joints to dissipate naturally."

"Ah, I see, so that's why it took you so long to come up after Mac called it off."

"Yup."

"I thought you were the boss, though."

"I am," I said.

"Then why was Mac calling the shots?"

"You need someone clear-headed to call the shots," I said. "When you're down that far, you can get nitrogen narcosis – sometimes called 'rapture of the deep' and your judgment can become significantly impaired."

"So you keep someone on the surface in charge?" he asked.

"Yup. That would be why we have a dive master," I agreed. "Didn't any of the guys tell you any of this?"

"They said to ask you when you resurfaced. I don't think they like me much."

I choked on a laugh and said, "I don't think it's that bad. I think it's a couple of things to be honest. One, they don't like the way you treated me. Two, they really don't know what to say in front of the suits. The last thing they want to do is offend the guy who holds the purse strings. Remember, they do this because they love this, but love doesn't keep a roof over their families' heads or food in their bellies."

"You're saying they're terrified of me?" he asked, stopping, and I stopped too, glancing over.

"Pretty much."

The look on his face then earned him some points with me. He looked momentarily stricken, then troubled.

"How new are you at this, Mr. Lennox?"

"At what?" he asked.

"Observing an operation in action."

"My first time in the field, so to speak, on something like *this*," he said. "Typically, I'm in corporate boardrooms and I've got to say – that's an entirely different animal, Ms. Barker."

"I believe it," I said nodding, putting my feet into motion. I was hungry.

He fell into step behind me and we talked back and forth through the line at the mess and taking a seat across from one another. He was, surprisingly, an attentive listener.

"Believe me, Mr. Lennox—"

"Jake, if you please, Ms. Barker."

I didn't know if I was honestly comfortable with being on a first-name basis with him. I mean, I hadn't thought about what that could mean. Still, I didn't want to be rude and ruin the rapport we were building so…

"Believe me… Jake. I understand every day we aren't doing something down the Devil's Arse—"

"Wait, *what* did you just call it?" he demanded, nearly choking on his food with his laughter.

I smiled and laughed a little myself.

"It's what Eamon Bligh called it in his journal," I said. "One of his crew named it and it stuck."

"You're serious!"

"Oh, yeah," I nodded, grinning. "There were some characters on his crew."

"Okay, you were saying, I'm sorry."

I laughed. "It's okay. It caught me off guard too. We've been trying to be careful and a little more PC with one of the Bancroft Group in our midst. It's a force of habit when investors are around."

"I understand, but I would like to think we're past all that now."

I nodded. "Maybe," I murmured. "Anyway, as I was saying, I know it costs money every time we face a day with no exploration but there's not a penny that anyone could spend that's worth one of my crew's lives. I will *never* put them in a position where they feel they have to take unnecessary risks in order to perform to anyone's liking. I don't care who is holding the purse strings."

He nodded thoughtfully. "I believe our miscommunication has been cleared up, Ms. – Avery."

I nodded and said, "I certainly hope so, Jake. I don't want anyone else to get hurt, or worse, die on my watch. I can't have it."

"Nor do I want it." He searched my face for a moment and said, "What I *do* want now, is a look at that journal."

I laughed and nodded and said, "After we finish up here, I think I can arrange that."

Truth be told, it'd been a minute since even I had spent any time with Eamon Bligh. Well, with his words, anyway. The journal was fragile being a two-hundred-and-eighty-five-year-old book, but fragile as it was it was also in *remarkable* shape. Like, unbelievably good shape for its age. That had a lot to do with the equally remarkable climates of the library rooms it had been stored in for a decent chunk of its life.

"Did I hear you say you were going to look at the book?" Nils asked from down the table.

"Yeah," I said. "You want a peek?" He nodded his head eagerly and I smiled. Nils was a Dutchman who had a thing for old books, maps, and other sundry historical writings. He was one of our resident archaeologists and had been working alongside Mac on the desalination process on the flask we'd found. That, and he'd been eagerly awaiting any other artifacts we could dredge up from the depths of the Devil's Arse.

Truthfully, I was glad Nils overheard us and it wasn't *quite* an accident that I'd said something loud enough. I still didn't trust Lennox to not make a move – so it would definitely be nice to have a chaperone.

Lennox and Nils followed me to my tent, and I opened up the safe that contained the journal, taking it out of its protective sleeve only when I had it in the environmentally sound box. Neither one of the men were allowed to touch it with their bare hands. Rather, they were given white cotton conservationist gloves, and I left Nils in charge of turning the pages which were brittle at their outer edges.

"Wow, she kind of looks like you, doesn't she, Avery?" Jacob asked.

"What? Who? Emma?" I asked, drawing near.

"No," Nils said, his voice thick with his accent. "Her."

I frowned, not knowing what they were talking about.

"Do what now?" I drew up close to Nil's back and peered over his shoulder at the old, charcoal drawing on the page, likely done with a bit of burned wood from one of the pirate's fires. On the page was a woman who *did* look like me, from the perspective of a man on his back.

She was riding him, breasts bare and pressed together by her straightened arms, looking down at him with her bottom lip grasped between her teeth. The image disappeared just below her elbows. Her hands had to be pressed to his chest, and I shuddered internally to think just how many times I had ridden my dream lover in my sleep.

"Yeah, she kind of does," I said, my voice distant, my mind elsewhere, back with my unknown lover from my recurring dreams.

The men talked, my mind raced, and thankfully it was late enough they called it after only a few minutes when I had to turn up the lamplight in my tent. I couldn't wait for them to leave so I could decipher the script on the page.

"Goodnight, you guys. Tomorrow we parse data. We need a solid break between dives."

"Safety first," Lennox agreed and I smiled, finally feeling like we were on the same page.

As soon as they were out of the tent and only half a step down the path, I flew into the seat Nils had vacated at my desk to look at the image and its description again.

"What?" I mouthed, barely a whisper escaping my throat which felt squeezed tight by some unseen hand.

I didn't remember this passage, and I had been through this book, the scans of the individual pages something like a thousand times and more.

I booted up the laptop and felt like I was going insane.

I slammed the lid closed and stared open mouthed at the journal. There was a scanned page in the computer that corresponded but damnit, *it wasn't there before.* I knew it wasn't there before. *I've been through this book a thousand times!*

I deciphered the code the passage was written in ferociously but there wasn't much there. Just something about his siren, his angel, a phantasm that haunted him and yet brought him peace, trying to suppose who she was and why she came to him when he dreamed.

"No," I said and closed the book gently. "No, no, no, no, no."

I carefully put the journal back in its safe and tucked the gloves away.

I felt hot and cold, every nerve in my body abuzz and jangling, every hair on my body standing at attention as I fought to regain my breath I hadn't even realized I'd lost in the first place.

"Walk it off, Avery," I muttered and did just that, batting the flap of my canvas explorer's tent out of my way and tilting my face up to the stars.

I closed my eyes and caught my breath, but I couldn't stay here. I didn't need one of the guys to happen upon me *losing my collective shit.*

I mean, there was *no* explaining this without looking like a crazy person.

I was grasping at straws by the time I reached the edge of the Mirror Pond behind its copse of trees and vines. I mean, I was even willing to blame it on the rapture of the deep at this point but I'd never heard of the rapture following anyone up to the surface.

"Ooooh, God." I groaned, stepping over to the pond and putting my hands on my knees. I took in some deep slow breaths in through my nose, out through my mouth and *refused* to be sick.

When I opened them, I nearly yelped. I certainly jumped... because staring back at me where my reflection should be was my dream lover, his green eyes wide and face echoing the shock of my own.

The waters distorted as he reached his hands through and heart in my throat, I dipped my hands through the surface and *grasped flesh;* his hands closing around my own.

I didn't think, I just dug my heels into the rock at the side of the pond and *pulled,* and the man I'd dreamed about every night since coming to this island stepped up and onto the bank beside me.

His chest heaved, water running in rivulets from the ends of his auburn hair made black by water and moonlight, dripping silver from the end of his nose, collecting in his long, dark lashes like a constellation…

"Oh, my God…" I whispered in a mixture of awe and shock. "You're real. You're really real."

CHAPTER FOURTEEN

*E*amon Bligh...

The water was cold, but only for a moment, and I had the sudden and horrific feeling as though I were falling. Time seemed a syrupy thing and my head spun like too much drink, and then I stumbled. The air was suddenly thicker, warmer, and hung with a dampness. She was still there, my siren, holding onto my hand with both of hers.

This isn't how this normally goes; I should be asleep for this.

"Oh, my God..." she whispered in disbelief. "You're real. You're really real." She swallowed hard, her fingers tightening around my hand as her blue eyes bored into mine. "Oh shit," she said, "Oh shit, you're real..." Her voice was heaven sent, light and lyrical.

"Aye," I said hesitantly, feeling the word in my mouth, as I spoke it experimentally. "Aye, real I am." She grabbed me in a tight hug, and the strength I suspected of her was there, though she drew back quicker than I liked. Her hand went to the grip of my cutlass and her eyes went wide.

"You seem to be most real, as well," I said. "Speak again, tell me your name, siren!" My excitement could not be contained. All of our other encounters, as deeply pleasant as they had been, were all wordless. In my dreams, she did not speak, and I was somehow unable to.

"Avery," she said. "My name is Avery." She stared at my cutlass and said, "This is Eamon Bligh's sword." She drew the blade free from my sash. It was a startlingly forward thing to do, but as in dreams, I could not speak, although here it seemed I was entranced and thus my silence. "This-this can't be Eamon Bligh's sword. His sword is in the Charleston Naval Museum, in a case, and its half rusted away. They didn't properly take care of it, left it—"

I took a finger under her chin and lifted her face from the cutlass to look at me. "Aye, Avery. You said that is my cutlass; I seem to need no introduction then. Since if that is Eamon Bligh's cutlass, and that be *my* cutlass, then I must be Eamon Bligh, would you not agree?" She seemed to pale a little despite my charming smile that I turned upon her in full effect.

"You're real," she said again.

"Aye, and I think you might be a bit of a parrot?" I gave a small laugh.

"Am not!" she said, shaking her pretty head as though to clear it. "How, how are you here? I dream about you, and not just from reading your journal." Her confession turned her cheeks red and I raised a brow.

"I dream of us as well; dream of you, my siren goddess. I would make the guess that you've used some sort of curious magics to bring us together, so that we might tryst in earnest," I said, stepping slightly closer to her. It made as much sense as anything else. "Sailors and witches are not so distant; I know the name of Circe and Scylla."

"Wait, what? I'm no-I'm not a witch!" she said. "Wait!" she exclaimed. "Let me see your hands."

I offered them to her, but not before tucking the cutlass back where it belonged. She seemed reluctant to yield the blade, but did, and was deliberately probing, looking at my hands.

"I had a dream you came to me. You had a severe laceration to your scalp, most likely a concussion, and your hands were badly torn." She traced down the lines in my palm, calloused and weathered from rope, salt, and tar.

"Aye, I remember fragments of this," I said. "You used your peculiar magic to mend me. When I awoke, the crew stood by as if in deathbed vigil."

"Come with me," she said and came near to dragging me in her enthusiasm. I followed her dutifully. There was a certain delight to watching her walk in front of me, with those curious tight underpants she wore. The camp she had was as queer as her clothing; strangely patterned, a barely there imitation of some French garment. She led me to a very large tent, the fabric very near to that of sailcloth. She peeled back the entry way and urged me inside, pulling me along after her as though I would deny her anything.

"I've been here!" I said, and she put a finger to her lips.

"Not so loud, the others will hear you!" she admonished.

"Do you mean to tell me you are alike, stuck upon this island?" I asked, my voice lowered. She looked at me, bewilderment and excitement battling in her eyes. "How do you know my journal, and my cutlass?" I asked. "Where are we?"

She fiddled with some strange device and with a soft hiss, it flared to light. *She had a witch light!* "I'm a treasure hunter," she said.

"Aren't we all?" I asked with a quirk of my lips.

"I'm a *specific* treasure hunter. I, and the people I work with, are looking for your gold, if you are Eamon Bligh."

"How can you even be looking for it? I doubt the king even knows it's been taken," I said.

"What... what year do you think it is?" she asked me with a curious look.

"The year of our Lord seventeen-thirty and a year. October unless my eye is mistaken," I answered. She gave a laugh and covered her mouth, shaking her head.

"Its June," she said. "June, *two thousand and sixteen.*"

I was quiet. I considered what she said, most made little sense, or none at all. I decided that perhaps this wasn't the time for such conversations.

"Avery," I said, savoring her name as I savored her voice and strange accent. "I've dreamed of you, and we've held such intimate congress as to make a sailor blush. I've been pained by my curiosity. I am very happy now, I know your name, and I am close to believing this is real." I reached out and caressed the side of her face.

She gave a small shudder, her eyes closing, and I knew that she was still my siren, even if she were much more verbose and excitedly vocal than she'd ever been before. I pulled close to her and kissed her. She seemed startled and tense at first, but she quickly relaxed. She trailed a hand down my shirt and kissed me back for a moment and stopped.

"Okay," she whispered, stepping closer in the circle of my arms.

Inside her space was a vaguely familiar bunk. I had no recollection of dreaming of the rest of this place, but it did not seem so foreign as the other places had been with its rows of empty cots before a great empty fireplace.

Here, there was a desk. Unfurled on it was a collection of maps and charts, some hand drawn, others created with lines so fine and deft that I shuddered to think of their cost, or the effort that had gone into making them. There was also a great wealth of books, with curiously slick and glossy covers, and more of her witchcraft devices and a strongbox. Well at least that was a somewhat familiar sight.

"Eamon," she said, and I looked away from the charts spread on her table. Her eyes sparkled in that beckoning manner and I turned my attentions back to her. I removed sash and cutlass, boots and the rest until I stood before her in shirt and trousers. Our lips met again, and it was sublime. Better than a dream, this reality.

"You are a beauty," I exclaimed, before putting my lips to her neck. I kissed her, and held her, and I felt her fingers pull at my shirt. This was no new thing, we had done this many a time before in my dreams, in my own bunk… Yet this seemed so different, much stranger, *more real*. I removed her top and lavished her neck with kisses. I wanted to devour her scent with them.

She moaned softly; her hands tangled in my hair as I took her breasts. I cupped them, squeezed them, and took first one nipple in my mouth, and then the other. I greeted them as if we were friends long separated and I longed to become reacquainted with them, but wanted neither to feel more favored, or left out, compared to the other. I felt a tremble in my hand, a frisson of excitement that vibrated from the base of my stiff cock, through my heart, and into the base of my skull.

I relieved her of the short pants, and found beneath them another set of underwear, this more curious than I expected; a barely there scrap of cloth to cover her nethers – almost pointless, ridiculous in their construct.

Those too, I removed and felt that boyish tremor of excitement again, one that settled into a deep ache between my legs. I restrained myself, and once her tuft was free, I did not aim straight away for it. No, I wanted her to sing softly for me. I kissed her stomach, and the flat above her nethers, down to where instead of unruly blonde curls, there was naught but that small welcoming patch of downy hair.

She tightened her grip in my hair as I breathed kisses around her sex, and I found her fragrance intoxicating. I kissed her on the lips of her sex, gently. She pushed her body against me, and I was aware that her excitement had brewed up as much as mine had. I tasted her, my tongue parting her secret lips and seeking inside of her. She moaned, and she rolled her hips, subtly showing me where she wanted my tender kisses.

I obliged her with a fraction of my attention diverted so as to remove my trousers without disturbing our intimate encounter. It was almost a palpable relief when I was no longer bound, and I felt myself swing free. She whispered a litany to herself. I caught snippets of God, and yes, and what sounded close to the sniffles associated with joyous tears. I felt my own joy, her pleasure was my own.

I stroked myself slowly as I sought to draw her out, her breathing quick and shallow. I felt my own excitement drip from me, and I feared that if I gave too much to myself, my ardor would overcome my reserve. I had no desire to disappoint my Avery in such a fashion.

"Fuck me," she said. *"Please."* The words were midnight whispers.

I slowly withdrew and kneeled before her. The apex of her thighs glistened and begged for me. I laid her upon her bunk and rose, kneeling between her thighs, slowly rubbing the head of my cock between her lips, slick with her arousal. I teased her, but I also remembered our first phantasmal encounter, and how she had ridden me, her sex pressed against mine. I slid my shaft between those pink lips, savoring her moan and the heat that I felt. She made the familiar needy sounds; begging whimpers that told me she was ripe for the taking, and take her I did. Gently, gently as a man in the throes of his desire could.

I entered her slowly, painstakingly. While we had been dream lovers for some weeks, months perhaps, this was our first *real* encounter and I would savor it. She bit her lip, her eyes almost starstruck, dreamlike and dewy as I gave her my entire length. We stayed there for a time, moving slowly against each other. This was different, and though my ardor remained strong, it felt different. My chest felt tighter than my bag, and I could think of nothing more perfect, nothing more beautiful, nothing I deserved… I was a pirate after all. I didn't deserve someone so flawless and good.

She drew me in, and we held each other close, kissing, lip to lip, sometimes just smelling her hair, kissing her neck. I felt as if I were becoming part of her, and she a part of me. The thrust of my cock and the tightness of her body around mine was just coincidental. I felt moved, my emotions were stirred, raw and aching.

"Avery," I whispered in her ear.

"Oh, God, Eamon, yes?" she answered breathlessly. I had

intended to relay that I felt love in my breast, and that my heart and her heart were the same. A stricture overcame me, and my words, as in the dream, failed me. I felt her squeeze me tightly, her arms above, her cunt below.

Our eyes were closed, and I felt something hot wash over me. She shuddered and there were teeth in my shoulder. I gasped with the force of my own release. It seemed to go on and on, as if I were draining a sea of passion I had been holding in reserve.

Eventually, my senses returned, and I became aware of the world inside her tent again. I realized how heavily I must have been pressed atop her and removed myself. Rather than complain or protest, she seemed to reach for me. I had softened to an extent but remained inside her. When I pulled out of her, she gave a moan that seemed to come from so deep inside her that perhaps it was not her, but her sex given a voice with which to speak its satiation.

We were still for what felt a long time, our sweat-sheened bodies stacked together. I was aware of her contented breathing, and the rise and fall of her breasts as she did so. It was also part of my attention that my flaccid length was lain against the inside of her thigh. Moving it would dispel what magic we had created with moans and kisses, so I was still.

I think for a piece, we slept.

When I woke from a skimming drowse, she rested her head against my chest, her fingers tracing the scar on my flank. "You never wrote about what happened, how you got this," she said. I covered her hand with my own.

"I was gifted that on my first voyage in His Majesty's service," I said. "I was a faithful king's man then, and barely more than a cabin boy at the time. I knew my ropes and knots, and had studied at the university to learn navigation, how to read the stars, and the way of maps and the rest of being a learned man."

"Were you wounded in battle?" she asked.

"Aye, but those were less generous with souvenirs, and took more limbs and lives – splinters, powder burns, the like. But this," I said, touching the scar, "this was given to me by a man of my own crew, a gunner's mate. We were ashore in St. Martin, the crew having a merry time with spirits and the painted ladies. One of my mates decided that one of the lady's ought to grant him a charity. Her services in thanks to the crown. They quarreled, and he made as if he were going to strike her." I looked down at her, her eyes were bright.

"I stopped him and told him that he was a man of the King's Navy and not some common brigand. Nor was a lady, even a whore, his for the taking when it suited him. His ire was raised and bolstered by a fair amount of Dutch courage, and he drew steel on me. I was headstrong, and drew steel as well, ready to fight." I remembered it, the heat and sweat, the way his eyes were bloodshot and angry. "I felt so righteous and full of my own vigor. We crossed blades and left a mark on each other. He left me with this... I was close to death for a time, but I recovered." I felt her tense as I spoke.

"What of the other man?" she asked.

"He was given time in the brig. The captain said we were sailors in the king's service. We were to uphold order and the king's law. Bludgeoning whores was the handiwork of pirates and mutineers." She relaxed and I felt her give me a tight squeeze, her sweaty naked form pressed against mine.

"Mm," she hummed before saying, "Come on, we should get cleaned up." I agreed, but she didn't take us back to the Mirror Pond or further down to the beach. Rather, she took me to some wood-craft knock-up. The sun was waking, starting to rise and paint the sky in lavender and yellows along the horizon as she turned knobs and other sundry mechanisms in the box. I didn't follow what she did with her devices, but she made a steady rain spew from a metal spigot and stood under it, beckoning for me to join her. I did, and the water was fresh and cool.

Why would the people of this time waste drinking water to wash with?

She had soft bottles of fragrant smelling potions, and a curious sponge. Her quick hands brought it to a lather, and with that foam, she scrubbed me and the scent of it filled the stall. It was the source of her delightful fragrance and why she always smelled so clean and fresh. Her attention at my manhood roused my passions, and I felt invigorated. She bade me to return the favor, handing me the sponge and a different bottle. They were not glass, smooth and hard, yet remaining somehow supple. Not leather, certainly an unknown make to my mind. I squeezed it as she had and the fragrance bloomed out of it as it fountained over my hand. She laughed and took the bottle away from me. "Easy, a little goes a long way and I only have so much," she said.

I did as I was instructed and used the sponge on her. It became almost hypnotic watching the pearly foam dance down her body. She caught my stare and laughed softly. She turned and rinsed the froth from her and made me do the same. I felt as if I had been made new. There were more bottles, and the next concoction, it seemed, was for hair. She poured some of it in my hands and then some in hers and started massaging it into her own hair. I reached to do the same, but she swatted me back. "Silly, that's for *you*," she said.

I did as she did, mirroring her stance and motions, while she did what I can only assume to be a hair washing dance that made her bottom bounce around in a small jig. She laughed and the sound was musical and light and caused my heart to flutter in my breast.

There was more rinsing and she seemed very pleased by all of this and fawned over my hair as if it were some unusual thing. Her hair was longer than mine, but not by so much. There was naught a barber on any ship's crew that I knew, and even fewer among pirates. A cut and a shave were, to be sure, tended in port.

"Hold still for me, promise not to move," she murmured and I stood as still as stone while she dabbed a different fragrant foam on my face, this one slightly spicy, different from the rest. She produced a strange tool and she asked if I knew what it was, and I confessed my ignorance.

"Okay, I mean it now. It's really important that you hold still for me."

"Aye, I shan't move."

She took it and slowly drew it down my cheek, sweeping away the growth there. It was a razor of sorts and she gave me a clean and close shave that I had not had in some time. I marveled at the smoothness of my cheeks and my neck.

"Is that how you tend yourself, so neatly?" I asked.

"Tend myself?" she asked. I gestured down to the deftly trimmed tuft between her legs. She gave a laugh and was apparently quite amused by this.

"No, uh, I prefer waxing."

"Waxing?" I asked.

She laughed slightly and said, "Another time. I don't want to overwhelm you."

She took a handful of the foam and she covered my cock and bag with it. The attention put fresh wind in me and I hardened in her hands. She made an approving sound and held me and started to work with the razor. She worked deftly, and eventually kneeled in front of me. While I assumed this was to better inspect her handiwork, I came full hard in her hand and had to stifle a groan. This also amused my siren, and I saw that my dreams were not all fantastic and that there was truth to them. She stroked me a few times, and then, pleased with her work, wiped the last of the foam clean.

My cock stood naked and proud. And then she took me in her mouth.

My breath left me; her lips wrapped expertly around me. I had to brace myself against the wooden stall, and if I looked down, I saw that angelic face, contrasting with the devilish pleasure I felt. I made the mistake of looking up and saw our reflection in the hung mirror, her golden hair, hanging in wet sheets, her head bobbing. She squeezed, and I felt her tongue molten against me, like nothing I had ever felt before! I lost myself. My thoughts scrambled and I managed to croak her name…

"Avery…" my voice was weak. She released me from her mouth and looked up at me with smoldering eyes. "I…"

Le petit mort

I felt my entire body tense, and I heard her laughing like the siren she was. I floated for a moment, my passion pulsing from my body, and then my legs were rubbery and weak, like a man the first time on deck in a storm.

"I just showered," she admonished.

"My-my apologies," I gasped softly. Pearls decorated her neck and her chest.

She stood and rinsed again while I gathered my wits. She was a sorceress as sure as Circe. *Angel, siren, sea witch.* I sighed. I was gladly damned to her embrace.

She is looking for the lucre... what happened to my crew?

The thought came unbidden to me, and I remembered it, the creeping dread and how I felt like the gold was a slowly tightening noose around not just my neck, but every neck on the *Honor*. I rubbed my throat for a moment, and the cool smoothness brought me back from my dark reverie.

"Wait here for me," she murmured. "Promise you won't move."

"Aye," I said, cupping her face, stroking a thumb along her cheek. She stepped out of the wooden box and disappeared.

Avery presently rejoined me, and she held a change of clothing for me.

"We need to have a way to explain to my boys who you are and why you're here," she said. "These first." She handed me loose fitting underpants. "We have a communal laundry, they won't notice a few pieces gone missing," she said.

I donned the underpants, and then the pants... those were familiar. It was a stout fabric, not unlike canvas, but many times finer in make. The last thing she handed me was a minimal impression of a shirt. There was no billow in the sleeve, the chest fit tight, no cut. This was a strange and confining garment to say the least. It was colorful, a blue I'd ever seen in nature and never in cloth. The icon on the breast unfamiliar to me.

"I can't just tell my dive team and Lennox that we're now hosts to an eighteenth-century pirate, who's treasure we happen to be searching for," she said.

"Is this Lennox, the man who captains this venture?" I asked.

"No, no," she said. "He's... he's a company man, like the South Seas Trading Company. He works for the people *I* work for."

"I know the name," I said. There was the heaviness of the lucre in my stomach.

"Eamon, times have changed in the last two hundred and eighty-five years. *I'm* the one in charge, here. I'm the captain, I guess, but I'm not the captain-captain, he stays on our boat." She gestured to the mainland side of the island. I followed the wave of her hand. "That's to say, I'm the commander, I guess."

I laughed lightly and she frowned. *A woman, a commander of anything but hearth and home?*

"Truly have things changed so much?" I asked, well pleased. *Oh, that Emma could know this, she would be well pleased...*

"They have, but no one is going to believe you are who you are. We'll both be – er, um, taken to the asylum. Thought quite mad, and so we need a cover story," she said.

"Fly a false flag, as it were," I said, amused and gaining an understanding.

"You are... a reenactor from the Charleston Pirate Festival," she said.

"Charleston hosts a pirate festival?" I asked.

"It's more like a Ren faire, but yes," she said. My expression must have conveyed my lack of understanding. "It's a bunch of people in Charleston who like to dress up like pirates and fantasy novel characters and pretend it's the eighteenth century, and they know the details. It's perfect. You are a pirate festival actor, and you play," she held her hands up in a theatrical framing manner, "the dread pirate, Eamon Bligh."

"But I am he," I said.

"Perfect!" she said. "Just keep at that. You are an actor playing yourself. A descendant of his and you refuse to break character. That's also why you're here. You're a method actor, so you studied

Bligh, and you… read a copy of his journal, and that's why you wanted to come work with us. Historical authenticity," she said, sounding well satisfied.

"Avery! Where are you?" someone called from the direction of her tent.

"Just a minute, Mac!" she shouted back. "Make some coffee, we, uh, we have a guest!"

CHAPTER FIFTEEN

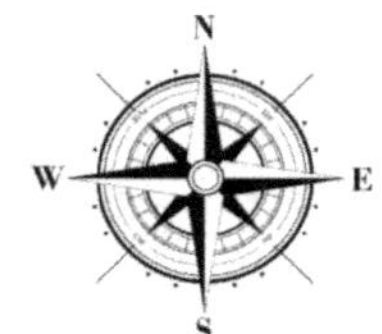

*A*very Barker…

"Whatever you do, no matter how surprising something is, *promise me* you won't freak out," I murmured. I fixed Eamon's deep green eyes with my own and he searched my face.

"Freak… out?" he asked, slightly amused. "Do you expect me to become a storm?"

"Uhhhh," I groped for an explanation but it was too late, Mac came around the corner.

"Woah, princess. Who is this?" he demanded.

"Mac, I'd like you to meet Eamon Bligh. Descendant of our pirate, Eamon Bligh."

Mac looked me up and down critically and said, "You're kidding me, right?"

"Nay, a jest is a poor way to make a proper introduction," Eamon said and smiled. *Damn,* I now understood what the term 'rakish grin' actually meant and it was panty melting. Unfortunately, it didn't do a damn thing for Mac.

"Can I talk to you?" he demanded of me.

"Absolutely, be right back, Eamon."

I did *a lot* of fast talking, dropping info about the pirate troupe of reenactors. How Eamon rarely broke character, and how things were about to get interesting but also how this Eamon could probably help us as he had access to letters between the original Eamon and his sister Emma that we didn't.

I absolutely *hated* lying to Mac with a passion, but I also knew absolutely nobody on this island was going to believe the truth – and why should they?

"How did he get here?" Mac demanded.

"Late night charter," I said without blinking. "I didn't want to say anything because we couldn't be sure he could get the time off work to be here."

"Not sure I like it," Mac said, unsettled. "Why's he gotta talk like that?"

"I told you, he *never* breaks character. But I promise you, Mac, he could be valuable. It takes *a lot* of getting used to, though," I said.

"At least he doesn't *dress* the part," Mac said, chewing the corner of his bottom lip thoughtfully as he eyed Eamon.

"He does," I said with a laugh. "Should have seen him last night."

"What, he stayed with you?" Mac scowled and I gave an impish smile and a little shrug.

"*Avery*," he admonished and I patted him on the arm.

"I'm a big girl, Mac," I told him. "And that man's *a snack.*"

"I'm not listening to this!" Mac shooed me with his hands, spun on his heel and walked away toward the mess.

Eamon drifted up beside me and asked, "Have you taken the diet of the cannibal islanders, or has the meaning of snack changed?"

I laughed and shook my head. "No. Come on back up to my tent. I need to introduce you to computers before you have the chance to freak out about them in front of everyone."

To his credit, Eamon didn't freak out like I thought he would. He simply sat in my chair at my desk looking like the wind had completely been knocked from his sails as he stared at the video of *Dreamy* doing her thing beneath the surface on the screen.

"'Tis a time of great wonders," he said in a choked whisper.

"There's a lot that's happened in the last two hundred and eighty-five years, Eamon. I need you to act like it's all perfectly normal."

He reached up, grasped my waist, and pulled me down into his lap. I put my arms around his shoulders and pressed my forehead to his and let him have as long as he needed.

"'Tis all perfectly normal," he murmured. "Normal beyond the imagination and comparison."

"I'm right there with you," I said dryly. "We're supposed to dive again tomorrow."

"I would go with you, on this venture," he said and the pleading in his voice… I wanted to. So badly.

"I can't," I said, my heart twisting with sorrow as I drew back to look into his eyes. "It's too dangerous. I can't teach you all you need to know in an afternoon, Eamon. It takes so much. There's *too much* for someone that's never done it before to remember."

He caressed my cheek and said, "But this spy box would let me observe this dive?" He waved a hand, indicating my laptop.

"Yes," I said with a smile. "You need to meet the rest of my crew. There are more computers and monitors and tomorrow will be much better."

He captured the back of my head with his fingers and dragged my mouth to his. I smiled against his lips and kissed him back enthusiastically, a happy glow settling in the center of my chest.

"Avery?" Kurt's voice sounded from outside the tent. Eamon and I both jumped slightly but it was too late. Kurt batted the canvas flap aside and was in before I had a chance to do much other than pull away from the kiss. I looked up at my best friend from my seat in Eamon's lap.

"The fuck?" Kurt asked, eyebrows askew.

"Kurt, meet Eamon Bligh," I said.

"You serious?" he demanded.

I smiled. "You haven't seen Mac?" I asked.

"No. Again, I ask, what the fuck, Avery?"

I gave Kurt the same explanation I'd given Mac and he laughed, hands on his hips, shaking his head.

"Sorry, dude," he said, knuckling the inside corner of his eye. "It's cool. You do you and all with the historical thing. Jesus, Avery. You had me going for a second there. I thought you'd lost your fucking mind. How come you didn't say anything?"

I sighed and stood up. "I lost my mind a long fucking time ago, Kurt. You know that. I didn't want to say anything about Eamon coming because we didn't know if he could get the time off work. Things sort of happened quickly and he was here before I knew it."

"Right," he said, sounding skeptic. I knew I would be answering to my bestie about both the lap sitting and the kiss he'd caught us sharing, but I would be putting *that* conversation off 'til the absolute last minute.

"You two coming down to the mess? Everybody's wondering where you're at," Kurt said coolly, and I knew I'd stepped in it – hip deep and sinking fast. It wasn't like me to keep anything from him and he wasn't okay with it. I didn't know what to say, so I ignored that too for the time being.

"Yup," I said, popping the 'p.'

Eamon pushed to his feet and I smiled up at him.

"You hungry?"

"Aye, I feel as if I've not eaten in three times a century," he said. Kurt shot me an amused look. Just because he was irritated with me didn't mean he would take it out on Eamon. Kurt wasn't like that.

"Cool," I said. "Let's eat."

We went down to the mess, chatter stopping, heads rising from over plates and turning to look at us and the new person in our midst. The looks ranged from confusion and curiosity to a few frowns of mistrust.

"Alright everybody, meet Eamon Bligh, direct decedent of our pirate, Captain Eamon Bligh, and historical reenactor. Eamon has had access to family historical documents, including some letters –

he's here to add insight into the search. We've been corresponding for quite a while; I just didn't say anything because we weren't sure if he could be here. Things fell into place last minute and here he is. Everybody, stop and take the time to say 'hello' when you get a chance."

As predicted, the entire crew chorused 'Hi!' at the same time. I laughed and shook my head and Eamon grinned. We got in line and dished up some breakfast; a hearty oatmeal that stuck to the ribs. The conversation, however, remained light – everyone getting a kick out of Eamon's accent and old-timey way of speaking. They got an even bigger kick out of him not 'breaking character' and how he spoke of his time in the King's Navy as though he *actually* had been there… *little did they know.*

I was nervous as all get out the entire time, too. Kurt eyed me from down the table as I forced a smile and laughed with the rest of the men.

We took the Gator up to the caverns and Eamon's green eyes *glowed* with his first ride on something with an internal combustion engine.

We were running *so short* on time for me to inform him about *anything* modern, really, but he stuck with me, and as promised had not freaked out. He had, at worst, remained stoic, expression tight around the edges and set in stone.

We got up to the caverns to find Pete cussing up a storm. I jumped off the Gator before it could even stop moving and went over to him.

"What's wrong?" I demanded.

He looked up at me, fury in his watery blue eyes, cheeks ruddy with his rage and said, "C'mere." He took me out of earshot of the rest of the crew up here with us.

"I couldn't be sure," he said, "but now I'm *damn sure.*"

"What is it, Pete?"

He sighed and said, "The fuckin' actuator was fuckin' *fine* last night, Avery."

"What actuator?"

"The one that causes *Dreamy's* arm to extend and retract," he said. "It would be one thing if I hadn't *just checked it*, but I ran checks last night, and this morning? Busted."

I shook my head. "Pete, *Wet Dream* is getting *old* for an ROV of its size. Shit, her software is outdated – there's a lot of things that could go wrong."

"I'm telling you, Avery, this is sabotage!"

I barked a laugh, rolling my eyes and said, "Not with the sabotage thing again…" even though a slightly creepy sensation was working its way from the back of my neck down my spine. "Seriously, come on. What would *anyone* here have to gain from sabotaging things, Pete?"

Pete looked at me, the misgivings clear in his eyes as he swept his trucker's hat off his liberally salted ginger hair and scratched his head.

"It doesn't make any sense otherwise, Ave," he said, scowling. "I'm telling you, this wouldn't just *break* like this between checks. Check with Keith. Unless someone took her down without my being here, in which case, I'll have their balls dangling from my rearview mirror when we get back to shore."

I nodded. "Hey, Keith!"

"Yeah?" he called back as Pete put his hat back on.

"Any record of *Dreamy* diving last night?"

Keith made a face at me. "No! I wouldn't take her anywhere off the clock, so to speak."

"Check the logs?"

"You're nuts," he said, punching keys on the main console to bring up the logs. He scanned the screen and I caught Eamon watching me.

"Mm, nope. Nothing."

I turned back to Pete and shrugged.

"How long until she's back up and running?"

"Huh," he barked a scoffing laugh. "Not today," he said.

"Shit," I muttered, sighing. "It's been long enough…" I stuck out my bottom lip, mulling it over and called out, "Kurt, what do you think?"

"What do I think about what?"

"Conditions are good, and *Dreamy's* out of commission. I would have preferred we waited to dive until tomorrow but we *are* over the safety hurdle to dive again."

"Shit," he said. "Let's do it!"

I caught Mac's eye and he gave a nod.

"Check the tanks, let's suit up."

A rowdy cheer went up and I turned back to Pete.

"I'm not saying something didn't happen," I said and sighed, shaking my head. "*Dreamy's* obviously busted, but *sabotage* Pete? Really?"

I knew he drank, usually a little too much, but now I was starting to wonder if it was a problem.

He grunted and huffed out a dissatisfied sigh. "You be careful," he said, jabbing a finger at me and I raised my eyebrows.

"I didn't know you cared," I said with a slightly reckless grin.

A muscle in his jaw ticked.

"We may not see eye to eye, Avery, but believe me, I know how good I got it."

"What a coincidence, Pete," I said, turning slowly. "The feeling's mutual. There's no mechanic better."

"I got the parts, I think, to fix this," he said and dropped the component onto a six-foot folding table he was using as a portable workbench.

"I believe in you," I said.

"I ain't no fuckin' fairy," he grumbled and I laughed.

"What was that about?" Mac demanded as I drew near. Eamon was under Keith's wing as Keith showed him all the monitors and equipment – what each switch and button did while Eamon asked questions 'in character.'

"Nothing," I murmured, distracted. "Just Pete being Pete."

Mac snapped his fingers in front of my face and I frowned, glaring up at him.

"Not sure what you and pretty boy back there have going on, don't care, Avery, but you need to be alert. I'm not sending you down there any other way."

My anger softened into affection and I nodded.

"No, yeah, you're right. Sorry, Mac."

"Don't be sorry, just *stay alive*," he said and walked away. I went over near Kurt and started suiting up.

"You good for this?" he asked, grinning.

"I'm good," I said and only cast one backward look to Eamon.

I almost had myself convinced, but Pete's dire warnings were still rattling around inside my skull and Mac's command was sitting uneasy.

CHAPTER SIXTEEN

*E*amon Bligh...

The world has become a strange place, but there are a few constants that have not wavered. The sun still rises and falls east to west, the ocean is still the same hue, and men who are of the sea have changed little. I see them, and in them I see not the faces of my now apparently long deceased crew, but their spirits. I see seamen, men who would have been officers, men who were fighters, and those whose keenest weapon was their mind or the product of their hands.

Mister Mac Davis, he was a fine captain's man, a man who could be depended on. He had a good comradery with the men. His company would be wise to cultivate.

Misters Keith Alby and Pete Mackey, they were men of this new age, and knew the spy boxes and strange devices as I knew my sextant and reading the stars. I might have a mind kin to theirs, but that would require much of me, to catch up with this strange new and wondrous time.

Of the rest, they were in common with cabin boys, soft and untested, impatient, with bored sullen stares and fidgeting hands. Mister Cody Lee managed to stand out among these swabs for being somehow both educated, and a boy. Hawkins in his youth would have been able to best this lot without assistance.

There were two of her crew whose intentions drew my concern. The first was a common enough seeming, Mister Lennox, and when I saw him, I could not help but think of some trading company man, with cold eyes and the deft hands of a money lender. His sort, they were trouble, but so long as the king and his purse were contented, they were contented. The other was the hard man, Mister Wallace. When they named him a mariner, a modern Navy man, I knew him.

This was another thing that had not changed; this Mister Wallace was a man who knew Death, and had danced with it, and dealt it out. The rest of this crew, they didn't know the scream of dying men, or the tang of burned powder, but Mister Wallace… Mister Wallace knew the business of killing. It was in his countenance.

This diving business was deadly serious, and their devices were strange. The sobriety of the venture was obvious. They donned costumes that clung to their bodies, and then festooned themselves with hollow lines, belts, a great number of strange devices, and a great metal can on their backs. This was also strange, until Mister Alby informed me that while the caves might have been dry during the Pirate's Golden Era, these days it was almost completely underwater. Avery's admonishment to not become overwrought came to me. The Golden Age of Piracy sent a shudder through me, but I could not betray that misgiving. I agreed and mentioned that in the surreptitious letters between old… dread… pirate Bligh and his sister never mentioned the caves being anything other than dry.

I contained myself; thoughts had been growing in my mind. If the crew of *Honor's Price* and myself had been successful in our grand venture, the gold would be gone. But if the lucre was still in the cave, then reason would dictate that after leaving Eamon's Folly or Ghost Island, we never returned. Maybe we did return, and found the cave flooded and impassable.

Given the amount of gear and devices this crew had, this barrier had prevented any sort of exploration of our hiding place. Maybe, maybe we were too clever for our own machinations, and hid the king's gold so deep and far away that only the Devil could reach it now.

There was a good deal of activity, as the various things Mister Wallace and Avery wore were put through their paces. I did not know the names of these things, but the more I saw them use them, the less seemed their mystery and the more they appeared as just strange tools – strange tools for a dangerous deed. Without ceremony, the two vanished into the water.

The spy boxes relayed what their own eyes saw as if they were our own eyes. They could speak as well, but their breathing sounded strange and deliberate. They went down a great distance, and my own recollections matched what my eyes were seeing. The entire crew was tense as the two descended the shaft of the Devil's Arse, and it was Mister Wallace who entered the cathedral first. His lamps illuminated the great chamber, and seaweed wavered over the crystal roof, refractions of their lights through the crystals I knew to be there heavily muted by the wavering green.

"I'm out of the shaft, entering what looks like what the journal called the cathedral," Wallace said. He turned and we saw Avery enter behind him. Our descent was slightly different, as gravity demanded we slide all the way to the bottom, and not go drifting through the chamber like fish.

"It looks like a lot of silt has accumulated," Avery said. "We will track the chamber in a clockwise circle. The treasure should be here somewhere."

"Can we speak with them, as they speak to us, Mister Alby?" I asked. He looked up, removing a device from over his ear, and handed me yet another object, smooth and black, connected to his desk by means of a corkscrewing cable.

"Press that button, wait half a second, then speak. What you say into the mic they'll both hear, then let go of the button, otherwise they can't talk back to us," he said with an amused look. I gave him a nod.

Press the button, *click,* wait but a moment and – "You will be wanting to look to the north wall, there will be a spot in it that is reminiscent of a church nave. If the lucre remains, that is where it will be." *Click.*

"How long have they been down," Davis asked. His concern was plain.

"They still have plenty of time," Mackey replied, tapping the clock on his wrist. I had already decided that I would also have one of those modern marvels for my own. The spy boxes were obscured by a swirling cloud of sediment. They had followed the north wall of the chamber, drifting over it like some immense solid sea jellies, until they found the nave. The tension in the surface crew had become greater, as if we were with them in the domain of Davy Jones.

Something gleamed on the spy box, and my stomach turned to lead. The crew cheered. The radio produced a great amount of excited gibberish and it was lost in the adulation. These men had been hard after this for a time longer than I knew, but I did not share their jubilation.

"I'm bringing a few bars back to the surface," Avery said, her voice still tight with excitement. "Uff! Okay, maybe *one* bar. This stuff is heavier than it looks." She held one of the tapered bricks up to where the spy box lenses would capture it. The gold still held its polish, and I saw the relief of George II knocked into it. I saw something else hadn't changed.

The lust for gold shines as brightly as the metal of the sun itself, and I heard it in their voices, and I saw it in their eyes, as sure as the day as we took it from the *Queen's Mercy.* Mister Lennox was close to joy, but in his face, I saw not the lust for gold, but relief. I did not know what company he worked for, but I knew the way those beasts fed on its own men.

"We've found it," he said. "Avery was right, the gold, the journal, this near cursed venture."

"Tis cursed, Mister Lennox," I said. "A great number of men were slaughtered over that treasure, the number I cannot guess." He gave me a questioning look, and he noticed that I did not share their excitement.

"Slaughtered?" he asked.

"Aye, the men of King George took it from the Americas and do not think they were running gold mines in that year. This gold was taken from the savages, looted from their temples and melted down into bars for the king's coffers. The crew of the treasure ship fought to the bloody last to hold it. The *Honor* lost more than half of her own crew and even with less than a score of men and ten times the king's ransom in gold still came near to violence over it. How many have died since..." I paused, minding the words of my tongue. "How many have died since Captain Bligh hid the treasure here?"

"I actually don't know," he said. His face twisted in concentration, as a man of numbers and figures is prone to do. "I think two dozen, maybe more. Accidents mostly."

"Aye, and we should keep a sharp eye for accidents, and for avarice," I said.

"Remember, Ave, Kurt, you've gone below normal depths, and you have to ascend slowly, give the nitrogen in your bloodstream time to dissipate," Mister Davis said into the mic, expertly clicking the button on the side. They responded. Avery seemed terse at being reminded how to do this task. I could imagine her lips pursed out with such annoyance. Mister Wallace replied with the precision that I expected from a king's man.

Then there was a blinking light. Alby and Davis became agitated by this, and Mackey leaped up as if a fish had nipped his sack. Everyone's jovial nature was replaced with black tension. "What is the meaning of this?" I asked Lennox.

"I don't know. I'm not a diver," Lennox said.

"Blast this burdensome lucre, and this folly of an island," I said, my voice rising to the deck voice of a captain. "Mister Davis, what is the nature of this red light?" I demanded.

"Avery's telemetry is saying that she's running low on gas," Alby said. "Which isn't right."

"She should still have well over an hour in the tank," Mackey said. Alby rotated and checked a different spy box, one full of words and numbers. He shook his head.

"Kurt still has sixty-six minutes left on his tank, and he usually burns gas faster than Avery does," Alby said.

"How far down are they?" Davis asked.

"Too far," Alby said. "They still have one more decompression stop to make, and that should be a twenty-minute pause. Thirty if you go by the guidelines."

"What's the warning level set at?" Davis asked.

"Ten minutes, and again at two, like always," Mackey said.

"Why don't she just come up?" I asked.

"If she does, all the dissolved gas will come out of her blood at one time, and she could suffer a massive stroke, or a pulmonary embolism, or a brain aneurism. She comes up too quick, she could be crippled for the rest of her life like her father or she could die," Davis said.

"Mister Wallace?" I asked.

"Same predicament," Davis said. "No one's immune to decompression sickness."

"Can we take her more of those, a new one?" I asked, gesturing to the silver tanks that were near arms distance from me.

"Where the hell is Cody?" Davis swore. "This is literally his job."

"Well his vest, and tank is right here," Mackey said.

"If that son of a bitch took off for a smoke right in the middle of an ascent, I'll have his ass in a sling," Davis said. "Hurry, go get him, run!" Davis cried and Lennox nodded and took off toward the entrance of the cave. I saw the look in Davis's eyes and I knew then, it was the look of a man calling for the doctor for a man he knew was already dead. It wasn't calling for help, it was the assuaging of the conscience. A man doing everything he could, knowing that in hindsight, this moment would haunt him, and if there was a single thing he could have done to change the course of events and didn't do, it would be the same as if he had committed the deed himself.

"Avery," Davis said. "We're going to get Cody down to you as quick as we can. There's been a snag, but it's okay, you have to stay calm. If you panic and breath too fast, you'll burn up your air supply. You know the drill, shallow inhale, pause, breath out…"

I felt my chest tighten. I quickly removed my borrowed thong shoes, and the other things that would slow me down underwater and started taking deep breaths. This would be no different than swimming under a ship, a crewman's dare, or seeing how far down an anchor chain you could pull yourself.

"Give me a good one, and be quick about it, lad!" I said in the captain's voice. Mister Mackey was quick on his feet and gave me one of the cylinders.

"You can't do this," Alby said. "You don't even know how far down they are!"

"We'll settle words about this when I come back," I said and leaped into the Devil's Arse.

I dove, kicking as best I could. The shaft only had one direction, and there was no getting lost. The light dimmed, and I felt the weight of the water start to press against me. My ears crackled and I knew my depth was close to where the cabin boys fled for the surface. It seemed like an eternity, pushing until my chest burned, and my arms were made of flame. The cylinder seemed to weigh as much as one of Baxter's twelve pounders.

Dim light shown beneath me, a pair of lanterns, and I knew them for the lights on Avery's face mask. Knowing her to be so close sent a charge of renewed strength through my body and I kicked. I swam less and less and found my way down more by handholds. She came near to colliding with me and when her eyes met mine, they were wide with fear. I did not know if those were tears, or if her mask was leaking. She grabbed my arm and I used this connection, leverage. I pushed the cylinder to her chest, its own mask and line trailing behind it. She grabbed it, her hands quick on the top where the device controls or valves were located and then a torrent of bubbles blew out of it and she replaced her own full-face mask with the smaller one attached to the tank.

I patted her on the shoulder, and my lungs reminded me that this was no place to remain leisurely. I fled for the surface and felt as a dolphin when I finally broke free. The air was stale and reeked of the cavern but it was the sweetest thing I had tasted since my kiss from my siren. Mackey and Davis pulled me from the water, and I had started to shiver. The cave water was colder than I accounted for and in quick order I had a blanket, and whiskey in my hands. I was thankful for both.

"I've never in my life seen anything like that," Davis said.

"No shit," Mackey said. "I mean, I think even a professional free diver or pearl diver would balk at going down that far…"

"That far in a damned cave, with no light," Alby said.

"No light, no suit, no air. *Jesus* man, that's some Aquaman shit right there," Mackey said. There was emotion in their voices, quivering and gripped tightly like it was some sort of serpent, an asp that if they released it, it was sure to strike.

Lennox returned with young Mister Lee in tow. He held something crumpled in his hand and looked red faced and scared. "Where in the hell were you, Cody?" Davis demanded of the young man. He went to reply, holding up his hand, some small white package wadded tight, presented as if it were an excuse. "You're done with this enterprise. You were needed, did you know that?" Davis's voice rose. "You're our damned rescue diver, and Avery has a busted tank, fifty meters down – *fifty fucking meters* and *five minutes* of air. You should have been here. You should be down in that water this very minute!" The boy's eyes flicked to where his gear was, and he made like he was going to grab it. "Oh no, you think it'll matter now?" Davis was indignant, voice rising with every barked sentence.

"The pirate reenactor took a spare tank and carried it down to Avery. She's fine. We just happened to have a pirate lord who can do this sort of thing," Mackey said. "Namor the fucking Submariner here just saved *two* lives today. Avery's and yours." Davis put a hand on Mackey's shoulder, a gesture for him to cool his spleen.

"Lee, go back to the *Sapphire*, you're fired," Lennox said. He didn't have the same ire as the others, I could feel it. Avery was without a doubt their captain, and these men, her crew, –they would die for her. If need be, die in her place. Lennox seemed to know this as well. Company men rarely lasted long if they were droop-eyed or slow of wit. "Next trip to the mainland, you can catch a bus home."

"But—" Lee protested.

Lennox raised his hand. "Right now, you're only fired. If you literally say another word, I'll have your dive credentials audited, blacklist you from this entire sector, and will personally kick you in the balls. Don't think I won't." He gave the boy a stare like ice, and Lee wilted and retreated.

We waited quietly, watching the steady progress of bubbles coming up from the shaft to burble in the pool. The adder of emotion was still wrapped around many of them – a few eyes wet from tears, tremors in hands, shaky fingers. I had seen this, had felt this. After my first naval engagement, when the cannons had thundered and after the white-hot terror of the boarding action of pistols and cutlass at close range. There had been no danger to these men, but such was their loyalty to their captain that they felt as if they too had been caught between death and revelation.

Eventually, a head broke the surface and it was not Avery, it was Wallace. He seemed calm as he exited the water, and a moment later, Avery finally appeared. Dragging two tanks seemed to have slowed her down a bit. I stood to assist her, but immediately noticed something else was amiss. As she climbed out of the pool, she threw the tank to the ground and ripped the mouthpiece from her face, peeling the strange hood of her tight garb from her head. She shook the water from her hair and grabbed at her belts, fingers scrabbling at the catches and buckles. Quickly, angrily, she shed her gear. The crew tried to speak with her, a garbled mess about her safety, about what happened with the tank, about the gold, but she silenced them with a firm raised hand and a shriek that was equal parts fury and what I could only imagine being the emotional hurricane that brewed in the breast from dancing with death.

She stepped off, turning in wild flight for the mouth of the cavern and I rose to follow her out. Davis put a hand to my chest. "Mister Bligh, you should just let her be."

"Yeah," Alby said. "She is probably going to be in a shit mood for a while and it's best to give her some space, you know."

"She dropped the gold sample when her tank failed," Wallace said. "She's mad at herself. You'll just make it worse, pirate boy."

"A risk I'm willing to carry upon myself, bootneck," I said and left the cave to follow my siren.

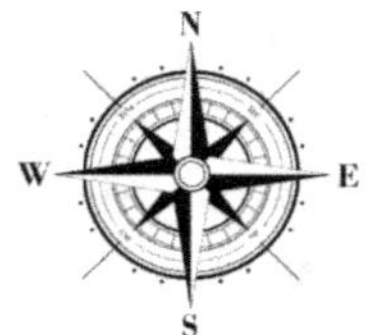

CHAPTER SEVENTEEN

JUNE 2016

*A*very Barker...

I didn't look at them. The panic and emotion crawled up my throat and spilled out my mouth in a rage and pain-filled scream.

I'd almost bit it down there. I had almost bought the proverbial farm. I had almost panicked and had been ready to kick for the surface, damn the consequences, when he'd appeared.

How had he done that?

"Avery!" someone called my name and I flung a hand up over my shoulder to wave them back as I stomped out the mouth of the cave, bursting into fresh, clean, *warm* sunlight. I wanted to pause, to soak it in, but I wanted away from my crew before I could let myself have the luxury, because the moment I stopped was the moment the dam was going to break and I was going to sob like a terrified little girl.

I didn't want them to see me cry was the main thing. I didn't need them to see me fall apart.

Close, far too close... and where the fuck was Cody? Why had Eamon brought the tank down to me and how? Did he seriously just pull a fifty-meter free dive like that?

My thoughts and emotions were racing, almost as fast and as caustic as the adrenaline that was pouring through my veins as I ripped aside the canvas flap to my tent and stepped through. I sucked in a great lungful of air, then another, and again. My breath sawing in and out of my chest as I fought and lost against the rising tide of panic and *what-ifs*. The wave cresting and swamping me as the close call sent a shiver down to my bones. I looked up and over as the tent flap moved and Eamon, still damp, met my watering blue gaze with his green and I couldn't help myself.

I felt my face contort, the tears slip, and he was there, crushing me to him and holding me tight and I let myself have this. I clung to him, buried my face against his broad chest beneath the thin cotton of his borrowed tee and I let it out. Spilled it all in a deep, cathartic, and noisy as fuck cry.

"There you are," he soothed. "I have you."

"I'm sorry." I hated how my voice cracked but I couldn't stop it. Couldn't rein it in even though I tried, even though I wanted to so badly.

"Nae," he said, dismissing my apology. "Looking Death in the eye like that? Death, he don't blink. You dance and show him no fear. When you're done dancing and still alive, then you do what you have to do. You scream, you weep, you tear at your breast... you let it out. If you keep it, if you hold it, you hold that piece of death inside you... like poison. I nae wish that for you, so you let it go."

I sniffed and looked up at him, the starkness of what he'd done a shock to the heart as it sank in.

"You came for me," I uttered.

"Aye," he murmured, caressing the side of my face. "Always will."

I captured his face between my hands and stood on my toes to crush my mouth over his. His arm curved around my back, his hand which had been at the side of my face curved around the back of my head, his fingers tangling in the wet, clinging strands of my hair as he held me tightly to him.

I felt my heart crack wide open and nothing but love poured out for this man. Impossible as it was that he even stood with me in this time and this place.

The kiss became fevered and fervent, hands grasping at and whisking clothing aside, dropping it to my tent's floor. He lifted me, and I hauled myself up his muscular body wrapping my arms around his neck and shoulders to hold myself up, twining my legs around his hips as he entered my body, his cock hot and thick, my body not quite ready for him, but I didn't care.

The stretched-full sensation of having him inside me was sweeter than that first breath of cavern air had been when I'd ripped my regulator out. I was *alive* inside, living for his warm skin pressed against mine, for the feel of him moving against my walls, plunging deep within me, touching all the right places deep and deeper still as he sat me on the edge of my desk.

His thrusts were powerful, papers and charts sloshing to the ground as he plunged deep and ground inside of me, both of us looking down the lengths of our bodies where we were joined.

I stared at his face, at the intensity of his expression, of the heat in his gaze, of the peace and freedom settling in every angular line and the curve of the smile that graced his full lips.

"Oh, God, *Eamon*," I groaned breathlessly and let my head fall back as I closed my eyes, reveling in the sensations he wrought, reveling in being *alive* and *unhurt* when things could have easily gone the other direction.

Passion fizzled in my veins, hauntingly reminiscent of the bubbles that'd been in my blood that could have so easily permanently damaged me or even killed me had they not had the time to properly dissipate, had Eamon not given me that time.

Eamon kept at me, holding me tightly, thrusting deeply, driving the close brush with death from me and replacing it with hot, pulsing, beautiful, *life*.

I parted my thighs a little further, gripped his ass with my hands and pulled him into me and he fucked me so good. He fucked the fear and the pain away, replacing it all with him, larger than life, and I was overjoyed to have him in my arms.

He was relentless, winding me up, taking me higher and higher, holding me fast, his green eyes, the color of the sea, meeting mine, the color of the sky, and it was the final nudge I needed.

I came, exploding around him, body writhing and pulsing, voice failing me, breath drawn from my lungs in a very different type of death. One that I would gladly dive into time and time again with him. *Only* for him.

We plunged, the both of us, into the deepest purest pleasure and as I clung to him, beneath the shelter of his body as he braced himself around me on my desk, I don't think either of us wanted to come up for air.

"Eamon," I murmured, and looked up, pressing my mouth to his in a gentle kiss.

"Yes, my siren?" he asked, tone muted, sexy and seductive and making me shudder all over again.

I opened my mouth to tell him just how I felt when Kurt's voice came from outside the tent.

"Avery?"

"Oh, shit," I murmured as Eamon scrambled off of me.

"Kurt, yeah! Don't come in here! Just a sec!"

We scrambled into our clothes to Kurt cursing me out. "Oh, Jesus, Avery, what the fuck?"

I rolled my eyes and glanced at Eamon, who with a sparkle in his eyes and smile on his lips gave a nod. With a sigh I called out, "You're good, Kurt. Come on in."

Kurt batted aside the tent flap as I leaned my butt against the edge of my desk, my pussy still throbbing pleasurably in my shorts with the sense memory of Eamon's presence.

"We going to talk about what happened down there?" Kurt demanded and I frowned at him.

"What is there to talk about?" I demanded. "I don't even know *what* happened."

"Avery, you almost *ran out of air.*"

"No fucking shit, Kurt," I snapped at him.

"You scared the shit out of me!" he yelled.

"You? How do you think *I* feel? If it hadn't been for Eamon, I would have drowned or worse! Where the fuck was Cody?"

"Mac wants to talk to you," he said glowering, and I was seriously confused. Just what the fuck was Kurt's problem?

"Where's he at?" I demanded.

"Mess," he grated out.

"Rest of the crew?" I demanded.

"Yep."

"Not sure why your panties are in a bunch," I muttered. "Didn't happen to *you.*" I pushed off the desk and made to go past him and he caught me by the upper arm.

I glared up at him and Eamon finally spoke. "Unhand her, sir," he said, his voice calm and deathly quiet.

"Shut it, pirate boy," Kurt snarled. "She's my best friend before she's your booty call."

"Kurt!" I snapped and he let my arm go, his warm brown eyes fixing on mine.

"Shit, I'm sorry," he muttered. "What you just said, though? That's not fucking *fair,* Avery. You scared the shit out of me down there! I thought I was gonna lose you."

"I still don't know what happened. My tanks were registering as *full.*"

"Me either," he said with a glowering look. "Let's go find out."

I nodded and turned back to Eamon, holding out my hand to him. His tense posture eased and he took it, his long fingers curving around the back of my hand and grasping it firmly. I took a deep breath and let it out slow, letting his touch ground me.

Kurt went out before us and we followed him to the mess tent. No one remarked on Eamon holding my hand, which was a damn good thing. I wasn't in the mood for any shit. Mac gave me a nod and jerked his head. I went to him, towing Eamon along and we stood separate from the others who had all stopped talking and were looking on with bated breath.

"Mac?" I asked dispassionately.

"Pete! Keith!" Mac called and Pete and Keith came over to join us.

"What happened?" I demanded.

"Tank was tampered with," Mac said without preamble. I looked from him to Pete to Keith.

"Define 'tampered with,'" I demanded.

Keith explained it with a few asides from Pete on the mechanical end of the spectrum. That someone had let some of the air out of the tank, had recalibrated my dive gear so it read as full. How, whoever it was, forgot to calibrate or didn't know how to fuck with the computer systems. I listened and Eamon shifted, standing at my back, hands gripping my shoulders to fortify me as I crossed my arms over my stomach.

"You think they were trying to kill me?" I asked quietly.

"Can't say, baby girl," Mac said and didn't sound happy about it.

"Who among you would wish you harm?" Eamon asked gently, and we all turned to look over the rest of the crew who had resumed talking but were all pretty much universally casting furtive glances at us.

"Where the fuck was Cody?" I demanded.

"Out for a smoke," Mac grated.

"Where is he now?"

"The *Sapphire*. Lennox fired his ass before I got to. You should have heard him. I was almost impressed. Cody's waiting for the charter to pick him up."

"I'd like to talk to him before his charter gets here. Keith, Pete, keep everyone else here. Mac, grab Kurt and let's go."

I marched past the rest of the crew, Mac and Eamon in tow, Kurt falling in with us at Mac's behest. I wanted Eamon with me, always, so I didn't comment when he stayed at my side. Glad for it, that there was a silent understanding in place that where I went, he was to stick with me.

I may not have been able to understand just how he was here, or what was in store for us, but *this?* This, I had some semblance of control over, and I wanted some goddamned answers.

I was hoping they lay aboard the *Sapphire Horizon.*

The four of us climbed aboard the Gator and Mac drove us down to the docks. I kept my fingers linked with Eamon's, hoping he could manage to keep his cool when he saw the *Sapphire.* The modern-day research vessel was worlds away from the likes of his old ship, *The Honor's Price.*

CHAPTER EIGHTEEN

JUNE 2016

*E*amon Bligh...

The ride on the alligator machine was tense, and I could understand the emotions that kept Mister Davis's knuckles white on the peculiarly small wheel. Sabotage was no small charge, and few things were considered worse; mutineers and betrayers and such. Avery's face was a mask, pale, like all of her blood had pooled in her belly and left the rest of her cold. The Marine was defensive, and more than once on the ride to where this *Sapphire* lay at rest, he touched his knife. My lip twitched, and I was keenly aware that my own cutlass was wrapped and stowed in a locker far from my hand.

I would be well served keeping a weather eye on that one.

The *Sapphire* was a sign. If Avery were my siren, my angel, then the *Sapphire* had left from distant moorings in a land of jasper and porphyry, alabaster and silver. The hull was as large as a Royal ship of the line, but her rigging, it was strange and canted over the stern, and there wasn't a square inch of canvas. The bow was as sharp as a knife, and she looked as if she could race across the ocean, propelled by the will of God. No gun ports, no oar locks, no sails. And she was a gleaming white, as if carved from stone. I must have been gaping.

Avery's hand tightened on mine, and her admonition of self-control refreshed itself in my mind. This was a brave new century, and perhaps they had lowered the masts, or their ships were as clever as their spy boxes and their metal tubes full of air. I could only take this on faith.

The gangplank of the *Sapphire* was completely normal, a white painted wooden length, and upon closer inspection, the hull was made of a fortune of metal. A metal ship, with no sails? Truly this was an age of wonders.

Inside, the wonders did not cease, and I started to feel crowded by the strangeness of it. There was a familiar seeming. We had gathered in what would have been the state room, or the chart room by the look of it. It was all closed in, the walls painted like the inside of a fine establishment, festooned with ornament, device, and cunningly rendered paintings, of a level of detail so fine, the odd subjects of them baffled my mind. What cunning artist would so expertly render images of children holding fish, or curiously framed images of swimming underwater and scabrous barnacle-encrusted garbage from the bottom of the sea? I saw Avery in some of the tiny paintings and recognized a few of the others. The detail was such that they were as if seeing a memory.

"The first issue," Mister Davis said, "is the claim of sabotage."

"There hasn't been any sabotage," Mister Wallace said with no small amount of contempt. "Pete and Alby just broke their toys and wanted to blame someone else, and the tank? We send the tank back to the manufacturer and tell them what a piece of shit it was. No one was hurt, and they'll kiss our asses and send us free stuff so we don't smear them."

"Where were you Cody?" Mister Davis asked pointedly.

"I was having a smoke," Mister Lee said. We had all easily over-looked the whip-like young man, and I saw anger in his eyes. "I was having a smoke because in seven dives, eight dives, I've been fully suited up and didn't have to do shit. Then I was told that I'm only here because the insurance writer says there has to be a rescue diver."

"You've gone on dives with us, Cody," Avery said with reproach.

"Kurt said I didn't even have to hang around! Shit, man! You did everything but tell me to go have a smoke," the young Mister Lee said defensively.

"Fuck you, Cody," Mister Wallace said, bristling with hostility. His fingers brushed the handle of the knife, but only for a second. "I didn't tell you to wander the fuck off!"

"You told me that I didn't have to sit staring at the pool, that I could play on my phone, or go have a smoke if I wanted. You told me the only reason I was there was so Lennox and the insurance company could check it off their list," Mister Lee said. His ire – I knew how that tasted.

"*You* fucked off. Don't try to put that off on me!" Wallace said menacingly.

"What were you even doing with Avery's tank?" Mister Lee shot back like a cannon.

"Aye," I said, louder than I intended, "What were you doing with Avery's tank?"

"Why don't you stay the fuck out of this Long John Silver," Wallace spat.

"I'll have to you answer the question, boy," I said.

"I don't have to answer questions from weed enthusiasts and wanna-be loser pirate cosplayers," Wallace said. "If I was going to play pretend pirate, I sure as shit wouldn't dress up as a penniless beaten loser who was hung and buried in a whore's grave," Wallace said. His hand rested on the handle of the knife he wore.

"What did you say?" I demanded coldly. I felt Avery grab at my shirt, pulling me back. Part of me knew that this was precisely one of the moments she'd warned me about. That this was something that I should just let go. If everything was to be believed, this was some distant past of theirs, but it was to be sure the future in store for *me* and I had to know what that could mean for my sweet sister, Emma. If the lucre was still in the cave, then what did that mean for her? I hadn't asked my siren what my own future held, and Avery had never seen to see fit to divulge it. But now, here it was. *Damn me for a fool.*

"Ho, ho, ho! This is too rich. You can't seriously be that fucking ignorant. It's like you don't even know the idiot you decided to dress up as!" Wallace crowed. "You're going to tell me that you didn't know that Eamon Fucking Bligh was dragged straight to Charleston? That the dumbfuck was so hell-bent on saving a woman who was already dead that he ended up captured, beaten, tortured, and then hung like a common criminal, his body cut down and buried in a crossbones graveyard with the likes of whores and lepers?"

"Visit that graveyard often? To pay respects to your mother, perhaps?" I asked coolly even though his words ravaged me down to my very soul. His hostility boiled over and he came at me. I was glad to see that his first impulse was not the knife. That would have made things more difficult. I accepted his charge and we crashed into one side of the cabin. There was a great amount of shouting and confusion from the others. I was glad to see that Mister Lee and Mister Davis took great importance in placing themselves between our scrap and Avery. That was one less concern to my mind.

We crashed into a wall, Wallace giving a furious shout which I met with my own mocking laugh. He had not drawn his blade yet, so this might just stay a scrap. Scraps could be good for morale, or they could lead to a mutiny. I gave him a few blows to his kidneys; he was stout and took the hits well.

Old Captain Blaine had let a few fights go on, let the men get the piss and vinegar out of their systems. Those fights that were too serious, those he didn't let happen. Tossing a man in the brig and a body overboard was bad business. Wallace tried to slam me down into the table, and I didn't resist. We crashed through the table, scattering charts and papers. I caught my legs around his chest, he rained fists into my ribs, and I gave him a few to the head. He recoiled and pulled away.

"Aye, fight already going out of you, Mister Wallace?" I asked pointedly. I released my lock on him so that he could break away. We regained our feet and my blood was singing, I hadn't had a good fight in what felt like months, and I could feel the bile I had pent up. I could imagine him being some distant ancestor of John Forsythe; I knew there was no such lineage, but the notion buoyed me up. Wallace's face was red, chest heaving, all wrath and fury, and I laughed at him.

"Some Marine you are. The king would have you swabbing decks and dumping pots," I taunted. "A right proper king's man would have had me on my arse in a minute, and my neck in a noose in a day."

"I'm not a Marine," he said and slid the knife from its sheath, his eyes going dark on me. "I'm a Navy Seal, motherfucker!" Now he was going to be serious about this, the sort of dance that Blaine would have stopped in an instant, but there were no other fighters on the ship aside from the two of us.

We will have our dance, oh yes.

He was quick with the knife, holding the blade in a downward position, as he would slash and stab, but he met only air. I side-stepped a strike. Another slash only managed to cut air. If I'd had my cutlass, this would have been over in an instant. He fought like a Frenchman, with his knife. I had killed a Frenchman or two, and their knives were certainly sharp.

This is not his true weapon.

A good knife fighter should have had me, a small space, myself unarmed. I saw my opening, and I gave him a great open-handed strike to the face, as a prostitute would slap an insulting patron. His head rocked back and my palm stung from the blow. He staggered and spat blood. His eyes were full of anger. I was not fighting him properly.

He changed his stance, and his knife came in a different direction and he drew blood from my arm, and then a slash across the chest.

Now we will truly dance.

I armed myself with some modern device, long and black, made of metal. It was blunt like a belaying pin, which I was well accustomed to. The knife clanked against metal, and Wallace sought to run his blade down the side of the metal club and rake at my fingers, but I wouldn't give him the pleasure.

I swung, finally going for more than playful jabs and taunting smacks to the face. I gave him a hard strike to the arm, and then to the ribs for good measure. His knife was too small, too light to offer resistance blocking, and he grunted. He slashed again, the black metal blade all but lurching toward my eye.

He overextended his strike, and I gave him the full swing of the club right into his midsection, taking the wind out of his sails. He dropped the knife and collapsed to his knees. Wallace held his hands over his midsection and struggled to draw in a breath. "Give him room, lest you want to be cleaning your boots," I warned. He drew a ragged breath, finally, and heaved up his last meal on the deck. "It's over Mister Wallace, and when you have your winds, you will be telling us the details of your treachery."

Davis pulled the Marine's hands behind his back and used some curious device to bind them. I picked up his knife, a flat black thing with sharp teeth, the sort that would make a barracuda proud.

The rest of the crew looked a mixture of shocked and horrified. Avery looked to be beside herself and could only stare at Mister Wallace in disbelief. "Any of you lads skilled with a needle and a knot?" I asked. The cut on my arm would need tending and I could feel the rush of excitement leaving me. I would rest well this night.

"Avery?" I asked, drawing her attention away from Wallace to look at me. There were tears in her eyes, and I was disquieted. I wanted to ask her questions, about my fate, about Emma, about everything involved including the cursed gold and the ship. They knew, and I felt the fool for not knowing these things that were obvious to them. I felt a tremor in my hand. "There are things that I need to know…"

She lowered her hands from her mouth, slowly. "It'll be fine," Davis said, and gave her shoulder a fatherly squeeze. "We'll confine Kurt to quarters for now, and maybe in the morning he'll be more inclined to talk civil-like and we'll get this all figured out."

Avery led me not to the captain's quarters, but to the infirmary of the ship, which itself was all gleaming white, with brushed steel, and almost everything was made of metal, glass, or the new material that was seemingly everywhere, *plastic*; strange but useful stuff, that.

There was a giant cylinder dominating the room, and it was encrusted with its own portholes and a great number of pipes fed into it. I had thought that I had seen the full of this place, but here was a wonder out of the minds of the most deranged futurist.

"It's a decompression tank," Avery said softly. She withdrew a bundle from a white box attached to the wall. "If you come up too fast, we can put you inside it, and it simulates pressure at depth. In an emergency, like today's, if a diver has to surface too quick, we can decompress them here, minimizing the health risks and danger. There's an even bigger one up on the deck for multiple people if we need it." She examined the cut on my arm and began cleaning it. Her hands were cold.

"This device would have been of use—" I ventured.

"Yes, it would have, if we were on the water. But we're cave diving in the middle of an island. It would take too long to get anyone from the Devil's Arse to the tank. They would have already suffered the full consequences of a rapid ascent." A stinging solution gave me a start, and I hissed involuntarily.

"It's your own damn fault for getting in a fight with Kurt," she said, bitterness lacing her tone, her voice as cold as the North Sea.

"Is there truth to what Mister Wallace said?" I asked.

"Truth to what?"

"I am a fish out of water, but you know the currents. He said that I died, beaten, penniless, and was given to Jack Ketch in Charleston, where there is a pirate festival now," I said.

She hesitated; her attention was most decidedly not on answering my question. "What of my sister? I wrote of her in my journal, which you seem to know quite well."

"She's dead," she said, clipping a thread. "You're dead." She still wouldn't look at me, high spots of color in her cheeks.

"Two hundred and four score years, it is fair to say that everyone from my time is dead," I said softly. "I have not asked of my fate, but you know it. Tell me… please."

"Your sister, Emma, died before you did, but the exact date isn't known. She was indentured and died in childbirth. There's no mention of the identity of the father, or if it was consensual or forced," she said, and I felt the needle stab, as she started making the stitches in my arm, closing Wallace's knife strike. My mouth tasted sour. I knew how the indentured were treated. They were slaves in everything but name, and there were many a story from the plantations in the colonies, escaped Negros were not afraid to speak their truth once they were away from their master's whips and dogs. I clenched my fist.

"You were captured on the island, jailed in Charleston. The magistrate had you locked up and there was a prisoner uprising. The records said you hanged in the aftermath. They kept your journal, but I imagine they couldn't read it. Not with the code and cipher it was written in. It was sent to your sister as part of your last effects, but they had no way of knowing that she'd been dead for months – maybe even died as much as a year before. Your journal ended up in the plantation's library. As for you? The location of your actual remains are unknown, and local apocrypha says that you were buried in an unnamed and unmarked crossbones cemetery, one that was used to bury prostitutes, slaves who were killed in escape attempts, and those who died from STDs," she said.

"What are STDs?" I asked.

"Syphilis," she said and tied the last knot in the stitch. I felt as if the Reaper were standing in the room with its cold bone hand on my shoulder. My mind's eye conjured up the image of my own rotted corpse being laid in the fetid Carolina soil, tossed into a pile with those who had been consumed by the French malady, and the poor men and women who had sought freedom from cruelty and found death at the end of their suffering.

"What of my men?" I asked. "The rest of the crew of the *Honor's Price?*"

"Killed on the island or buried at sea, I'm not one hundred percent sure. There wasn't a whole lot said in any records or documents about the rest of the crew. Only about you. Accurate historical records from that era are hard to come by, Eamon. It's been two hundred and eighty-five years," she said. "It's a miracle I even have your journal, that it survived." She put the healer's tools away and spun to face me. Her hand was fast, and I found myself suddenly looking to my right, the side of my face stinging.

"What were you thinking?" she demanded, her expression anguished. "Kurt is a Navy Seal, he could have *killed you.* By everything I know about him, he should have! Easily!" Avery snapped, her face red and tears in her eyes.

There was a pause, I didn't know what to say, but I also wasn't sure of some of the other things she had said.

"Do you know what that would have done to me?" she asked. "Do you have any idea what you mean to me?"

"What I did was the thing that needed doing," I said, reaching to take her face between my hands. "Don't forget that he tried to take you from me," I said softly. She jerked back from my touch as though she'd been the one in receipt of her hand. There was a flash behind her eyes, *ire.*

"I've known Kurt since we were children," she said and the ice was back in her voice. "We went to the same school for Christ's sake!" she snapped.

"Aye, and your tank?" I wished her to *think.*

"Cody is a kid, and he didn't see anything. He said what you wanted to hear," Avery said.

"Wallace is a devil," I said. "I know his type."

"Of course, you would say that," Avery said. "You're a pirate."

"Aye, I am a pirate, but I'm no devil and more to import, I am no fool," I said.

"Eamon's Folly," she snapped back at me. "Trusting John Forsythe and the rest of his men? Wrecking the *Honor's Price* on the rocks. No, no, you are no fool, Eamon. You're a bull-headed idiot!" she snarled. She slung the medical kit onto a counter with a great clatter and swept from the infirmary, slamming the door behind her.

Her words stung.

I sat for a while in silence. Then, motion came to me and impelled me to wander through the guts of the *Sapphire* in search of the galley. A ship in this new era was, in many ways, still a ship as I reckoned. After some searching and opening doors at random, I found the galley, and attached to that, the ship's stored goods. No locks, no guard, these people were far too trusting. Even the best-natured captain on the most disciplined ship in the king's fleet still kept locks on the doors to where the spirits and food were stored.

The ship's pantry was certainly strange, and surprisingly cold once I mastered their silver door's handles. Inside were boxes, all neatly labeled with clean letters, and a wealth of fresh produce. I helped myself to a handful of apples and continued my search. My mouth was parched, and I needed a fire in my belly. The cold room didn't yield any spirits, and I continued through and into another room, this one full of metal containers wrapped in colorful sashes proclaiming their contents. Peas – one such label boasted. Not what I was looking for.

Then, I found my prize behind a wooden door with a latch, old-fashioned to this era but more familiar to mine. A large number of bottles of spirits lined boxes in the narrow little room beyond. I knew some of these, others were strange, but I certainly recognized the three letters for rum, and I took one of the many bottles.

Surely with stores like these, it wouldn't even be missed.

I went to the rear of the *Sapphire* and sat on the gunwale. I ate one of the apples and availed myself of the rum. I keenly missed the wise council of Morgan Dougal, or the sour voice of Mister Baxter and his face tattooed with black powder burns. My mind ran through the events of the day; the sabotage, saving Avery from death in the flooded caves, the shouts and accusations. The way we had made love, Avery and I, so urgent. And then the fight with Wallace, and her defense of him. These people were soft, their ways made them weak. My mind boggled at the fact that my siren defended the honor of the man who attempted to slay her, to turn her ire readily on me – the man that had saved her from the clutches of Davy Jones.

To hell and Davy Jones with this crew of landlubbers.

I took my leave of the *Sapphire Horizon* the same way I greeted her, down a gangplank that would have been as familiar as any in the King's Navy, leaving the ship and its flameless lights and wizard's devices behind. The trek from the indention in the island that pretended to be a bay, I walked the distance back to the side of the island that was familiar to me. My mind chased after itself, like a dog intent on catching its own tail. The things that had been said likewise ran in singsong circles.

Emma might or might not already be dead.

I am caught and hung in Charleston.

I am a fool for trusting John Forsythe.

That is who betrayed me, who betrayed us. It had to be him.

I knew that if I could go back, I could put some pistol shot in his black heart and make a quicker pace for Charleston. My betrayer in his grave, there would be no one to give us up to the king's justice, and there remained a chance that I could still save Emma. Avery had said she hadn't known precisely when she died.

My dear sister, surely, I could take some of the lucre and see that she was attended by the finest doctors in the city. Even if that cost me my life but saved hers, that was a price I was willing to pay.

A pox on this gold.

This gold, that was the folly. So many had died for it, and Avery had almost died because her childhood friend had the lust for gold in his eyes. Gold changed men. It changed a man faster and far worse than anything else in God's own creation.

I found myself, chest heaving and close to being emotionally overwrought, standing at the edge of the Mirror Pond. I cannot guess how long I stood there, my eyes boring into my own reflection, and remembered that a short time ago everything made sense. The only thing in this blasted place that made any sense at all was a glass bottle of rum.

I closed my eyes and leaped into those waters, as smooth as silvered glass.

CHAPTER NINETEEN

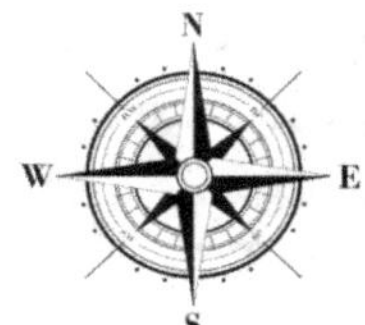

*A*very Barker...

"We gotta talk about this, princess." Mac didn't look happy and I wasn't any happier. I thrust Eamon out of my thoughts for the time being, hurt and angry but confused more than anything about the whole damn day.

Kurt was acting like a maniac and completely out of sorts – way off his baseline. Eamon shouldn't have been able to get to him the way that he had which told me *something* was going on. I shook my head and said to Mac, "We *will* talk, Mac. I promise. First, I gotta talk to Kurt and find out what the fuck is up with him."

"I'll go with you." Mac's tone brooked no argument, but he was about to get one, anyway.

"No way," I said. "This is my mess to handle. You can't hold on to the back of the seat forever, Mac. I gotta learn to pedal and keep the bike upright on my own."

Mac chuckled and shook his head, tucking his hands in his armpits, crossing his arms over his chest in the way that he did when he didn't want to admit I was right. It was the classic Mac sign for not liking it but knowing he was about to let me do it anyway. It made me slightly nervous – I wasn't a cat, and I didn't always land on my feet.

"You didn't give me or your dad a chance to even teach you. You pulled the training wheels off your bike yourself and went out with Kurt and taught yourself to ride."

I nodded; it was true.

"Same principle, Mac," I told him and felt a little sad about it.

"I'm here if you need me," he said kindly. I nodded.

"Think he's cooled off enough?" I asked, hesitantly; hating how I sounded like a scared little girl. I'd never seen Kurt come unglued like that before, and I had to say – I was *terrified* about what it could have potentially meant for Eamon. Kurt was no slouch – he'd let my pirate lover off easy. That slash to Eamon was little more than a love tap… of course, I think Eamon had returned the favor. Last time I'd seen Kurt puke like that was on my twenty-first birthday.

Neither one of them had been out to hurt each other over much, but here I was, all the more damaged for it, and the ensuing confusion that sowed in me was tapping into my rage. I took a deep breath after exchanging a few more words with Mac and went to Kurt's on-ship quarters.

I knocked.

"It's locked from the outside, Avery – what're you doing?" Kurt called out and I sighed. I unlocked the door, the key sticking out of the deadbolt and opened it up. Kurt looked up from his bunk, elbows propped on his knees and it looked, almost, as if he'd been crying. His eyes red rimmed and glassy.

I leaned a shoulder against the doorjamb, feeling weighted down and heavy. I couldn't even be *happy* about finding the treasure. The old adage *money can't buy happiness* so very true – especially now. I kept my focus on Kurt, even though it desperately tried to wander to Eamon.

"What the hell is going on, Kurt?" I asked, and I hated the pleading that crept into my tone.

He sighed and dropped his head into his hands and took several deep breaths trying to keep his shit under control and that *scared me.* I'd *never* seen Kurt like this. Not even when we were kids.

"The tanks got switched," he said. "It was supposed to be my tank." His voice cracked, and I felt the shock down to the very depths of my soul.

"*You* tampered with it?" I asked in disbelief.

"You gotta believe me, Ave. It wasn't supposed to be you."

I slid down the doorjamb and sat cross-legged on the floor in front of my best friend, staring up at him dumbly.

"But *why?*" I demanded. I knew it was bad. The hurt was there, but it didn't hurt – not yet. You could always tell how bad it was when it didn't hurt right away. If it didn't it was *bad.* Catastrophic, even. This was like that. Exactly like that.

I stared up into my best friend's face and all I could think was *he'd genuinely tried to kill me...* even if what he was saying was true, he had been trying to kill himself.

"Gwen's got me by the shorthairs," he confessed. "I got in on some bad bets – she said she would pay them off but that I had to do something for her first. She wanted me to tank the expedition. I didn't want to, but these guys, they're bad news, Avery. They're gonna kill me and they're gonna make it slow. I figured if I could break enough shit, we'd be forced to give up. Lennox would pull the plug and that would let Gwen swoop in and find the gold, but you?" He shook his head violently. "You just *inspire* like nobody's business. Lennox wasn't taking the bait. Wasn't gonna hedge his bets. I was running out of options and I figured I was going to be dead anyway – the tanks, they got switched. I never meant for it to be you. I swear to God!"

I stared up at him as he babbled and felt the tears slick silently down my face.

"You *tried to kill me,* Kurt. At the very least, you could have crippled me for *life.* I'm not even *thirty* yet!" I struggled to my feet and stumbled backward out into the passageway.

I found Mac and Lennox there, standing outside the door,

looking just as shocked as I was – except the shock was wearing thin with Mac – the anger rising to the surface.

"I need a minute!" I blurted and spun on my heel and walked away from all of them.

I didn't want or need Lennox to see me cry and it had nothing to do with being professional.

The hurt was here now, looming large and threatening to swallow me whole.

I found myself walking right past my tent and up the island's central lane, though I didn't remember the trek from the *Sapphire* at all. Up, up, and up, toward the caverns, I went, and I was severely winded by the time I reached the top. I'd been a little foolish if I thought I was going to be alone up here.

Keith and Pete looked up from *Dreamy* at the same time as I scuffed through the cavern's entryway, breathless from the steep climb on foot.

"What's eating you?" Pete demanded, but his soft expression belied his typical surly tone.

I sniffed and ignored the question in favor of asking my own.

"How's *Dreamy*?"

"She's coming along," Pete said grudgingly, and the boys turned back to her and showed me what they were up to.

We worked on her for a good bit and finally, I sighed with exhaustion but felt marginally better.

"Get some sleep, kid. This'll be here in the morning," Pete grunted.

"Thanks Pete, thanks, Keith. I'm going to turn in."

I was calmer and felt ready to talk to Eamon. I just needed to find him.

I left the cavern and went down to check my tent first – not there. I don't know what made me think to try the Mirror Pond, but it was my next stop. My heart seized in my breast when I found the empty rum bottle on the ground by the pond's glassy surface.

"Oh, God… Eamon, no," I murmured.

"Avery!" it was Mac's voice calling my name.

I turned and crashed back through the brush and he came up the path in my direction.

"There you are—"

"Not now, Mac. Seriously," I said and I went into my tent. No, his things were still here. Cutlass, and his pile of old clothes.

Shit.

Shit, shit, shit, shit, shit!

"Ave, what's going on?" Mac demanded.

"This is absolutely going to sound crazy, Mac… but I need your help."

His expression crushed down into a frown and I started spilling my guts, about Eamon, about the journal, about the whole thing.

I took him through it from start to finish and he sat down heavily on the edge of my bunk while I sank into my desk chair.

"You're dead serious right now," he said and rubbed a hand over his mouth, the scruff on his cheeks rasping against his calloused palm.

"As a fucking stroke, Mac," I told him and didn't mince words. He stared at me and then I caught the look. The one that said he was about to tear it all down.

"Don't, Mac!" I said coldly.

"You can't!" he cried.

"I'm going to!" I cried right back. "I can't *not*."

"Avery, what do I tell the crew?" he demanded.

"I don't know. I just know I have to *try*. I can't let him go, Mac. Not like this. I love him. I love him with everything that I am and I *won't let him go*. You've got the treasure but there are some things far more important than money – isn't that what you and my dad always told me?" I demanded.

"What if we never see you again?" he demanded, and I straightened from where I was putting Eamon's cutlass and clothes into a thick plastic bag. I pressed buttons on the safe and pulled the Glock out of it, checking the magazine, knowing it was loaded. I always kept it loaded. I pulled the two extra magazines out and dumped it all in the bag.

"I'm coming back," I swore. There was no doubt in my mind. "And I'm bringing Eamon with me."

"Jesus Christ, Avery. This is crazy!"

"I know, Mac! I know!" I whisper-shouted back at him. "I'm still doing it."

I threw in a case of power bars, a bunch of bottles of water, and sealed the bag with its random assortment of supplies and grabbed a length of nylon rope. Mac stood and put himself between me and the entry and exit to the tent.

"You're serious. You're going to try."

"I *have to*. I can't let him die. I can't let him die thinking I don't care."

"Baby girl—"

"Stop, Mac. You have to know, someone has to tell my father," I said.

His mouth thinned down into a straight line and he took a deep breath and held it. He finally let it out in a sharp explosion and said, "I'm not telling your daddy shit. You can tell him yourself when you come back with the fucking *pirate*."

"Thank you," I breathed.

"What do you want me to do, Avery?" he asked, and it was the first time he sounded lost.

"Operations as normal under your eye. Tell them whatever you want about me, just keep them all on task recovering the gold. You are all rich. Be happy with that."

He snorted.

"Money can't buy happiness, baby girl."

"I know, I just told you, that's why I'm doing this," I said with a crooked grin.

"Come on, show me how this pond thing works."

"Not entirely sure," I said, leading him out of my tent. "I'm about to find out."

We went back to the edge of the Mirror Pond and I tied the rope around my waist and secured it around my bag of supplies.

I'd done something similar once before in South America with

Kurt when we had to dive to get up into an underground air pocket to climb through some chambers in a cave behind a waterfall system to dive further in the very same cavern system further down the line. That'd been a trip. We'd found things of archaeological evidence and significance but no gold. Still, sometimes the greatest treasures known to man had no sparkle to them. Sometimes you couldn't see them at all. It was the greatest love you had ever known in your heart, one that spanned centuries and untold distance across time.

I wasn't willing to let Eamon go. Not now, not ever. And so, with one backward look over my shoulder at Mac who stood helplessly by the tree line behind me, I put my hands together, took an arching leap of faith, and dove headfirst into the smooth silvery water of the Mirror Pond in front of me.

I pulled myself down into the depths, sweeping my arms out in front of me into a wide arc, pulling them into my breast, and sweeping out all over again. One, two pulls, the water sweeping past my tightly shut eyes warm as bathwater, a feeling of disorientation like I was falling but not and on the third stroke, I broke surface! Sucking in air with the scent of rich earth and green growing things, I opened my eyes to star scatter above my head beyond anything I had ever seen before.

No light pollution to diminish them, maybe? was my first, hopeful thought.

I trudged out of the water onto the overgrown bank and hauled my bag of stuff up after me.

It was *dark*. Super dark; and I needed to figure out *fast* where to go from here.

CHAPTER TWENTY

$\mathcal{E}$amon Bligh...

The pond was an anomaly like no other on God's Earth, and in my travels, I had seen a few things beyond the tropics of Capricorn and Cancer – floating mountains of ice and strange creatures, the great whales, and a myriad of birds and fish. None of them compared to stepping through the flow of time. In truth, I had expected my attempt to return to my own century, to 1731, to end in me splashing about in the pond like a fool. When I had initially arrived in my siren's time and place, it had been with Avery's hand pulling me through. But my worry was unfounded, and the pond revealed a hidden bottom that broke to the surface of a different century.

When I clambered from the edge of the water, I knew that I was in my own time again. The sky was clear, the air had a different scent to it, and there was a whiff of burning. I looked up and saw a pillar of smoke rising from somewhere inland, interrupting the stars. I discarded the flip-flops and ran for our encampment. Fire was a folly, especially a large one. It could be seen from a great distance, the smoke during the day and ember glow at night.

Had a storm struck, and lightning smitten something and set it ablaze?

No, the smoke was black, and black smoke was pitch, and we had a small abundance of that. This was a signal fire as sure as anything, and that meant that I had been too late to stop the betrayal. I would kill Forsythe for this. He had jeopardized everything and everyone with his black-hearted ways. *Who was he signaling?* There would be no pirates cruising these waters. This was the territory for the Royal Navy, smugglers, and coast-hugging ships, small-time tradesmen and fishermen.

My heart bade me to run, but my mind said I should see first, and I listened to this advice. Ascending a large tree was easy enough, though it pained my stitches and reminded my feet that they had too long lived in boots and had forgotten the rough and honest truth of a life on a deck and in the rigging. There was a ship in the harbor where *Sapphire Horizon* had made her berth, or would make her berth, in a few hundred years. The sails were furled, and I saw the gun ports were open and the black mouths of cannons protruded. I counted quickly, eighteen guns on her port side, in the glimmer of her lantern's light, making her at least a thirty-six-gun frigate, two gun decks, and likely carrying eighteen pounders. This jackal of the sea would have devoured *Honor's Price* if she had been able to catch her and put her to the king's justice.

The king's colors flew from the mast and I flexed my hand and realized with some colorful language that my cutlass and boots were tucked away in a footlocker in another blasted century. I considered heading to the encampment, but if the frigate's sails were furled, she had been there for a while. That would mean her marines would have had time to row ashore, and we had prepared no defenses against such an approach. Nae, that would be a bad idea, so I made for the narrow path that led back to the cave and the Devil's Arse. My loyal crewmen were likely to be there, if any had eluded capture.

Except that the blasted path did not exist in this time, and I had to make my own way through, devoid of anything more than Mister Wallace's black knife shoved into the pocket of the future trousers. I made good enough time and was nearly rewarded with a blind death. A pistol shot splintered the trunk of a tree mere feet away from my face as I was about to enter the clearing at the cave entrance.

"Stop bloody shooting!" I shouted.

"Sorry, Captain!" Baxter replied. "The island has recently become infested with a number of Englishmen."

I entered the cave and found it well defended. Baxter had his swivel guns and a few of the crew armed with their pistols, cutlasses, and boarding axes. I searched their scant number and noticed several important faces missing. Morgan Dougal and John Forsythe were both absent, but so was young Hawkins.

"Give me your report, Mister Baxter," I said.

"I thought I already did," he said glibly, reloading the swivel gun.

"Who is left and what has happened?" I asked.

"We were summarily betrayed, Captain," Baxter said. "Someone was setting fires on the island, smearing trees with pitch and setting them ablaze. We tried to catch the scoundrel and even considered leaving but found our two longboats were damaged beyond repair."

"How would you damage a rowboat beyond repair? The island is covered in trees and we have a spider's lifetime of rope."

"Hard to return a boat from ashes," Baxter said, touching the brim of his cap.

"You could have said the saboteur gave our escape plan to arson," I said dryly.

"Aye, sir, but what would be the fun in that?" he asked. Before I could fully appreciate Baxter's sense of humor, there was a shout, and I heard familiar voices.

"Don't fire! Don't fire!" A darkly familiar voice rose above the others. Baxter pointed the barrel of his swivel gun up, as did Mister Hammond. I felt my eyes go wide with incredulity. The voice I heard was none other than John Forsythe. He and several others came into the cave with great hurry. Forsythe had been wounded in the arm, and as soon as he had cover, he started reloading his pistol. If I had my pistol or cutlass, I would have ended him on the spot.

"Fine for you to rejoin us, Captain," he said pointedly. "Would asking your bearing the last few days be cause for a challenge?"

"It would take too long to explain," I said.

"What sort of... garb... are you wearing?" he asked, regarding the colorful advertisement blouse and pocketed trousers. "And where are your armaments?"

"Part of the same story. I'll have this one first, if it is pleasing to you," I said harshly.

"Oh, this is a fine story, sir. After you went missing, we had a number of words, and a search of the island, and then a great deal of pistol and blade pointing," Forsythe said.

Several pistol reports sent splinters of rock flying from the mouth of the cave. Baxter gestured and Hammond swung his gun and let fly. There was a sharp roar, several trees shuddered, and I heard the sounds of several men moaning in pain, and in the dark, a flash of red material. Royal Marines, and they were down.

"We decided to leave, and found our ships burned, and I thought, forgive me, sir, that you had found a new way off the island and decided to maroon us here." He stuck the barrel of his pistol around his sheltering boulder and fired. There was a wet bubbling scream, and I knew that for a man shot in the neck. As Hammond furiously reloaded his gun, Baxter handed me a pair of pistols – his pistols.

"I did no such thing," I said, firing a round into the body of a particularly large man emerging from the tree line. He took a knee and keeled over. "But I would know the name of the knave who set that signal fire."

"Oh, Captain," Forsythe said. "I quite imagine you would blame me."

"I have entertained the thought," I said. I still had my shot and he was reloading.

"Save that round for a man that deserves it," he said hotly.

"You would have me believe you have nothing to do with this?"

"You are an educated man, Captain. You've made sure that we

reprobates know this. Had that I summoned the King's Navy, would I not be on the shore with the officers in their powdered wigs and not being shot at in a hole in a rock?" Forsythe asked.

"If not you, then who sold us to Jack Ketch?"

"It would be the crewman conspicuously absent, sir," Baxter said.

"Where is Hawkins? Dougal?" I asked.

"Dead, and sitting comfortably," Forsythe spat.

"Morgan Dougal?" I asked, dumbfounded.

"Aye," Baxter said. Hammond and the others gave their nods, supporting Baxter and Forsythe. "Dougal had been a king's man, part of the Royal Navy, and now he's gone back." I felt as if I had taken a cannonball to the chest. I had sought Dougal's council, and he had my ear. What had his purpose been?

Survival.

It had always been survival, *his* survival. He was a cook, he didn't fight, didn't man a cannon or cutlass. My mind struggled with this revelation, but I was not afforded long. More pistol and rifle shot flew, and I became more concerned with the disposition of powder and lead.

"They don't know about the cave," Forsythe said. "Which means he's not told them about where we stored the gold."

"Why wouldn't he tell them?" I asked.

"Because he's playing cards with them. As long as he holds the location of the king's gold, he won't hang alongside us," Forsythe said. "Have your senses left you as you departed us?"

"No, you're right. Dougal won't give them the lucre until it benefits him the most," I said. The marines ceased their assault on our blind and withdrew. This was a cause of great relief as our ammunition was low. We tended the wounded, and I learned how many of my crew had fallen or were among the dead. We thought ourselves lucky until the crack of thunder.

The first whistling projectiles struck the encampment and there was a roar. The air filled with debris. "Fused shot," Baxter snarled and handed me my spyglass. I put the lens to my eye to scan the frigate. The cannons gave distant flashes in the dark and a moment later their voices reached our ears. The encampment, over a month of work, was reduced to pulverized splinters and smoldering scrap.

"I feel that it is time that we evacuate this location," I said. "If they range those guns on us, this cave will not offer us anything but a very expensive tomb."

"What would you have us do, Captain?" Forsythe asked.

"I don't know," I admitted. "There is no escape. We don't have enough ammunition to hold off the entire complement of that ship, and no answer for those eighteen pounders."

"We could make an answer if we could sneak on the ship," Baxter said. "A spark in the magazine and that frigate is kindling in the sky."

"A shot in Dougal and they never recover the gold," Forsythe said.

"A fool's errand," I said.

"Look at these boys," Forsythe said. "Barely marines. Look how poorly they charged, and how wide their shots were. This is no veteran crew, no great and terrible captain to be feared. I suggest now that we have a proper captain, the advantage is ours."

"You've gone mad," I said. "But your madness, they won't expect it. They've a ship full of wounded men, and maybe they don't believe Dougal if he tells them our number. We take the fight right into their teeth," I made a fist, "and we take their ship."

The remaining men cheered.

They were brave, and I saw something different in Forsythe. He cheered, but I saw death in his eyes. We were speaking courageous and bold words, but if we took this course, it was simply picking the manner of our demise. The rope? A rotting cell? Or a valorous charge, bared steel and pistols firing in defiance? There was a poetry in it. Quite to my surprise, I had the luxury of writing these thoughts into my journal. I thought of Avery, who had just so recently roared into my life like a storm. Her sketches were still there, though they did not do her justice, and I felt that this was a folly. Was this going to be my last folly?

No. Emma.

I would not die on this island. If nothing else, they said that I died a broken man in Charleston, not on this island.

We crept from the cave under the velvet night sky, before the sun drove the stars away in a bonfire of colors. These men were fresh as babes, still suckling on their mother's teat, and the small number of watchmen were quickly and quietly cut down with cutlass. Mister Wallace's future knife accounted for several retirements from the King's Navy, a fine weapon it turned out to be.

Hammond led the charge up the gangplank and was cut down by the senior marines on the deck, suddenly coming to their senses. One of the marines was caught by a pistol shot and crumpled, and the second took Forsythe's cutlass across the breast and screamed. There was shouting and screaming. A handful tried to take command, and then we gave them their second rude surprise – Mister Baxter's first swivel gun shredded men at close range, firing a terrible wad of nails and sharpened pieces of junk metal.

I took a shot to the shoulder and nearly dropped my pistol.

Things grew quiet, and I saw that the fight was over, and I was still alive, but the ship was not ours. Our shot was spent, and the crew of the frigate had appeared in their greatly reduced number, but still well-armed.

"Now that this nonsense is over," a short but imperious man spoke, mounting the main deck from the direction of the captain's quarters, "I should like to hear your name, pirate Captain." He was followed out by two other men, one portly with red side whiskers and a taller man with the bearing of a captain.

"Aye, that one," Dougal said. "That one is the captain."

"Mister Dougal," I said, "there is a special level of hell, reserved for mutineers, and betrayers." He looked surprised as I lifted the pistol with my wounded shoulder and pulled the trigger. He went down, painting the man next to him with blood.

I had a moment to revel in my victory before a knock to the back of the head sent me stumbling to my knees. My mind reeled.

Captured.

This is how I end up in Charleston.

Fate is cruel.

I woke sometime later, my hands clapped in irons, and there were two other men with me. I dwelt in twilight, and I knew both of my cellmates to be deceased. One was Morgan Dougal, the lower half of his face a ruin from my shot; everything from his nose down was a deeper gorier red than his side whiskers. The other was a sunken-eyed man, flesh bloated and pale. Captain Blaine stared at me, and I could feel the admonishment, the disappointment, in his gaze. I had lost his ship, lost his crew, and believed good lies and not good pirates.

When I awoke again, I was blessedly alone, and my head felt like a lantern cast to the deck, shattered and full of broken glass. When my jailors discovered my roused state, I was the subject of great interest, and my hands and face were given a coarse washing, and a semblance of care was given to my hair. My shoulder had been tended; a spot of blood soaked through the packet of clean bandage bound to it. After I'd been cleaned up, still clapped in the king's favorite jewelry; fashionable black iron at the wrist and ankle, I was unceremoniously drug to the captain's stateroom, where I was awaited by a committee.

Splendid.

"I would know the name of the man who stands in front of me," the short man in a white wig said.

"I would know the same of my questioner," I said, my voice cracked and weaker than I cared for.

"Very well, I don't feel like playing this game a third time. My name is Commodore Acton Goodchilde, and I am acting *posse comitatus ex Oceanus* in the name of the South Seas Trading Company, in good stead with Captain Clive Everett of the King's Royal Navy, master of the frigate *Norrington*. Does this suffice to answer your question, man?"

"Eamon, Eamon Bligh," I said. The force of his personality was buffering like sailing into a storm.

"I would ask you, politely, as to the disposition of a lightly armed merchantman, which you might have seen in your travels, the

Queen's Mercy?" I was dumbfounded at how quickly the king and his agents had acted, and how much ill luck on our side led to great luck on theirs. "You can dispense with pretending you never encountered the ship. Your two mates who were taken alive and awares have already confirmed that your ship encountered the *Mercy.*

"How do you know; how did you find us?" I asked. The short man gestured and one of the guards who brought me into the room responded by reminding me of proper decorum when speaking to an important man of a chartered trading company and adjutant of the king through the application of his fist into the side of my face. He made sure I was paying attention by repeating himself twice more. I spat blood.

"Answer my question and I will answer yours," he said.

"We sank the *Mercy* and lost two out of every three members of our crew for the trouble," I answered.

"And you assumed command of the ship, yes?" he asked.

"That doesn't answer—" my retort was cut short, the guard again reminded me of what was proper etiquette and what was unacceptable. There was more blood and the side of my head throbbed. "Yes," I said through gritted teeth.

"Wonderful, and thank you, sir," Goodchilde said. "Would you care for a refreshment? I could offer you tea, wine, perhaps a good shot of my own personal spirits? I am quite fond of Jamaican rum."

I whispered the word rum. I was offered a glass and the captain himself poured it for me.

"We have had a time following your trail, but there were markers left in your wake, with the most important having been a large wooden barrel with details about your ship and what was taken from the *Mercy* and your suspected heading. How? Did we already have a man on your ship? No, no, we did not. That fell to your own man, who took it upon himself to throw this valuable information overboard, in such a manner that we might find it. A Morgan Dougal, a man of your own confidence, by his own words."

"He doesn't have many words now, does he," I said. I closed my eyes. I knew the fist was likely coming, but it never landed.

"You have a certain spirit, Bligh, and that is quite amusing," Goodchilde said.

"He's a pirate, nothing more," Captain Everett replied.

"Oh no, he is a pirate *captain*, but besides that? A learned man, formerly of the Navigational college, son of the executed Bligh family. No sir, he is much more than *just a pirate...* he is a very interesting man, indeed," Goodchilde said. "Which means that he didn't make stupid decisions, he made *inexperienced ones*, which are completely different. Your man Dougal sold you and your crew out for a chance to rejoin the Royal Navy and go home to his dear wife and family. *Tsk tsk*, you made sure that didn't happen." I gave him a bloody-toothed smile. "I would be most satisfied with that as well," he said. "Well played, and *mea culpa*, I should not have allowed Dougal on deck to gloat."

"Better luck next time," I said.

"Indeed, and thank you," he said. "I will most certainly endeavor to keep that lesson in mind for future use. I would offer you advice, but it would have a certain futility." He gave the slightest hint of a shrug. "But let us cut to the quick of it. You and your men took the *Mercy* and liberated her of her treasure, a very significant amount of gold. I am sure you would have recognized it. It consisted of several very shiny, yellow, metal bars with His Majesty's profile hammered into it. Very striking, hard to miss."

"I'm not familiar with those things," I said. I flinched as the guard made to hit me, but Goodchilde gestured and the guard again stayed his hand. The relief was short lived when Goodchilde approached me himself. He grabbed me by the forearm with one hand. The other he placed on my shoulder, the wounded one, his thumb almost instinctively finding the wound in my shoulder, slipping beneath the bandage.

He dug into it, and there was no preparedness for that sort of agony. I screamed, and he dug in without mercy, twisting his thumb, fresh blood blooming through the folded bandage over the area, staining the scraps of the shirt I wore beneath. I fought, twisting my body away from the torture, but the guards grabbed my chains and held me down while Goodchilde dug. His expression never changed – not a sneer, not a scowl, not even a sparkle of distaste in his eye. His flat affect more terrifying than any of these things.

"Shall I describe the gold again?" he asked.

"You'll never find it," I said through gritted teeth. "It will remain lost for two hundred and eighty-five years before anyone else lays a living eye on it."

He laughed then, a mocking bray and said, "Such a specific number! What makes you so sure?" he asked.

"Because it is almost two score fathoms deep," I said. "Right up the Devil's Arse." Goodchilde fixed me with his cold eyes. His face could have been carved from stone and displayed no more warmth and emotion. "It's gone to you and the king," I said with a savage grin.

"What reason do I have then, to keep you alive, if my king's gold is missing?" he asked.

"Funny, I didn't think that you were going to," I said.

"That was decided already, you are right. But now, there is no reason to even bother taking you to Charleston. We will hang you and the rest of your pirate crew from the yardarm and deliver your bird-pecked corpses to Jones's Locker," he said.

"What?" I said. "No show for the governor and the people? No Jack Ketch and dancing jigs?"

"You are a very peculiar pirate, Bligh. Your audacity is inspirational and amusing, and I will take your request into consideration. With as much damage as you and your crew have done, costing the king a great amount of war funding, a ship, a crew, and a not insubstantial number of this ship's marines and sailors, it would indeed be a waste to simply render you into fodder for sharks and gulls."

"Aye, such a waste would be a pity," I said.

"Give him his journal and writing tools. It would not do for such an educated man to be denied a chance to chronicle his last thoughts and words," Goodchilde said.

"Dougal said he wrote about the stolen gold in his book," the captain said.

"And I have already read it," Goodchilde said with a smug curve to his lips. "Clever of you to write it in code and cipher, but do not think I am not a cleverer man than you." Goodchilde spoke down to me. He turned his attention back to the captain of the *Norrington*.

"The Devil's Arse is a cave in the center of the island. Upon our return to Charleston, you will lead a detachment of your best men in expedition back to the island to explore the cave and return the king's bounty to the *Norrington*. You'll gain the commendation you desire, and I will earn a profitable and pleasant posting where I will live in peace and not chase pieces of flotsam thrown from pirate ships by their betrayers."

I was hauled up by my jailer. "One last thing, Bligh," Goodchilde said. "Thank you for eliminating Dougal for us. We were never going to honor the promises we made to him, but of course, you probably already knew that."

I was returned to the brig, and it was as Goodchilde said. I was given my journal, ink and a quill, and the bottle of rum. I was a condemned man, and it was perhaps my finest folly. I could have just stayed on the *Sapphire Horizon,* accepted that it was a new time with new people. I could have still been with Avery…

I sighed deeply. Avery was lost to me. Emma was most likely lost to me as well. I had to concede my folly in returning to this time, that my place in it now was through naught but fault of my own. I'd been played for a fool because I *was* a fool. Morgan Dougal had betrayed the entire crew after gaining my ear and I'd not once questioned his loyalty.

Damn my eyes.

I was left with far too long with naught but rum and my thoughts, and even emptying the bottle did little to empty my mind. I filled the journal with my thoughts, the thoughts of a foolish pirate who came close to holding everything and who had lost it.

No, I didn't come close to holding everything, I did hold everything. I was the captain, a great treasure in Avery, and there was some gold hidden away in a cave.

Avery's eyes, the color of endless skies, haunted me every time I closed my own. To think, I had let her slip my grasp.

Nae again, she did not slip my fingers... I threw it all away. What a fool I am. Eamon's Folly should be the title of my life.

We'd left Ghost Island, and if what Goodchilde said was true, the gold had not been recovered. I could feel the sway of the hull. A ship at rest is quiet, but when she is under sail, the hull is a symphony of squeaks and groans and the *Norrington* was under full sail, now.

We remained underway for a lengthy time before I was disturbed again, and this was to bring a new prisoner to share the singular cell I occupied. Hung between the two marines was what was left of John Forsythe.

I felt a slight increase to my morale, both with John being alive, and the fact that one of the marines who bore him was bandaged and apparently wounded. I wanted to ask him when and where he was struck. Was it their foolhardy charge toward the cave, or was it in our terrific charge to take the *Norrington*? I wisely did not taunt the man, and they unceremoniously dumped Forsythe to the floor, a sack of potatoes that groaned when they kicked it and departed, clanging the black iron gate of the cell shut, punctuating the fact of our incarceration with its metallic ring.

"John, John, how do you be?" I asked, my voice barely above a whisper.

"Fresh as rain, pretty as a flower," Forsythe said. "Help me sit up, Eamon." I did, leaning him against the side of the cell that was the brig. I gave him some of the water I had been keeping for myself, rationing it against the likelihood of want. He accepted, and coughed, the action staining his lips with red.

"Are there any left besides us?" I asked.

"Nay," John said. "Tis just the two of us left of the *Honor's Price*. I'll speak freely now; my hours are being counted."

"You are too mean by twice for Death to come looking for your ugly face," I said. He gave me a twisted smile, amusement in his eyes.

"Oh, my captain," he said. "I fear what they have in store for you."

"They will hang me in Charleston, I imagine. Jack Ketch or Davy Jones gets us, one or the other," I said.

"Nay Eamon. That man with the Devil's calm smile, he has plans for you, and it will be the sort of thing that the noose will be a means of escape, and not a means of punishment. He's an evil man, and I would fear him."

"What do you mean, that you would fear him? Do you not fear him?" I asked.

"Nay, I do not fear anything, Eamon. My wounds, they are fatal and I feel my death coming. It won't take long. That is why I am here; I am supposed to die in this cell so you get to see it happen. To what end, I cannot guess. I am not a questioner or torturer," he said. "I would thwart their plan," he said after a good while. "I would seek to make final amends with you."

"There is no requirement for this," I said. His eyes were dark, and his bruised face was damp with sweat.

"You are a good man, Eamon Bligh, and good men make for terrible pirates," he said. "As it happens, I was a most excellent pirate, which I assume your logic would mean me to be a terrible man, and your logic and reason would be to rights. Don't let them take that from you, being a good man." He took a shuddering breath with much difficulty, grunting and closing his eyes a moment before continuing.

"Being a good pirate is an easy thing, you just have to be cruel, and care nothing about anyone but yourself and the coin in your pocket; poxes and daggers for the rest." He coughed and his strength failed him. I gave John more water and tried to make him more comfortable.

"Tell me about the sister you mean to save," he said after a while. I did, I told him the entire story, of how I suspected the Blighs back in England came to be crossways with the king, and how my father, a highly regarded king's man ended up being labeled a traitor. How my mother was locked in a gaol until sickness took her, and of Emma and her bookish leanings and soft voice. How she had been sold to some plantation owner in Carolina as an indentured woman.

I told him about Avery, and the Mirror Pond, and he seemed to gain some comfort from my voice, and I let him hold the empty rum bottle. Sleep took him after a while, and his breathing was very poor. He succumbed to his injuries not long after that, the death rattle shaking his body, and then he was still.

I slept some and was restless as well. I read my own journal and traced the lines I had made in an attempt to illustrate Avery's face, and my mind was consumed with darkness, knowing what fate awaited me. There is no passage of time inside a ship, nothing to indicate the time of day or night, just the motion of the hull, and the creak of the timbers.

The guards came for me, grabbing me roughly out of the cell while another guard grabbed the mortal remains of John Forsythe and drug him in a different direction. The sun stung my eyes as I was pulled up on deck, and I saw the noose hanging from the yardarm and felt a surge of panic, felt the terror in my bowels. I could see the port of Charleston through the loop of the noose, and had I eaten anything, I would have brought it back up in an instant.

The docks were lined with people, and it seemed that this was more than just the usual business, they were watching us as we glided through the harbor and dropped anchor. A guard forced me into one of the longboats, and then I was rowed ashore, covered by strong marines well-armed with pistol and truncheon. "They're going to make a spectacle of you, pirate," one of the men said. "Going to make sure you take a long time to die," the other added. "You and your mates killed and harmed a lot of good men on that blasted island, and you're going to get the slow death for each one of them."

I closed my eyes and swallowed hard as the mantle of my impending fate settled upon my shoulders. As a result, the ride to shore seemed to take longer than the trip from Ghost Island to the port. There was a prisoner's cart waiting for us, waiting for *me*, and I was fairly certain that the driver took a longer than needed route.

More than once, we encountered crowds, and they jeered and heckled and threw things at me. Women spit on me, and children threw rocks and other road debris at me. The wooden slats of my cage kept anything large from getting through, but it was a fractional comfort. I saw the hate and anger in their eyes, and how much they were going to cheer when I danced my jig for them.

The gaol in Charleston was buried under a stone walled building and being drug through the portal took me to another place. It was dark inside save for the flicker of a few candles and single-pitch torch, replacing the bright sunlight and rainbow of colors with a monochrome wash of red and orange against the rough stonework. Benches were arrayed against the wall opposite the cells, and those cells were fashioned from flat black iron, stout rivets, and heavy locks. The air was hot and heavy, poisoned with the brackish smell of sweat, piss, and despair.

Wordlessly, I was deposited in the last cell in the row, the furthest from the entrance. The sound of the metal lock grinding and engaging was no different that the lid of some ancient Egyptian sarcophagus being pushed closed over a living man trapped inside.

I wept.

CHAPTER TWENTY-ONE

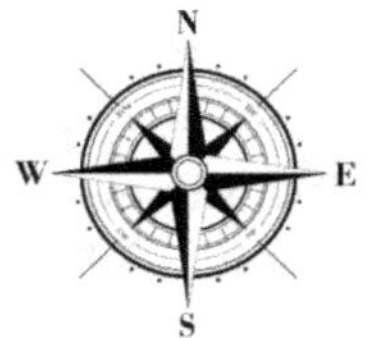

OCTOBER 1731

*A*very Barker...

I dragged myself out of the pond to the darkest night of ruin and mayhem I'd ever encountered. I skulked around in the woods listening to men shout and followed their voices down to the beach while further up the mountain the crack and boom of shot went off like it was a fucking modern-day war zone.

The only thing more disturbing than the sound of shot was the ensuing silence.

This was not good.

A ship glittering with lantern light was out in the bay, anchor dropped and the union jack stirring in the slight breeze from her mast and another, larger than life, off the stern. The scent of gunpowder and burning wood wafting through the air at me from behind me, further up the mountain and the jungle-like woods had my stomach in knots.

Watching Eamon and his crew attack the ship had me squeezing my eyes shut with dread, even as I scrambled to come up with some idea of what to do next.

With the sky turning pastel with the dawn's early light, I watched them throw a pirate to the sand on the shore and jumped, clapping my hands over my mouth as they leveled a one-shot pistol at his back and blew the back of his head out through his face and *laughed about it.*

Holy shit.

My mind was reeling, in a freefall of panic, but I already knew – Eamon was not dead. Not yet. He was either on that ship, or he was about to be put onto it. In either case, I needed to be on that ship, too. My best chance at any kind of rescue attempt wasn't going to be here with all these red-coated thugs and assholes. It was going to be in Charleston.

For this, I had to be stealthy and sneaky as fuck. It was going to be a long, hard swim and climb and I was running out of the cover of darkness.

I withdrew back into the tree line stealthily in a sort of backwards combat crawl that Kurt had taught me when he'd gotten out of the Navy and we'd been doing all those cave dives in hostile territory down in Mexico. There were some gnarly dudes, mostly cartel types, that wouldn't have looked twice at kidnapping my blonde haired and blue eyed ass for a turn in their sex trade, so I'd put myself through the wringer with Kurt learning all types of self-defense and evasion of capture tactics – which is precisely how I'd known he'd thrown the fight with Eamon.

Nothing against the ferocity of my pirate lover, but against a fully trained modern-day Navy Seal? I didn't think so. That fight had gone down way too easy for the both of them and though I hadn't recognized it in the right away after the fact, while the adrenaline was still buzzing through my veins, I think deep down I'd known something wasn't adding up. I don't think I was mad at Eamon for the right reasons, either. I think I was mad at him for accusing Kurt of being the saboteur because equally deep down in the bottom of my soul, I had known he had to be right and I hadn't wanted to believe it.

I'd never gotten the chance to apologize, but then again, I didn't think he would be so rash – I'd underestimated how overwhelmed he must have been. Gotten too familiar with him through his written words, which he'd always had time to write them after the fact – when he'd had time to calm down, when he'd had time to analyze. *Shit*. It was a big mistake on my part thinking he could be levelheaded in the moment. That *anyone* could be that cool given the circumstances.

Right here, right now, was my instant fucking Karma for being so short-sighted.

Adrenaline fizzed through me, a caustic substance that set my nerves on edge as though I had a raw, low grade and annoying electrical current buzzing through my arms and legs, swirling about my head as I clutched the dive bag of Eamon's items plus some extras to my chest. I edged my way into the surf, way down the beach and away from the ship the knot of nylon rope secured around the package and my waist.

I couldn't let them see me get into the water. I had a much better chance of remaining hidden while swimming with the ability to duck below the surface than I did traipsing out over the golden sands of the island.

It seemed the majority of the men from the ship were still on the shore, and there were very few actually on board, yet. So, what I needed to do was make the trip out there *now* while the timing was best and find a place to hole up.

We were only a couple hours from shore via modern gas-powered vessel, but this was wind power and if they decided to hit old Charleston, we were a good couple of days out. I hoped the protein and granola bars I'd thrown in the bag and the few modern plastic bottles of water I'd tossed in would hold me for the journey. I wasn't thrilled at the prospect of climbing that anchor chain with this much weight dangling from my waist but I was just gonna have to tough it out.

Eamon's life was literally depending on it.

I swam out to the ship. A glorious East Indiaman by the looks of it. Huge, with plenty of places to hide if I played my cards right.

It was a long fucking haul, dragging my ass up hand over hand, notching my foot into the anchor chain where I could find purchase. By the time I reached the anchor chain's portal into the ship, my arms *burned* with fatigue and felt like Jell-O, but I wouldn't, I *couldn't* give up.

I clutched the package I'd hauled up with me to my chest and shivered with the cold of the seawater that drenched me. I couldn't do anything about it except keep my teeth firmly clenched against any involuntary chattering as I crept, quiet as a church mouse, through the guts of the ship.

Storage. I need to find the ship's stores. Plenty of places to hide there.

I ducked behind a cannon at one point, wedging myself into shadow while a red coat went by. Only letting my breath out slow when I could be a thousand percent sure he'd departed, only to suck it in sharp and freeze as he came *back* by with an armload of stores.

Thank you, Jesus! I thought to myself, as he'd just given me a stellar indication of where I was supposed to go.

I tell you what, the one thing the movies and history books couldn't prepare you for when it came to the real thing was oh, my God, the *smell.*

I crept through the smoky dark of the ship's lower decks the scent of unwashed bodies in too close a space assailing me at every step, matched only by the stench of the tallow burning in the lamps and lanterns at regular intervals. Those fetid smells were layered with overtones of human waste and rat piss, and I didn't honestly know how I was going to do it.

Eamon is depending on you, you know you're in love with him, so whatever it fucking takes, bitch. That's how you're going to do it. It's literally 'do or die' time!

It wasn't the type of pep talk I would give one of my crew, but it was the one I needed in the moment and I was feeling so guilty I let fly on myself with no mercy.

I found a storeroom full of crates and barrels and got lucky when I managed to find a tight space behind some of them in a far back corner. It looked good. Even if the ship were to pitch, the items were solid and stacked in such a way that if they shifted, I wouldn't be crushed, just trapped. It wasn't entirely a comforting thought, but it was better than no place to hide and me getting captured, too.

I closed my eyes and could catch scraps and snippets of talks and conversations. The shouted orders across the ship's decks were absolutely clear as day, so was, unfortunately, the screams of men being tortured.

Just fucking perfect. I thought bitterly, as I set down the burden of my dive bag and unknotted the cord at my waist. I listened for Eamon's voice, desperately afraid of both hearing it and not... refusing to believe in any way that I was too late.

He's alive, Avery. He has to be... I told myself, over and over.

I spent the next several minutes shortening the length of Eamon's trousers and cutting out the arms on his shirt to make things fit my much smaller frame a little better. While his cutlass was just sharp enough to get the job done, and I could appreciate that the heavy weapon would help me fit in on shore, this was a job for my much sharper dive knife, which was almost an afterthought when I'd strapped it to the side of my lower leg in its sheath back at my tent. Man, was I glad I'd grabbed it now! It was much easier to maneuver in the tight space I was in.

Thankfully, I wasn't terribly cold anymore. The ambient air, fetid as it was, saw to that. I'd go as far as to say it was oppressively hot and close, but I knew it was bound to get a lot warmer and a lot stuffier as the sun continued to rise.

I went over what I had left in the bag, tucking the extra magazines for my Glock into the front pockets of my cutoffs beneath Eamon's trousers and the Glock itself into the back of my waistband.

I had a good bit of protein bars, like a case and a half, as well as six water bottles. I wondered at what the fuck I had been thinking tossing the lot of it in the bag – not that I was complaining – I was glad I had it now.

As for the cutlass and the rest of it? Shit.

I folded the dive bag and shoved it in the back pocket of my cutoffs, there wasn't such a thing as plastic in this century that I knew of, and I wasn't keen on leaving any kind of footprint behind. Lord know how much damage I was capable of doing to the future at the rate I was going. It weighed on my mind, but nothing weighed more than the thousand-pound boulder of worry in the center of my chest. I worried about a lot of things, but my worry for Eamon was paramount, taking over every waking moment of my stowaway status.

I heard a lot of things. Beatings, a blast from a pistol on deck. Cursing, shouting, threats and the clang of metal on metal, groaning, weeping, all somewhere on a deck or several decks above me. It was pitch black in here now that the door to my secret hiding place had been shut, a key turned in the lock – which made me sick. I'd done everything I could swiftly by lantern and the low light of the rising sun when the door had been allowed to swing wide, and now I had to do everything by feel.

I drank sparingly, ate less than I probably should have, but with only a scrounged and empty small crate to relieve myself in across the storeroom, I didn't want to have to go too often. Besides, if I could hear all of the things out there, surely, they could hear *me* if I made a wrong sound at the wrong time.

Hot, close, I felt the fetid breath of the devil himself on the back of my neck, as Eamon would say. I closed my eyes and tried to rest.

We were underway when I woke. I froze, blinking and realized *there was light* coming over the barrels. I held my breath as I heard them. Two men, in the stores just the other side of the barrels and crates I hid behind.

Oh shit, they're onto me, I did something, they heard something, oh, shit, oh, shit, oh shit!

I remained frozen, my hands sealed tight over my mouth,

breathing in slowly, carefully, and most of all *silently* in and out through my nose.

"Be quiet, damn your eyes man!" one of the two whisper-shouted.

"Apologies, I've been waiting for this all day."

The sound of hot and heavy kissing had me wide-eyed and blushing.

"Turn around!" the first man said, his tone eager.

"*Yes,*" the second man hissed and I squeezed my eyes shut at the rattle of buckle, the rustle of clothing, relief washing over me when I realized I had absolutely nothing to do with why these two were in here.

Panting breath, hot and heavy, the occasional grunt as they rutted just beyond me, I kept my mouth covered with both of my hands and closed my eyes, squeezing them tight against the insane urge to giggle like a preteen boy.

A groan, a cry of climax and the first man admonished the second to be quiet. They took long moments to catch their breath and then the valuable information spilled from their lips.

"Again?" one said in a pleading moan.

"Now?" the other said with surprise.

A chuckle. "No, tomorrow."

"We'll make within sight of the coast tomorrow," the first one said. They shared a kiss.

"Charleston won't be for at least another day," the second said softly.

"We risk much," the first one declared.

"Think the pirate will make it?" I perked up slightly and strained to listen.

"Their captain will."

"Bligh?"

"Aye, he'll hang for sure. A spectacle for all to see. A warning, a lesson."

"The other surviving man?"

"He'll be dead before we make port, Goodchilde will see to that."

The first one snorted and spat, and I had to guess that he held no love for Goodchilde. I didn't either by the sound of him.

The second pouted, and they began to do up their breeches. In the end, they decided *not* to risk another dalliance so soon and when they left, I breathed a sigh of relief.

My mind raced, and I closed my eyes and played things out over and over in my mind. I had no plan. That was the conclusion I reached over and over. I had no plan and I would just have to see when I got there. I would just have to keep winging it.

It wasn't comforting. Not in the slightest.

I woke up to shouts, bumping and thumping, and sat up sharply.

I had whiled away the hours with little more than my own thoughts until I wore myself down into sleep. I ate when I was all but absolutely *ravenous* and drank sparingly. I was hot, I was thirsty, and I was acutely aware that the sounds I was hearing were the sounds of the East Indiaman *docking*.

Hot damn!

I used the opened-up scrap of one of Eamon's sleeves to pack up my remaining water and power bars and tied off each end with some of the length of nylon rope, looping it over my body so the pack lay along my back. The rest of the rope was being used as a make-shift belt to hold the trousers up onto my hips.

I was barefoot, the modern shoes I'd had on in the pack with the rest of the food and water – I'd put them on later when I needed to, but right now? I was trying to blend in. I had *no idea* how I was supposed to get off the damn boat, whether it was day or night, anything.

I crept out from my hiding place and stood shaky and still a bit sleep addled when the damn door opened and a voice called, "Oi! How'd you get in here?"

I froze and picked up a crate that was doable and lucked out *hardcore* when the voice called out, "Doesn't matter, hurry up, boy! Get that to the docks, then!"

More boys and men trailed in past me and hefted crates and boxes and I tried not to cry with relief. I just kept my head down, fell into line, and carried my burden to the docks. I helped to unload the ship, snatching a floppy wide-brimmed hat from where it hung from a dock post and felt myself go breathless again when I looked ahead and saw them toss Eamon, limp between two red coats, into the back of a jailer's cart hauled by a rough looking man and a donkey.

"Where are they taking him?" I asked aloud and a boy my height, lanky and awkward as he wasn't done growing said, "Gaoler's Rock." He pointed up to a fortress jutting out over the water. "You new here?"

"Aye," I said trying to mimic Eamon's way of speaking.

"They don't like questions and they don't like lazy; I'd get back to work if I was you."

I tipped my hat and made for the ship, diverting at the last moment when I was sure the boy wasn't looking to make my way up the dock.

"'Ay! 'ay you!"

Shit!

I bolted, pelting up the steps, refusing to look back when I heard bootfall hammering up the docks behind me. I made it onto the crowded street and disappeared among the crowds into an alley, hiding in a doorway.

"An' just what d' you think you're in for, love? Runnin' from the dockmaster like that?" I looked behind me at the woman who'd spoken.

"Blimey! You's a woman!"

"Yeah – I mean, aye," I said.

"Come quick," she ordered and opened the doorway behind us and I slipped in.

"Just what d'ye think you're doing?" she hissed.

"I have no idea, to be honest with you," I answered and she cringed back.

"You have a strange way about you," she commented.

"You wouldn't believe me if I told you," I said.

"Name's Imelda, what's yours then?"

"Avery," I said.

"An' just what you think you be doing, Avery?" She was persistent.

"I'm not really sure I should say," I said eying her cautiously. She would have been pretty were it not for the scars from acne or a pox across her cheeks. Her brown hair was curly and pulled into a low ponytail and her, eh hem, décolletage was on full and prominent display.

"Are you lookin' for work?" she asked, eying me back. "Ye'd fetch a fair price and a man's eye with skin like that."

"What? No! I'm looking for a way to Gaoler's Rock. A way to get inside."

"Now why would you want to do a thing like that?" she asked jerking back in surprise.

"Suicide," I muttered, and she laughed.

"You're right about that," she said.

"Look, thanks for pulling me in, but I really gotta go—"

"They're gonna hang 'im, love," she said, looking at the cutlass on my hip.

"Not if I have anything to say about it," I shot back, and she cocked her head curiously.

"They they're going to hang you too, I'd reckon."

"Oh, ye of little faith, Imelda," I whispered, peeking out her door.

"Who is he to you?" she asked.

"The love of my life," I answered quickly, jerking back and easing the door back shut as men approached up the alleyway. I backed away from the door as a heavy fist fell against it and rattled the door in its frame.

Imelda hissed and swept back a curtain and shoved me through into what was sort of a pantry.

"Hang on! Hang on!" she shouted in annoyance and she went to the door and jerked it open.

I stood stalk still and listened.

"What d'you want?" she demanded.

"You see a boy run past?" an authoritarian voice demanded.

"Now how am I supposed to see through my alley door?" she demanded. "Get on with ye! There's no boy here."

There was an unappreciative grunt, and she shut the door after a moment and sighed.

"Ye can come out now, Avery."

I stepped out, and she sighed and looked me over.

"It's that cutlass that gives ye away," she said with a wave of her hand. "Nae but a kings' man or a pirate carries one of the likes of those." She sighed and shook her head.

"Good to know," I said coolly as my mind raced to figure out what the fuck I was going to do about it. I knew Eamon wasn't going to want to give it up, and I wasn't about to.

"You look like a pirate dressed like that," she said dryly.

"Any suggestions?" I asked.

"Aye, ye need to dress like a lady. Skirts'll hide the blade well enough."

"Wouldn't happen to have a spare dress lying around, would you?" I asked.

She shook her head and said, "A shilling or two would have you right as rain."

"I haven't got any money," I said with a shrug.

"My, then we are at a disadvantage, aren't we, lass?"

"Maybe not," I said with a raised eyebrow. "Let me ask you something, Imelda."

She put her hands on her hips and swept a hand out in front of her to tell me to go ahead.

"Why are you helping me?"

She stared at me and I stared at her, her hazel green-brown eyes searching my face, a sorrow and rage filling her expression, but that last one? It was almost helpless in nature. When she spoke, it became readily apparent why.

"They killed my boy, the redcoats did. Damn the lot of them."

"Killed him how?" I asked. I gave a long slow blink. She didn't look old enough to have a grown-ass man for a 'child.' Like, she honestly looked older than *me* but not by much and that could have been the scarring and pitting on her face combined with the clear indication of sun damage on her skin.

"Sailed off wit' him. Nay a day over sixteen," she said. "Ship came back to port, and he wasn't wit' 'em. They said he wasn't cut out for the sailing life, smirked at me they did. He was just a *boy*. Damn the lot of them." She dropped onto one of the rickety looking chairs around her rough-hewn kitchen table and I sank into one opposite her.

Tears glittered in her eyes with a particular mamma bear rage and I could see her pain and anger plainly – it was *no act*. I mean, if it was? It was pretty damn convincing, so convincing, I took the gamble and rolled the dice.

"I'm here for the pirate they just took off that ship and rolled through town in that gaoler's cart," I said, the old-fashioned term for 'jailer' tasting funny in my mouth. "Before they do the same to him."

She scoffed and gave me some side-eye. "And what do you aim to do about it, lass? You're just a wee thing."

"Doesn't take much to outsmart these brutes," I said, tapping my temple with two fingers.

"Aye, not a one or two of them, no," she said slowly, "but they're a sight more than one's and two's Avery."

"Let me worry about that," I said, sighing. "I just need to get *in* to Gaoler's Rock."

She snorted, "That's easy enough," she said. "A proper dress you'll be needing, though. You haven't a coin or schilling to your name?"

"Sadly, no," I said sitting back.

"This pirate, would it vex them terribly to lose him?"

"Oh, you have no idea," I said, rolling my eyes. She looked at me puzzled and I amended my speech. "Vexation for days if not weeks, perhaps, even, for the rest of their lives."

A wicked little smile painted her lips and she said, "You've no sorrow in your heart over stealing what you might need?" she asked.

"Can't say that I do," I answered honestly.

"This is what we'll do, then…"
I leaned forward and listened intently.

~

I HATED HOW LONG IT TOOK FOR ME TO 'NICK' A PROPER DRESS AS Imelda had put it, but I'd gotten it done. Now I had all of the things I needed to hide up under it, my tits mashed and bolstered up on full display, whore's makeup caked on my face and I was perfumed to within an inch of my life along with Imelda; the floral and sickly sweet cloud wafting around us wherever we went as we made our way through the dusk-darkened muddy streets – if you could call them that – to Gaoler's Rock the following night.

Imelda made her living in one of the nearby brothels, but surprisingly, didn't live there. She kept a place of her own, instead. She said it was to raise her boy away from that place and when he was gone? She couldn't bear to move into the main house and leave what memories she had with her son behind.

I couldn't say I blamed her. She said she'd gotten pregnant from a rape, also from a British soldier, when she was thirteen. No man would marry her when she birthed a bastard, so she'd made the best of a bad situation.

She had been heart broken when her son had grown and had decided to become a king's man, but she'd chosen to remain proud of her boy. She hated herself for not fighting him on it and the whole situation was all around tragic.

Now, here she was, getting her revenge in the strangest way possible helping a woman from two hundred and eighty-five years into the future do some damage to the pride of the British army operating out of Charleston. I had mixed feelings on actually *killing* any of them, but if it came down to a choice between me and Eamon? I knew exactly which way that was gonna go.

We easily made it past the gate and into the fortification, all Imelda had to do was knock and bat her eyes coyly at the soldier that'd opened the spy plate set in the heavy door.

I guess this was a regular thing the whores around town did – made prostituting house calls to the barracks set within.

The fates had been smiling upon my modern-day ass the whole way thus far, but I was feeling sure that shit wouldn't hold out forever. When things did go tits up, I was just hoping I would be ready.

Eamon's cutlass bumped a little less than reassuring against my leg beneath the skirts. I had on my shoes, the skirt length dragging along the flagstones and hiding them as we were let into the main proper of the fort itself. The sky stretched on impossibly large and open, glittering in the deep blues and pastel hues of deep sunset above us as we were led to another door across the courtyard.

"Oh, please, sir… before we get started, my man is serving a short sentence here in the gaol. Might I see him for just a moment, not for any relations, but just to say 'ello?" Imelda asked, batting her eyelashes.

"Oi, maybe after you're done," he grunted back, taking a big ring of iron keys off his waistband.

"Might I see the pirate?" I blurted in a rush – just as Imelda and I had planned. I raised the fan to cover my mouth so all he could see was my eyes and he grinned at me.

Apparently, like modern-day serial killers had their groupies, there was something similar to be said for pirates back in the day.

"Depends," the man said, coming at me, his teeth gray, brown, in some places *green*, and slimy. Breath fetid and apt to knock me on my ass alone despite the barrier of the fan I kept in front of my face.

He put his back to Imelda and put a hand to my hip, which remember what I said about my luck running out eventually? Yeah. Now would be that time, as he dropped his filthy mitt to my hip *right* over the hilt of Eamon's sword.

His brows crushed down under his tricorn hat and he said, "'Ello now, what's this?" just as Imelda came to the rescue, cracking the great oaf over the back of the head with the sapper she had hidden on *her* person.

She was a pro, apparently, because he went down like a ton of bricks, face-planting and slobbering in my titties as he went. I leaped back some and winced as Imelda immediately grabbed his booted ankles and hissed, "Well don't just stand there, girl! Help me!"

I helped and we both wrangled him into an alcove and sat him up on a low stool there. Imelda searched his person as I took up his keys, and heart pounding so loud I was sure the entire fort and jail could hear it beating like a drum, I looked around. Dude started to slide and I caught him along with Imelda, wincing as I dropped his keys with a clatter.

We got him situated and she gave him a quick pat down.

"Ah ha!" she declared, unscrewing the cap on a flask and taking a hit off it for herself. I winced, just thinking about dude's teeth and shook my head when she held it out for me.

"Suit yerself," she said with a shrug and doused the man with a little bit of the flask's contents for fragrance, situating the open container in his meaty paw.

"Did you get his keys?" she hissed at me and I jumped.

"Oh, right! Right here!"

I retrieved the ring from the flag stones with both hands, keeping them from rattling by gripping the keys tightly in my other palm. So tight, the metal dug painfully into my palms as I held a white-knuckled grip on them.

"He'll be in the deepest part of the prison," Imelda said with a sigh and I nodded. "The key you need might not be on this ring."

I nodded again.

"Come on, then." She jerked her head and gathered her skirts and I followed suit.

She literally had no fucks left to give and it was impressive. I was terrified of getting caught, raped, and God knows what else but wasn't willing to let it stop me, but Imelda? She had a completely different vibe going on. She literally moved around the jail and prison complex without a single damn care. Like whatever was going to happen was going to happen and oh-fucking-well.

It was both impressive and sad when I thought about it, to be honest. Impressive because holy good goddamn, she was fearless! Sad, because she'd likely lived through it all and it was nothing really all that new to her. At least, that was the impression that I got.

She took me to a door and sighed and said, "Try your keys, girl. I'll keep a watchful eye."

Seemed my guardian angel and Imelda were working it overtime because the second to last key? It worked. The tumblers of the lock grating and sliding back, the door latch swinging free. I turned and looked over my shoulder and Imelda and I both whipped our heads around the opposite way and up as voices bounced along the stone corridor from back the way we came.

"You go on, lass. Find your pirate lover – I'll find a way and keep the lot of these bastards distracted," she hissed. I went through the door and ducked down, locking it back up from the inside as Imelda called out to the two approaching voices, "Ah, good lads you are, I seem to be lost finding my way to the barracks!"

She gave a simpering laugh as one of the men up the way called back, "I'll say – how did ye get way down here?"

I closed my eyes, listening intently as they conversed just the other side of the door and until their voices faded away.

Holy shit, that was close.

I suffered untold amounts of cat calling as I went past the twin rows of open-barred cells filled with men to either side and gritted my teeth. Their racket was sure to bring out guards, and I almost went right past a room full of them out in the open, ducking back at the last moment and hiding just the other side of a support pillar, sucking it in and holding my breath as a redcoat stepped out of the side room and shouted, "Oi! Keep it down out here!" He retreated back into the room and slammed the door behind him and some of the shouting and cheering dimmed to the low roar of groaning and jeering.

I ducked, swept past the door and kept right on going until I found stairs leading down.

It was dark and dank as fuck down here, and I didn't like it one bit. I got myself out of the encumbering dress in front of the door at the bottom of the stairs when I realized that one, there was only one small row of cells down to one side beyond the small barred window, and two, this was the end of the line. There were no more doors. At the opposite end of the hall, there was a blank stone wall with just a guttering smoking torch in a bracket on it. The stone glittering in the weak firelight, slick with a brackish water. I didn't even want to know where it was originating from. *No, thank you.*

It stank to high heaven down here. Rank, like rotting flesh and piss – not all of it rat piss, but some of it. It was kind of amazing I could tell the difference and I honestly wished I could trade it for a useful talent right now, like picking locks.

I took the bundle of Eamon's old clothes and my provisions serving as the stuffing for the bustle of the back of my skirts out from the midst of the stolen cloth. My handgun and extra magazines were wrapped up tight in Eamon's old clothes and I got them ready first. As soon as that was handled, I got myself situated as before; except this time, I had a leather belt holding Eamon's sword and two old-fashioned pistols to my hips, but those were for him. The Glock was seriously all I was going to need and if it came down to my dive knife still strapped to my leg? Well, fuck. We were as good as dead.

"Come on, *please*," I whispered and tried the last key on the ring in the lock of this door.

No dice.

Fucking damnit.

I slipped my dive knife free and was trying to jimmy the lock when I hit the second lull in my luck. I was so absorbed in the task at hand, my focus narrowed as it was, I had no clue the jailer down here had snuck up on me until he had a grip on my shoulder. He spun me around savagely and fetched my ass up *hard* against the rough planks making up the door I was trying to get through.

He snarled and stepped into me, pinning me but he fucked up too, and wincing, hating myself for doing it, I slipped my knife between his ribs and plunged it into his chest cavity.

His eyes went wide and glassed over almost immediately. His mouth working, but nothing but the barest of sounds came out.

I'd done as Kurt had taught me, had slid my knife home almost textbook perfectly, and the reason dude wasn't screaming is because Kurt had taught me well, and I'd punctured and collapsed his lung.

I sucked in a breath and felt tears spring to my eyes and muttered to him, "I'm sorry," as he collapsed on me and my knees nearly buckled from his weight. He was way heavier than me and I shoved and he sort of flopped onto his back. I winced as my knife pulled free and shuddered as my mind made the comparison that it felt almost exactly like I'd stabbed a side of beef. Except this guy was no cow, his lips frothing with blood as he drowned in it and it was all my fault.

"I'm so sorry," I whispered as he reached for me blindly, trying to grab for me for anything to hold on to as he died. I didn't know what to do to make it quicker, my mind scrambling but nothing really sticking in my panic except *find the key! Get the fucking key!* as I rifled through his clothing and along his person as he lay gasping.

It took *forever*, way too long for him to die as I wrapped fingers around something hard and curved, straight in places and a bit stabby with knobby points through his pocket.

I pulled out a single iron key and felt my breath explode from my body in relief.

I tried not to look at him as I wrestled open the door in the narrow passageway and shoved it hard against his still gasping body and the pile of my discarded dress. I edged through the tight and narrow portal into the awful, fetid, dank and dark hallway beyond.

"Eamon!" I whisper-shouted and waited, creeping along the far wall out of arm's reach, skirting closer to the flat bars only when I had to go around the narrow, rough benches placed against the walls opposite the cells.

I was pretty sure the guy in the first cell was dead, the second and third cell lay empty, but that fourth cell?

I plucked the torch off the wall and brought it closer to the bars.

"Shit! Eamon? Eamon, wake up, baby. Turn over! Turn around and look at me," I demanded in a rushed, hushed tone.

Please, please, please, please, please! I thought desperately, and finally he stirred.

I nearly yelped with relief, clapping a hand over my mouth and sobbing slightly when he pushed his arms under him and his body up off the nasty, dank stone.

"Hang on, lover. I'm gonna get you out of there," I vowed and hung the torch back up to free my hands.

"Avery?" he murmured, and turned, looking up at me dazed.

"You're damn right," I grated, and set to work trying every key I possessed on his cell door.

Shit. None of them worked.

"A vision, no more," he said his voice filled with despair.

"Fuck that fucking bullshit!" I hissed at him. "I didn't travel back two hundred and eighty-five fucking years for nothing! Get your ass up!" I commanded. He blinked owlishly at me and like a coiled snake, struck out at the bars.

"You're here!" he hissed and reached through to caress my face. I leaned into the palm of his hand and sighed.

"Yeah, I'm here. I'm right here," I said. "And I'm going to get you out!"

"How?" he demanded and shook his head. "Nae, it's impossible," he said. "You must leave this place, my siren, before they catch you too."

"Fuck that noise," I declared and turned this way and that, looking for something, *anything* to get him out. My eyes landed on the stupid flat bench up against the wall and I froze like a deer in the headlights.

"No," I said incredulously, and turned back to Eamon and his cell. I went back and forth between the bench and the bars like watching some demented tennis match as my mind worked the problem in overtime.

"What is it?" he demanded.

"Stand back," I ordered. "I saw this in a movie once, and I have no idea if it'll work, but I have to give it a try."

Last-ditch effort, I man handled the bench into position under the cross bars of Eamon's cell door, wedged it in there good and with a deep breath and like I was a kid at the playground trying to launch my buddy off the other end of the see-saw, I took that leap of fucking faith and jumped on the other end of the goddamned bench.

The grate and squeal of rusty metal, and damned if it didn't fucking work! The cell door lifted, and the hinges popped free and the door swung, the lock groaning and giving way before I bolted up against the wall beneath the torch and the whole damn thing came down with a clatter that forced Eamon and I both to clap our hands over our ears and reverberated, echoing, off the stone walls.

"Times up, lover," I said panting, hands going for the belt at my waist. "If they haven't figured out a jailbreak is going down before, they damn sure know what's up now!"

It was no time for movie madness, but just like in the swash-buckling flicks on the big screen, Eamon grabbed me around my waist, hauled me tight up against his body, and kissed me soundly and I had zero fucking regrets in returning the favor.

CHAPTER TWENTY-TWO

*E*amon Bligh...

It is said, by godly men and poets, that it is always darkest before the dawn, and I did not think of this until the most unthinkable thing occurred. As I sat, alone, in the king's stinking gaol, with nothing but dank stone and doom hanging above my head, my sweet siren appeared. My wits, fogged by despair scarcely recognized her, even as she wore my own battered clothing.

We exchanged words, but these words seemed alien to my mind, the dialog of a dream, or attempting to remember the lines of an actor at play, many years past. But I felt my mind drawn to earth, and a bolt of lightning strike me through like an oak tree as my lips touched hers.

I knew her, and I felt as if there was a chance again. There was also the off chance that these were my final delusions as I sank into Death's embrace, but I cared not for that bit of dread.

"How did you come to find me?" I asked.

"Loverboy, I swam three centuries, climbed an anchor chain, hid in a storeroom, and lucky for you, I like pirate movies." She produced a brace of pistols and my cutlass from the inside of my own coat. "These are for you."

"Do your pirate movies include how to escape from the king's gaol?" I asked. I felt the reassuring weight of my blade, and the pistols. I checked them, and the powder and shot seemed good.

"Swashbuckling," Avery said.

"Swashbuckling?" I repeated.

"Yeah, swashbuckling. Swing the sword, shoot the pistols, swing down from the rope holding the chandelier…" she said.

"Your king must have far nicer gaols than mine," I said. "But I think I know your purpose." She produced her own pistol of sorts, a small black thing that seemed both toy like, and very serious. "Is that dangerous?" I asked.

"Very," she said.

"Good," I nodded, "save your shot for the right moment." She gave me a curious look accompanied by a feral grin but agreed, as if there was something dreadfully obvious about her small pistol that I was completely unaware of.

We found the body of a dead guard. I looked down at the man, and the patch of blood on his coat. "Your handiwork?" I asked.

"I didn't mean to, but I did what I had to," she said.

"Fine work, fine work," I said. I relieved the dead man of his gaoler's coat, breeches, and thankfully his boots, battered as they were, were neither overly large nor too small to wear. Avery seemed to chafe at the time it took, but the only sound that came to my ears was the rabble of prisoners above the narrow spiral of staircase before us.

"A woman helped me get in here, and she might be providing us a distraction, we might be able to sneak out the way I came in," she suggested. I gestured for her to lead the way, with a theatrical bow that I thought she might enjoy. She gave me a comical curtsey, and led us up the stairs, and through a hall with several clusters of cells with screaming and shouting prisoners to either side of us. I heard the clank and rattle of the gaoler's keyring, and I turned to look at her.

"Do you still have the keys?" I asked. She reached down and plucked them from the inside of my tattered and now sleeveless shirt.

"Seems so, yes," she said. I held out my hand for them and she gave them to me.

"Lad's here's your freedom, you just have to reach it," I said, and gave the keyring a toss into the dark.

"I don't think that is a good idea," Avery said.

"You're right," I said. "I think it a terrible idea. A very loud, problematic, and violent idea." I said. "But it will take them time to figure a way to reach the keys from their cells, minutes if God favors them, or they'll never find them if the devil means to have them. I leave these things to the winds of fate and a power higher than I possess," I said with a grin. She looked at me like she was in love with a maniac and was considering the wisdom of this fact. I gave her my best smirk, and we took off through the next door and down the hall beyond it.

We slowed, pressing ourselves to shadow upon hearing oddly the grumble of impatient men and the slap of skin against skin. I raised an eyebrow and looked at Avery. I had seldom spent much time in any gaol, and my first visit to the colonies was certainly more than I expected. She raised a finger to her lips, and we made to creep past the chamber the sounds were coming from. As we approached, it became louder and more obvious the source of the chorus.

There was a single woman, by her panting and moaning, and a number of men.

I ventured a look into the chamber and my eyes bulged at the site. A woman with weathered and pockmarked skin was bent over a small table, the sort that the guards were likely to play cards or dice at, and she was being taken from behind by one of the brutes, his black breeches around his ankles and his pale hands on her fleshy hips.

Avery stuck her head around to peer at this spectacle as well. The guard was not alone, nay, he had a goodly number of companions and some stood, their cocks in varying states of rigidity in their hands. The man taking her shuddered and his thrusting ceased as *le petit mort* took him and he gushed into her.

I felt Avery's hand tight on my arm, but I didn't dare move. The guard seemed to desire to languish in his position, and I knew the sublime pleasure of feeling my own ardor cool as a sword quenched in oil; the pleasure of growing soft inside a woman.

His compatriots found this rude and he was pulled back by a shoulder, dislodging his member. Another man, this one a burly man with a gnarled lump of a nose and a lumpy cock took his place after boxing the first in the ear. The woman gave a deep gasp as his cock plunged into her. The woman brought up her head and looked directly into my eyes, and I saw her notice.

"Imelda," Avery whispered.

"Come here, love," she said to one of the other guards, one vigorously tugging at his half-mast. "Come here and let me help you with that."

Avery gave the woman a sharp nod, that I saw this Imelda return it with little more than a squinting of her eyes and the upturn of a smile on her face. Two men both stepped forward and it seemed like they considered getting into a brawl over who was going to have her attention when she moaned to them, "Aye I have two hands and a mouth, don't be greedy, you."

I had been beaten, half starved, and my thirst was great, but even now I could feel a stirring between my legs, the sheer shock of it all. I didn't think I was alone; Avery's gaze was perhaps even more intense than mine.

"We should go," I whispered. We crept past the door and paused, the man with the ugly nose sounded as if he had taken a cannonball to the gut, but a moment later found the experience pleasurable.

Avery led us to a door, unguarded, and we stepped into the moonlight. I felt like I was being born from darkness, I felt her hand in mine squeeze and I returned the squeeze, feeling a broad fool's grin grow on my face.

"Oy, you!" a man shouted. He came toward us, in his shiny black boots ire sparking in his beetle black eyes. "You aren't supposed to leave the gaol until I come to relieve you," he said.

"Terribly sorry," I replied and I drew my pistol quickly and at point blank range put the shot in him just above the belly button. He screamed and grabbed at the bloody ruin that had been his gut and fell to his knees. "I feel the urge to inform you that I resign from my position in the king's gaol." He looked up at me, his eyes filled with pain and confusion. "The reason? The appalling lack of chandeliers. Simply ghastly," I said.

"Did you really?" Avery asked, eyes wide.

"Was that wrong?" I asked, as we hurried on our way.

"I mean, yeah. You just killed that guy!"

"Men die," I said with a shrug. "'Tis the nature of living. When we are safe, you will have to explain what chandeliers have to do with this."

"Now is *so* not the time," Avery said.

"So how," I asked, "did you get here?"

"The same way you did, the Mirror Pond," she said.

"Easy then, we go back, hop through, and we're back in your time with those hot showers and the ale in glass bottles," I said.

"You make it sound so easy, we can book a B&B, then just take a pleasure craft over to Ghost Island, with a mimosa break in the middle," she said smartly and though I know it was a jest, I had no notion of her meaning.

I gestured to the row of buildings beyond the gaol and raised an eyebrow. "This is not the time for leisure."

I took her hand and I drug her away from the gaol and toward the bilge row of Charleston, the taverns and brothels. There was attention building near the front of the nearest inn, shouting and certainly some interest in the pistol shot I'd let loose. A few whores had come out to watch the commotion.

"Aye there, lovie," one called out to us as we approached. "What's the fuss?"

"Seems like there is an escape attempt," I said. "To be sure it is quite the spectacle." Several others came forward and I pointed in the direction of growing noise.

"Were you hurt?" one of the whores asked, touching the blood stain on my new coat.

"Oh that? No tis from a prisoner, I…uh…killed him…" I said. There were increasing shouts and there was the sound of fighting. I pushed past the whore and into the front of the brothel, dragging Avery by the hand behind me. It was perhaps hotter inside, and the smell of floral perfume was near to overwhelming. Most of the people within seemed more interested in the oldest profession and heavy drinking.

"Is there a chance you have a room available?" I asked of the woman who was working the bar. She was older than the working girls, her hair streaked with white, but her bosom was pushed up no less than any of the others.

"We've got room, you and your friend wanting to share a girl, or one for each of you?" she asked.

"No, I would just see the room, and make a discrete exit," I said.

"I think not," she said. There was a scream and the door was kicked open. Several men in red coats came through the breach, one carrying a musket.

"I'll show myself up," I said, and grabbed one of the dusky green bottles from the top of the bar, whirled on my foot and sent the bottle flying through the air. The bottle struck one of the guards in the face and he went down bonelessly. The bottle bounced away from him and struck a table and burst, showering two whores and their prospective client with wine and bits of glass. The common room exploded in a roar of anger and as quick as that it was fists and improvised cudgels. The men looking for pleasure had no love for these men of the king interrupting their leisure.

"This way?" I asked, pointing toward a set of stairs near the end of the bar.

"Get out!" the proprietress shouted.

"That's my plan, so if you please?" I asked and grabbed two more bottles. I threw another one toward the guards, and missed, but they ducked as if I had thrown a grenade into their midst. *Cowardly land-lubbers,* I thought as I shoved Avery toward the stairs.

We mounted them two and three at a time, and it was rather fortunate that when we reached the top that the nearest door flew open and a man came darting out. He was a guardsman of some importance, judging by the decoration of his unbuttoned coat. He was unarmed, and without trousers, and being startled, very easy to throw down the stairs into the arms of his compatriots.

We ducked into the room he had very recently occupied and found it still was. A pair of women, nude, stared at us with large eyes. "Brace the door," I said, and crossed the room to the window. I heard the scrape of furniture across the floor, while I was forcing the window open. The fresh breeze blowing through was *glorious.*

"Come, Avery," I said, as I stepped out the window onto a narrow ledge. It was a steep drop for certain, but it was much wider than the yardarm that I dangled from a not so long time ago. Her eyes grew large, but I helped her out onto the ledge and she pressed close to me. I ached for her, but this was certainly not the time.

We crossed the span of the roof, leaped to the gable of another building and went across it as well. As we made our way through what could be seen as the rigging of Charleston, we became aware of the growing clamor in the streets. Groups of soldiers were leaving the docks and rushing toward the gaol, while some people seemed to be most interested in leaving that particular patch of townscape with a similar rush. Some were heaving bosomed serving women and whores, the young craftspeople of the area, and other such innocents. The rest wore the filthiest of clothes and some were still wearing the king's finest black irons. From our vantage point we were well above the swirl of the growing fray, and most of these landlubbers didn't have the sense to crane their necks up to look above the street level.

"Do you have a plan?" Avery asked as we took a bit of shelter against a brickwork chimney.

"Oh, a delightful one," I said. "Cause mayhem and ride it out like a ship in full sail before the storm."

"That sounds like a *terrible* plan, if you can even call it that," she said.

"Storms, especially the big ones, push the water before them," I said.

"Storm surge, yes they do. That doesn't really apply here… or at least I'm not following."

"A storm is a storm, and that is a hell of a squall down there," I said. "The prisoners are loose, the guards are not just looking for me, they're trying to contain *all* the king's guests. We add some more to that and we can blow this squall to a full-on hurricane and ride away like a seagull on the bow wind."

"What can you *possibly do* to make this worse?" Avery asked.

"Fire?" I said.

"You can't burn down Charleston!" she said sharply.

"Why not? It would improve the smell," I said. She rolled her beautiful blue eyes heavenward.

"Okay, you get a point for the smell thing, but a lot of innocent people could get hurt and die," she said seriously. "Lose their homes, and for what?" I waved the notion away.

"I have no intention of burning homes and craftsmen shops, I mean to strike there," I said, pointing toward the *Norrington*.

"You're going to set *the Norrington* on fire?"

"I'm going to try, because if it is on fire, they will be more pressed to put the fire out with an eye toward fixing the damage, rather than to pursuing us. I would also that they not pursue us in a thirty-six-gun frigate."

"Have you done something like this before?" she asked.

"Of course," I said. "Twice. Once in Barbados, we stole aboard Black Sam's cutter and slashed lines and stole his stores of liquor. The second time in Tripoli, some Barbary brute who had a notion of capturing ships and selling their crews to the Ottomans. Set that ship ablaze in the harbor. She burned to the gunwales and sank."

"Oh, well... okay then," she said.

An entire troop of red-coated men through the streets below us at a trot, and I recognized a few of them, their coats were torn, and some of them were still bearing bandages from their harsh encounter with my men. The marines from the *Norrington* had been called for and were heading toward the gaol.

"Ah, and there is our signal," I said. We found a path to the ground, dismounting to the street, and my legs nearly went out from under me when I landed. Avery caught me and kept me from falling. I thanked her as I regained my footing. My shoulder throbbed angrily, and I kept my off arm tucked close to my body as we moved through the undulating sea of people in the streets.

The way onboard the *Norrington* was easy, there were but a few marines left on the ship, mostly meant to oversee the remaining men who had been working at restocking her provisions, though most of them had vacated their posts.

A commotion in town was a good reason to run off to see what the fuss was, or to dash across the dockside avenue to one of the taverns for some of the continental whiskey or gin.

"Oy! You there," one of the remaining crewmen shouted. "Fight's the other way, the lieutenant himself gave the order."

"Name yourself, sir!" I shouted back.

"Mister Connelly, sir," the man replied. "Quartermaster of this fine ship."

"Mister Connelly, I commend your vigilance at remaining at your post, sir," I called as I mounted the gangplank and traversed the deck toward him. Avery came along close behind me, my shadow if you will. "I will have you know that I have captured one of the escapees from the gaol and will lock this scallywag in the brig here, if that is pleasing to you."

"We're not fit for prisoners," he said. "What with all the marines gone ashore."

"Is the captain still aboard? Or the king's man, Goodchilde?" I asked.

"No and aye, sir. Captain Everett is ashore in the audience of the governor or mayor, some important man with a great white wig and two daughters ugly as a donkey's arse. Mister Goodchilde *is* still aboard and doesn't plan on leaving the ship until such time as we return to England."

"Who's that prisoner that follows you like a mate?" Connelly asked.

"Eamon Bligh," I said. "Escaped and returned to the ship on his own recognizance."

"I don't remember Bligh having quite the sweet face," Connelly said, giving Avery a hard look.

"Oh, that isn't Mister Bligh, my good man. *I* am," I said. He jerked his head toward me just as I put my stolen boot in the middle of his gut and sent him head over tail down the cargo hatch. I made for the captain's quarters, Avery on my heels, and kicked the door open with cutlass and pistol in hand.

Avery slipped in close behind me and I could hear her protesting the foolishness of all of this and that we should be making our escape, not running around inside the second to last place we should be. Though to her credit, she closed the door behind us, sealing Mr. Goodchilde in with his fate.

"What is the meaning of this," Goodchilde demanded, bolting to his feet. His hair was flat, greasy, and thinning. No wonder he wore a powdered wig like a little lordling.

"I believe you have my journal," I said, pistol pointed at his guts.

"Bligh... how did you escape?"

"There isn't a prison that can hold the dread pirate Bligh," I said. "Now, about my journal."

"Funny," Avery said, ducking around me and showing her face. "Actually, that'd be me. I'm how he escaped. Who're you?" she asked.

I spoke over her, "My journal, man! Where is it?" I thumbed back the hammer on my pistol to emphasize my position. Goodchilde, to his credit, paled but remained firm.

"I… I don't have it."

"Dude, last chance! My man wants his book back, now where is it?" Avery shouted in her captain's commanding voice. She pointed her small black pistol at Goodchilde and he looked at the compact weapon confused by it, rather than threatened.

"Captain Everett has taken it to the governor's manse, for safe-keeping," Goodchilde said. I pressed toward him, forcing him back against the wall of the cabin and now that the positions were switched, he seemed much the smaller of us. I ran him through with my cutlass, with such force that the blade passed through his body and stuck true into the frame of the ship.

Goodchilde made a gasping, groaning noise and clawed at my arm, eyes wide with the shock of being skewered.

I tugged twice and then abandoned the blade, its work was done. I saw a much finer replacement for it at any rate. "Mister Good-childe." I picked up the silver chased slender blade, its scabbard like-wise silvered and traced with gilt from where it hung on the back of his chair. "Would this be Everett's sword, or perhaps yours?" The man glared murder at me as the front of his clothing darkened with his own blood.

"Give it to me and I'll show you," he said with a cutting glare.

"It's the captain's I would reckon. You seem like the sort who carries a pistol and gives his orders to others, never handles the steel himself. You can keep that cutlass, it's a fine if plain weapon and has served me well. This one I will have in its stead." I picked up the bottle of brandy from the corner of his table and knocked his oil lamp over tipping it among his papers and ledgers. The oil spilled and quickly lit the gathered papers and parchments he had been working over. I saw the seal of the South Seas Trading Company and felt a tingle of satisfaction as it was consumed by the flames.

"Give Mr. Forsythe my kindest regards," I said ruthlessly before dragging Avery with me from the room.

We mounted the stairs to the deck two at a time, and Avery hissed at me, "Was that all really necessary?"

"Aye, it was. What would it avail us if I were to burn my journal while it was on this ship?" I asked. "Would a wee stripe of a girl find my diary in an old plantation library if it were burned up this night?"

"Oh, shit. I didn't even think of that," she said softly, voice holding a softening of the steel in her resolve. "You surprise me."

"I surprise a great many people," I admitted. "Myself included."

"Your sword," she said.

"Aye, you said it was in a museum, which means that it should be left here as well," I said.

"If you burn the ship, though…" she said.

"It's in the harbor and those cannons won't burn, they will dig them out of the mud if they have to, I'm not worried," I said. I took a long pull of the brandy and it was a surprisingly good vintage. I handed the bottle to Avery. She shook her head. "How much is a bottle of 1731 brandy worth in what year was is, 2016?"

"A few thousand dollars, or more," she admitted and took a drink from the bottle herself. "Although that's some good shit. It's not gonna make it back with us." I chuckled and we made for the way up to the deck.

On the deck, there was a commotion as some of the crew had returned as well as a number of marines, they seemed worse for the wear, but were still armed and outnumbered the two of us easily. Several of the crewmen were at work pulling Connelly out of the cargo hold. His arm was broken, held tight to his side, but he pointed at us with his good one.

"Aye! That's the pirate, in the red! That's him that threw me down the hold!" he shouted. I brandished pistol and my new sword and cursed myself for not reloading my second pistol before returning to the deck.

The marines who had returned laughed and started to circle around us, their confidence high as they clearly outnumbered us so.

"Who's this chippy?" one of the marines asked, waving his musket and bayonet toward Avery. She raised her pistol and fired. The sound was louder than I expected and near smokeless, the man collapsed backwards and I felt a stab of regret. Too soon for firing her shot. To everyone's great surprise she faced the next man and fired again. Her pistol barked and barked again, as she released a hailstorm of shot across the deck of the ship, cutting down and wounding a great number of men.

"That's cheating!" a man shouted from behind a stack of crates. His gun was discarded and he had been injured. Avery dropped to a knee, and some device came popping out of the grip of her pistol. Dread overtook me as I thought the weapon destroyed. She clapped some sort of replacement where it had come from and depressed some component with her thumb. A piece of the top of the weapon jerked forward, and she raked another volley of gunfire at a group of marines who were heading toward the gangplank of the ship, sending some to the ground, and the rest fleeing in terror.

"Now what, lover boy?" she asked, pushing some dislodged golden hair out of her face.

"Those pony kegs there, those are black powder, for the cannons. We light them up, and the *Norrington* won't be going anywhere for a while, and the port will be slightly occupied with a ship fire, allowing us to slip out unnoticed," I said.

"That's almost romantic," she said. "A sail at sunrise, I mean."

"You are strange, sometimes," I replied. "But we should leave, unless you have enough wonder in that pistol to take out the entire guard." I kicked a few stray pistols away from reaching hands and stepped on a few extended fingers.

Avery moved quickly, snapping the pistol around in sharp movements, fired a few more times, and stopped at the gangplank. She looked back at me as I knocked several kegs of powder over, breaking one in the process. I pointed the muzzle of my pistol into the spilled powder and fired. The flash lit the powder and it went up in a crackling sizzle of heat. I bolted from sudden and growing flame and waved for Avery to depart as well.

We ran down the gangplank while the deck of the ship filled with shouting and then a surge of men in various states of injury trying, themselves, to disembark with the greatest haste possible. Most departed by jumping or dragging themselves over the side.

The smart ones leaped over the far side of the ship, into the harbor. Those who had more panic than sense leaped from the dock side of the ship, and they found that the wood and stone of the dock itself made for a poor cushion. One actually hit hard and then fell back between the ship and dock before vanishing into the water.

I pointed with my pistol, picking out a small fisherman's vessel, a single mast and sail, and manageable enough that it could be rowed if need be.

We were near the small vessel when the magazine of the *Norrington* caught fire and went up. The ship lifted out of the water, and her back broke, sending a great spew of fire and black smoke into the sky. It began to rain splinters of wood, bits of rope, and tattered confetti that had formerly been the furled sails.

"Right, that's the first time I've actually done *that*," I said, looking back at the pillar of black smoke blocking out the stars that marked the grave of the *Norrington*. Large pieces of the ship were scattered across the dock, and a number of windows were cracked and broken along the street. People slowly rose to their feet, seemingly dazed by the demise of the frigate. A cannon had been deposited into a rank of red-coated guards, their bodies crushed under it, but a few regained their feet and I recognized one.

It was the man with the great ugly nose, and the lumpy cock who last time we had seen him, had been distracted by the wiles of Imelda. He was uninjured, as were a few of his comrades. They had the coats not of marines, but of the gaol guards. I knew some of them, not by name, but by the shape of their fists or the bottoms of their boots. I had no love for any of these cruel men. He pointed at us and gave a bark, and the men who remained uncrushed by cannon or broken mast girded themselves and made a line for the two of us.

I lifted my pistol, and though at range, I figured that luck had been with me this long, so why not? I fired, and the shot went well wide of the lead guard.

"It's amazing that you can hit anything with a short-barrel smoot-bore gun," Avery said, dropping to one knee and raising her lethal black pistol. The black weapon barked its sharp and savage call and the guard's charge was turned into a rout, the leader falling, hands flying to his face as he went down.

"That's for my girl!" Avery shouted and fired several more times, sending the remaining men to the ground. We leaped from the dock to the fishing skiff, and I slashed the mooring line with the sword, and shoved us away. She ejected the strange device from the pistol and slammed another such in its place. "This is the last clip," she said, depressing the switch that allowed the top of the pistol to slide forward. "We need to make this one last."

Few dared to approach the edge of the dock as I raised the single sail and swung the yardarm so that it caught the harbor breeze. We were small and light enough that I needn't concern myself with the tide, or overly much with the current. We sat on top of the water more than down in it in a craft such as this. After a few minutes, when there was no obvious pursuit, Avery relaxed and stowed the pistol in her belt.

"A weapon of sheer terror," I mentioned as she took a place near the yardarm.

"I'll get you one when we get back to my time and teach you how it works," she promised.

"Do you know how to sail?" I asked, focused on our current present rather than our future for the time being. She stripped out of my butchered garb until she was wearing naught but her modern woman's coverings, scant as they were. Without a word, she took to the ship, and I knew this was not her first time with sail or rope. She caught me eyeing her weapon and she grinned.

"It's just a plain pistol, a few hundred years newer than yours," she said as she moved about the vessel coiling and tying off line. "And yes, I've been on a sailboat or two."

We let the wind and the waves carry us away from Charleston and along the coast. Avery knew the way better than I and she told me about how often they had taken a power boat from a similar port, though in her time they were arrived at what they named Fade Island in but a few hours' time thanks to something called the internal combustion engine. She also spoke of how much was different between now and then, how the coastline was changed in some ways but in others remained largely the same. I agreed, the sea was like that, it might never stop moving, but it never changed.

She produced some curious sweet bars from her small pack, the last of them, she confessed, as if I knew what they were. We found no provisions on the fisherman's skiff, but in truth, expected none.

We rested. The sail and the wind did the work and keeping a hand on the rudder was easy enough. I slept some, grateful to be out of the worn boots and bloody jacket. I quite enjoyed when I took the rudder and she rested some as well. She was stunning to look at, even wearing days of filth and weariness. Almost as if sensing my gaze, she removed the bralette top and stretched out on the bow of the small ship.

The boat bobbed on the water, and it seemed like there was nothing left in the world but the two of us and the wind. "You're staring," she said after a while.

"Aye, the scenery is very nice," I said.

"My scenery isn't too bad," she said. "Overdressed, but not bad." I obliged her by stripping off the dirty remnant of a shirt I had worn for far too many days.

"Better?" I asked.

"Better," she replied with a narrow-eyed smile. "How's that shoulder?"

"They tended it well, removed the shot and bandaged me proper."

"Let me see," she ordered and crawled to me. She loosened the bandages and inspected the wound, doing a curious thing and sniffing it.

"Doesn't smell bad, looks like it's healing. I think you're in the clear for infection."

"I see," I said as she rebandaged me and returned to the bow of the boat.

After a few minutes, she slipped out of more of her clothing, until she wore nothing but her smallclothes and a smile. I raised an eyebrow as she stretched like some cat, her breasts raised in praise to the sun, skin glistening with sweat. I felt myself becoming uncomfortably stiff. I unbuttoned the rags that had once been the blue trousers and discarded them. My ardor, though covered, was obvious. Her eyes traced a line down my chest that I could almost feel, and I saw a flick of pink tongue across her lips as she spied my manhood. I had seen similar expressions on captains as they decided that some continental merchantman was going to get the sword and cannon treatment.

I felt my own gaze intensify as she dipped one of her slim hands inside her small clothes. My armor came to its fullness, and soon began to ache as I watched. She sighed and moaned, her eyes smoldering on my chest and arms as her fingers moved in a secret dance against her own pleasure. I squeezed my cock and felt it throb. "How's the scenery now?" she asked.

"Tis a sight so pleasurable that it is near to painful," I said. She gave me one of her wicked fallen angel smiles.

"Painful, that's terrible," she said. "Maybe you should do something about that." I stood and removed the smallclothes I wore and felt a surge of relief as I came free from the confining garments. She made a noise of approval and removed her own smallclothes. I saw the flash of pink, her lady garden most inviting. I approached, bracing the rudder in place but not horribly caring about our heading at the moment.

"Dirty pirate," she said, and gestured for me to come closer. I did, until I stood nearly over her, the shadow of my cock silhouetted against the firmness of her belly. Her fingers continued their dance, teasing her womanhood and parting her lips. She gestured for me to kneel, to come closer. As I did, she reached up and grabbed me about the cock, her grip firm. I stifled a groan in my belly, and I dripped from just her touch.

She started tugging, and my groan could not be stifled, it could not be held in any longer. She made her own moans, eyes glued to my manhood. I mounted her, she guided me inside, squeezing all the right places with her hands. I shuddered as she took my full measure.

As I gave her all the passion I had, she wrapped me in her legs, and in her arms. She held me as fiercely as her cunt gripped me. She gasped, and her fingers dug into my back and neck. There was nothing left of my mind other than her singing in my ear and the vigor we shared between our legs.

I sought her kisses and stole them between moans and gasps. I found her buttocks and grabbed them, using them for more leverage, so that I could give her everything I had, *everything.*

I felt my pleasure coming, and hers was on the verge of crashing around her. It felt like tunneled vision, my perception fading out so that there was nothing but her thighs around me, her fingers on my sides, my cock inside her, her so wet and so hot. She bucked and grabbed a fistful of my hair, and I felt her spasm around my cock. I held, I held for dear life and it was a tremendous effort.

"I love you," I rasped, my lips pressed against her neck.

My sack and shaft seemed to turn to light and fire and I felt my seed explode inside her. For a small eternity I hung above her, her body wrapped around mine. Ages seemed to pass, pure and perfect bliss, and then the pulse would come again and more seed would erupt from me. She took it, and her voice was angelic, a choir of fulfilled passion.

Le petit mort.

I died, and as I died, I was reborn.

We lay together for a while, our hearts racing and breathing rapid, but slowing as we regained out winds and wits. "Eamon," she whispered. "Is this real?"

"Aye, tis real," I said, after what felt like too long of a pause. I myself wondered if this was real. Part of me thought it had all gone too well and that we should have been caught or killed a dozen times. A more rational part reminded me that this was very much real, and with some deep regret, I was about to be parted from her, as she released my softened manhood.

"Did we really do that; did we really blow up a ship and escape?" she asked. "I feel like I'm dreaming."

"This is no dream, and aye, we did do those things. I do apologize about the lack of a chandelier, though I am not sure there are any in Charleston." I said softly. She smiled at that. I wrapped her in my arms and didn't feel so weary. She sighed and pulled herself down into my embrace and I was only aware of her pressed against me, and the steady creak and snap of the boat as it went its merry way.

CHAPTER TWENTY-THREE

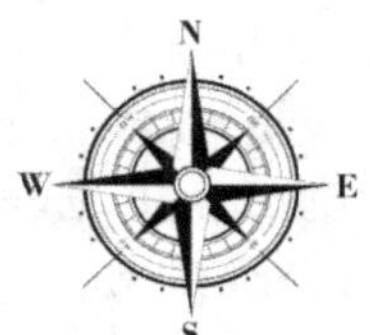

*A*very Barker…

He cracked me up. One mention of a chandelier and it was like he was stuck on it. I couldn't wait to get us back to *Fade Isle* and to my own century so I could show him all the piratey swash-buckling flicks from old Hollywood to modern day, from Errol Flynn to Johnny Depp.

Still, we needed to talk about some things first.

"Eamon?" I asked and he made a noncommittal noise to let me know he was listening.

"Mm?"

"Why did you leave?" I asked softly. "Was it something I did?"

He lifted his head from my chest, his ear pressed between my breasts, over my heart.

"Aye," he said carefully.

"Was it because I didn't want to believe Kurt had tried to kill me?" I asked, swallowing hard.

"Part of it," he answered carefully and wouldn't look at me.

"What else?" I asked, knowing full well that whatever he had to say, was likely about to hurt a great deal.

"Why did you not see fit to tell me how I met my end? To tell me of my sweet sister's fate?" he asked, and I closed my eyes.

Fuck. I am the asshole, here, I thought to myself.

"I was too far up my own ass," I said and he frowned in puzzlement. "Figure of speech," I said softly, raking back some of his hair off his forehead, running my fingers through it.

"I was so caught up in finding the gold and doing right by my dad and my crew I didn't even think about it," I said. He stared at me, eyes like pale emeralds which were typically so expressive, suddenly unreadable except for one thing: *go on.*

"It wasn't fair, and I'm sorry. It was a shitty way to treat you and I feel awful."

"Tell me," he said, swallowing hard. "Is my sweet Emma truly lost to me?"

I felt my eyes well, the vision of him grow blurry as I broke the news with a nod at first, "She died sometime at the end of 1730, as far as the plantation ledgers said. Cause listed was 'childbirth' that was it; there wasn't anymore. She's gone, baby. I wouldn't lie to you about that. I haven't lied to you about *anything* and I'm so sorry if I've made you feel like I have. Believe me, if there was a way, if she was alive, I'd go with you to get her come hell or high water – but there's not. I'm sorry."

He searched my face, nodded, bowed his head, and wept while I held him and I felt my heart break all over again with his.

"Thank you," he said when he'd regained his composure.

"For what?" I asked, sniffing.

"For being brave enough to tell me the painful truth," he said, laying a kiss in the center of my palm. "And for being wild enough to follow me back in time to save me from my own folly."

I smiled then and with a small laugh said, "Hopefully, the next time we decide to do something this monumentally stupid, we do it as a team."

He smiled at me then and asked, "Do you think there is a place for an old pirate in your modern times?"

I grinned and said, "Oh, aye. As long as that place is with me."

He grinned too and laughed, nodding, and said, "Agreed."

It took more time getting back to the island than it had to come from it thanks to some fallow seas. The calm was annoying, but we were determined, switching off and rowing for all we were worth until we were exhausted and the other took over to allow the other a rest.

Eamon was the star of our two man show, using the very stars at night to get us back on course. During the day, he used the position of the sun, and I cursed myself a fool for not thinking to bring a fucking compass, but who needed one with the likes of Eamon Bligh at the helm? He was truly impressive, absolutely magnificent, and I had to admit to myself and to him how absolutely in love with him that I was.

I mean, would I have honestly come back to the year 1731, chased all the way after him two hundred and eighty-five years into the past, if I didn't love him?

No.

At least, I didn't think so.

Still, I worried about Mac and the rest of my crew in the future. Worried about what Mac told them. Worried if the gold was still there, how much had been changed, just *everything*. I didn't know how long I'd been gone and if things had devolved into chaos and all I could feel on the subject was this desperate need to get back to them all. Of course, coupled with that anxiety was the anxiety of *how much had we changed?*

I suppose I had to be comforted by the fact that my own internal knowledge hadn't deviated over much. At least not that I knew... I mean, wouldn't it have if things had been changed too drastically here in the past? If we had affected the future too terribly much, I would know about it, right? Or would I?

I mean, as far as I knew, Eamon's sword was still in the museum in 2016. His journal had still led me to the treasure on Fade Isle, the

Isle was still a wildlife preserve, the caves were still flooded… all of the things required to bring me to this point were in play, but I still didn't fully understand *how*.

That was okay, though, I guess. It was definitely a good thing Eamon had thought of all that he did while we were in Charleston. I certainly hadn't been thinking of his cutlass, or about where his journal had ended up. I'd only been thinking about him, and myself, which *clearly* was something I needed to work on.

Priorities, woman.

I mean, there was still the whole problem of getting us back to the future.

I giggled as I always did when I thought that phrase in my head and Eamon looked up from where he pulled the oars smoothly through the glassy sea.

"Do not tell me the sun has driven you to madness," he said with a crooked grin.

God, he is so achingly handsome when he smiles at me like that, I couldn't help but think.

"No, just remind me when we get back home to play the movie *Back to the Future*, in addition to all the pirate movies and shows I have in store for you."

"Movies?" he asked, drawing out the word slowly.

"Magic spy box," I said, and he nodded slowly.

"You can watch dramas and plays, in them, but it's like nothing you've ever seen. Trust me," I told him. "You'll like it."

"I have no doubt," he said and the way he looked at me soothed my restless soul.

What soothed it even further was spotting *land* behind my man. I perked up as he pulled the oars through the water and the line on horizon grew slightly in height and greened out, fluffing up with the resolution of that greenery into a canopy of trees.

"Land, ho!" I cried excitedly and Eamon frowned at me.

"What?" He twisted in his seat and the crease in his sunburned forehead smoothed out. We were seriously hurting for water and were definitely crispy critters from almost two days and more of damn near relentless sun exposure.

We'd been lucky that this was a fishing boat and that we'd been able to catch supper last night, carefully cooking the fish practically a bite at a time over the boat's lone lantern's flame.

We needed fresh water and calories if we were going to survive and thankfully, the island in front of us had both. We just had to get to it.

As exhausted as we both were, the sight of Fade Isle, or Ghost Island as Eamon called it, renewed our vigor. We continued switching off, but our rowing had become more frantic, more frenzied, the closer the island loomed.

I fully admit to flopping on the sand and kissing the earth, Eamon laughing at me the whole while.

"Save your kisses for me, my siren."

"I have plenty for both you and this island," I said breathlessly, before getting up and helping him to haul the fishing vessel onto the shore.

"What do you think?" I asked, panting. "All the way into the tree line?"

"Aye, and keep your pistol handy, love. We've naught any notion on if they've left a fair bit of red coat behind or no."

"Aye, aye, Captain Bligh. You make a good point."

We hauled the boat across the sand, the both of us struggling with the careened vessel to get it into the tree line. Eamon using his fancy upgraded sword to slash down vegetation to camouflage the stern of the ship from prying eyes on approach from the sea.

We took a well-deserved break in the marginally cooler shade of the overhead jungle canopy and too soon, my man got to his feet and declared, "Come, we must get to a water supply or this will all be for nothing. Too soon we will be too weak to do anything."

"Find me some damn fruit or something on the way, and you got yourself a deal, Mister Bligh." He chuckled as he hauled me up onto my feet.

"Downgraded from Captain to Mister already?" he asked.

I snorted. "The captain's life honestly still for you?" I asked. A darkness passed through his eyes and I felt like a heel, knowing as I did that he thought on his lost crew. All dead at the hands of the king's men.

"Nae, my love," he said. "Nae, tis not."

"I figured," I said softly. "I'm sorry I brought it up in such a callous way." I put my arms around him and he held me tight. We stood like that for long moments, cuddling in the shade, taking an extended, but still too-short moment to softly grieve in the heat and humidity of the island's oppressive atmosphere.

"Come, my lady. Let us return to the caverns, it is our best defensible position should the king's men try to find us."

"Agreed," I said. "You sure kicked the hornet's nest back in Charleston. I wouldn't be surprised if they came after us."

Eamon chuckled darkly and said, "It was but what they deserved."

I shook my head, "They deserved a whole hell of a lot more than what we pulled off now that I think back on it, but we did what we could."

My heart was heavy with his story about his capture and his treatment at the hands of those monsters. At the treatment of his men and how they died... I followed him readily into the jungle as he occasionally slashed his way through the overgrowth to get us where we needed to be.

I didn't mind falling back. After all, he knew 1731 Ghost Island better than I knew 2016 Fade Isle. His time, his lead. I was okay with that.

We stopped at a spring and drank the cool water greedily and we ate fruit that he swore was edible and would do us no harm along the way. The fruit wasn't something I wasn't familiar with and I would have to look it up when I got back to Google. Custard-like texture that tasted like a cross between a banana and mango, they clung to trees in clusters, green in their unripe state, yellow and brown when ready to eat, falling to the forest floor.

"How much farther?" I asked.

"A steady hill's climb that way, a good quarter of the day left. We should make it just fine by nightfall." He gestured in a direction that just held more trees, vines, and passion flowers and I would have to take his word for it that the caverns lie in that direction. It just looked like more intensely sloping jungle to me.

"This is gonna suck, isn't it?" I asked.

"Suck?" he asked quizzically.

"Yeah, uh, suck. Be terrible or shitty," I said.

"Ah, yes, this is going to suck…" he agreed, and I smiled.

"If it's even more terrible than that, it's going to suck big fat hairy donkey balls," I told him and he grinned and laughed, nodding.

"Then it is indeed going to suck an ass's balls," he said.

"Sucking ass is a whole different qualifier of awful," I said hoisting myself to my feet and he looked up at me, pushing to his as well.

"So, to suck ass is not to suck balls?" he inquired.

"Nope, two different levels of suckage," I answered, letting him take the lead again.

We talked, delightfully so, and made good headway up the mountainside.

I was hoping against hope that he was wrong and that we would reach the caverns before dark, but nope. By the time we spilled from the trees it was getting hard to see and we had to duck a few times from the swoop of waking bats pouring from the cave's mouth.

"Should we risk building a fire?" I asked.

"Aye, far enough back in the cave where no light can be a beacon for our enemies to be sure," he said.

"Okay."

We worked to gather some sticks and I followed him carefully into the cave system, not knowing precisely what to expect.

In my time, it was flooded to the top with sea water, there was a scientific explanation for why it was the way it was, even though the caverns sat well above sea level, and I knew it in the back of my mind, but something about delving into a cave with bats squeaking and flying about overhead, the smell of creatures and the knowledge that they could have left men behind, or a wild boar or some shit, I know it was silly, but *there might be bears*!

Yeah, okay, maybe not, but I would not be comfy until we had a good fire lit.

"Ah, I see nothing has been found," he said and put out a hand to stop me. I blinked and looked down into the indescribable dark of the first drop.

"What do we do?" I asked and Eamon smiled and dropped his pile of sticks into the dark.

"We see if the supplies are still intact that I and my crew stowed with the lucre."

"I'm not gonna lie," I said, mouth dry and wiping my sweaty palms on the front of the thighs of my denim shorts. "I'm blind as a fucking bat down here."

"Ah, then I would say that you're in good company, my love," he said as one squeaked overhead on its way out.

"Great," I said rolling my eyes. "How do we do this?"

"I go first, so that I might catch you if you fall."

"Eamon, that's not comforting!"

"It wasn't meant to be, it was to be the truth."

He took my armload of wood and pitched it into the maw of darkness at my feet and I hated how long it took for them to crash and rattle at the bottom.

"I don't know about this," I said uneasily, and he turned. "What about your shoulder?"

"A bit stiff, but much mended. Watch me," he said, and I scowled.

"I can barely see you!"

He laughed and picked up a rope at our feet and turned, back to the yawn of chasm below us.

He wrapped the rope just so around himself like a classic rappel line and I felt marginally better. It was, at least, something I understood, or got. I'd be lying if I said my entire being didn't crawl with uneasy nerves and nervousness his entire descent.

"Wait there!" he called. "I'll supply you some light."

God, he sounded so very far away, his voice echoing and reverberating around me from down below.

A spark, a flare of brilliance, and I peeked over the edge into a pool of golden light. Eamon stuck the flickering torch between two giant rocks to one side and set to wrapping scraps of cloth soaked in something around another stick.

"How is the light from up there?" he asked, and I turned and looked at the mouth of the cave, then back to the hole.

"Fine, I don't think you can see anything from out there, let me go check to be sure."

I checked, and I was right. I returned to the edge of the hole and smiled at the anxious look on Eamon's face, and how it smoothed out when he saw mine once more.

"We're all good," I said giving him two thumbs up.

"Not until you're in my arms once more, my siren."

"Right, guess it's my turn," I said and sighed in trepidation.

Repelling down that rock face with that rickety, creaking, eighteenth-century rope was *not* my idea of fun, even if that rope was practically new-ish considering I was *in* the eighteenth century. I definitely preferred my modern climbing ropes with their nylon fibers and stronger tensile strengths.

"Let go," he called gently. "I've got you."

If it were any other man, I wouldn't have done it, but it was *Eamon* and I trusted him. Once upon a time, I would only have trusted three people with something like that. My dad, Mac, or Kurt… it was *nice* to trust Eamon but it was still raw, still painful, that I couldn't trust Kurt like that anymore.

There were a few reasons I wasn't looking forward to returning to my own century, and that was definitely chief among them. Still, there were *way more* things I couldn't wait to get back to – such as indoor plumbing and unlimited supplies of hot water.

I was pretty sure, at this point, I was going to be spending the next *week* in a hot shower. Like, eat, sleep, and revel in a bubble bath bliss for a solid seven days and seven nights. I could not *wait* to be home for that.

"Are you well, my lady?"

I turned. "Yeah. Just tired," I answered. "Mind's getting away from me."

"Let go, let me catch you, we are almost to our rest," Eamon declared, and I nodded.

"Okay, here I go!" I let go, made a girly squeak as the stabilizing factor of the rope left my hands and I caught air. Eamon caught me at my back and behind my knees with a grunt and I put my arms around him. He pressed his forehead to mine, and I closed my eyes and took a moment to relish in the strength of his arms around me, the strength with which he held onto me making me feel safe like I hadn't felt since I was a child.

"I love you," I uttered spontaneously and the smile he graced me with in the firelight told me everything I needed to know about us. That there would most definitely *be* an *us* and I was so here for it.

I laid my hand along the side of his face, pressed my mouth to his, and kissed him soundly as he let my body slide against his, setting me down and onto my feet.

We kissed like that, safe, secure for the time being in the pit, and I sighed in utter contentment.

"Come, I wish to show you the cathedral," he whispered against my mouth and I nodded.

"Okay."

We gathered our firewood and I worried about how bad the smoke would be if we lit an actual fire down here. I mean, it was *significantly* cooler in the caves, enough to make me shiver the deeper we went, but would the smoke be able to sufficiently vent and since wild animals weren't a concern down here, should we even light one?

These thoughts went through my mind as we carried a bundle each under one arm and lit our way with a torch with the other.

"No, not that way," he said, and I paused, looking up and around and nodded.

"Sorry, you're right," I said. "It looks so different out of the wat —" I froze mid-sentence and looked at Eamon.

"If the caves are dry now, how does the lucre go undiscovered and how do the caverns be under water in your time? Aye, hence why I say not that way. The powder stores from the *Honor's Price* lay that way, would be folly to bring flame to them."

"Oh, shit. You've thought a lot about this, haven't you?" I asked, falling in and letting Eamon lead me down the path to the treasure cave.

"Aye, I have. Our actions now decide your future, do they not? I wish it to be a future with me in it."

"Me, too," I said, and he stopped short.

"I am glad for that, Avery. I'd not imagined a life beyond what you told me the rest of mine would be. Though once I came to know you, to know that you were real, I would do anything to claim a long life with you at my side."

"I want that too," I said breathlessly. He set the pile of firewood down and took mine from me.

"Come, you could not see the cathedral in all its splendor on your dive, too many sea plants obscured the true beauty of the crystals beneath."

I stepped into the vast cavern hand in hand with my lover, my love, and as he raised his torch, I raised mine too and cast my eyes to a ceiling full of glittering stars that resolved itself into spectacular crystalline formations.

I gasped and stood, staring in wonder, and whispered, "It's beyond imagination."

"Aye, I don't remember if I told you that my words could do it no justice," he whispered back and I tore my eyes from the crystal cavern and looked at Eamon, and fell in love even harder at the look on his face as he stared at me.

He was staring at me with no less wonder than I'd stared at the crystalline ceiling just a moment before.

"Make love to me," I whispered, practically begging, and he smiled and drove his torch into the drift of sand to one side. He took mine from me, stepping into my personal space, wrapping a solid arm about my waist and hauling me in tight, close, to his bigger body, his mouth descending to mine to claim it in a fiery kiss.

I smiled on the inside, thinking about how many historical romance covers were based on this look alone as I put my arms about him and kissed him back fervently, holding my body close in the shelter of his as he cast my torch aside carelessly to grab yet another armful of me.

I could feel him pressed close, hot, and rigid against my belly. The length of his cock like a branding iron through our scant clothing, and it became a rush to divest each other of the scraps keeping our skins separated.

All thought or worry about the caverns being too cold left me as I warmed myself against Eamon and the fires of our passion for one another. He hauled me off my feet, and I wrapped my arms around his shoulders as he pressed me back against a smooth portion of the cavern wall.

Oh, so it's like that then? I thought, smiling into our kiss as he worked his hips against mine and pressed me back against the rough, cool stone, his cock looking for purchase against the slick, velveteen wetness of my pussy lips.

I groaned into his mouth as the tip of his penis teased my throbbing clit and he wrapped strong fingers beneath my bottom, hauling me up his body just that little bit more. His cock found my entrance, and I moaned as he brought me down over the top of him, my body sinking down onto his erection slowly.

He was so thick, so smooth, the girth of him filling me out and pressing against my walls and teasing sparks of pleasure to life as he moved inside me.

I clung to him, his little spider monkey, wrapping my legs around his lean hips as he worked them back and forth, plunging his full length up inside of me, letting gravity do half the work as I slid down his shaft to meet each thrust halfway.

God, he felt good.

I tipped my head back and panted and moaned his name as he made fierce love to me against the cavern wall, his lips and tongue working the sweet spot on the side of my neck, as he added just the sweetest edge of teeth to set fireworks off in my blood.

"Oh, God! Eamon! Don't stop, please don't stop!"

"Never, my siren, my beauty," he ground out, breath hot against my ear.

I stared at the wonder of the ceiling of crystal above our heads, reached out and gripped a chunk jutting from a formation near my right hip and held on as he worked me to a beautiful crescendo, my orgasm peaking, my voice echoing back at us, a thin wail of utterly devastating pleasure pinging through the crystals above and around us as I came around him with the suddenness and ferocity of a lightning strike to earth.

The chunk of rock I'd grabbed onto in our fervor bit into my palm and crumbled off its base into my hand and I swore I was going to keep it forever, just like I would have Eamon keep me, if he would have me, until our dying day.

I was willing to commit to this man and only this man that hardcore. He was, after all, the man of my dreams.

"Oh, Avery," he whispered harshly next to my ear as his breathing calmed and the sweat on our skins cooled in the cavern air. "How I love you."

"God, I love you, too, Eamon," I murmured back and guided his lips back to mine with a hand on his face, the reddish gold scruff of his cheeks tickling against my palm.

"I would make you my wife, if you would have me," he murmured and I drew back, smiling from ear to ear.

"I thought you would never ask," I said and kissed him vigorously. He pulled back, checked my face, and laughed, spinning me out beneath the crystals and whooped, the sound of his joy echoing back at us as I clung to him, hopefully, for the rest of time.

I laughed with him, the joy in my heart unmatched. Eamon Bligh was absolutely my greatest treasure find of *all* time.

CHAPTER TWENTY-FOUR

Eamon Bligh...

I toyed with the name in my mind, Avery Bligh, or maybe Barker-Bligh? Her new time had new customs. Certainly not Bligh-Barker, that brought to mind the image of a circus barker, shouting but with the consumption. It had not been a week; it had been the better part of a *year*. In the span of less than seven days I had gone from capture to a prisoner on the brink of despair, to destroying a frigate of the King's Navy, killing an important man of the South Seas Trading Company, and finally taking flight in a stolen boat to become engaged, as it were.

There would need to be a suitable ring, a jewel to match the beauty of my siren, and that should be easy enough to acquire in her future time, since the lucre would still be there. That nagged, that the caves were flooded in her time, but not in mine. It was a curious thing, that.

The answer was obvious, but the real question was *how*? The caves were flooded because we were going to flood them, to keep the captain of the ill-fated *Norrington* and the rest of the king's men from using my journal to return and find the gold. After all, Goodchilde had spoken the contents of my book aloud in the presence of the captain, and though I doubted the man could decipher my journal on his own as Goodchilde had, he didn't really need to. Goodchilde had made great fanfare and flourish by naming the location of the lucre to these caverns. Which brought me back to the present... or future, really. How to flood these tunnels.

The water depth was important, it was what protected the gold, at least until the future and its breathing devices allowed for treasure hunters like Avery and her crew to dive deep into the flooded caverns to find it. There was enough black powder to make a large explosion, aye, that was true. There was uncut fuse in the supplies, and there was also a great amount of sail cloth and pitch, that could be used to ignite the packed powder; to force it to bang instead of just burn.

The stockpile itself, oh that had been a Godsend. The food stores were still good, and after our passionate confessions of love and desire we had eaten well of them. It was no lord's feast, for certain, but after my stay on the king's hospitality, and her time stowed away, salted beef and pork, cured fish, and hard biscuits were a Christmas feast. As much temptation as there had been to indulge heavily in the casks of rum, as cheap stuff as it was, we showed more restraint that I had thought possible.

Was this what love and a honeymoon were to a married man? To a normal man who lived his life not by wits, steel, and pistol. Such a life could be wonderful, yes? Yes, it could. I wandered the cave and finding no new things to aid us in our plotting, returned to my rightful and God-given place next to my siren and slept again.

Time passes strangely in caverns, with no celestial bodies to mark its natural progression. The bowels of the earth remain the same temperature and I was sure there could come a hurricane and this deep? We would be none the wiser. I was sore and stiff from sleeping on a raft of canvas unfurled on the rocks, and found Avery awake. She sat with a torch, her eyes on the vaulted wonder that was the cathedral.

"Imagine, the two most beautiful things in the world, both in the same place at the same time," I said. She gave me a smile and her eyes sparkled.

"Flatterer," she said. "Silver tongued pirate."

"Guilty, my angel, my siren," I said, and gave a half bow.

"We have to get back to my time, the future," she said.

"You have movies to show me," I said.

"How do we do that?" she asked with a rueful smile.

"The same we've done it each time, through the Mirror Pond when the moonlight is on it," I said, "With intent in our hearts." I added, tapping a fist to my chest.

"That's it?" she asked.

"Well, that's how I've done it. To be fair and honest, we might be the only two time travelers in either of our times," I said. "And we've both made the voyage now. That is not my immediate concern, however."

"What is your concern then," she asked.

"The caves flood between now and your time, but there is no reason that I can see other than us. Some of these caves are above the tide, are they not?" She nodded. "If this is so, how has the water gotten in, and where?"

"I actually have the answer to that. The how is, obviously now, that we blow a fucking hole in the rocks to flood the chambers out. As for the where? There have been flow tests done in the future, before even my time on the island, where previous expeditions found the channel that the sea water flows through. Then there was something about hydraulic pressure, the tide pushing the water in and how there are chambers and channels beyond these and the way that they formed keeps the water trapped so that yes, while the water level fluctuates with the tides, inside the caves the water level rises and falls with it, but only a few inches. Something about an air dome, and drainage rates, it was all very scientific," she said.

"Do you recall where this channel inflow is?" I asked.

"Vaguely," she said.

"The caves flood because we flood them," I said. "If we don't, Captain Everett of the *Norrington* is still alive, and Goodchilde was able to break my code and cipher and told the man the location of the gold... If the two of us can rappel down here so easily, nothing will stop the king's men from doing it themselves; and if there is no lucre, no gold to be found? Then by extension, there is no reason for young Avery Barker to ever come to my folly of an island," I finished.

"Causality," she said thoughtfully.

"If you say so, aye," I agreed.

"Time traveler's bane," she said. "Everything we do here and now will affect the future, but in this case if we don't flood caverns, then we never meet, and if we never meet, then neither of us travel through time, and nothing in the past is changed. If we do flood the caverns, well," she spread her hands to either side of her shapely hips. "Then here we are. It's one big circle at this point."

"Be all that as it may, we flood the cave, give the lucre in Davy Jone's keeping, and we go back to your home with bottled beer and hot showers and spy boxes. Once there, the king cannot follow us, and bears us no threat." I said.

"You make it sound so easy," she said with a half-smile on her lips.

"Navigation is navigation, and it's just about getting where you want to be," I said. "A good navigator makes it easy; a bad navigator gets you lost or wrecked."

"Maybe it *is* that easy," she admitted. "All in all, you're an *exceptional* navigator so I'll follow your lead. What do we do?"

We took a breakfast of more dried ship's stocks, with a surprise being found by way of a bag of dried apricots and some biscuits that were slightly less hard than stone. As we ate this tooth resistant breakfast, Avery told me of the eateries of her time, and all the different cultures and cuisines that were available.

To my defense, I had known of most of the nations she spoke of, though had seen few enough of them even in my own travels. She seemed most genuinely surprised that though ignorant of some continental cuisines, that the curries and spice of the East Indies and India were known to me. The only answer I could produce over a rasher of salt dried pork was that India was open to the crown, and the Italians were less tractable to the king.

Surveying the caverns on foot took longer than Avery expected, she knew the caverns, this was true, but by her own admission she had barely stepped foot in them. She was more aware of drifting through them, well above the bottom, and hanging in the middle of the chambers. The walls would be dangerous, rocks and snags to hang their lines and air hoses, or a place for bubbles to gather to further disorient divers. We eventually wound our way to a deep place, well beneath the cathedral, and it took some climbing and a bit of bravery to dare some of the tight passages to reach it.

We finally came to a spot that was different, a rough crenellation in the stone that seeped salt water in small amounts. Reaching the place had been the most difficult at the last as the gallery itself was a nest of salt crystals, some were sharp enough to draw blood from a careless handhold.

"I... I've never seen any of this," she said. Everything was coated in white, like ice had frozen the rock, some slick, most sharp.

"The ocean, she is close here," I said. "This is the place to set out charge, and opening this will flood our treasure and protect it for centuries."

We took to task the moving of the kegs of black powder into the salt gallery, and I broke a few kegs to pour the powder into the dry cracks, and then on the other kegs. When it went up, I wanted it to go up fast, a great thunder in the bowels of the island. Hours crept into a day, and we ventured up from the darkness for fresh water and to forage for more of the island's exotic fruit.

Avery spotted their tracks before I did, boot prints in the mud around the edge of the Mirror Pond. Perhaps it was complacency set upon me, but I had nothing more than a long knife in my belt, not even the sword, but Avery had been more to keeping her wits and still bore her pistol. We followed the trail around the pond and toward the seaward side of the island and found ourselves no longer alone on this damnable rock. It was no frigate or large ship of the king's armada, it was a two-masted merchantman; Dutch built by the shape of the forecastle and rigging but flying the king's colors.

"I suppose the captain of the *Norrington* has commandeered himself a new ship," I said softly.

"Determined assholes, aren't they," Avery said.

"Some men serve the king the way that the clergy wish everyone served God," I said. "Some even more so. Stay here, I'll get a higher look." I clambered my way up one of the stouter trees to survey the scrap of beach the captain had taken his ship to and tried to count his men. There might have been a half dozen redcoats on the ship, and beach. Charleston had been expensive for the king's men, it would seem.

"How much shot do you have?" I asked, descending.

"I have ten, eleven rounds left," she said. "Kurt would be disappointed in me for not having a round count."

"Mister Wallace, all things considered, should count himself proud," I said. "Your marksmanship and courage are unquestionable."

"That's still something that has to be sorted out," she said. "Things with Kurt, I mean."

"Aye, but we'll chart that course when we get to it. We've got half a dozen redcoat marines, plus possible three officers and the captain. There are crew, but they look like pressganged fishermen and not navy men, so they won't be up for a fight," I said.

"Still, that's a lot of people," she said.

"Too many, yes," I admitted. "We only have to worry if they find us and the cave. He didn't find the depths of the caverns last time," I said.

"They have your journal and your map," she said, "Cipher or not, you said that asshole gave up the goods."

I nodded. "We lay a trap for them," I said with a smile. "We won't have a repeat of the scrap on the beach."

We retreated to the cave and laid out our plans. There wouldn't be time for the making of proper villainous traps, no digging pits or setting spike traps, or deadfalls. What we did have was a number of pistols and plenty of powder and shot. I readied as many of the pistols as I dared and stuffed them in belt and bandolier, while Avery minded the entrance of the cave. The last pistols readied, I girded myself with the captain of the *Norrington*'s own blade.

"You certainly look the fearsome pirate," Avery said.

"Aye, and I feel it as well," I said. "Six pistols and a blade make any man feel like he can topple the walls of Jericho."

We looked upon one another and with a nod to indicate our ready, left the shelter of the cavern depths and took up the ready.

"This is a fool's errand," one man growled. He held a rifle and bayonet in a warding position. The men skulked behind him, hacking at the green with blade and knife. Others cursed and spat, they were as green as the flora around them, the men who had remained on the ship during the initial foray on the island, and they knew that their marine brethren had charged this hill and many of them had died and those who hadn't died had come back with grievous injuries. Their morale was low. My shot took the complainer in the span between neck and shoulder, the next shot took one of the men in the thigh.

I retreated quickly, running ahead of the screaming and shouting, and random shot fired blindly into the greenery. The entrance to the cave was waiting, and Avery kneeled with her pistol ready. I gave her a nod and tossed the two spent pistols toward the cave. Two down, four left. As the men in red came on, the captain was among them, his hat giving him away. Foolish.

"Advance, advance you cowards!" the captain shouted. "There are only two of them!"

"There aren't many of us left either," the leg shot man roared back at him. "An' they have the high ground!"

"I'll see every one of you feckless bastards dead before I leave George's gold in the hands of brigands and pirates," the captain snarled.

"That's all you'll find here!" I shouted. "Death for men in red." I ducked and heard shot rip through the foliage above me, none were close but one didn't tempt the Reaper. "Oh, now I know you're George's men, missed me with every shot! I'm glad you're not Dutch, one of you might have hit me!" I taunted.

"Damn you Bligh!" the captain shouted. "I'll see you in irons again!"

"Already tried them on, sir, a poor fit! You should try them!" I ducked as a pair of pistols fired and did considerable damage to a tree.

"Arrrrg, you got me!" I shouted. One of the captain's men cheered. "Not you!" I cried. "The other fellow!" I heard them bustle and come out into the clearing, putting themselves between my concealed spot behind my line of trees and the mouth of the cave. So long as I kept up my distraction, they would be inclined to pursue me and not venture into the cave. Once they had their backs to the entrance, we would have them in a crossfire.

I heard Avery's pistol make its now familiar rapid loud popping sound, and I knew that something had gone awry. I came from around the tree with pistols in hand and came near to colliding with a marine carrying of all things, a blunderbuss. I kicked furiously and fired both of my pistols, and his miniature cannon roared in reply. I staggered back, hit the tree and fell. He too fell backwards and for a moment a red mist hung in the air. I patted my chest, my arms, feeling for the injury that was so severe that my body refused to acknowledge the pain of it. What would it be, disembowelment by a spray of shot? A perforated chest, lungs torn away, heart turned to pulp?

I found nothing amiss, nothing damaged save for a torn shirt. The blood was his, one pistol had taken him in the shoulder, the other had been a fair bit higher and had removed a portion of his face. I trembled at the closeness of Death. There were powder burns on my sleeve from his weapon.

"Surrender," I heard the captain say, but he was not facing me. "Surrender and I will show you clemency, such that you do not deserve."

"Go fuck yourself!" I heard Avery retort.

"Your companion is defeated, and I assure you that unless you surrender, that cave will be your tomb," Everett said with the abrasive certainty that only an English captain can produce.

"Lay down your arms, and surrender, and I will see personally that you are given a fair trial, and I will very specifically not shoot you like the dog that you are." I pulled the last two pistols I had and put both of them in his back.

"Who now is going to be shot like a dog?" I asked. "That would be my fiancée that you're threatening and I'll not be having that, no sir, I will not." I bit off the last and snarled.

"You'll hang for this," he said through gritted teeth.

"Drop your weapons, or the last thing you'll see is your breakfast sprayed on that rock there," I said.

"You're out of shot," he said.

"How many pistols do I carry?" I asked. "You don't know, because if you did, if you were dead certain, you would either drop your piece or you would call me, and then I would blow your guts out," I said.

"I do not know," he said after a pause.

"Aye, you don't. Be a good sir now and disarm yourself. A pirate I may be, but I'll not shoot a surrendering man. I'm a fair bit more honorable than your own men, wouldn't you agree?" I said. He dropped his pistol and raised his hands. I knocked him in the back of the head with one of the pistols and he dropped to his knees and then over onto his side.

"Avery, it is safe to come out, there's no fighting left," I said. She rose from her concealment and I saw her arm red.

"It's just a scratch," she said. "I'll be okay."

"We should make haste with our preparations and be on our way back to the *Sapphire*." She nodded, and we tied the captain's hands and made sure that the injured men were in no position to rearm themselves. They looked at me and saw their deaths, I was a pirate, and they showed no mercy to my kind. I considered ending them, but they, the three of them who remained, were disarmed, defeated, and consigned to their fates. They were tied to trees and then we returned to our work, going as quickly as we dared.

The pitch took the longest, and I set the fuse with hands that were shaking. Some was the exhaustion that followed intense action, and some was the fact that there was easy a man's weight in black powder that we were about to detonate. This in and of itself was foolhardy, but what in the last few days had not been?

Avery went above as I lit the longest fuse I could fix together and then I too scrambled for the surface. It was nearing sunset as I came out of the cave as fast as I dared. Avery grabbed me in a hug as I emerged, and then the ground shook and a great gust of pulverized dust came vomiting from the throat of the cave.

"What have you done?" the captain asked, looking up from where he had been tied to a tree.

"Your gold has been blown up, and it was my pleasure, sir," I said. He looked aghast, and part of his expression told me that he might have preferred being cut down in action rather than return alive with the lucre blown to hell and lost.

"I can hear the water!" Avery shouted from the mouth of the cave, "Its flooding! It's flooding!" She gave a hoot and laugh.

"You're mad, the both of you," he said, aghast. "*Mad.*"

"My good sir, I do beg the pardon of your release, but my bride to be and myself are soon to be late for an important rendezvous." I held out my hand to Avery. "My lady." She took my hand in hers, and I gave it a squeeze. "My love, my siren, my angel, are you ready to go home?"

"Yes, so much yes," she said.

We walked away from the bound men, taking the barely visible path leading down toward the Mirror Pond.

"You can't leave us like this!" one of the men shouted.

"Where are you even going? Lunatics, the both of you!" the captain shouted.

"What about them?" Avery asked.

"The crewmen will eventually come looking for them, and will untie them, and they'll find the cave flooded. Our duty is done. I have no taste for killing a man who is unarmed and, on his knees, besides." She nodded.

By the time we reached the Mirror Pond the moon was well and up, reflecting in its still waters. With a laugh we ran the last few paces and leaped into the water like children.

CHAPTER TWENTY-FIVE

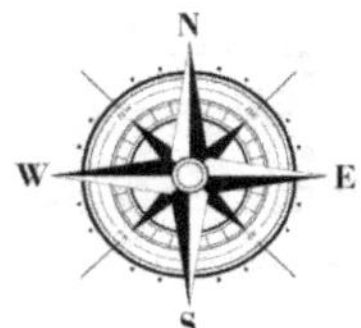

JUNE 2016

*A*very Barker...

We pulled ourselves through the water, each refusing to let go of the other's hand as we dove deep. The water was cool, the shift in time disorienting, and then the feeling of pulling ourselves down into the depths shifted to the sensation of desperately pulling ourselves up to the surface and the new future that awaited the both of us.

"Avery!" Mac cried and Eamon and I both surfaced gasping.

"Lord almighty," I heard him say aghast as Eamon and I tromped through the mud at the edge of the pool, the water running from us in silver rivulets under the glaring light of the moon above.

"Mac!" I cried overjoyed and practically fell into his arms. He hugged me tight and squeezed looking up at Eamon.

"Where did you come from?" he demanded. "Avery, what happened?" He held me out at arm's length and inspected me as best he could.

"How long have I been gone?" I demanded, and he shook his head, mouth hung open at the state of me and Eamon both.

"A few seconds? Maybe?" he said skeptically, and I grinned.

"Well halle-fucking-lujah!" I cried. That made things exponentially easier in that there would be no need for explanations to the crew. Mac was the only one who had to know anything.

"Why?" Mac demanded. "How long do you think you were gone?" he demanded.

"Uh, a week? Maybe less, maybe like six days? Ish?" I said.

"I don't know if I can believe this," Mac said. "You're both pranking me. You're pulling my leg, and it isn't funny, girl!"

"I assure you, good sir, she is not," Eamon declared.

Mac searched me over and lifted my injured arm. I sucked in a breath between my teeth and said, "Ouch! Mac! Damnit!"

"This ain't no scratch," he declared, and I shook my head.

"Graze from a musket ball," I told him. "First things first, Eamon and I need a shower and some real food and then I'll be more than happy to explain. You got the Gator up here?"

"Out past your tent."

"Good deal, take us to the *Sapphire Horizon*. I want a *hot* shower."

That's what we did, too. We stopped at my tent for some clothes, Mac ran us down closer to base camp and went in to fetch some of Kurt's clothes for Eamon, then, leaving the sounds of hard partying behind, he ran us back down to the *Sapphire Horizon* and provided enough distraction for Eamon and I to steal aboard and head for the facilities to clean up – but only on the stern promise that I would bring my happy ass straight to the sickbay for Mac to doctor me up.

Eamon and I spent at least an hour under the hot spray together, kissing, touching, washing each other clean. He spent long and patient minutes with me in his lap, shaving his face for him, and held a wet washcloth to my still-bleeding arm, though the bleeding had significantly slowed.

Putting antiseptic on that shit was gonna suck, hardcore, and I let Mac take his perverse pleasure in administering the stinging spray and subsequent numbing ointment while we filled him in on all that had happened.

"I seriously don't know how we're going to keep a lid on all of it Mac, but I need your help. Eamon has to stay."

Mac grunted.

"I maybe know a guy," he said. "Same guy that knows the right guys when it comes to currency exchanges wherever we go. I might be able to get a hookup on the papers he's gonna need, but Avery?"

"Yeah?" I asked, holding my breath, damn near forgetting to breathe.

"You can't tell *anybody* else *any* of this *ever*," he said gravely.

"Not even Dad?" I asked softly.

Mac shook his head. "I'm not sure even your daddy would believe this," he said. "But I know what I saw in that pond tonight, and," he hiccupped a disbelieving laugh of his own, "it was like looking into a mirror, for real," he said. "Except, it wasn't my reflection on the other side. It was you two, jumping in."

"Seventeen-thirty-one," I said softly and traded smiles with Eamon.

"What was it *like*?" Mac demanded.

"I believe, you would say, it sucked," Eamon declared. "Both ass, and balls, and an ass's balls."

Mac stared at us both in disbelief as he put what Eamon was trying to tell him together, his shocked face split into a slow grin, a bubble of hysterical laughter working its way up his throat until it went from a laugh to a roar of mirth.

The laughter was contagious, both myself and Eamon falling in with the fit of the giggles as I leaned into Eamon's side. He put an arm around me and I stuck the hand of my freshly bandaged arm into the pocket of my fresh, clean, khaki shorts. Wrapping my fingers tight around what I thought of as my 'engagement crystal.'

"Okay, okay," Mac said, wiping tears from his eyes. "You've gotta work with him on that."

"The modern colloquialisms?" I asked.

"Yeah, whatever the fuck just came out his mouth."

I grinned.

"Mac, we got the rest of our lives to work on it and I'll get right on it, just as soon as we recover that gold."

"Agreed, my love," Eamon declared, and I looked up at him. He brought his mouth to mine and we kissed, right there. Right in front of Mac, and it felt oh, so, right.

EPILOGUE

*E*amon Bligh...

Honor's Ransom sat in the lee of a small island; anchor dropped in a lagoon so clear that it looked like a lens that magnified the bottom. The sailboat was much smaller than both *Honor's Price* and the *Sapphire Horizon,* but it could be handled by just two people, or one person if they were skilled and patient. The last few months had been harrying and busy.

Avery's company had successfully removed the lucre from the underwater caves on Fade Isle, and considering the value of the gold bullion, it had been easy enough to convert it to the currency of the twenty-first century. Sometime between 1731 and the modern age, the Cayman Islands had somehow gone into banking with a fervor that would have put the crown to shame.

There had been a massive court hearing, where Mister Wallace had proved his mettle, revealing the clandestine plot from Avery's sibling, Gwen, and her machinations to ruin the family business to the point that Avery would have been forced to sell or surrender her share to Gwen. Wallace confirmed and produced documentation to prove malicious intent. The worst of his actions were quietly left out, and the matter of his debts were settled away, along with a stint in a hospital of some sort for gambling addiction. It was a strange new world, and sometimes, it was too much.

Such was the case with these *movies* Avery had spoken of, filled with motley caricatures of pirate men, none of them making sense. Likewise, the mainland had been more than I could handle, with cities bigger than I had ever seen, the constant noise, the electric lights, and absolutely nothing familiar to me. It was like being in an ocean that constantly assaulted me but never offered the solace of drowning.

I looked down at the bow of the ship, where my *wife* was lounging. She wore nothing but a gold and crystal ring, taken from the lucre and cathedral fragment hat she'd brought back with her. The only other thing on her person a large pair of peculiar dark lensed eyewear called sunglasses. I let my eyes trace the sun kissed and glistening slope of her breasts, the curve of her hips, and the delicate line of her throat and felt that tightening of my chest.

"Do you want to know what time it is?" I asked. The face of my watch was the most delightful machined blue steel, with parts smaller than I imagined possible, resistant to water, *gorgeous*. Like her.

"Not particularly," Avery said. "Time doesn't matter right now." She rolled over and got to her knees before standing. She walked up to me with her siren's waltz, hypnotizing me with her hips. I sighed as she came and sat in my lap, her perfect golden breasts all but pressed in my face. "If you want to fiddle with something, how about you fiddle with me instead of that watch?"

I kissed her neck and shoulder, cupping her bosom and her bottom with opposite hands. "Heaven," I whispered between kisses. She ground her hips against me, but the advantage was hers, she was already nude and I was clad in modern bathing shorts. She pressed her advantage, and I knew the inferiority of my position and that I was in no position to offer resistance.

"I can tell when you are thinking," she said, reaching down to squeeze me between the legs. "You make this certain face, and I know that you're thinking too hard. Hard... mm," she purred.

"I will never weary of this," I said as she pulled my cock out of the swimming shorts and started rubbing the end between her secret lips.

"I should hope not," she said.

"I never thought that I would be your husband, any woman's husband, let alone one as magnificent..." I trailed off as she guided me into her and sank down into my lap until we were pressed hip to hip.

"I never thought that I would ever marry, I wasn't going to be anyone's wife," she said, and she rode me. I leaned back and held onto her. I was never going to tire of this, this angel who saw fit to have me, pull me from my own degenerate century and bring me into hers.

To take me, scars and piracy, and all as her husband. Nae, I was not good enough for her, not by a hundred times, not by a thousand... I was filled with these tender and romantic notions, and all my resistance failed, and I came inside her. She finished herself off and gave me a long lingering kiss before dismounting from me.

Sometime later, she spoke.

"I found something interesting at an archive on St. Kitts," Avery said after a while. She had availed herself of her pocket spy box; a smartphone, she called it.

"What have you found?" I asked. I looked up from the book I was reading. I had centuries of catching up to do, and I had discovered books helped better than the large spy box. That thing had been as relentless as any storm I had ever seen and the feel of paper and parchment in my hands soothed my soul in counterpoint. Avery was absorbed in her hand-held spy box and I knew to be patient, to wait her out. That she would come back to me in her own time and finish her thought.

"Oh, what are you reading now?" she asked and looked up from her device.

"*Dracula*," I said. "Mister Mackey said I would enjoy it, and Mister Alby suggested that I read *Frankenstein* or *Twilight* after this." This amused her, by the laugh she gave. Such things happened, some of the books that were recommended were indeed the sort of thing I liked, and some were jokes at my expense, and I didn't know which it would be until I was a few pages into it.

"The curator of the St. Kitts archive has what she claims to be a collection of charts and records from the South Seas Trading Company." She looked up and raised an eyebrow.

"Oh, you mean King George's personal gold shipping service?" I asked.

"The one and the same," she said with a cheeky grin.

"You aren't all worked up to visit a different century again, are you?" I wondered.

"Don't get me wrong hubby," she said. "I will be happy with you forever, but this is a vacation, and I can't spend the rest of my life lounging naked on a boat. We don't need money, but it was never the gold, that wasn't the real reason."

"The adventure," I said. She pointed a finger at me, the other she brought to the tip of her nose.

"You got it," she said. "I found my pirate lord and a heap of gold, but there are still wrecks and secrets to find out there." She smiled. "Oh, and I got an update on your citizenship papers."

"Did you now? Do tell."

"Yup, it only took some money and polite words and once the paperwork goes through, you'll be an American citizen," she said. "One more thumb bitten toward king and crown."

"Oh, I like that," I said.

"I thought you might."

I settled back in my seat, smiled at my wife, and gazing out over the crystalline waters asked, "So where, pray tell, does our next adventure lie?"

Avery laughed, and I turned back to her, her smile radiant, her blue eyes a match for the sea surrounding us.

"With me, always with me," she said. "Other than that? Somewhere off the Florida coast in hopefully what will only be eighty feet of water."

I grinned and nodded, with my siren by my side I was perhaps ready to conquer any sea.

ALSO BY TIMBER PHILIPS

Hallowed Be Thy Light

Hunter's Choice

Love in Purgatory

The Witches of Loving

1. Love Springs Eternal

ABOUT JARED KINGPACAL LAIN

Jared KingPacal Lain hails from the Great Smoky Mountains, a place of both beauty and dark things, where he explores strange fiction, hidden secrets, and venturing away from the main path to find hidden pleasures, wonders, and horrors.